MY SON THE AMERICAN

My Son The American

A novel

by

EUGENE CHRISTY

Adelaide Books
New York / Lisbon
2020

MY SON THE AMERICAN
A novel
By Eugene Christy

Published by Adelaide Books, New York / Lisbon
adelaidebooks.org

Editor-in-Chief
Stevan V. Nikolic

For any information, please address Adelaide Books
at info@adelaidebooks.org

or write to:

Adelaide Books
244 Fifth Ave. Suite D27
New York, NY, 10001

ISBN: 978-1-952570-89-6

Printed in the United States of America

For Janet and Patrick

VOLUME II
OF THE TWENTIETH CENTURY
QUINTET

To those soldiers who must often have wondered WHY they were

going where they did . . .

Omar N. Bradley
Dedication to *A Soldier's Story*

Contents

Chapter 18
Father Coughlin Speaks **281**

Chapter 19
The Indian in the Woods **292**

Chapter 20
The Rules of the Game **304**

Chapter 21
Black Sheep, Lost Lamb **310**

Chapter 22
Bulletin **321**

Chapter 23
Sons of Italy **336**

Chapter 24
Tony and Harry **355**

Chapter 25
Return to Alta Villa **363**

About the Author **417**

Chapter 1

Ciao, Boston

When, at odd moments, looking out the train window, his forehead leaning up against the rattling pane, he registered the fleeing presence of a flat countryside, out there; of what seemed to be endless low-lying scrubwoods interspersed with low-level cities or towns, or simply train platforms which disappeared as soon as they wheeled up, his inattention lapsing; he became barely conscious of the passage of time, of drifting in and out of listless dozing.

In 1911, it took six hours for a local train from New York City to crawl up the Connecticut coast and go weaving through Rhode Island all the way to Boston. But for young Tony LaStoria, at twenty-two years of age, devastated as he was by the death of Laura Antonelli, in what all the papers agreed was the tragedy of the century, the Triangle Shirtwaist Factory Fire in New York City, it may as well have been an eternity.

Not only was he leaving the city he loved, New York, and all the friends and family he had known for the past dozen years, he was departing life as he knew it. Nothing could ever be the same again. New York he knew as intimately as the lines crossing his own palm; what could Boston hold for him but exile?

On the train north, unseeing, unfeeling, Tony stared out the window. The rest of the time, he looked at the floor. He did not want to look at the other passengers. They might look back. They might venture conversation. He did not want to talk. Rarely did he lift his gaze from the ground anymore. What was there to see? The things he saw, he didn't need eyes for them. He saw them when he closed his eyes, not when he opened them.

In these dreams, these nightmares, waking or sleeping, at night or in daylight, Tony saw again, he re-lived again, those moments leading up to one last awful moment, when girls, leaping from ninth-story windows, their clothing trailing smoke, their hair on fire, in one last desperate gamble for life, fell flailing through the air to their final fates on the concrete below. Again he cringed as bone met sidewalk, again he shut his eyes tight to shut out the sound of exploding flesh. What searing coincidence, what conniving chance had contrived to lead him to be there, to be there to witness, with his own eyes, at that precise moment, the undeserved horrible death of the innocent creature he loved?

When she was alive, when he lay in his bed dreaming of her, then, he had been able to conjure up only her shoes. Now, her face appeared to him, every time he sought rest. And in that face, her eyes looking into his, for that fleeting moment when their eyes had met, that day, that one time, on the streetcar, those deep and clear and expressive brown eyes looking up into his, with the question that was in them, the protest, that fixed him, a lover stabbed by a look, pierced through the voicebox, robbed of any response.

Over and over again he excused himself, stood up, felt flush, and awkward: and yet their eyes met again, for that instant of time.

Dead. Never to come again. Never to be reborn.

But still, from beyond life, it was as if she had granted him his most fervent wish: *that he be able to see her face;* that face, which in life, she had, except for that one time, kept away from him, kept averted, kept to herself, from shyness, from modesty, from anger.

And also, from across the divide, from death, she reached out to him, to make sure she never lost her grasp on him; for Laura Antonelli, the young woman who was, the innocent girl who had been, for her spirit, for her memory, for whatever her ghost was composed of, this was the one chance that she would ever have to live again.

If this was love, thought young Tony LaStoria, *why was it so full of agony?*

The answer, that he would never find love again, that this was to be his permanent condition the rest of his days, stared back at him from the dull, streaked window, as they stood, patiently puffing in some lowly, anonymous station where more and more passengers departed and more and more people struggling with their luggage stepped on board this train.

They moved on. When, at odd moments, watching through the glass, he absorbed, in desultory inattention, the flatness of the countryside, he was roused half-heartedly to calculate how far he had come, and how far there was yet to go. It seemed to him that he would have to go all the way back to the beginning, to the day when, as a mere boy, a child of ten years, he had run away from home in Alta Villa, to cross the ocean on his own, unaccompanied by anyone or anything but his own thoughts.

And that was why he was glad he would not have to see Uncle Eugene anymore, Zi'Marietta, the cousins, even Harry Spritzka, all the people who tiptoed around him in his grief, who, out of consideration for his feelings, said nothing, asked no questions, made no comments on the weather or the supper or the day's work or the events of the world. All those telegrams, from the humming wires of daily existence, which usually form the urgent business that people are most compelled to feverishly communicate, those telegrams he would not have to tear open and read ever again.

The people who loved him wanted to spare him from that.

But that didn't matter to Tony. He had to get away from anyone and everyone who loved him, who cared, from anyone who ever so much as knew him. They were all reminders. They all stood in for one who was not there among them anymore. Nor could he take the chance that, in spite of their constant vigilance, one of them might let slip, a word, a reference, a look. For after all it was everywhere all the time on every newsstand, written on every grocery receipt, burned into every wall, *that she was dead.*

And every time he thought *that thought,* that terrible thought, so final, so committed in its finality, that *thought,* which he tried not to think, which he tried to hold off, but which nevertheless returned on slippered steps, creeping up behind him, whispering, breathing: *she's dead.*

Dead. Dead. Dead. Dead. *Dead . . .*

When he arrived in South Station, in Boston, he wandered aimlessly through its cavernous hall and eventually emerged outside into the streets of a non-descript, low-roofed place; masquerading for a town, it was an area that was simply there, without any distinction, leaving no impact, or even impression. It might be called a city, but it did not seem to him like New York at all. He began walking away from the station in no particular direction, and when he stopped walking, it was because he saw a sign saying *Rooms to Let*, and he wanted only one thing, that this room where he would live should not be in an Italian neighborhood, where he might be called upon to act humanly among human beings, for he wanted only to be a stranger in a strange place, where he had no ties, no friends, no relations, no connections, where he could pass among the living like a ghost.

He was grateful for this: that he could plunge himself into work; work, work, work; into what he knew beforehand would be a vain attempt to fend off his own mortal miasma; but which, at least for fourteen or fifteen hours a day, might permit him to hold off the moment of drowning.

And for this one saving grace he was forever in debt to Harry Spritzka, the friend of his youth, the man who, now, would be sending him money, in compensation for his faithful work on Harry's behalf. Harry Spritzka, the one person to whom he had ever given his trust, the one person who had never let him down.

To Tony, this town was the frozen north. The image he had of it before he actually entered on its streets was the picture Domenico the Iceman had put in his mind, of the ice-gang on the Penobscot, chopping gigantic blocks out of the river.

Because he wandered into the South End on his first day in Boston, he stayed in the rooming house he had first found for the next two years.

The people of that neighborhood, he found, were happy not to have to get acquainted with him, and concerning them, he was just as glad that they seemed to have very little to say, and would rather cross the street than have to say, "Good morning." Tony supposed this was the famous Yankee reserve he had heard of. It didn't matter: his business was his own, and he did not want to know theirs.

This business of his, which, after all, was supposed to be the reason he had come to this God-forsaken place, this work of his he did not think of as a profession.

That was for doctors.

Or a vocation. That was for the priesthood.

But as an *occupation,* yes, that was the word.

For to be a tradesman, one would have to have his own shop.

The way to look at it, Tony thought, when he thought about it, was that he practiced his trade of tailoring, within the occupation of factory manager.

To call himself a supervisor, or a superintendent, seemed to him absurd, as if he were to dub himself a "vice-president" in Harry's company. Titles did not stir Tony. He never liked it when people called him "boss." That was Harry's role. Harry Spritzka relished that role, he tasted power, and he liked it, he wanted to exercise his control, even his whims, on others.

If it were not for Harry, Tony would not be here in Boston, running a *model factory* (let's face it, *a sweatshop)* in a back street near the Fort Point Channel, just across the bridge, in easy walking distance, from his solitary room in the boarding house.

Nor would he be setting up a factory-outlet store on the first floor, modeled on the one they had operated on West 37th. Or stretching the boundaries of his own ignorance of retail, challenging what he knew to be his limitations, trying to find the space and hire the kind of people he needed to open and operate Harry's first commercial location, his first *Richard Paul*

Men's Clothing store in the Boston market, which ended up in a very visible corner spot, with a trolley line and a major crossroads, at the junction of Harvard Street and Beacon Street, in Coolidge Corner; not in Boston at all, but in Brookline.

Fortunately, for Tony, Harry was far away. Just where, just now, Tony liked him.

Everything in his life that had ever been associated with New York, Tony pushed away. He only wished he could put it all behind him once and for all.

But there was this modern invention, the telephone, and so Tony heard it plenty from Harry.

The Boss claimed to be too busy, overworked, overstretched, and successful, in his rising, multiplying business, too busy empire-building, to actually get up to a backwater like Boston. *So, what's this week's report? How many pieces? Never mind the other crap. Get to the bottom line.*

Taught to him by his family, given to him, yes, by his parents, also, bestowed upon him by his father (he had to admit, the only inheritance he would ever receive from that man) Tony's precious trade of tailoring was the only thing that kept the wolf from the door. A man of the cloth, yes, that's what he was, and it made him think, ironically, that title was a, what's the word? *misnomer,* yes, when applied to the clergy. Sewing, stitching, measuring, fitting, this trade of tailoring he would practice in a sweatshop; these were the habits of mind, the inborn traits, which preserved him from having to beg for pennies playing his mandolin in the streets or subway entrances or outside public latrines on the Boston Common.

Not that he currently possessed that long-lost mandolin. Like everything else, his friends, his cousins, his hopes, his dreams, his emotions, he had long ago left it behind in New York City.

Unlike Harry Spritzka, Tony LaStoria possessed no salesmanship. No fever of pressing dollars into the flesh of his hand. No mania for persuading others to give so that he could take. Tony did not know how to do what came so naturally to Harry, to sell himself, from a pushcart. If Tony had tried to open his own corner shop under his own name, he would have sat there empty-handed with nothing in his lap to sew. He would have starved. Because he would not have rushed into the street to beg, cajole, pester, push and command people to come in.

What Tony knew was that this way, he did not have to live *there* anymore. All day long, he need not pay hardly any attention at all, things ran themselves. He had run far enough away to almost hope that he could forget. He could sit in his office, stare out the window, wait for the end of another day, and walk home alone, *to be with her.*

And in this manner, day-in and day-out, two years went by, and to Tony, nothing had happened.

The same could not be said of the people that he employed every day.

They were more or less the same people who worked in the sweatshops of New York. Only the faces were different, because even the names were similar, the usual sprinkling of Italian names among the predominant middle European names, the Heinies and the Polacks, with a couple of differences. There was no Lower East Side in Boston, packed with Russian and Lithuanian and Polish Jews. Instead, here they had the Greeks.

And of course, these employees were all women.

As in New York, the male positions were reserved for the cutters and pressers. So once again Tony found himself overseeing a gaggle of young women: who all wanted to get married so that they could get out of the sweatshop.

If he had wanted to, in theory, Tony could have taken his pick of Polish swan or Greek raven. But he wasn't interested.

And for this very reason, he was an object of fascination to the girls.

Where had he come from? New York? Really . . . and so, what's the story? He's not bad-lookin.' Do we know anybody who knows him? Anybody who knows anything about him, anything at all? He's from the old country? Originally? How about that. You would never know. He doesn't have an accent, except for the way he says, "Caw-ffee." In fact, that's all he ever says: "Caw-ffee." *Ask Brooklyn. What did she find out about him?*

"Brooklyn" was the nickname the girls gave to a young Italian girl who, like Tony, had come up here from New York. She was the only one in two years who had ever succeeded in actually having a conversation with him.

Brooklyn said, "He likes to keep it on a professional level. That's what he told me. Yeah! I ast him. Why would he want to associate with the likes of youz, anyhow!"

Brooklyn had approached Tony one day about a raise in the piece-work rate.

Tony said to her, "I thought you were a nice kid. Are you gonna give me trouble?"

"I would love to. Whaddya doin' Saturday night?"

"You. Typical New York. You come right to the point."

"With you, a girl's only got one shot at it."

Gradually, over a period of several months, only because she would not give up, Brooklyn got him to let her in his office, one day when she brought him *Caw-ffee.*

"You smoke too many cigarettes," she said.

"Thanks for the caw-ffee. Now get outta here."

"Not until you tell me why you're so sad."

He looked at her, as if she were something from another world: a mind-reader, a person with subterranean powers; a dangerous woman, who could throw him off balance, completely.

"What? You think it's not written all over you?"

Tony put the coffee down on his desk. He sat back in his swivel-chair, put his hands behind his head, and looked at her, and past her, and at her. Slowly he said, "It's none of your goddam business."

"Somebody broke your heart. What happened? She ditched ya?"

Tony said nothing, but his demeanor was forthcoming. Brooklyn could see him swaying back and forth between losing his temper with her and caving in.

"I ain't gonna stop till I find out. So, you might as well tell me now."

Tony had turned into a statue, seated in a swivel-chair that was broken and would not turn.

"Okay, forget about the piece-rate. Why don't you put me to work in the office for you, here? I can type, you know. I ain't as dumb as I look. I can make myself very useful to you. And I know a very nice family over in the North End. Why don't you let me introduce you?"

Chapter 2

The Life of Gigi

A young person of only seventeen, a girl named Gigi, who had lived as long as she could remember on Prince Street, in the North End of Boston, had no way of knowing what was to come next, for herself, or anyone else. Except that she had it all planned.

Gigi believed she could foretell the future.

And in her future she saw a bride in a white dress, at San Leonardo's, at the end of her own block, on the corner of Prince and Hanover Streets. She was the bride, and the handsome young Italian guy in the picture was her groom. She did not yet know his name, but that was of little consequence. The important thing was that Gigi did not care to learn English, so he was going to be Italian, and they were going to speak Italian at home, with all their kids, because that was what Gigi preferred.

She had once heard someone refer to something nice to eat, a nice, creamy Neapolitan, when she was a little girl, as "food," and when she asked what that meant, and they told her *"cibo,"* she thought, what an ugly word, what an ugly sound!—foo-oo-d! Not at all appealing and attractive and appetizing like *cibo,* which made your mouth water in anticipation. Who would ever want to eat *"foo-oo-d?"* She made up her mind immediately never to bother learning such an ugly language.

Besides, what would she need it for? She was only going to stay at home and be a mother, like her own mother, and have a husband to provide for her, as she had her father to provide for her now. That was the way of the world, and it seemed only right and natural to Gigi, and, in a way, predestined.

When Gigi imagined growing up, she always saw herself as a young and beautiful bride, blossoming into motherhood: then to be surrounded with a brood of children, who were more or less like the dolls made out of scraps of cloth stuffed with newspapers, with which she had surrounded herself when she was a child, and whose faces she painted on with watercolors.

Gigi had never once seen herself looking for a job in a factory. Why would a beautiful young girl like herself with enlarging bosoms want to go hide herself in a drab and dingy place like that, smelling like machine-grease and flannel-dust, and have to sit still, without fidgeting, all day, and be at the beck and call of every man, young and old, with popping eyes and pinching fingers, who only wanted to nibble your neck.

Nobody had ever tried to nibble Gigi's neck, but she thought about it, and she would certainly entertain luxurious, languorous thoughts of her neck being nibbled, but she was saving her neck for her bridegroom.

Besides, her father, Pasquale Fabrizio, would have cringed at working in a place like that. He was a butcher, probably the furthest thing from say, oh, a tailor. A tailor sat all day with his work in his lap, pinching his fingers together and losing his eyesight. Gigi's Papa strode around with blood on his hands. Anyway, who ever heard of a lady butcher?

So it was simply not in the stars in Gigi's family that the girls should grow up to become job-seekers, in need of a skill or a profession, or even pursue a family trade.

Well, there was skinny, purse-mouthed, pouty and simpering Anna-Vittoria, the elder daughter, whose name meant "Victory of Grace." Their first daughter, she was named by her mother, Anna-Lisa. Anna-Lisa wanted "Anna," after her own mother, but Gigi's father, Pasquale Fabrizio, for some reason remembered the Vittorio Emanuele who was King of Italy before Umberto I, and after Umberto I, that is, the Vittorio Emanuele II, *Secondo,* and the III, *Terza.* Anyway, who could keep them all straight? And what did it matter? The clown-princes of the far-distant house of Piedmont had very little to do with their own *paese,* which happened to be Volturrara, in the mountains southwest of Avellino. Especially here in the North End of Boston, where every town and village had their own street, and every *paese* their own neighborhood street society, with their own clubhouse; where someone from the next street over was considered a foreigner.

Her parents, Anna-Lisa and Pasquale both, were disappointed in Anna-Vittoria. After two sons, they had been looking forward, so much, to an easy time with a young flower who would brighten their windowsill, but instead they got a weed, who soured their flowerpot.

With their second girl, they gave up and named her "Gioconda," which meant, simply, "happy." And here they were fortunate, because that's exactly the way she turned out, a round, smiling, cherubic little chattering meatball, all waving arms and legs, who became her father Pasquale's little pet, because she was such a relief from the dour and complicated Anna-Vittoria, who liked nothing better than complaining.

Their sons, Aldo and Agostino, were the ones that Anna-Lisa and Pasquale sent to school: public school, naturally, that didn't cost you.

There was one, and only one, parochial school in the North End, and that was an Irish school, started by that patronizing bastard, Archbishop O'Connell, who condescended to call it, when he opened it in 1907, *St. John's School for Italian Children,* as if they were a colony of African aborigines to whom he had sent a mission, to convert them to Catholicism!

The Irish, even though they were Roman Catholics, were proselytizers worse than the Beacon Hill Unitarians who also infested the North End, prowling the streets attempting to convert illiterate villagers from the southern end of the Italian peninsula, whom these proper Bostonians deemed to be so ignorant that they did not even realize they were "Eye-talians."

The boys, Aldo and Agostino, were the ones who survived. Originally, there were two others, but they died very young, one from infantile bronchitis, and the other from diphtheria. The remaining boys had to be prepared for a life earning their own keep; in other words, grubbing for money like the rest of us. Otherwise, who would there be to care for Anna-Lisa and Pasquale in their old age and infirmity? You had to think of these things.

Anna-Lisa and Pasquale's own aged parents lived on the top floor of their dark and dingy tenement, half wood and half brick, squeezed into the packed row of Prince Street; two sets of squabbling in-laws who managed to behave, in spite of their years, like idiot children.

Up there was the only light that crept into the whole building anywhere. The bottom two floors were shadow and gloom morning and afternoon every day of the week. Prince Street was so narrow you could cross it on foot in three steps. So the grandparents, double the headaches as they might be, still, they deserved respect. They had earned the right to a little light in their lives, simply because, after all this time, they were still hanging on, right down to the end. Thanks be to St. Jude, patron of lost causes, that by hook or by crook Pasquale Fabrizio had managed to buy this rickety old building, and though he owed his life to the *Banca Italiana* in North Square, he could go about boasting that he owned his own home, that he took care of his own family, and that of his wife to boot.

The Fabrizio daughters, even Anna-Vittoria, *prugna secca* that she was, with a narrow, elongated, hollow-cheeked seed for a face, they sheltered, kept at home, kept away from the world. In fact, as long as nobody objected, or knew, or cared to know, why should the two girls go to school? Daughters could be taught what they needed to know at home: how to keep house, how to cook, clean, wash; how to keep house, how to make change, so they didn't cheat you at the Haymarket when you bought a watermelon; in other words: how to keep house. Let them mind their manners until they were old enough to get them married off. As long as they knew how to roll out the dough and cut the macaroni into strips, they could keep some man happy. As the whole world knew, the road to a man's heart ran through his belly.

That did not mean that the girls grew up ignorant. Far from it.

Anna-Vittoria had the nose of a shopkeeper and the hearing of a cat, accumulating bits and pieces of information like coins, and shutting them up in her cash-register.

Gioconda, the bambina of the family, was spoiled to death by her favorite brother, Agostino; and even more by her Papa, who was the one who gave her name the pet form of "Gigi." This little girl loved to sit on her father's lap and put her arms around his neck and hug and squeeze. And she got her brother Agostino to read to her from his schoolbooks until she knew as much as he did, and even taught herself to read, with his help, of course. Or else, what's a brother for, if you can't twist him around your finger?

But Gigi was also, like a cat, stealthy, though her realm was the world of a big hunting cat's insatiable curiosity, a curiosity that hungered after, not morsels of meat, but secrets: signs, and symbols, and numbers. In Gigi's world, everything had a meaning, and it was usually a hidden meaning that had to be interpreted, but only by one who could see *within,* and *beyond,* below the surface, the obvious, the outward, *to the real,* which lay curled up underneath.

This feeling she had, which she developed into a talent, and then, a way of life, a way of thinking, began when she was small and told stories to her dolls.

These stories began with a mother and father, of course, and in a house with children. But these children could be dogs and cats or pigs. Cats she knew, but barnyard animals she had never actually seen. Nevertheless, her Papa had told her about the three little piggies, and the three blind mice, and the three bears, and of course, he knew all about pigs, and mice, too, from the butcher-shop. As far as bears go, well, maybe back in the old country, up in the mountains, where he came from, maybe they had bears over there? Well, what did it matter? The point was, Gigi's imaginary families could be lions, tigers and bears, also, even eagles. Or, people. Or, kings and queens. Or, gods and goddesses; those gods and goddesses whose pictures she had pored over in her favorite books, those divinities who lived on a faraway mountaintop, with the eagles.

Her mother, Anna-Lisa, was the one who told stories to Gigi, about those mountains, far away, in another world, in the old country, where Anna-Lisa herself had spent her own childhood.

Anna-Lisa portrayed those mountains as hidden from view in cloud-banks, which would then be swept into sparkling vision by a sudden onrush of brilliant, hot sunshine, towards the end of the morning mist.

She explained to Gigi how a child could sit on the wall at the end of the village and watch the shadows of the clouds skipping and skimming across the bearded faces of the mountains across the valley. The mountains wore beards because the trees were entirely covering them, like whiskers.

Life then, in the old country, was nothing like today, when they were cramped into a narrow, tottering slum where you didn't have room to stick out your elbows.

To Gigi, it was a magical place, the "Old Country." Her mother never mentioned that back then, back there, they were as poor as the dirt underneath their bare feet. That you had to fetch water in *acqua caraffe* from a well or the public fountain to bring into the house. How you had to go outside to do your business. Why should she stuff such ideas into Gigi's head? Time enough to be always worried and beset with things. After all, she adored Gigi as much as her husband did; though she was a little jealous of the special closeness between those two.

But who wouldn't love Gigi? She was the light in the dim first floor of their house. Everybody loved Gigi!

And Gigi loved everybody.

Sometimes, as she grew a little older, as she grew up a little, as her breasts developed, and her mother explained: that was so she could nurse the children when they came along; sometimes Gigi was swept away by an oceanic tide of feeling, which came over her at times, unbidden, in waves of love, like the undertow at Revere Beach that her father, Pasquale Fabrizio, always warned her of.

Yet Gigi, she could become so overtaken with these rolling surfs of emotion that she wanted to spread her wings and envelop the whole world in a bursting embrace.

Except for that hideous sister of hers, Anna-Vittoria. That one! It was just impossible to include her!

Gigi's mother told her that the clouds skimming over the bearded mountains were like the wings of ghosts, or angels. You could see that they were actually the transparent reflections of their ancestors; their grandparents, favorite aunts and uncles, long dead, who had returned to visit their old home place. Yes, even Anna-Lisa, Papa, too, had a grandmother: long gone now. But ghosts were nothing to be afraid of. They were your friends; they came to remind you that *there was another world.* The only thing you had to fear was being afraid of them. *That* they didn't like, because it offended them; they were kind-hearted and would never hurt you. They were your family.

This information Gigi hastened to share with her dolls, which were her family, her children, whom she practiced on, for the day when she would be a mother herself, and have her own, real children.

Gigi modeled everything she knew about how to live on the ways that she saw her mother practicing. To Gigi, her mother knew how to be a woman, and a wife, and a mother. *And* to be the one to take care of her own parents, and her husband's. Gigi's mother took care of everyone. That was how Gigi wanted to be, one day.

Then there was the dream-book. This was a fat volume, as thick as a Bible, loaded with numbers, which came to you in dreams. It was called *La Cabala.* Gigi's mother used to send her to stand on a chair and fetch down the dream-book from the cabinet where it was kept next to the square tin of white flour. Then they would sit at the kitchen table consulting the dream-book. Anna-Vittoria would drift by and turn her nose up in the air. Secretly, she was envious. Why her mother chose not to share *La Cabala* with her Anna-Vittoria would never know.

But Gigi knew. It was simple. It was because Anna-Vittoria did not dream. She was too discontented with life to have any dreams. She was not open to them. She did not invite them. So they did not come.

Anna-Lisa would begin her session with Gigi by saying, "So—did you dream last night?"

"I had a dream this morning."

"Were there any numbers in it?"

"Not that I remember."

"Well—was there a house in it? What was the number on the house?"

"Oh, yes. There was. It was Rossi's, across the way. Number 79."

"Ah. *Va bene.* So we have a seven and a nine. That's a good start. Now, what room were you in? *Il salotto?*"

"No, I was in the bedroom. But there was a pig in the bedroom."

"A pig!"

"I always dream about pigs. Because Papa has to butcher them at work."

"*Va bene.* A pig is the number 4!"

"I have never seen a pig, but I see them in my dreams."

"You're not missing nothing."

The book they were consulting was worn-out and dog-eared, but you could still make out the title on the grease-stained cover: though people usually referred to it as *La Cabala,* it was actually entitled *"La Smorfia Napoletana."* From this, Gigi's mother Anna-Lisa interpreted that it was actually written by Morpheus, the Greek God of Dreams. "How else we gonna come up with some winning numbers for your Papa to play in the nigga pool?" Anna-Lisa used to say.

Once in a while, they hit, but they never became millionaires. The point was that if they hit anything at all, it proved the book was right!

In any case, you didn't want to go against *The Book.* They were very superstitious about that book. They didn't need any more bad luck than they already had.

To Gigi, who had never seen a Bible, much less read one, or even a Sunday Missal, this one book opened up entire worlds of imagination.

If there was a Greek God of Dreams, *allora,* it must follow that there must be other gods, too. And her mother had told her about roadside shrines that they used to have back in the old country, and grottos, tucked away in the mountains; and things like what it meant if you dropped a spoon, or if a goat wandered into your garden. Not that a goat would ever wander into your garden, or that you would even have a garden, in the North End of Boston, but, you had to use your imagination. So that's what Gigi was learning how to do at the hands of her mother: how to use your imagination.

Gigi, from her earliest times, was taught to understand that almost everything meant something else. And when her brother Agostino brought home books from that school of his, even though they were in English, which Gigi did not prefer, she coaxed him into borrowing other books, in good old Italian, from old ladies in the neighborhood. And one of them, the one she treasured most of all, and never did ever give back (hoping the old lady had died, or more likely, forgotten) was all about the ancient gods that lived on the tops of mountains in Greece, and Italy, too, back in the olden days, even before the Madonna and her son Jesus Christ came along.

This book was called, "Storia di un'anima," and it was written by a man called Ambrosio Bazzaro, and the date Gigi found inside was 1851, so she thought to herself, it must be true! *it's so old, even this book is ancient.*

She loved the book because it had beautiful illustrations, all woodcuts, of cloudy mountaintops with palaces and temples where gods and goddesses with names such as Minerva and Apollo lived like one big happily quarreling family, constantly in and out of adventures and trouble, flying around on winged sandals and horses that flew near the sun. Each illustration had a caption which she read so many times over that she memorized them: and thus, learned to read.

The feeling Gigi got from this book was not the same feeling she got from the dusty and musty interior of San Leonardo's, down on the corner of the street, with the wine-colored candlelight flickering from brass rails and the piteous, skeletal form hanging on the cross; or from the old women dressed all in black sitting under the small tree in the courtyard in front of the church, gripping black rosary beads in white knuckles.

That was a dark and discouraging vision. Even the stones in that courtyard seemed to be smudged with charcoal. They conveyed a foreboding, that wore you down with sadness and hopelessness, which then clung to the air around that church; and Gigi much rather would like to think of the light, and sunny, high ramparts where the other gods cavorted.

So she adopted these cherubic and robust athletes and lovers as her own. Although, as young as she was, she knew enough not to tell anyone. *It was her secret, and hers alone.*

And all this time, from her youngest days onward, certain forces that roamed at large in the world were conspiring, unbeknownst even to Gigi herself, to prepare her, *La Gioconda,* for her very own wedding day.

Perhaps the gods had looked down on her from the mountaintop after all.

Chapter 3

The Kiss

Harry Spritzka was worried no longer about his old friend Tony. He was worried about everything else, but not Tony. Two years had gone by, and every detail on every sweatshop or retail store in his burgeoning empire kept him awake at nights, but from Tony he received little that could have troubled him. Everything seemed to be well under control up in Boston, proceeding normally, making progress, making a buck. Sometimes it almost seemed that Tony had become a voice on the telephone, disembodied, not someone who had lived inside Harry's own shirt. The past recedes quickly in New York. Harry had even found a new lady friend called Mimi, a rather posh young woman, who brought him face to face with the new century at the Armory Show. After all, it was now 1913. Things change. People leave. They leave *you*. And since when had he received so much as a postcard, nevermind a phone call on his birthday?

For Tony, nothing had changed, not since a certain day. And he wanted nothing to change.

But sometimes he felt at a loss. He did not seem to be able to put a finger on it. Something was missing. Perhaps he had run out of it, whatever it was. Steam? Gas?

As the months wore on in Boston, Tony, still living in a room by himself in the boarding house in the South End, began eventually to feel a vague sense of dissatisfaction gradually creeping over him. All he knew was that something was changing, and he did not want it to change. He still had no friends in this town. His friends were in New York, unless you could call Brooklyn, in his office, a friend.

She did. She called herself Tony's *only* friend. She kept at him till he finally talked to her. Like someone human. Not grunts and "hmmphs." It took all her patience to break down his resistance. But if she did not, how was she going to accomplish her plans?

And Tony himself, there was one thing he had left behind in New York which, after a long time, began to press on his mind, and even become insistent. His mandolin.

When Laura died, he had put it aside. It was as if he could not bring himself to touch it. There was no song in his heart that he wanted to play. And the instrument reminded him of so many things that could no longer be. At first, he hid it from his own sight. Then, when he was leaving the city, Uncle Eugenio noticed that Tony was packed to go, but no mandolin. But the uncle did not dare to bring it up. Until he forced himself to. And then, poor Uncle Eugenio was blamed for trying to do the right thing. Tony reacted as if he had been slapped. He was not grateful to be reminded, but angry, and he snatched the mandolin by the neck from Zi'Eugenio's hand.

And that was how it happened that he was in the same foul mood later in the day when he left the mandolin in Harry Spritzka's office, on purpose, hoping never to lay eyes on it again, though it may have seemed to Harry that his friend Tony simply forgot himself, out of sheer preoccupation.

Harry then decided that he didn't want this instrument in his office, either. Why be reminded constantly of something he did not care to dwell on, *the loss of Tony?* His bosom buddy. Someone in his life that even his new love, Mimi, could not replace. But what to do with that stupid mandolin? That cursed reminder? Where could he put it? Who to give it to? So he brought it to his father's shop that very night and left it in the care of Tony's old friend, Litvak, the tailor, in the back room. Not everyone would want something so useless hanging around if it could not be played. But Litvak, yes. He was the kind to keep good care of this mandolin because, even if it never uttered another sound, the very presence of it spoke to him of Tony and the affection, the trust, which, of old, had grown up between them, an old man and a boy.

And then finally Tony wrote a letter to Uncle Eugenio in Camden, New Jersey, the first letter he had sent to anyone in two years, or, for that matter, in his whole entire life. He got the address from Harry, over the phone.

Where was the mandolin? Tony asked in the letter. For some reason, embarrassment, or sensitivity, he had not asked Harry when he had him on the phone, even though he recollected, or thought he did—no, after two years, he had forgotten where he had left the thing. And so he said nothing about it and only asked Harry for Zi'Eugenio's new address down Philly way. Harry would know because Harry had sent him there.

A hunt for the lost mandolin now ensued in Tony's mind. He actually became anxious over all this while waiting for his uncle's reply. For one thing, he had realized it was necessary to provide a return address if he expected to hear back—but this was the first time he had let anyone, anyone at all, know where he was. Not even Harry knew a street address, only the business address, and the phone number in Tony's office. Not even Brooklyn, from the office, had been to his room.

It was almost as if ice were cracking on the East River, or better, the Penobscot, and urging Tony, in splutters, that it was time for the waters to resume their course.

More time went by while Zi'Eugenio was inquiring after the mandolin from Harry and Harry was contacting Litvak.

Finally, Tony got his answer, and that meant a trip to New York.

He left the shop in the hands of Parisi and Mello, the cutters, and Brooklyn, if truth be told, and gave himself no more than one week to get to New York and back.

He worried about the shop, which everyone now called Spritzka's, as if it had been there always, brown and dour, squeezed hip to hip between seven-story redbrick mill buildings in the industrial section across the Summer Street Bridge, around the corner past the curve of Melcher Street, at No. 10, opposite the foot of Necco Street.

The shop was, is and always would be, the terminus to one end of Tony's daily round. His life had become a return trip back and forth to work, between two buildings of redbrick in a brownstone and brick low-rise town called Boston.

In New York, of course, he stayed with Harry.

He wished he hadn't. It was painful to be reminded of his old life. So much had changed in two years. Harry himself did not seem like the same guy.

That was Miriam, or Mimi's, doing. Harry was blind, deaf and dumb to it, but to Tony, the transformation was like the lights of Times Square had come on. Though it was impossible to refine Harry's rough soul, this young lady had smoothed down the ragged edges, and combed the woolly surface. He was still a beast, but now, a soothed beast.

Miriam Lowenstein, Harry Spritzka's fiancé, wore on her ring finger a perfectly ostentatious diamond he had given her, but she was in no hurry to get married. First Harry had to build her a house. She was the scion of a family of German Jews from Carnegie Hill and her father was in the banking business, and that meant that Harry had a lot to prove to him. The father was a ringleader of the Jews of the Upper East Side who called themselves "Our Crowd," who looked down, congenitally, on Jews from Poland or the Ukraine or Lithuania. That accounted for the size of daughter Miriam's diamond.

However, the father dismissed Harry's chunk of rock as a bauble. Mr. Lowenstein the banker was waiting to see whether this young Jew was going to keep his daughter in the style she was accustomed to.

So Harry purchased a lot on East 91ˢᵗ, right next door to Otto Kahn, the investment banker, whose mansion was on the corner. Naturally, Harry couldn't put a Rivington Street hovel in there. So when Tony arrived, and had to search for the address, he was ushered into what had become an Italian Renaissance palace, under construction.

Tony looked around and said to Harry, "Where do you get the money?"

Harry said, "It's 1913, Tony. Tony. Business is good, you know that. They're expecting a war in Europe."

"How do *you* know that?"

"Tony, don't you read the Wall Street Journal? Ever hear of the Rothschilds? Max Warburg? It's my business to know, Tony.

Robert's, too. You know, my brother's a genius, you know that, don't you? Now listen. The gunmakers, the steelmakers, they're gearing up. Economy's pumping. Wall Street soaring. *We* are still expanding. Spritzka Enterprises. New *Richard Paul* stores opening, new factories, new real estate. I can't keep up."

Tony looked at his friend as if he didn't recognize him.

"What? It's my business to know these things." Harry hooked his thumbs in the bottom of his vest. "I keep my nose to the ground."

Tony gazed on the Italian stonemasons standing on scaffolding with trenches and trowels sculpting concrete lions into balustrades. "I didn't know business was that good."

"I don't believe in letting money lay idle," said Harry.

Tony looked more aghast than impressed.

"You should be proud—this is all being built with the best Italian craftsmanship!"

Tony shrugged. "I never saw a building like this back in the old country."

"That's why you left."

"So, you don't go up to the Speedway anymore on a Saturday afternoon?"

"Tony, that's long gone. You know what they use that for now? People go up there to take the family out for a Sunday drive in their motorcar! After all, it's the best place, the only place, for views of the Hudson, not all cluttered with barges and tugboats. Tony, those days are gone, things have changed!"

It was Harry's brother Robert who was the contractor for the new house. He was expanding, too, trying to branch out from land-lording and turn himself into the next big thing, a *developer.* Construction, and hotels, that was the wave of the future for Robert Spritzka. Tony had to ask himself if he really knew these brothers. *Did they even remember a time when it was Tony who gave Robert an introduction to Don Serafino? That they owed it to Tony, that five-hundred dollar loan from the Don that gave them their start?*

"So, do I get to meet Miriam?—or you hiding her?"

"Mimi, Tony. Call her Mimi. I call her Mimi. She likes it. Makes everything cozier."

They all went out to dinner that night, at a Bavarian restaurant called *The Munich-Haus,* and that was even more painful for Tony. He picked at the sauerkraut as if it were food for pigeons. Mimi was all she was advertised to be: gracious, courteous, kind—and condescending, Tony thought. He didn't hold it against her. He thought, *how could she help it? Why would she know any better, being from where she's from?* He, Tony, was a part of Harry's life that had nothing to do with her, and evidently, she thought it well behind him. She was bringing Harry along and had no intention of anyone dragging him back into the gutter he came from.

But Tony did like her perfume. And she wore a dress with elegance. Always a thing that Tony took notice of. Tony thought, maliciously, *so—he's gonna marry his own mother!*

But on the train home, Tony was restive. Home. *Boston.* How had that ever happened? And yet, he no longer liked New York—it was not his town anymore. Not the same place at all. The streets were crowded and noisy, but it was a different kind of noise, big engines, cranes, pneumatic drills, automobiles crawling along, like dogs on a sled, nose to tail, sniffing exhaust. Where were the families strolling in the street, on the way to Mulberry Park on a Sunday afternoon, chattering, happy-go-lucky, heedless? *Gone. All gone. Replaced with cement lions . . .*

It was just as well that he and Harry were no longer friends. That was another splinter sticking in his eye on the way back to Boston. Almost with bitterness, Tony thought—*just as well—I can't afford to go to the wedding—what in the hell could I get them for a wedding gift? And how much would it cost me? More money than I'll see in a month! I work for him, and that's all. Let it go. Let him build his empire. I got another row to hoe.*

But there was something else. Tony looked forlornly at the mandolin, lying in his lap. As usual, the train was crowded, and he had to hug it to himself. But he felt no impulse whatever to play it. It comforted him to feel it, the neck, leaning against his heart. The same way it felt comfortable to see old Litvak again, when he went to fetch it at No. 68. Even Harry's parents, looking a little more worn and torn, but not really aged, were glad to see him, *since they knew he wasn't staying!*

But worst of all was coming face to face with the idea that Bubelah was gone. She had died, and Tony never even knew. Nobody had thought to let him know, not even his best friend, Harry.

What was happening to all of them? Tony sat on the train back to Boston and the swaying motion, that cradling back and forth, had him close to tears.

Could it be that Bubelah was the only person who had ever loved him? *He could not remember if his own mother had loved him.*

And Laura Antonelli had never had the chance.

It occurred to Tony to ask himself, rocking back and forth in the train seat—*will I ever have the chance?*

Because what bothered him more than anything, when you came right down to it, was that Harry was getting married. And maybe Mimi loved him. As hard as that might be to believe. And maybe he even loved her. As hard as *that* might be to believe. And maybe they were going to be happy, together. But, in any case, together. And he was going home to a room. To nothing. And nobody.

When he got into town, Brooklyn was waiting for Tony at South Station, when he emerged onto the sidewalk, pulling the strap over his head to situate his mandolin.

"Are you all right? You look terrible!"

"Everything's fine," said Tony.

"Thank God you're back!"

"Why? What's wrong?"

"Nothing! Everything's fine, like you said. I was just worried you wouldn't get back in time."

"In time for what?"

"For Sunday—that's what."

"What's Sunday?"

"You'll see."

They were walking out to the street. Tony had his suitcase and his mandolin. He stopped her.

"What are you cooking up, Brooklyn?"

"You want me to spoil the surprise? Don't worry, I got everything arranged. She's a beautiful girl—her name is Anna-Vittoria."

"Anna-Vittoria who?"

"Fabrizio, that's who! Her father's a butcher. Where I get my pork-chops and a leg of lamb."

"What are you, a matchmaker all of a sudden? Who asked you!"

"You need a woman for what ails you!"

"So that's what this is all about! Why don't you stick your nose into your own business?"

"She's the oldest daughter, and her father's getting anxious. I told him all about you, and how you're the perfect young man to take her off his hands."

"I'm not about to get married to anybody!"

"Who said anything about marriage? We're just gonna go to Sunday dinner, on Prince Street, in the North End, that's all! That is, you are. I gotta check my appointments. I'm a very busy individual. So you're just gonna get acquainted, that's all! What's so hard? You look like a scalded cat! Don't worry. She's a nice girl. You'll like her."

Tony was about to say, *I don't like anybody!* But before it came out, a car swerved to the curb, and he held Brooklyn back using the suitcase in his hand. "Watch out!"

"I see him, I see him! You watch out!"

"I am. And I'm not getting married to anybody, either."

"Yeah. That's how you watch out for yourself. If you didn't have me! And frankly, I'm getting tired of escorting you to the coffee shop on Saturdays, your big night out, or to go see some bow-legged horse running in circles down in Hingham that oughta be, by rights, in the cemetery for old nags in some God-forsaken place like Malden, at the end of the trolley line."

"One time, you dragged yourself!"

"I'm not so fond of hoss manure, like you. How's it workin' out with your little side dish from the diner?"

"The Irish girl? She's nothing but a pain in the *culu*—like you!"

"Right. But you don't need me to arrange no introductions to any nice families for you, with a nice girl for a daughter, who speaks Italian, not some Irish floozy!"

"You got some mouth on you!"

"You're a big conversationalist yourself!"

"I'm telling you right now, Brooklyn, I am not getting hitched to no Anna-Vittoria or anybody else for that matter!"

"You're not gettin' any younger, you know!"

"What is this, a meat market?"

"That's rich! A meat market! Well, her father is a butcher. At least you'll never go hungry. She's a nice, well-brought up young lady. She cooks. She cleans. What more in the world could you ask for? But what am I, crazy! I'm wasting my breath! Like as if you know what's good for you! Whaddya do in that room all the time, anyway? Play solitaire?"

On Sunday, Tony went to the house on Prince Street as if he were going to a hanging, his own. All he wanted was to get this out of the way. Once he was past this, he could resume living. Living his own life, such as it was. *Goddam that Brooklyn, did she know how to get under a man's skin?* She wouldn't leave off pestering him all week in the office till she finally got her own way. In the end she made him feel ashamed for breaking promises *she* had made! How in the hell did she do that? Oh, yeah. *They'll be insulted. Are you trying to insult them? You too good to go to their house, is that it? You wanna make them feel offended? How would you like it if somebody did that to you? You invited them over, and they refused to come? Don't you realize that's the worst possible insult you could inflict on anybody, to refuse to sit down and eat with them?*

In the end Tony gave in, just to shut her up. And now, the big two o'clock Sunday afternoon, four-course dinner, from olive pit to watermelon seed, for which he had arrived strictly on time, *so as not to insult anyone,* was finally over, and he had been asked to go in the front room and sit by himself, with his hands folded in his lap, cooling his heels, while the family who had so kindly and considerately invited him to inspect their daughter, Anna-Vittoria, shut the door on him, to confer by themselves, *God knows why,* privately, out of his hearing.

And here he was, sitting, in a room by himself, the Fabrizios' *salotto,* the only one in their house with a window looking out on the narrow confines of Prince Street; a single lousy, narrow window in a narrow house, and he couldn't even stick his hands in his pockets, while he sat there on their *divano,* for fear of them taking him for some *buffone* from the farmlands, with pig-shit still crusted on his boots.

So he had to sit there, on his good behavior, angelic as a choir-boy, while all the time the devil inside his head was asking him, *but how did you let yourself get into this fix? Are you stupid? What are these people to you? You don't even know them. So, they come from Volturrara. Still, you're lucky they're not from Alta Villa itself! God forbid that you should be actually related! but how do you know? the kids could come out like a mule with only three legs, soft in the head like a grape you squeeze, squish! leering at you out of a lopsided face!*

And take one good look at that Anna-Vittoria! How in the hell's a kid gonna come outta her! She's so skinny, if she turns sideways they could use her for a lamp-post! And a personality like she spent all day sucking on lemons! Even her little toothy-mousy mouth is puckered up sour! Can you imagine lying in bed beside her! You might as well crawl in a coffin and try to put your arms around the corpse! To take one look at her would shrivel up St Anthony himself! Ah fa Nabala!

On the other hand, that sister of hers, whadda they call her? Gigi?—she's got a set! Ah, now there's a couple of pillows you could rest your head on!

But what are you thinking? Are you crazy? The father ain't gonna let that happen. He wants to get rid of the oldest first, he's got to. And this is his one big chance. He saw you coming a mile off. No wonder he was falling all over you. He even spoke English with you, in front of them! You want some more soup, Tony? Have a little shot of anisette. How do you like the sauce? good, huh? I found myself the best little cook in the world, right here, isn't that right, Anna-Lisa? And I made her a Fabrizio, first chance I got. And she's not stupid either—she told her father, Papa, it's the veal-cutlet for me! Just like Anna-Vittoria—.

But Anna-Vittoria raised her eyebrows and twisted her chin at her father, and stopped him short, when she heard her name get mentioned.

And Tony sat there thinking of that now.

He realized something—something important—*she* did not want *him!*

What a hell of a fix to get into!

And she's got a helluva nerve, that simpering little cat-foot! the kind that goes sneaking around the house flattened up against the wall like you don't see them! I hate cats!

And she's got the notion that she don't like me!—that I'm not good enough for her!

From that moment on all Tony could think of was getting out of there.

He looked at the window. He looked at the window desperately. Going back out that shuttered door, past them—out of the question. But the one window in the room was closed.

It suddenly occurred to him how warm it was today. He pulled at his collar. Something was cinching him so tight that beads of sweat were coming out of his forehead. *Ah, the hell with it!* He looked at the shut door facing him with dread. He imagined it bursting open and Signore Fabrizio walking in hitching up his pants for a man-to-man talk with him—settling down on the couch next to him—putting his arm around him. *The man looked deeply into Tony's eyes and asked, will you take good care of my daughter?*

Tony was not going to wait for that fatal door to open. He was going out the window if he had to. He said to himself, *I'll give them an insult they won't forget!*

He had raised the window and had his whole upper body out and he was calculating how he would lower himself down onto the sidewalk by one leg and how it wasn't too far and how he didn't want to fall over in the street and make an ass of himself and what if the passersby who were already curiously taking note of a man coming out of a window were to all laugh at him lying there in a heap on the sidewalk—when the door of the front room behind him burst open!

"Where do you think you're going!"

Tony was shocked to hear a feminine voice! Behind him! He was staring straight at the sidewalk, about to pull his right leg through the window. Could he look back, over his shoulder, from that position, without losing his balance?

"Come back here, you *toro grande!*"

And a hand on the collar of his tailored pinstripe suit-jacket was pulling him, manfully, back into the room!

And he thought to himself—*my God, she's strong.*

She was so vigorous that, pulling him back in, she bumped the back of his head on the bottom of the raised window, so that when she had him straightened up and turned around to face him, his hand was going to the back of his head, and she growled at him, with a gleam in her eye, "You remember my name, eh?"

He had time to say, "Uh," when she interrupted him impatiently. "Of course you do! I'm Gigi! Everybody knows Gigi! And everybody loves Gigi! Now come over here with me and sit down!"

Tony took a deep breath, which allowed him to straighten up a bit, and he got a better view of the expansive love that she was offering him, in two big bundles, like paper bags full of groceries, and he smoothed back his hair, with both hands, and went to straighten his necktie, but impatiently she grabbed his hand and yanked him by the wrist onto the sofa, where she landed next to him, practically in his lap.

"Put your arm around me," she commanded, and her dark eyes were angry when he did not immediately. She pulled his left hand out from between their hips, where she was sitting on it, and was pulling it around the back of her neck, when he said, "Slow down, slow down, you know? I don't speak Italian every day."

"That's all right, I talk for both of us."

"I have to think of everything I say."

"Well, what's to say?" She patted his hand, now on her shoulder, and resettled herself against the curve of his arm encircling her neck. "You like that shoulder?"

He said nothing, but he did smile, he couldn't help it, *it was that devil again!*

"I know you like that shoulder. And that's not all you like."

She had placed her forehead against his, and she was looking into his eyes, and grinning mischievously, and she said, "Go ahead! You can look down. I know you want to. You know you want to. Eh!—you're a man! Don't be shy! I'm Gigi! And these are for you. You appreciate a couple of good things when you see them. Take a good look. Don't you want to see what you're getting?"

Tony took another swallow of air. "I don't know," he said, carefully, in dialect, "if I understand."

But speaking did not save him from looking down. That was involuntary. And what he saw was magnificently seductive. A breathing, curving mound of skin so close you could see it and smell it and taste it in all its glorious milky whiteness, and a twin sister, rising and falling alongside, breathing together, keeping each other warm and blossoming.

"That's all right," she said, her chest rising, "I understand for both of us."

Slowly, she began to lean back against the curve of his arm around her neck and her sway and pull and emphasis led him onward until their heads were leaning together on the back of the sofa, their shoulders were comfortably settled, and she said to him, "Kiss me."

He hesitated.

"*Va bene,* I wait. For you, I wait a long time. I saw you, big *culu,* going through that window. I brought you back. Because the minute I saw you at my father's table, I wanted you. Forget about that string-bean, Anna-Vittoria. If I saw her lying in the street, I'd spit on her. You think I was going to let her have you? And my father, forget about him, too."

Tony was trying to think at the same time he was trying to keep his hands to himself like some sort of gentleman; at the same time he was trying to breathe without gulping air, and trying to think of how to express himself in Italian, and trying to be polite and courteous, and not offend anyone; especially her, this commodious, fragrant, intoxicating, buxom body pressing into him, him, a gentleman, who, when his pulse was racing, and his heart pounding, and he was beginning to feel himself hardening, down there, a very wicked and bad, and delicious, sensation, was suddenly no gentleman, but a ravenous beast, with bestial impulses pulsing in his blood, and he managed to say, "Did I hear a commotion out there a minute ago? Behind that door?" He noticed now that she had closed it again, and they were alone. "While I was sitting here, by myself, waiting?"

"That was me, telling my father, and my mother, who's marrying who. And no, you weren't waiting. You were trying to get out the window."

Tony swallowed, and he was thinking he had the devil in his arms as well as in his head.

"I'm waiting," Gigi announced. She nestled her head comfortably into the crook of the elbow of his arm, that was ranging along the back of the sofa. "Take your time." She looked warmly into his eyes, back and forth, like someone with a match in a dark room searching for something. Again, she spoke. "Do you know when I fell in love with you? Do you know why?"

Now Tony was searching her eyes, to see if he could believe anything, everything, she was saying.

And Gigi said, "It was when I heard your name—LaStoria."

"When did you hear that?"

"Oh, before you came. And, then, when you were here, and you sat down at my father's table—then I knew."

"Knew what?"

"That it was true."

"What's true?"

"That's my secret."

"You have secrets?"

"Don't you think so?"

"Yes."

There. He had uttered it. The fatal *yes.*

"Don't you have secrets, too?—Antonio?—*my* Antonio?"

"*Si. Ho uno segreto. Ma, solo uno.*"

"And will you tell me?"

"No. I cannot."

"No. You cannot. You will die before you tell me. That's why I love you. You understand that a person can have a secret.

And you will not ask me about mine. But—tell me this—can you give only one kiss to Gigi?"

On his lips were no words, but in his heart Tony was saying to himself, *May God forgive me.*

"I ask you for only one kiss. And then we'll see. Maybe one kiss is all you need. Maybe one kiss is all you dare. You are a strong man, my Antonio. Maybe you can stop after just one."

But he could not.

Chapter 4

Wedding-Night

Gigi said, "We are going to have nine children!"

The exclamation escaped her lips the way a bubble of air might escape the water.

She and Tony were leaning on a railing down by the wharf-side adjacent to the North End neighborhood where the Fabrizios lived. Ever since their first kiss, they had announced their engagement to the world by walking out together in the evenings, arm in arm.

On this particular evening, they had been visiting a jeweler on Hanover Street, to pick out wedding bands, gold.

"And a lot of gold to wear," Gigi continued, as an afterthought. They were leaning their foreheads together, over the railing, gazing at the water, and then again at each other. "Bracelets. Necklaces."

Ever since their first kiss, they had been kissing at every opportunity. It was hard, in front of people, and obviously, you could not openly, on a public street, so they were hiding their heads together, at the wharf-railing, with their backsides turned to the world.

When Gigi made her announcement about the children, her grip on Tony's hand had tightened, her fingers squeezing, as if emotion had made her reactions involuntary.

Tony wasn't worried about the gold. He had a feeling he wanted to buy his Gigi everything, especially anything she asked for. But he was alarmed by the children. Nine! "How do you know about the children?"

"I just know. Don't ask. It's *my* secret."

She was looking at the water now, not him, and her look was drifting away, on a ripple, wavering, as if transfixed by peering underneath. She was floating far away from him in her mind.

He knew enough not to probe further.

That she would withdraw, and retreat, behind a screen, he had discovered; a wall went up, and she was in another place all her own, where no one was admitted, not even him; this he already knew.

That, too, seemed to him involuntary.

Sometimes her eyes would go back in her head. She would enter what seemed to be, or could only be called, a trance.

Then just as suddenly, without warning, she would come back, and be sitting here in the room with you.

If you asked her where she had been, she reacted with surprise, as if she honestly did not know that ten, twenty, twenty-five seconds had gone by when she was not there.

She was very mysterious, and very insistent, and very impatient. He was fascinated by her.

But she was also warm, almost on fire, simmering, with a glow, aromas, steam rising, like a pot on a stove. You wanted to put both arms around the pot, but not be burned.

He knew he did not love her, but he knew also that, now, he could not live without her.

It troubled him that everything was moving so fast. They were going to be married, without waiting, within two weeks from the first time they met! Gigi did not want to wait, and whatever Gigi wanted, heaven and earth had to move, her father, her mother, her sister Anna-Vittoria. Because Gigi stamped her foot, the family quivered.

It troubled Tony not because he did not want to marry her: for that, he could hardly wait. Each day now was an eternity spent in waiting until he could finally escape the shop and go to her in the evening. When he walked back alone to his room in the South End late at night, he did not even notice where he had been going, what streets he had passed, who, or what, he had seen, and yet, all of a sudden, he was back at his own front door, without being able to say how he got there. It troubled Tony because he had promised Laura to always love *her.* He had made a vow deep in his soul and now he was about to betray that vow.

So, when Gigi retreated, into that vacant state when her eyes went out of focus, back in her head, and you knew she was looking inward at a world, a world in there, where no one else could go, then so did Tony retreat, to redeem a little his lost individuality, which was being soaked up by her vast, overpowering being; each of them was edging back off a precipice, while still, they held on tightly to each other.

And it was then that Tony thought, *if I do not love her, if I do not fall in love with her, then, my vow will be kept.* Because it was then that the thought of Laura entered his mind, while Gigi was *away,* and when he thought of Laura, he found he could not let go of her corpse.

But even as Tony felt an impossible, unthinkable, but inescapable attraction pulling him spiraling downward towards the whirlpool that was Gigi, so Gigi felt a mysterious connection to him: though Tony would never have been able to imagine that. To her, he was a volcano, a smoking mountain, something fearful to watch, but at the same time, you could not take your eyes away from it. *Would a wave of the ocean encircle the mountain, or would the volcano set the sea on fire?* He was—what? A stranger, who had walked into your village street, and you had the feeling you had always known he was bound to come. He was a story you had heard before, and that's why you knew the ending already. He was: a city in the distance, to which all roads led; you had never been there, but you knew that's where you were going.

Although he appeared as a man, to Gigi, who had always lived in a world of her own making, he was something else, something more, something out of a past long ago and far away, across an ocean in another time. He only appeared to be a man.

And Gigi was impatient to be married because she had an empty, hollow hungering for every sensation that he was going to give to her, a void inside her, the size of the deepest ravine of the ocean floor, that ocean which came from worlds away to lap the very seawalls of the North End where she lived, which brought with it, in waves, that emptiness which *he* had come, according to the promise of life, to fill.

She did not need to know anything else.

Tony could not have imagined this. He thought that he was following her. He was *her* follower. None of this was his doing.

It was all happening *to* him, *because of* her. He was happy, even contented, to be her follower. He need not therefore decide anything. Everything would be taken care of for him.

In this mysterious fashion Tony became one of the family, overnight, the family whose members all were held in Gigi's sway.

But for Gigi all was transfixed in the mirror in reverse. She was *his* acolyte. She was ready to fall to her knees to climb *his* mountain. She was a pilgrim at *his* shrine asking only favors, only a blessing, just his hand on her shoulder.

All this was highly amusing to Gigi's mother. They had always been confidants, in a way that no one could ever be with that other thing, Anna-Vittoria. And it tickled Anna-Lisa to no end to think about the surprises this mischievous witch of a beguiling daughter had in store for her on her wedding night!

Of course, Anna-Lisa was not going to spoil it for Gigi by telling her anything. *Let her find out on her own! Better that way.*

And Gigi also was her mother's co-conspirator in this willful blindness.

Of course, Gigi had always known, whenever her mother and father had closed the door, and shut out the children, that something was going on in there. There were the noises they would make, and it wasn't just the bed sighing.

After all, in their family, they were always hugging, kissing, holding onto one another, back and forth: all except for Anna-Vittoria.

And sometimes Mamma, or Papa, would have a certain look come over them, a look of pleasure. Of a secret thought that made you smile to yourself. What was that secret satisfaction?

But Gigi did not care to ask. Or to find out. To her, life was a mystery, and she liked it that way. *Why would anyone want to draw down the blue out of the sky?*

All her mother would say was, "Just you wait!"

And a gleam would come into her eye. Eyebrows a little raised. While they were peeling onions together at the sink.

"Oh," said Gigi's mother, "I'm going to cry!"

"I'm waiting."

"Don't worry, he'll know what to do. He's a man. They always know."

Gigi wanted to ask her—how do they always know? But she knew better. She would save that question for her wedding night, and her husband. Husband! How that word affected her. Her whole life was going to be changed. By him. And she was going to enter new worlds, worlds she could hardly conceive of, in reality, though in her dreams she was intimately familiar with them.

"You just let him," said her mother. "That's all. Just let him. You don't have to do anything. He'll do everything. You'll see. He'll teach you."

And then it was the morning of their wedding.

Everything was white. The sun was high in the sky by eleven in the morning but the light flowing down into the cradle of the North End streets was neither golden nor yellow but pure white. Gigi's wedding gown was white and the purple pansies and red carnations of the bouquet she held in her hands before her, like a child going to communion with hands respectfully folded, their brilliant splash only accented the startling white of her wedding dress. Even Gigi's smile, as she walked from her front door only a short way to the corner of her own street where they were to be wed inside San Leonardo's, was bouncing, white with sunshine, teeth sparkling, as she turned her head one way and another to catch the reflections of suddenly surprised onlookers, who saw a bride walking in the street on her father's arm, and who, in their turn, burst out into smiles. It was only natural: when you see a bride smiling and happy, it makes you want to smile in return, especially on a busy Saturday morning in August, with the North End thronged with people in the streets. If it was a funeral, you might bow your head, make the sign of the cross, and hurry on your way, but a wedding makes you want to stop and gaze on happiness and drink it all in, bask in the glory and feel the sun caress your skin, and you welcome the tingling heat on your bare arms.

At the center of this passing spectacle, Gigi too felt the warmth of the sun on her arms, but that heat spread also underneath her bodice down her ribs along the curve of her stomach and down into her thighs so that she felt the sun not reflected from her, but captured inside her, and the heat of the sun became the source of her radiance, from within, so that, as she passed from the brilliance of the day under the portico into the darkness of the interior of San Leonardo's, as sudden and refreshingly cool as a grotto in the high mountains, she glowed.

And then she passed through the *cerimonia* as if walking in a dream. And she recited her lines as if given a part memorized before birth. And she looked back at her father only once, as he unhooked his arm and let go of her. And then she saw her bridegroom, waiting for her, and he tilted his head slightly, and smiled tenderly, almost a trifle sadly, as if a bird had just alighted on his windowsill, and he knew that it was bound to fly away again, and the moment would be gone.

And then it was all over, and Gigi passed back under the portico from the cool shade back out into the intensity of the sunshine, and she squinted at the world, and tried to memorize what had changed, what was so different, but she could not exactly say, except that it felt that everything was transformed into something dazzling and new. And she wanted to hold onto that feeling as long as she could.

Then there was music and *cibo* and dancing and singing and people at a reception held in the brown-wainscotted rooms of the Italian Protective League, on Hanover Street. That was the doing of her father, who, being a merchant, was a faithful member, dues-paying and vociferous, anxious to hold the police accountable for protecting him from predators such as *La Camora*. And again everything seemed to Gigi slowed down as if a lengthy and languorous dream were passing before her very eyes and she had the time to linger on every word or glance.

For she had dreamed so long of this day far in the future and now she was at last surrounded by the day and the night when the fulfillment was being born before her very eyes, astonished by every phrase falling to her ears and every look swimming up to her eyes.

And then she and Tony were alone.

Alone together, in a room with a closed door.

A bedroom with a closed door.

They hadn't needed to close the door at all, because everyone had left them alone, and gone down into the street to celebrate with friends and neighbors, to prolong things, just a moment, on the front stoop, and then, down the street to the cousins' to spend the evening, and give Gigi and Tony a little privacy on their wedding night.

So they were married in the morning at the church on the corner and they were to spend their first night together for the rest of their lives just a few doors away.

Tony gently closed the door and turned to his bride sitting on the edge of her bed. For a moment he simply looked at the magnificence of her presence, spread out like a garden of white daisies, dahlias and begonias, all white, on the side of the bed.

It was her white dress that was spread out on each side of her. A wedding gown that they had picked out together.

It had been an occasion in which Tony was able to indulge himself and his somewhat hidden, fastidious taste. A special occasion, not to be repeated. He was not a tailor by birth, heritage and upbringing for nothing. Gigi was a beautiful young woman, as fresh as the brilliant yellow flower the Americans called a black-eyed susan, and, like that flower, she was dark in the center, but spread her golden wings far-flung, wide and embracing, and she deserved to be clothed in something silken and finely spun on her wedding day.

So Tony had brought her to Bonwit Teller, a sanctuary of satin and lace domiciled in the cerulean blue Victorian house with the mansard roof on the corner of Newbury Street, and paid for the gown himself. He wanted her to luxuriate in the day. He had the money. But could she find what she wanted?

They had found it off the rack, as it happened. A simple, flowing Greek-inspired design that gave her ample bosom support under the breasts as it cinched high above her waist.

When she came down the aisle in San Leonardo's on her father's arm, that morning, in that dress, she was gliding, and you would not know that she walked on mortal feet, because the swishing long gown hid them right down to her slippered toes, so that she seemed to move like a goddess.

And now she was seating herself, waiting for him to join her.

She patted the bed at her side.

But he wanted to gaze awhile first. So he leaned back against the door as he closed it gently with one hand behind him.

Then he was beside her, and they resumed the kissing, the kissing which they had barely interrupted since the day they met.

But this time Tony did not restrain his hands. This time he wanted recklessly, come what may, to let his touch roam over the body that he felt beneath the silk, this time he wanted to possess her entirely and completely, and as he supported her with one arm behind her waist, he was filled with a fervor rising from below, and as their kiss deepened, he wanted to press her down upon the bed—but then she stopped him with her hand, pressing him back.

"What's that?" she said.

"What?"

"I heard something."

"I didn't hear anything."

Her eyes were as black as olives.

"There's someone at the door," said the bride.

"There's no one in the house!" said the groom.

"Someone's there. I know it. Go look. I'll wait here."

Tony rose slowly, and turned away. He was embarrassed a little because his arousal felt like it was going to burst his satin-striped black wedding trousers. *But how silly!—she was his wife now!* And yet he could not reassure her, and when he turned to face the door, he felt actual trepidation. *What if there was someone there? Who could it be?* He only knew that Gigi felt it, powerfully, and had pushed him away. And now he was filled with it, he had caught the sensation from her, it felt almost like dread. But he could not show that he was afraid of anything, in front of her, at this moment.

When he opened the door, he was holding his breath.

There was no one there, the rest of the house was empty and dark.

Tony breathed again. He turned to her and said, "There's no one there."

"*There was! There was, I tell you.* And when you opened the door, he was gone."

He returned to her side because he could tell she was frightened. He smoothed her hair and gently urged her to lower her head onto his shoulder until she surrendered. She had gone rigid there, for a moment. And once she was resting her cheek on his shoulder, he continued to pat her head, as you would a frightened child.

But he felt a grieving shadow pass over them, and he had wanted nothing to spoil this night for her, or for himself.

And Gigi was thinking that her mother had told her to just let him have his way, and, like a child, she wanted to do what her mother told her.

Tony was feeling disturbed, and troubled, so he made up a lie, quickly, and told her, "It was Jesus who came to the door."

She looked at him doubtfully, so that he redoubled the lie, and although he did not believe it himself, he said, "Yes, Gigi, *He* came."

He could almost feel his finger wagging.

"*He* came, to change the water into wine, for our wedding."

But Gigi did not believe that.

She had felt something terrible—a presence of foreboding—a thing that was only half-human, but more than half bestial, a thing of corruption, like something dead.

Gigi did not know what kind of messenger had been sent, by what god, or whether a divinity itself, but it was something wild, perhaps bearded like a nanny-goat, perhaps rutting, a runaway pig, a wild boar, in heat, from the dark forest of the bearded mountains, mountains bearded with trees, gnarled and grotesque, overrun with vegetation, crag-like mountains, with ridges, and steep, hopeless ravines, ringed with garlands of grey mist, laurels of ghostly cloud, mountains that she had never seen, but which her mother Anna-Lisa had made vivid and real.

Gently, Tony took her by the shoulders and lowered Gigi, suggesting to her, wordlessly, to lie back on the bed. He stood and lifted her legs for her, which she primly kept closed together, joined at the knee; Tony repositioned her lengthwise, to fit the way the bed ran, instead of sprawled across it contrariwise. He went to the other side of the bed and gently rolled her body up on her side. She let him. She let him do whatever he wanted. She was following the commands of her mother. She was a good girl. And she was going to be a good wife. And a good mother. She did not know how. She was suddenly terrified of the thought of all that she did *not* know.

Of only one thing was she sure: *there had been someone at the door.* And he was in the room with them now. Her husband had let him in. When he opened that door. Not in body was he there, but as a spirit. A ghost. A *spettro. Si,* that was it. *Not Jesus, but The Holy Ghost. The third member of the Trinity. The Third Eye. Which sees everything . . .*

Tony lifted her back, propping her up with one hand while he rolled down the bedcovers. He sat on the bed beside her, and he managed to massage the covers down around and below her feet, and then let her down onto her back again, where she lay in her wedding dress, looking up at him, wordless, but watching his every move. All this time she had not taken her eyes off him.

He covered her and drew the bedclothes up under her chin. Then he stood up again beside the bed and unhooked his trousers and let them fall. He stepped out of them, and then took down his underwear.

He stood there in his stocking feet, strangely moved, no longer concerned whether he were aroused, or flaccid. That no longer mattered, he only wanted to climb in and hold her. He stood there in the top half of the English morning suit in which he had been married that day, and the tails of his white shirt trailed around his thighs. He disrobed until he was standing there completely naked, and then he climbed in and lay down next to her under the covers.

Tony took Gigi in his arms and tenderly stroked her brilliant dark hair. Without shutting off the electric light, he told her to close her eyes, it was time to rest, time for them to sleep, and that in the morning, they would wake up together, man and wife.

He stroked her hair tenderly and breathed in deeply the breathless fragrance of her long dark tresses, which smelled so good, so intimate, so like the fragrance of flowers which haunted the bees.

When Gigi had gone to sleep, Tony finally relaxed, relieved, and he lay there thinking. He shut off the lamp so that he could lie in the dark, to think better.

Now that she was asleep, he was alone again, and he felt his head aching with all the toasts of red wine from the wedding reception.

He felt like he wanted a cigarette, but he did not dare to get up. He could not leave her alone. So he continued just lying there on his back in the dark looking up at an invisible ceiling.

Whatever is troubling her—it is just as well, Tony thought. In a way, he was mightily reprieved.

As he lay there thinking, the first place his mind wandered into was the shameful place down on Allen Street, that night when Harry Spritzka had pushed him up the steps to the assignation of a Jewish whore; and he pushed the thought away, or tried to, because it burned like a flame, singeing his tattered conscience, or what passed for his soul: a soul damaged, broken and stained by that one original sin.

And these bitter thoughts sunk him in a *cul de sac* from which the only possible way out was—*Laura.*

How he loved her.

Was it *She* after all who had come to the door? *To beseech him to remain true and not to betray her?*

Chapter 5

My Son the American

In the end, they had not nine, but seven children.

And Tony would come to think that this was a lucky number.

For, by that time, Gigi was almost worn-out with child-bearing, and in fact, the doctor, and the midwives of their Italian-exile community, as well as her nosy, interfering sister Anna-Vittoria, had warned her, on her life, not to go through another pregnancy.

Though Gigi's powers of foretelling the future seemed to have suffered their downfall, whenever Tony looked back on the beginnings of their life together, he always thought of the wedding-night, when the door opened.

And out tumbled all those children. As if they had always been there.

He almost believed that they had been *out there* floating in a shapeless form, waiting to be born; that, in truth, not only would they be bound to out-live their parents, as was the natural course, but that they *pre-existed* them as well.

Tony could not quite explain this to himself or anyone else. It was a feeling without a theory. He became convinced gradually that his children were not simply under his feet, climbing on his furniture, and making a mess of his house, but were somehow droplets of eternity, clothed in human form, blown here by a wind from forever.

In the end, Tony LaStoria liked better to remember the beginnings, when he and Gigi were both young, and it seemed that it had never before rained on the streets of the city, and that when it did, the sun came out to kiss away each raindrop from the steps of the house, the curb at the factory door, the black railings around the front garden of San Leonardo's, and the forehead of his child-bride.

Gigi, in the beginning, she thought she had never so desperately needed her mother before, nor had she, in her wildest dreams, imagined what married life truly was.

The very next day after the wedding night, when the family came back home, descending on the poor newly-weds before they were half-ready, Anna-Lisa pulled aside her daughter and said, conspiratorily, "So, what happened? Tell me all about it!"

"What are you talking about?"

"Last night, you *thorn-bush!*"

"Nothing," said Gigi, airily.

She certainly wasn't about to start telling her mother about any doors opening.

"What do you mean *nothing!*"

"I went to sleep. Is that what you want to know?"

"Hmph," said her mother. "He's certainly not the man your father was, then."

"Ah—but you didn't ask about this morning!"

"No!"

"Yes!"

"He's a strange one, that one."

"Mamma! How did you know! Did he show you the tail he keeps tucked into his pants? His tongue, like a snake? His hands, like oil?"

Actually, Gigi had sat up in bed, afterward, demanding to know, "Where did you learn that? Who taught you? You have been with someone before!"

Tony laughed, because he was sitting up too, next to a warm and pliant naked woman, who had no shame now, and revealed everything to him without thinking, who only a day before was hiding herself in folds of modesty, and now was heaving her breasts at him tempestuously.

While he himself felt a deep surrender to a spreading satisfaction rising from deep within his upper thighs and lower back, so that everything seemed glorious, and he did not hesitate to confess. "Well, yes, of course."

"Tell me, immediately!"

Tony held nothing back: as long as it did not involve Laura.

The Jewish whore down on Allen Street, that was nothing; that he could explain; and, inwardly, secretly, now, smiling to himself a private smile, he was thankful to Harry Spritzka for making him go through that. Or else upon his wedding night (or morning, as it turned out) he might have fumbled through everything, instead of guiding his expectant bride.

After all, she was a mere child of seventeen, and he was a man of twenty-four, a man of the world.

"You men!" said Gigi. "Pigs! that's what you are!"

"Gigi, I was drunk!"

"I don't care! Drunk or sober! How could you!"

"I didn't really have much to do with it, myself."

"So, your first time, you couldn't wait! You had to pay for it!"

"I never did that!" said Tony, outraged in his turn, remembering that the whole thing was a treat from Harry, on his nickel.

"Is it going to hurt like this, every time?" Gigi was suddenly miserable.

"Oh, Gigi. Let me look."

Tony was pulling back the covers—Gigi was trying to stretch them up to her chin. "Don't be a clown!"

"Let me kiss it, and make it better," said Tony, with a pout.

"Why do you want to make fun of me!" Gigi wailed.

"I'm not! Let me look!" But he let her get away with the bedclothes. He had seen what he wanted to see: blood on the sheets.

"Are we going to do that again?"

"No, of course not. Why would I want to hurt you?"

"But maybe it won't hurt so much."

"But, don't you know anything? What do they teach young girls at home these days? Did your mother never explain anything to you?"

"I would not have believed her!"

"But, how do you think babies are made?"

"Not like this!"

"Gigi!"

"This is what I have to do to have a baby?"

"Oh, now you want to make me feel bad, because you're surprised! You know, Gigi, ignorance is going to be the end of us!"

"Maybe we should try again, eh? Maybe it will get easier. If I just get used to it? I don't know . . . my mother never seemed to make a big fuss about it!"

"Have you never seen two dogs?"

"We don't have dogs like that in this neighborhood!"

"Two—pigeons, then!"

"That's what we're reduced to! Birds that shit on themselves!"

"How can they just let blind ignorance come over the eyes of these young girls," Tony was muttering, "as if the most natural things in the world were deep, dark secrets that they had to hide from the prying eyes of children!"

He was working himself up into an unreasonable fury.

"Antonio."

"What?" There was something in her voice, the way she said his name, something new. His own name had never sounded so sweet to his ears. He said, "But how did you think babies were made?"

"At the butcher shop! In the meat-grinder! And my father would bring them home wrapped up in bloody paper!"

That was hardly the end of the surprises in store for Gigi.

She became pregnant almost immediately, and when the news was confirmed, for certain, and she really believed it herself, finally, she burst into loud tears, and Tony was furious. "You don't want to have my baby!"

"Yes, but not so soon!"

"What kind of a woman are you?"

"The kind who loves you. I would like a little time to spend with you, to get to know you, and now I never will!"

"You have the rest of your life!"

"It's not the same! I will have to share you. I want to keep you all to myself!"

"Gigi! I didn't know you felt that way!"

"How would you know? You don't love me, so it's not the same for you!"

"How do you know I don't love you!"

"A woman always knows, believe me!"

This business of being married was going to be perplexing, that was all that Tony could conclude. *No matter what you say, you're always wrong!*

Gigi said, "Furthermore—you will love the children, you will fall in love with them, and then you'll forget all about me, I'm just their mother, you know. Believe me, I know you!"

"But what do you want me to do!"

"Nevermind. You can have them, the boys, that is. The girls I will keep for myself. We're going to have nine of them! Five of one, and four of the other!"

"And which will be which?"

"How should I know? Don't ask so many questions! You think I know everything?"

"You told me you can see into the past. I mean, the future!"

However, there were many things Gigi had not foreseen at all. She had thought that child-bearing would turn out to be no more than, oh, a case of indigestion; a little stomach upset. She did not know that she would come to feel like a stranger trapped inside someone else's body! A strange body with a mind of its own, constantly rebelling against the rightful owner. A collection of provinces, revolting turn by turn against the lawful queen. Places you didn't even know you had. What is this nonsense about fruit of thy womb? You would have to be as saintly as the Virgin Mary herself to put up with such revulsion and repugnance and disgust with your own loathsome self. This is not like, you move your bowels, and it's over, you feel better. This is like some quivering worm crawling up inside you. Some foreign snake trying to invade your innards. And will it ever be over, finally, and done with? Nine months, they say! Nine eternities is more like it. You would like to reach inside there with both hands and rip the whole thing out and get it over with, once and for all. But no, you have to suffer. And smile! While you suffer. And listen to people tell you how beautiful you look, pregnant! You're expecting. You should be happy. I'm happy, all right, when I feel like a sausage-skin with the butcher stuffing gizzards up me with his doubled up fist!

Once it was known to be a fact, that Gigi was pregnant, her mother promoted her. Before that, she had been a child. Now, she was, overnight, all grown up, and therefore, could be treated like a sister, like an equal, and confided in. No more making up fairy-tale explanations for the facts of life. Incredibly, Gigi thought, her mother took an almost perverted delight in her daughter's discomfort.

"Now, you see."

"See what?"

"What I've been telling you all along. You who were so smart. Now you find out I was right!"

"You never told me anything. You shut the light and let me stumble around in the dark!"

"That was for your own good."

"A lot of good it did me. Did I tell you I had a dream, mamma?"

"About what?"

"That volcano."

"Vesuvius? Ah. You never saw such a sight. Hump-backed. Like a donkey on her knees."

"Well, it's going to erupt!"

"Is that what you saw in your dream?"

"No. I saw a man in my dream. A guide. Standing by the door of the volcano."

"It doesn't have a door. It has a mouth, like a yawning cavern."

"All right, then, standing by the mouth of the cave. He was going to guide us down into the bowels of the earth."

"Who?"

"All of us schoolchildren."

"You never went to school in your life! But I know you can read—you thought you had me fooled, but I saw what you were up to with Agostino."

"I can see Vesuvius, though, and not in a book, either. In my mind's eye."

"Yes. The Third Eye. Can see many things. You know, the last time Vesuvius erupted, there was an earthquake that destroyed San Francisco."

"Do you believe that what happens over there can reach us over here?"

"Well, how do you know it can't? After all, the earth is round. How do you know that Vesuvius doesn't go right down through the center of the earth itself and come out the other side, like a tunnel? That's what happened in 1906. You were only 9 years old then. You don't remember."

"I do too remember!"

"-but I *do*."

"Well—it's easy to see into the past. It's already happened."

"And you can see into the future?"

"Yes. I know there's going to be another eruption."

"We all know that. Tell me when."

"Oh, not for a long time. Uh . . . not until, uh, let me see . . .1943. Does that satisfy you?"

"Good," said her mother, with a shudder. "Then it's a long way off."

"It's only twenty years."

"What's the matter with you? That's thirty years."

"Oh," said Gigi, with a giggle, "you're right. So much the better."

Gigi told Tony all about it when he came home from work that night. They had a room of their own, but they had to be quiet. Her father's house was too narrow for thick walls. They were lucky the older boys, Aldo and Agostino, had moved out long before, or there wouldn't have been room for Tony to move in. And Gigi would not have wanted to have any babies without her mother right there. Her sister was useless, but her mother was a different story. Gigi might embroider fantasies in her imagination, but when it came down to where her bread was kept, she knew the location of the pantry.

Tony felt an involuntary shiver when Gigi mentioned eruptions. It came back to him with a rush: that dusty road of weary walking in the shadow of ominous rumbling when he left home and struggled on foot all the way to Napoli. Was he really ten years old at that time? He recalled with a shiver how that cursed mountain had frightened him on that long-ago afternoon. He said, "I never liked that volcano."

"Quiet," said Gigi.

"We're forever whispering!"

"Don't you want me to tell you all about the day? And what my mother said? Then, you have to be quiet—stop bumping around like a sheep."

"How do you know sheep bump around? You never saw a sheep in your life!"

"I can read a book, you know."

"Too bad you couldn't predict what number's coming out in the nigger pool tomorrow." Being from New York, Tony could pronounce the letter R on the end of a word: Bostonians called it the *nigga* pool.

"My powers are not meant for low and corrupt purposes like that!"

Tony enjoyed their discussions in the evenings. Without realizing it, Gigi was telling him everything he wanted to know about her. He was avid with curiosity, and he never had to ask so much as a question. All he had to do was wait, and everything would come pouring out.

"I want you to do something for me," said Gigi, tracing one finger along his forearm.

"What?"

"I want you to bring me two spools of thread—from that factory of yours—one white, and one black."

"Why? You going to start making clothes for our baby boy?"

Gigi flashed him an angry look. "And what if it's not a boy?"

"I think it's going to be a boy. At least, I hope so. Every man wants a son. But if it's a girl," he shrugged, "we try again."

"I know you, you'll hate me if it's a girl."

Tony did not want to say anything more, because he was very superstitious about this, and he did not want to start an argument, which, with Gigi, was all too easy. "Why do you want these two colors?"

"I don't know. I just do. It's nothing to do with the colors! Don't be stupid!"

When she got her two spools, Gigi let them sit for a couple of days. She just waited for them to tell her what to do with them. One day she picked up the white one, and began to unravel it. She took the black one, and started to intertwine the colors. But this left her very dissatisfied. This was not it at all. She left them alone for a couple of days more, putting off her mother's questions, and her sister's ridicule. Then another stale afternoon came with nothing to do but rub her stomach and her aching back and her sore calves and wait for her husband to come home with something delicious for her to eat, from the bakery, something creamy; and she found herself unwinding the black spool till it was all over the floor, and the empty spool was hanging by a thread. Then, she did the same with the white one. She felt that she had to. When there were two pools of dark and light all over the floor next to her bed—then she took up the black spool, empty, and began to ravel it up again. Everything became terribly tangled, between black and white. She had created an inscrutable web that she had to struggle with her fingernails to extricate herself from. But the thought occurred to her, *ah, it's not the unraveling that I must be about . . . it's the raveling up!*

When she was done, she balanced the two lumpy spools on her tiny chest of drawers, facing one another; misshapen, bulging; for it was impossible to get the thread, by hand, wound up tight, smooth, and flawless, like it was in the beginning. Nevertheless, Gigi felt a strange, supreme satisfaction. She had made a discovery. A discovery all her own. She need never tell anyone about it. Not her mother. Not her husband. But she knew.

Now the next time she and her mother were cooking sauce for the macaroni on the tiny cast-iron white-enameled stove in the narrow pantry, where they had to wedge each other in by the elbow while they were slicing cucumbers or celery, it came to Gigi that she must keep stirring the pot. Again, she said nothing to her mother. But somehow, a little later, she made a connection between stirring the pot and the eruption of Vesuvius.

Then, she finally had the dream. Which explained it all. And it turned out that it was the guide on the mountain, the man with the telescope, who was the key to everything. For it was he who asked her for the thread, which he said he must have so that when he plunged down into the midnight hole of the volcano, as he called it, he could find his way out again.

Gigi avoided telling her mother any of the substance of her surmises by playing the game of the Cabala. Every day, without fail, her Mamma would interrogate Gigi on her dreams. Then together at the table pushed up under the lone window at the back of their kitchen they would consult the book. Every day Anna-Lisa would write down the numbers and send either her husband Pasquale or her son Agostino, to place a bet with the bookie; Agostino dropped by usually once a day (the other one, Aldo, he never came to the house anymore). Agostino would go down to the bakery or the trattoria or the Protective League, to play the nigga pool (certain American expressions Anna-Lisa, the mother, had picked up, inexplicably came out with a true Boston accent, though she spoke no more English than Gigi, the daughter did!). Or she would send Agostino, if she thought she had a really hot combination for the Daily Double, to place a wager on the horses running at the New York tracks. And then there was Tony.

Tony was available to be Anna-Lisa's runner because he was the boss over at Spritzka's shop, and so he could come and go as he pleased. So it happened that for the second time in his life Tony was conscripted into somebody's private gambling habit, and it gave him occasion to recall, with a smile, Savastano's barbershop.

Life had not simply changed since then: it had flipped, swerved, and detoured. Only last year Tony was living in oblivion in a rooming house in the South End. Now he was crammed and crowded into a family where he was the only outsider; but he was in a family again. After two years alone. Often he wondered at what had come over him as he obediently did Anna-Lisa's bidding, whatever it was that she wanted at the moment, Gigi, too; without questioning any of it. *As if he had always been there, an appendage of the Fabrizio clan!*

If the truth were told, the one thing he missed about the old days was the racing life in New York. In Puritan Boston there was no such thing. There, in good old New York, there was a wide-open town, where anything goes. Here, was a tight-lipped, blue-nosed, shamed sense of the forbidden attached to life's enjoyments: drinking, eating, love-making, playing—and gambling. It was Boston where the anti-gamblers acted like the old-time abolitionists all over again. It was Boston that had infected the whole country with an anti-gambling epidemic that even closed down New York's racetracks in 1911 and 1912. Thank God, down there they had recovered their senses. Up here, in the frozen north, they had one season at Rockingham, far away in New Hampshire, back in 1906, Pasquale told him: and even though it was 35 miles north of Boston, it frightened them so badly they never let it happen again. What do you do with such a town? In a place like this you can't stroll through the paddock like an uncrowned king and survey the spectacle of thoroughbred horseflesh: *it's banned in Boston.*

Therefore, Tony went after it with a renewed passion. He became involved in a long-distance romance with a memory. All through the medium of betting at the bookie's.

As for coping with the rest of his confinement in Pasquale Fabrizio's narrow brick house on Prince Street, with a pregnant bride and her omnipresent sister, mother, and brother, besides, Tony discovered the Boston papers.

There was the *Boston Post, the Traveler, the Daily Record,* and *the Globe*, morning and evening editions: simple. You just act like a guest in a hotel, which gives you prerogatives. You're paying for the room (with your body and soul! wrapped up in the role of a son-in-law!) so you set yourself up after dinner in a chair, or on the couch, spread open your newspaper in front of your face, and you don't have to talk to nobody. People walk around you. They scratch their heads. They hesitate to interrupt the great thinker in his absorptions.

And in the meantime, in this roundabout fashion, Tony actually discovered a world of interest in the newspapers, a world which by and by began to seduce him. He began to expand his realm, a little beyond the daily round of home and family, with all of its conceits, complaints, idle gossip and thick stupidity, the mindless small talk; *but what can you expect from small people with small minds?* His workaday life in the office and on the factory floor he now was so practiced at that he could do it with his eyes closed. Over and over again the same every day. Repeating endlessly the same round of identical tasks: *you could do it in your sleep by now.* His life now had become so automated, he even began to take the subway to work. He had only to walk as far as the Haymarket station, go down the steps, then ride all the way to South Station; then he had a nice stroll on foot across the Summer Street Bridge to work in No. 10. And the subway station put him right in front of the newsstand every morning, where he picked up a paper, and a cigar to give to the old man, his father-in-law: *keep him pacified.* And at home, when they said, for the thousandth time, *how did you like the eggplant tonight*—Tony could respond with, "The Austrians have given an ultimatum to the Serbs."

"What do we care about the—whoever they are!"

"The Hapsburg monarchy."

"Them, too," said Signore Fabrizio. In his own house, he pontificated, nobody else! "Who are these Serbs, anyway! Never heard of them! They have a lot of balls, coming from nowhere!"

"Pasquale!"

"It was a Serb," said Tony, "who assassinated the Archduke Franz-Ferdinand last month."

"Listen to my husband," said Gigi, with a wicked gleam darted at Anna-Vittoria.

"Oh, that's good," said her father. "You have respect for your husband. That's very good in a wife. And what about respect for your father, eh?"

"Papa, Tony knows more about this, only because he reads the newspapers. And you should, too."

"It's far, far away, in the old country," her father insisted. "Got nothing to do with us."

Tony passed him the *insalata*.

"Oh, thank you. Your wife should be so courteous. Maybe you can teach her some manners."

That was the whole trouble with the Fabrizios. They had their own language. Half the time you had to read between the lines. Tony felt like a telegraph pole in the middle of the house and they were transmitting messages to one another, through him.

Then all of a sudden, there was a baby.

That was all they needed, to add to the general consternation.

In the newspapers everybody was declaring war on everybody else, and the very next day, Tony was the proud father of a son.

And he had to go through the pains, the crying, the screaming, the turmoil, the agonizing of childbirth, personally, himself.

Where would he go to hide from it? It was all happening on the other side of a thin wall. The place was overrun with women, from the midwife of Prince Street, to the nosy neighbors. And in the next room, oh! the shrieks, the outcry, the cursing, all called down on the head of the man who had done this to poor Gigi. If only he could shrink into the floorboards. There was no question of putting up a newspaper in front of his face. He had to sit there and swelter under the gaze of his nonchalant father-in-law, who was acting as if nothing at all was perturbing *him*. While Tony sat with his palms sweating, the old man sat puffing on a stogie! Which Tony had bought or him! For all the world as if he were watching a pleasant afternoon sail by, down at the harbor! "Nothing to worry about, son!" said he. "Don't take it that way. They always say such things. Believe me! Her mother was ten times the foul-mouthed witch! Gigi's an angel, compared to that one! It's normal, the first time. After that, eh!"

"Shouldn't we get the doctor?"

"Only if it's necessary. Otherwise, he won't come."

"But maybe he could give her something!"

"He doesn't want to step on the toes of the midwives. They're nothing but trouble!"

Just then, Gigi called out, "Where is that bastard! Why isn't he here! If I ever get a-hold of him, I'll kill him, before I ever let him touch me again!"

Tony buried his face. His teeth were clenched.

His father-in-law was laughing at him—he was enjoying this!

Tony thought he had never felt so humiliated in all his life. He could not endure this for another minute! Nine long months! And he had felt every pang, every stitch in the side, every back spasm, every bolt of pain shooting down the hip or the back of the calf. No one could tell Tony that he did not feel her pain!

And to think that he was the cause of it all—he was mortified.

How would he ever make it up to her? Not in a million years. And who could tell him why it had to be this way? Why did we have to suffer the agonies of Christ on the cross just to be born? To come into this cursed world? Something that was supposed to be blessed like those touching pictures of the holy infant in his bed of straw; or cradled in his mother's arms beneath her benevolent gaze, La Pietà! turned out to be like pulling all your teeth out with a pair of pliers!

Then came a baby's cry! From behind the wall. From the other room. One of the neighbors came running out. "It's a boy! You have a son!"

His father-in-law was pulling him up, embracing him in his beefy arms, twirling him around the room, a pair of dancing bears. Tony didn't have time to let it register, the idea, the incomprehensible idea, that he had a son. And the first thought that entered his head, crazily, was this: *my son is an American! Born right here. This day. On American soil!*

Why had he not thought of this before? He could have slapped himself awake. But there was no time. The room was in an uproar of crying, smiling, hand-shaking, back-slapping congratulations. Where did they all come from? How did they all fit into this room, never mind the building, as narrow as a rowboat!

It seemed that everyone wanted to be his friend. People he didn't even know were instantly his closest compatriots. They crowded around: he was the center of attention; then they all melted away. Where did they go? They disappeared! They went to see the baby, and the mother!

And Tony was the last one allowed to enter that tiny, crowded bedroom, with the bodies three deep around all sides of the bed, so that he was left to stand on tiptoes at the back, just to try to catch a glimpse of them.

Then someone was placing the baby, wrapped up, into his mother's arms. The room divided and came apart at the seams as they tripped over one another to get out the door, past Tony, who was left standing there.

When he came to the side of the bed, and saw her face, framed in her dark, disarrayed hair spread out fanlike over two pillows propping up her head, he felt tortured with guilt.

How could he have done this to her, when all she had done was to love him? How she had suffered, *suffered*: for him, for his sake, to have *his* baby!

He picked up her other, free hand, where it rested on her belly, gently by the fingertips, and he could tell it felt limp and powerless. He sat down as gingerly as he could on the very precipice of the bed. He just wanted to gaze at her mutely to let her know how sorry he was. All he could manage to say was, "Gigi."

"I'm exhausted. Here, you take him. Hold your son. And don't drop him, please."

"He's so tiny."

"And so red. Oh. Did you ever see such a color? Purple and red."

At that moment Tony was speechless. He had no idea how to hold this thing. He felt he should hold up the head: it wasn't holding up itself! He didn't want to hurt it. How could it be so light, so small, so disjointed? You were afraid to move, you might pull it apart. How was he ever going to manage being a father?

"Oh. I'm so tired. Take him away. Take him to my mother. I have to sleep."

Again, Tony looked at her, and tried to say something, he didn't know what, with his eyes, hoping she would understand, but he didn't know how to put it into words, and he was ashamed to discover that, at a moment like this, he didn't know what to say.

"Go, Tony. Just go. It's all right. I want to sleep now. God, how I want to sleep. Fourteen hours, this took. Fourteen hours."

Gigi's head fell away on the pillows, and when once she had looked at the wall, her eyes shut, of themselves.

Just like that. And Tony crept away with his American son to find his mother-in-law out in the hubbub of the other room.

It was three weeks later when Tony found the words. They were sitting on the beach, on a blanket, in Nantasket. It was a warm summer day, late in August. It was a weekday, and the beach was mostly empty. There were no weekend revelers crowding the boardwalk and clamoring for amusement. No long lines of people in bathing suits standing knee-deep in the water. They were alone with the seagulls, sharing the emptiness of a blue sky without any clouds to be seen, hearing the gentle lapping of low tide on the golden sand. Nantasket had a fine white-gold sand, not clumpy and grey like Quincy or Revere. And it was far enough out of town so that you had left all the worries and whistles and horn-blowing of the city behind. The day was so fine that you wanted to paint of picture of it, to remember. Tony had built a cushiony armchair out of sand for Gigi and the baby to sit in, padded with blankets rolled up, and real scatter-cushions, shaded under a beach umbrella, and the thought occurred to him, strangely, that she looked, sitting there, gazing out over her realm of blue ocean and silver wave-caps and azure sky, like the Queen of Egypt: the successor of Cleopatra, sitting on her throne, with her son, the Crown Prince, the future Pharaoh, surveying the world at their feet.

Tony left them in their little would-be tent and walked along the sand down to the water's edge. Far enough so that he felt the wetness under his bare feet, where he stopped.

He wanted to gaze out over the immensity of the ocean. From horizon to horizon. He wanted to listen to the rhythm of the heartbeat he heard welling up from the sea, like a pulse from the depths of darkness and fathomless deepness.

The world was so wide, and they were so insignificant, lost in the vastness.

Across that infinite ocean was another continent, another world, beyond his gaze, impossible to know. *But he had come from there . . .*

How? From there, to this moment? It seemed like a dream. It could not have happened. And yet it did.

Then he took a few more steps into the water. *If I just kept going . . . could I walk all the way back there, on the bottom of the sea?* He kept going. *No . . . the waters would close over my head, and I would drown.* He took two steps more, feeling the splashing surf pass up over his knees to inundate his thighs. Though the August day was quite warm, the water here was cold: out in the Atlantic, the warm waters of the Gulf Stream were diverted eastward when they bumped the crooked arm of Cape Cod, forming a warning fist to the ocean. *The waters would rise up over my head, and then I would be drowned, and then I would be dead, and re-united with Laura . . .* suddenly he felt impeded, as if by a hand in his chest. A wave crashed against him, causing him to stagger a bit, and waver.

Gigi, in her makeshift tent with the baby, was watching him. She felt a certain sense of satisfaction in thinking that he was important enough in the world to do as he pleased; to bring her and the baby to this place of hubbub and frolic on a quiet weekday when nobody could bother or hinder them, just because he felt like it. To tell the rest of the world to go to hell and just spend the day with her.

She wanted him to always be free to do exactly as he pleased, always. She wanted to bestow on him that freedom. And she felt in her heart that, without her, *what would he be?*

Tony returned to them on their blanket. To his wife and child, in their little pavilion made of rolled-up blankets and throw-cushions. His Queen and his Prince.

He threw himself down on his back on the blanket. He felt exhausted, not physically, but by his encounter in the water with an enormous spirit of perplexity. A spirit too powerful to contend with. He was filled to the lungs, not with seawater, but with doubt. His gaze now wandered next to the faraway sky, as just now, he had looked deeply into the sea. *What is up there, through the end of the blue?* It seemed so thin and airy. You would be able to puncture it with a sewing needle. To penetrate the empyrean. To reveal what was on the other side. Lying there on his back, gazing upward, he seemed to be floating. He had a sudden sense of disorientation: he wiggled his shoulders ever so slightly so as to feel solid sand supporting himself so that he would not fall away endlessly through the hollow of the vast blue empty heaven. Was he moving? Floating? Or was it the sky, so far above them, imperceptibly passing from right to left?

Then an immense and overwhelming sense of sadness overtook him, unawares. The newspapers were full of headlines, maps, tales of atrocities, bulletins of the rape of poor Belgium by brutal Huns, who were inhumanly merciless. But it was not that. It was a sense of private, personal loss that overcame him. This vacuum was fleeing away from him, at this very instant, receding to an impossible distance, where he would never be able to grasp hold of it again.

Laura. She was up there, in the sky.

And he was down here on the ground.

She was no longer with him. *How would he ever reach her again?*

It came to him that this was the way it was meant to be, after all, in the end.

A mere moment ago was suddenly a lifetime ago, when he had stood at the water's edge, and asked himself—*should I wade in? Should I go to her? Should I simply step into the sea, one foot after the other, and just keep going till the waters roll up over my head and I drown? So that I could then be with her . . .*

But instead he had turned back, to be with his wife and child.

And now he knew that this was his place in life. *I will have to live out my life to the very end of my days—and Laura will be waiting for me, then. At the end. In the sky. In a paradise made alive, made real, by her presence, beyond death.*

If he could ever reach her there.

How was he supposed to manage that?

He knew only that at this moment he had to turn to Gigi, for rescue. Rescue from himself. From his impossibilities. *I want to live!* To live! *Here* and *Now. I don't want to die. Because life is so alive, and I cannot leave it. I cannot turn my back and go away, as I have done before; as I had done in Alta Villa; in Napoli, in New York. I cannot abandon my wife and my child as I have done my mother and father; as I have done Uncle Eugenio; as I have done Harry Spritzka. This I could never do.*

Tony propped himself up on one elbow. He looked at Gigi.

He said to himself—*I have heaven, here on earth.*

He felt his soul flooding over, and he said to Gigi, "I love you."

She took his hand, and said, "I know."

"No. No. Gigi, how can you know? It's because you have given me something I never had, something I never hoped to have, that I never dreamed was possible, in this life. You have given me happiness, Gigi. Happiness."

Chapter 6

La Grande Guerra

The butcher, Pasquale Fabrizio, was stuffed with pride at the birth, in 1914, of his first grandson. The daughter he doted upon, Gigi, duly named the boy "Pasquale," after her Papa. But Tony LaStoria, the boy's father, soon invented his own nickname for little Pasquale, an Americanized nickname; and the fortunate son was thereafter sentenced to go through life known to everyone as Patsy. His array of titles included: My son, the American, my brother, Patsy, cousin Patsy, my husband, Patsy, Uncle Patsy, and so on. But before the first-born boy could become my brother Patsy, there had to be another child. That was Maria, who came two years later, in 1916.

And after that, every two years, there came another child, first, two girls.

Gigi named her first girl Maria because, as a newly fertile fount of *bambini,* it crossed her mind that her former devotion to ancient gods, who after all, were un-christened pagans, would somehow become known to a jealous Mother of God; and that she had better appease the Mother of Jesus. (It always gave Gigi a shudder to think that the most beautiful baby boy born in the history of the world had to die that savage death on a cross of suffering. And his mother, supposedly God's mother, who supposedly adored her son, was yet powerless to save him? If that had been Gigi, and her son Patsy, she would have crawled up the cross to take his place before she sacrificed him. And so right then and there Gigi had lost respect for the Holy Mother. To Gigi, she was just a plaster saint.)

Still, to be on the safe side, she named her first daughter, Maria. Better not to antagonize the gods, of whatever grotto, or you were asking for bad things to come. Although, personally, Gigi ranked the gods second to the ghosts, who were real, (and moreover, were your own family, your ancestors.)

Then came Margherita, two years later, and Gigi, who had established naming-rights with her first-born Patsy, named this second daughter after Queen Margherita, of the Italian Royal House of Savoy. (Actually, it was her father, the butcher Fabrizio, who named this daughter—in fact, he insisted.)

Now Tony LaStoria could not understand what in the world his father-in-law saw in the House of Savoy. After all, weren't they just figureheads? And weren't they Piedmontese, from the faraway North? To any of the *paesani* of the South, where the Fabrizios, and the LaStorias, too, came from, they were as remote as Alpine peaks. And even though a Great War was being conducted over there, a symphony of guns, and operatic howitzers, conducted by be-ribboned General Toscaninni's, Tony himself had no use for the governments on either side. It was none of his business, or Pasquale Fabrizio's, either.

But when you live in the domicile of your father-in-law, where it becomes necessary to please and placate your wife; and your father-in-law, the butcher, reads pig-entrails, not newspapers: divergent points of view can occur.

Although Tony was following avidly the course of events, in his newly-adopted passion for the Boston daily papers (the drama, the suspense, the maps of the battles, the horrific tales of atrocities and heaps of dead and wounded littering trenches, which were nothing more than ready-made graves!) he still had no use for the Royal Houses of Europe. They were the ones who were dragging the whole world, it seemed, through this folly, this *opera buffa*.

Except for us. Here in America. Because we have a President smart enough to know better. Wilson will keep us out. This was an article of faith with Tony. He refused to even discuss it with his father-in-law, who somehow managed to hold that royal mannequin, Victor Emmanuel III, in higher esteem than the President of the United States!

One thing was certain: the war over there was good for business over here. Boston had been swept away on a wave of prosperity. Long before 1917 arrived, there was more of everything: more jobs, more people, more movement, more money, more cars, more bustle, traffic, shipping. The somnolent backwater of Boston was coming alive with activity.

Tony, however, would always think of it as a city of low horizons. Nothing could change that. He was a New Yorker, transplanted here, and these streets of cobblestone Boston he could never call his own.

New York City. Since his boyhood, forlorn, heartsick in Alta Villa, New York City had always been the capital city of his imagination; ever since that long ago day when, as a child of ten, locked away in perpetual torment in the that narrow house made tomb-like by the *miseria* of his father, he made good his escape; ending his unwilling exile, returning to the greatest city in the world; which, owing to that cursed man, *he had seen with his own eyes.*

But there were momentous things going on his own life, nevermind the faraway newspaper world of the European continent. In the shop at No. 10 Melcher Street, on a daily basis, he had his hands full with the new contracts coming in from not only local and regional department stores but even foreign agents of the warring governments in Europe, who, whether English, French, Austrian or Italian, were ruining military uniforms faster than they could replace them. And that did not even figure in Harry Spritzka's frantic expansion schemes getting phoned in from New York every other week. Always Harry wanted Tony to tell him everything had been done *yesterday;* and how many pieces, too. Tony had to go out and get a driver's license and put his hard-earned money into a reliable automobile of his own because every other month Harry was sending him to Taunton or Brockton or Fall River or Lowell or Worcester or Manchester or Providence to rent yet more cheap floorspace in New England's redbrick cotton, woolen and shoe-mills, built as far back as the 1840s, or amid the frenzy of the Civil War; and in each case he had to open a factory outlet in-house but, more importantly, locate, research and buy up yet another corner-lot, streetcar-location for a new *Richard Paul Men's Store* (soon to be known as *Richard Paul Men's and Ladies' Fine Apparel,* so as not to discourage the ladies, who, Harry knew, did most of the buying).

Harry Spritzka was building his expanding manufacturing operations and at the same time inventing, selling, and advertising the idea of *Richard Paul Stores,* which he expected Tony to understand had to be *branded* into the minds of the buying public, which meant the housewives and mothers who culled the newspapers for coupons and allocated family budgets. *We gotta hustle,* Harry would always say on the phone, *we gotta strike while the iron is hot. Don't think of all the new revenues pouring in, Tony. Think of what we're losing if we don't.* In the go-getting, hustling climate of the current hysterias, Tony could no longer afford to see himself simply as a factory manager: he had to figure out how to turn himself overnight into a General Manager of a Division of a far-flung Corporation. With the expense account and gas expenditures to match the traveling he had to do.

Now, with everything on his plate, having to pay to park his new 1914 Buick overnight in a garage in the overcrowded, narrow cobblestone streets of the North End; missing his suppers at home with the family, as often as not; still, now, he would not trade his hard-won, newfound happiness, his sweet Gigi, his own Patsy, and Maria, (and whatever children were yet to come, as Gigi was never not-pregnant); he would not trade this new life, however hectic, challenging or tiring, for anything, even New York. And they, Gigi, the kids, the Fabrizios, were here, in Boston. So it was Boston now, not New York, to which he would return after every overnight in Providence, Hartford, Worcester or Manchester or Lowell or Brockton. And in Boston he would remain, even if he could never become a Bostonian at heart. For you could not eradicate New York from Tony LaStoria's memory, which is to say, his soul.

Here, in Boston, the North End was everything Italian. The population was swelling with more and more arrivals from the old country every day. The war was driving people across the ocean: either they were trying to escape, trying to return, or trying to profit. Their part of town had grown from an outpost of gathered townsmen to an entire overseas Italian city, with a population now verging on forty thousand Italian-speaking inhabitants, crowded into an elbow of ancient, 18th-century streets, the very oldest part of this old, round-shouldered Puritan city.

The entire North End had been turned into a great debating society. The women were left to gossip of their own affairs on the front stoop with the children, or over the fire-escape laundry lines, their primitive telephone system. The men all gravitated down to the corner of the street, where they smoked their pipes, cigars, and cigarettes to their hearts' content, out of earshot of the nagging, complaining, interfering armada of kitchen-drudges, their wives. Here the men, the husbands, the fathers, the brothers, the cousins, the sons-in-law, the fathers-in-law and brothers-in-law, lounged on the park benches or hung on the lamppost outside the front garden of San Leonardo's and dove headlong into the great affairs, the momentous events of the day, a self-appointed street Congress, quite capable in their own minds of legislating an end to the war, of directing the battles in France, of charging uphill to victory, of burying the barbaric Huns, of orchestrating the peace conferences, of dividing up the world, of parceling out the spoils.

And their steam-engines of baggy wind were fed by the steady rivulets of returnees arriving from their hometowns, back there, in the Old Country, with news of who was in the Italian Army, up on that frozen, unimaginably Alpine Austrian front, who was wounded, whose cousin was killed, whose family should now be grieving over the loss of a loved one.

Down in North Square, the Scavolas were doing a land-office business in Italian passports. Married men were leaving their wives and kids to go back there and enlist in the Italian Army, and bringing their sons with them, whether Italian-born or American, before it was too late and the whole show would be over.

Just exactly where one's loyalties and obligations lay was the topic of the day. Some said they were fine right here, and to leave well enough alone, and mind their own business. More said it was their patriotic duty to go back and aid the mother country in her hour of distress.

The anarchists were said to be meeting nightly in the North End, in some secret place. Nobody knew, or wanted to know, where. But there they plotted, planning bombings and attacks on munitions plants and shipyards, because they were against the whole thing, this insane slaughter that some of their *paesani* insisted on calling *La Grande Guerra*. They were certainly not standing out in the open on the corner of Hanover and Prince Street, debating with the rest. Their minds were made up. The anarchists talked only to themselves because they were the only ones who agreed with themselves. A crazy bunch! With their philosophy of life, you could rule out wine, women and song. Everything was death and destruction, we're all slaves of the system, death to the capitalists!

The trouble was a lot of the "capitalists" were gathered on the corner of Hanover and Prince. They might not have a great deal of capital, but they wanted to; their pockets might be empty, but their hearts were full of greed.

Pasquale Fabrizio and Antonio LaStoria were right there among them. Tony's attendance was mandatory, if he wanted to live in his father-in-law's house. Fabrizio was a well-known local merchant, with his own shop in the Faneuil Hall markets, and many of the men standing there smoking were eating his pork and beef and mutton-chops off their supper table that very evening, so he was listened to with respect.

Which annoyed Tony to no end. He had never met anyone so ignorant and so opinionated in his life. Bad enough he had to sit still for it at home, but to be dragged down here, and expected to bow down before every infallible syllable from the pontificating lips was a little much, don't you think?

Nevertheless, Tony did not hesitate to rub the old man the wrong way. Whenever Signore Fabrizio brought up the King, Tony countered with Wilson. Whenever Pasquale brought up Marshall Badoglio, Tony countered with General Pershing, hero of the Pancho Villa campaigns. Pasquale said, "Fight," Tony said, "Stay out!" Pasquale said, "We better wait till spring and the mud dries off the roads," Tony said, "No, attack now, when they least expect it!" Between the two of them they had every argument known to man, squared off, ends rounded, and fought down to a draw. Neither one of them wanted to give in to the other, in front of that audience they had down on Hanover Street. Their spectators arrived each evening looking forward to puffing their pipes through at least ten or fifteen rounds, and thought with amusement of what the hell it must be like with these two living in the same house.

Finally, Tony said to himself: How that man likes to argue! I'll never win! Or hear the end of it. He said to Gigi, "We gotta go, amore."

At this time, they had two children of their own, with another on the way, and there was just not enough room in that narrow place on Prince Street.

To his surprise, Gigi said, "Okay!"—her one word of English, unless you counted "Okey-dokey, smokey," which made her giggle, and in her mouth, came out *"Occi-docci, a-sa-mocci!"*

So they found a flat of their own for rent in North Square. They moved babies and baggage in one night.

North Square was an Avellinese neighborhood. With its own church, *Sacred Heart.*

In the North End of Boston, the street you lived on, the church you went to Mass in, was dictated by your *paese:* the Sicilians lived near the fishpier, down on North Street and Fleet Street. The Abruzzesi were over on Endicott and North Margin. The Calabrese, nobody wanted anything to do with them. They were only one rung above the Sicilians, but even the Sicilians had no use for them. For some reason, they lived far away, in Tony's old rooming house neighborhood, the South End, by themselves. They were among the foreigners with whom Tony had found no need to speak, in those days when he had lived for two years by himself, apart from the human race. They had their own dialect, and to Tony's ears, it was a foreign language. As long as the Avellinese occupied North Square, Gigi was comfortable there: no language barrier for her. So Gigi said, "Don't worry. Mamma's not far away."

They needed Mamma, back in Prince Street, to watch the kids for them.

Tony was now smoking Chesterfields. He rather thought they gave him an air of distinction, as if he were an English gentleman. He was now known in the North End by his customary white shirt, as once, so long ago in New York, he had been known in Little Italy as the boy bold enough to talk back to the Don.

And in general, Tony was well-tailored, as befit a tailor by craft, who also just happened to be a manager in a now-thriving factory, down on Melcher Street, No. 10, in the South End, across the Summer Street Bridge; who was capable of handing out jobs, *especially for that daughter of yours you don't know what to do with; send her to see Tony.*

Tony himself had every expectation of one day occupying a place in this town of low horizons at least as lofty as that of his father-in-law. All he needed, which he lacked, but which the other possessed, was longevity.

All in good time. Meanwhile, he and Gigi, when she wasn't pregnant again, were doing the town. After all, her husband made good money, thought Gigi. And she intended to spend some of it, in his company.

There was plenty to do, and plenty of places to go, even in this backwater of Boston, which, come to find out, had its own pretensions to culture, and took, actually, an inordinate pride in its own peculiar institutions, such as the magnificent home of Isabella Stewart Gardner, crammed with Art that no common person of the city had ever been privileged, or even permitted, to gaze upon; and magnificent piles such as the Boston Public Library, by McKim, Mead and White, or the brownstone monolith of Trinity Church, by H.H. Richardson; or the sacrosanct Emerald Necklace parklands reservation, by none other than Frederick Law Olmstead.

So Gigi was pleased to find that it was no problem to steer Tony in the direction where she needed no English. When they brought the babies over to Prince Street to be watched so that they could go out, she would observe, flippantly, to her mother, Anna-Lisa, "My husband is taking me to America tonight!"

They went to the Italian band concerts on the Boston Common and the Italian Music Hall on Tremont Street and to the *commedia dell'arte* in the North End, and also to Symphony Hall, to hear Toscannini when he came up from New York as guest conductor. It was their last chance to see him, as he was known to be returning to Italy soon. He had been conductor of the Metropolitan Opera and the New York Philharmonic for the last eight years. Every Italian in Boston worth ten cents turned out to see him at Symphony Hall.

On these occasions, if English came into the conversation, Gigi was happy to let Tony do all the talking. She would simply hang onto his arm and bask in his glory. In these situations, she took pride in his self-command, his assurance. She thought he was genuinely a sophisticated creature, which he must have gotten in New York: he shared that theatrical glow with Toscanini himself.

Gigi loved every minute of her excursions. She felt that they were having the time of their lives. She intended to make up for the fact that she was always pregnant in one night, if she had to. So there would be dinner, dancing, the opera, the theater, the symphony, and she could wear proudly the gold that her husband bought for her: bracelets, brooches, very slender necklaces; tasteful gold. Appropriate to her station as the wife of a prosperous man. To whom she clung, decorously. With the other matrons who had Italian she chatted happily about children and recipes; always with one eye out for any other woman who allowed her gaze to rest on Tony's ravishingly handsome face a trifle too admiringly. In these moments, she would clutch Tony in the crook of his arm sturdily, and steer him the other way. Yet she was inordinately proud of her handsome husband, that he would attract looks from well-dressed women at the symphony.

Tony was happy to be her escort. He thought she made him look magnificent. At last he was the epitome of all he had ever wanted to be, truly, a noble person at heart, simply miscast in his life's beginnings; now, after all, in the end, coming into his princely estate.

And at the end of their evening out, there was lovemaking. Safe at home, back again, in their own little love-nest in North Square, having picked up their sleepy children at her mother's, little Patsy and Maria, and walked home with them nodding on their shoulders, a couple of streets over, not far; and lovingly they would tuck them into bed, kiss them good night, and at last fall in love with each other all over again.

For Tony, these were nights of passion. His happiness had not ceased for one moment since that day on the beach at Nantasket, when he realized finally the gifts he had been given. And Gigi felt the same.

Gigi felt above all that her trust and reliance in herself, in her own dream of life, had been justified. That she had been right all along. And that this was the way things were meant to be; from a time immemorial to humankind, long before any of them existed in the form of human flesh; predestined, by that other world hidden behind the screen of this one, that world where fate and destiny were real things, not, as was taught here, mere fancies of a childish imagination.

And so she was able to surrender herself, completely, and think only of him. And she gave him everything. She left nothing of herself. And after that, they went to sleep happily in one another's arms, with their legs intertwined, rubbing their feet together, intimately, cozily, falling . . . asleep.

Tony never thought of Laura anymore. Or if he did, she was far away. *As far away as his own mother.* His mother was in the distant past, Laura in a far-off, impossible future, which might never occur, because the way he felt now, he might never die, he might just decide to live forever, young, strong, money in his pocket, a beautiful wife who loved him down to the ground. He had *il mondo* hanging by a thread, and the tailor's scissors were in his hand. Of the women in his life, his mother, and his famous lost love, Laura, Gigi, and only Gigi, was the one who was here, here and now. *And they were going to live forever, both of them, together.*

Now if Tony could only evade Pasquale Fabrizio. To accomplish this, he devised a stratagem. Pasquale Fabrizio had his clubhouse at the Italian Protective League, on Hanover Street. He was the follower of a dead man named Siano, James Siano.

Long before Tony's arrival in Boston, this man, Siano, had established himself as the leader of all the *paesani* of the North End. Siano was one of them, through his parents, although he himself had been born in Boston, way back in the 1880's, his family being a part of the earliest wave of immigrants from the South of Italy.

As a native-born American, he was the first man with an Italian surname ever elected to the Boston City Council. Then he became a state senator up on Beacon Hill, under the golden dome of the Massachusetts State House. A remarkable achievement, unprecedented at the time, but destined to be cut short in 1906 by Siano's sudden death, when he was only twenty-nine.

It was not only Siano's wife Florence and their two little children who mourned him, it was Pasquale Fabrizio and the rest of the North End, who turned out *en masse* to walk behind the hearse on the day of the funeral High Mass. They had lost the only champion they had ever known, the only man who could speak for them, who could not speak for themselves. Many times Pasquale exclaimed to Tony that they would never see his like again.

The Italian Protective League was Siano's creation, and Pasquale's undying loyalties were lived out under that roof.

On rainy evenings, in winter weather, after that son-in-law of his took his beloved Gigi and moved her out of his house, that's where you would find Pasquale Fabrizio, smoking his stogie, having a glass of wine, playing cards or backgammon with his cronies.

So, Tony joined the Sons of Italy.

When a suitable length of time had gone by since the wedding, but even before he moved out of the house to his own establishment in North Square, Tony made his move. He had met some people on his own who encouraged him, people who were a little beyond his father-in-law's tight circle.

One was Father Conte at San Leonardo's, the pastor, who got wind of Tony's prosperity and solicited Tony for charitable contributions.

There was the Home for Italian Children, an orphanage, run by the Franciscan Sisters, down on Centre Street, in Jamaica Plain. The war in Europe was now killing North End husbands, and leaving North End mothers destitute. With six or eight fatherless children to keep, without a job outside the home, and the family breadwinner killed on the Austrian front, fighting in the Italian Army, what could they do?

In addition, there was the School for Italian Children, a nerve-racking project of Father Conte, who was being pushed by Cardinal O'Connell, who was infuriated that the Italians in the city did not send their children to his parochial schools. Father Conte advised Tony that if he had money to spend on the nigga pool, then he must have money for people less fortunate than he was.

Tony could only shrug, and hope that his luck might improve alongside his generosity.

From Father Conte, another do-gooder learned of Tony, and also sought after his acquaintance. This was the editor of the local Italian-language newspaper, *La Gazzetta del Massachusetts*, a man called Stephen DiBenedetto. A man, like Siano himself, with Italian parents, but born in Boston, who succeeded, in the wake of the State Senator's untimely loss, to somewhat of the leadership position the dead man had held. DiBenedetto, because he held himself aloof from running for office, as a newspaper editor, had more projects and pursuits than even Siano himself, and it was DiBenedetto who drew Tony towards the Sons of Italy.

DiBenedetto said to Tony one day, having stopped him on Hanover Street to introduce himself, that he knew many deserving people looking for work. Could Tony help?

Tony said, "We employ women, mostly. Stitchers. The two or three positions I have for men, I already have two cutters. They're not going anywhere. But I'll see what I can do."

Tony had been in Boston long enough to know that the North End was the distillation of everything Italian in the city. Now that he was living there himself, every day, and night, through marriage, he had become one of them, finally, in spite of himself.

More than ever, with all the upset going on in the world at large, Tony LaStoria was unable to remain the outsider; his New Yorker identity could no longer give him a wall between himself and them. And he had to admit that he was among the more fortunate. He recalled vividly his own days of destitution when he had arrived a penniless ten-year-old in the world's biggest slum. He knew the North End could not survive, let alone thrive, without the mutual-benefit societies that lined every street, according to each street's *paese,* that formed the social network: the card clubs and wineshops for the men, the religious welfare organizations for the women, the children, the elderly, the sick and infirm of mind or body; these were vital to the residents.

There was no help coming from the government, whether city, state or beyond—and often, not from the Catholic Church, either, which was much better at holding out an empty basket to collect than a full basket to distribute. And the North End Italians were not about to kiss the ring of Cardinal O'Connell, either.

The people of the North End had to depend on themselves, and themselves alone.

So Tony gave. He gave as much and as often as he could. It almost seemed at times he never stopped reaching into his pocket. Along with his white shirt, his expensive belt, his smart suspenders, the Chesterfields peeking from his breast-pocket, there was the jingle of coin in his pocket that gave him the self-assurance of his success, his status.

Tony loved the feel of money weighing down his pockets, solid copper, nickel-plated coin. It gave him actual pleasure to reach in and give it away. He could see people's reactions. He knew he was gaining a reputation; Gigi complained that he would give them the shirt off his back. But Tony saw his generosity reflected in Stephen DiBenedetto's face, when he saw that he was being awarded deference, and respect, by the Editor.

The next stratagem DiBenedetto employed in his campaign to involve Tony LaStoria in public affairs came in the form of free tickets. To Fenway Park.

The Editor was promoting baseball in the pages of *La Gazzetta* as a part of his overall drive to Americanize the Italian district as rapidly as possible. He himself was native-born but he saw all his endeavors, especially his opinion-making newspaper, as affected adversely by the poor opinion of Italians in general held by the wider American public.

This wounded DiBenedetto's deepest sensitivities. Perhaps at bottom he was more than a little ashamed of his fellow

Italians because of their seemingly perverse attachment to *La Via Vecchia,* the old way. And he also observed the counter-current among the younger generation, some of them, born here, towards rejecting their parents, who were seen as hopelessly outdated, in fashions, habits, and customs, and incredibly stubborn. The younger generation were openly embarrassed by their mothers and fathers.

DiBenedetto advocated playing baseball because he felt it was absolutely the quickest route to Americanizing the youngsters, and he resented the elders, for their blind and wilful resistance. He wanted, he expected, all his friends and allies, to agree. Therefore, he called up Tony one forenoon, having found out his office number, and said, "I have an extra ticket to today's game. One o'clock. Can you get out of work?"

"Of course," said Tony. "I'm the man in charge."

They went, and Tony was grateful for the pleasant afternoon, in talkative company. But he did not greatly care about the ball game. He himself had never been enthusiastic about team sports as a youngster. He might have gotten as far as pick-up stickball with Harry Spritzka and his gang at times, but no further than that. And come to think of it, in the narrow streets of the Lower East Side in Manhattan, growing up, it was the new-fangled game of basketball that drew the kids to the Henry Street Settlement. But, ah! now, if there had been a racecourse that afternoon available in Boston!

Tony was still firmly attached to the back of that horse, Fiorello, riding through the streets of New York in the early dawn, delivering ice. Consequently, he loved nothing better than hanging around a paddock full of finely-bred specimens; thoroughbreds were the princelings among horses. They made Tony feel monarchical himself, as he attended to the Sport of Kings.

But, in this backwater of Boston, there was no Harlem Speedway, no Jerome Park. And his companion, DiBenedetto was a Red Sox fan. "Whaddya think of that kid Ruth, huh? Can he throw the pea, or what?"

"He's all right," said Tony. "But he's a lefty." DiBenedetto looked at him quizzically. "You know, lefties, they're all cracked!"

Ruth was nuts, and diBenedetto was a Republican, so the afternoon, to Tony, was only half a failure: they could talk baseball, but not the war.

"Wilson thinks he's conducting classes at Princeton: he's ruining the economy!" said diBenedetto.

"President Wilson has kept us out of the war," said Tony.

But then the Great War, as the papers, including diBenedetto's, habitually called it, came home to Tony's doorstep. It turned out in the end that it didn't matter that the United States was not officially in the war: the war still had tentacles.

Chapter 7

Boston at War

Tony got a call one evening when he was malingering, late, in his office at No. 10 Melcher Street, from the barber in North Square, to say there was a riot going on right under Tony's windowsill, and he'd better get home as quick as he could.

It was the anarchists, aided and abetted by the Wobblies. It was now early December of 1916. The Wobblies had come to Massachusetts as far back as the year 1912, shortly after Tony himself arrived in Boston.

In the old days, Tony and Harry Spritzka had taken their part, playing their own role as Owner-Operators of the Manhattan garment industry, on the other side of the long strike of the I.L.G.W.U., in 1909; as Management, they lost that Strike, though Harry, the business-owner, fought it ferociously (Tony, less so, as he was secretly a sympathizer with the striking girls.) That Strike of 1909 had had the most dramatic consequences of any strike in American labor history. Prior, that is, to the devastating Triangle Shirtwaist Factory Fire of 1911, in the Washington Square neighborhood of Manhattan.

That event, that Fire, was the singular, never-to-be-forgotten event in Tony LaStoria's existence. Even now, married to another woman, Tony divided his life into before-and-after Laura Antonelli. She was Tony's first love. She occupied that pre-eminent, unparalleled position in Tony's life. There can never be another first love, in anyone's heart. Laura Antonelli, then, was the young factory girl, the teenage stitcher, with whom Tony had been so desperately in love, only to watch her fall to her death from an upper-story window on that tragic day, March 25th, 1911, a Saturday, as Tony could never forget.

When the Fire came, not only did Tony lose Laura Antonelli, in his personal life, but the Fire's repercussions were still playing out every day in Tony's daily business life, right now, in the present of 1916, five years down the road; where he now operated a garment factory in Boston with a mandatory fire-sprinkler system installed; frequent fire drills; inspection visits from the Boston Fire Department; and, of course, no locked exit doors; and the same would have been the case were Tony now serving as floor manager in a similar garment-making sweatshop in Philly or Chicago: such was the impact of the notorious Triangle Shirtwaist Factory Fire, which cost the lives of 149 young women.

The Wobblies had insufficient strength, numbers or influence back in 1909, to take a real part in the I.L.G.W.U. Strike in New York. Their titular head, Big Bill Haywood, managed to be present at the infamous Cooper Union, the night that began it all. He was on the podium with Gompers while Tony watched from the back of the hall. That was the extent of the Wobblies' participation; that strike really belonged to the International Ladies' Garment Workers, and in fact, was the making of them.

But in 1912, here in Massachusetts, another long, terrible winter strike had erupted in the textile city of Milltown, in the

Merrimack Valley, along the New Hampshire border, thirty miles north of Boston.

This strike had turned into the next major uprising in American labor history, and promised to have similar, far-reaching consequences.

This time the Wobblies were prominent organizers and agitators. They sent Big Bill Haywood, but also Joe Hill, as well as the famed feminist and suffragette, Elizabeth Gurley Flynn. Haywood would speak from the bandstand on the Milltown Common, while Hill played his guitar and sang his organizing-songs afterwards, in the workingmen's clubs, and in the women's child-care halls, Gurley Flynn marshalled the mothers to form the backbone of the strike.

There were more workers of Italian origins in the Milltown mills than anywhere in Massachusetts outside of Boston, and, as the anarchists flocked to Milltown on the heels of the Wobblies, both of these groups assumed leading organizer positions in what had become a General Strike up there, a Strike which shut down every mill in the city, from the giant American Woolen Company on down, and put 20,000 workers out picketing in the snowy streets.

Italian surnames were splashed all over the Boston papers during those days. Ettore and Giovannitti, Renoso and DiOrlando. The purple press dubbed it "the Bread and Roses Strike," because of the role women had taken in it. Mothers who were trying to send their starving children by train, to relief societies, in other cities were attacked, bludgeoned and trampled at the Milltown train station by mounted police.

Again, as in New York, public opinion was outraged and the strikers won, after 63 days of frozen winter picketing under the bayonets of the State Militia.

And the Wobblies now had a permanent presence in Massachusetts.

Then, on the eve of the Great War, in 1914, out West, on their home-ground, where the Wobblies had originated, as the I.W.W., *The International Workers of the World,* in the mines and lumber camps of Montana and Utah, in 1914 came the infamous Ludlow Massacre.

An immigrant tent colony had settled at the Rockefeller-owned Iron Works, near Pueblo. This colony, like Milltown, in 1912, like everywhere, had many Italian mothers and children. Demonstrations and agitation over wages, hours and working conditions, again, like Milltown in 1912, like Manhattan in 1909; but this time when the mine operators called in the state militia to quell the strike, troopers raked the demonstrators with machine-gun fire, and burned the entire Ludlow tent camp to the ground. Two Italian women and thirteen Italian children were burned to death in the melee.

These were the cohorts who were now rioting in North Square, in the North End of Boston, in early December of 1916. The anarchists and the Wobblies of Milltown and Ludlow. Though their ideologies kept them apart, the Great War brought them together, in opposition to war, to capitalism, to a host of society's ills. And together they were rioting, right under Tony LaStoria's windowsills, with his wife, Gigi, and their two children, inside.

The cause of the demonstrations this time was the construction, earlier, in the fall of 1915, on the Commercial Street waterfront, the very northern border of the North End, of a 50-foot-tall steel tank that would hold in excess of 2 million gallons of molasses.

When the tank was finished, it brought dozens of overlarge, overladen ships bearing thousands of gallons of molasses from Cuba, Puerto Rico and the West Indies north to Boston

Harbor. A company called United States Industrial Alcohol hired dozens of North End Italian men to distill the molasses into industrial alcohol for use in the production of munitions and high explosives destined for the European nations at war with Germany. Many more local residents were engaged as stevedores, longshoremen and teamsters unloading and transporting the raw and manufactured gallons. The North End became a beehive of war-work; with a population now pushing forty thousand and streets throbbing with vitality; as people, pushcarts, hacks, delivery trucks and wagons competed for space on the narrow, twisting byways, it also became a target of those against *La Grande Guerra:* the Great War.

All this conspired to put money into Tony LaStoria's pocket, and anarchists under his window.

Tony LaStoria and thousands of other local residents may have looked the other way or somehow ignored the realities right under their feet, but the North End of Boston had gradually become widely notorious, during the last two years of war in far-off Europe, as the national headquarters of the American anarchists. And they were led by a *paesano* from the South of Italy named Luigi Galleani.

Galleani was a thinker, and a writer, who edited his radical newspaper, *La Cronaca Suvversiva,* or *The Subversive Chronicle,* out of the North End. The Justice Department in Washington called him "the leading anarchist in the United States," and his newspaper, "the most rabid, seditious and anarchistic sheet ever published in this country."

The riot in North Square began with an IWW open-air meeting, held in front of the Sacred Heart church. The police who were there feared that incendiary remarks might inflame a gathering audience. Or they had other information. Or they were misinformed. Whatever the truth was, the police were nervous, and warned the IWW speakers not to speak out, and ordered them to refrain from handing out radical literature. When one of the cops proceeded to require bystanders to move along and clear the sidewalk, the riot began. A disciple of Galleani named Fargotti, a militant anarchist, slashed with a butcher's knife at a patrolman, slicing the officer's blue overcoat and injuring the policeman's hand. Shots rang out from the crowd nearby. One officer wrestled a .32 caliber pistol from the grasp of a demonstrator. A general melee broke out, so noisy and confused it caused a pregnant Gigi, watching from her window, to run away to the back of the flat with Patsy and Maria and her new, unborn baby bouncing in her belly; and the rioting could be heard over on Hanover Street, blocks away. Additional officers from the Salutation Street and Hanover Street police stations came running to assist. Dozens were arrested, and police found a loaded gun in Fargotti's pocket.

Tony got there as quickly as he could on the subway, running all the way home from the Haymarket station, but the riot was by then long over, although Gigi seemed to be still shaken.

The next day the headlines all over the country were all about Italian anarchist violence in a major Eastern city, and they did not mean New York.

After the riot things moved quickly and it seemed that life became more complicated by the day. The New Year was 1917 and now the war was no longer so far away. Tony had gone to see his new friend, DiBenedetto, about another problem altogether. Something he could not bring up with Gigi, or her father. "I had a visit in my office, the other day."

It was deadline day for the weekly in his office and DiBenedetto seemed distracted. "So?"

"He said Messina sent him."

Now the editor looked up. "Oh. Them."

"You know who I mean."

"Yes, yes, yes. What do they want?"

"Ten dollars a week."

"For what?"

"Protection." Tony shrugged. "Call it fire insurance."

"Well, what are you going to do, Tony?"

"I don't know. I thought I'd talk it over with you. I need advice."

DiBenedetto stopped entirely now, to swing his swivel seat and face Tony. "I can't tell you what to do. You gotta do what you gotta do. I only know these people are a stain on the whole North End, and they should be stamped out. They give a bad name to everybody. If I had my way–."

"I'm with you, Stephen. I'm on your side. But I gotta lotta people work for me, depend on me. I got an owner, far away, in New York City. I'm responsible down to the last penny, to him! How is it they don't bother you?"

"Tony, they're afraid of the power of the press. They're not like the anarchists, who glory in the publicity, who want to take credit, for Chrissakes. These people, the Sicilians, they are scum of the earth. They hide behind the name of *La Camora*, and expect people to bow down to them. That Messina, he's new, just came last year, and already?"

"I see," said Tony.

"Messina, he doesn't want his name in the papers. He wants his name spread by word of mouth, spelled out by fear."

"Okay, okay."

"And as long as you, Tony, and people like you, and your father-in-law, wanna play the nigga pool every day, as long as a man wants to have his way with somebody not his wife, as long as the housewives wanna buy olive oil on the cheap off the back of a stolen wagon, as long as people want cigarettes for a nickel a pack—."

"Okay, okay."

Tony left. He had not come for a lecture, but help. Advice, at least. He left feeling there was no help here and no way out. Tony himself had no such power of the press as diBenedetto thought *he* had. He left the editor's office with his friend muttering behind him, "And the police! They're a big help! They're all taking their allowance every week. Goddam Irish!"

Tony was thinking, *and who's to say diBenedetto's office can't be fire-bombed? He may* think *his pen protects him!*

Tony could see no way out. It was a very long time ago, now, when he had thrown down a shoeshine rag, and defied a don. Back then—what did he have to lose? Nothing. He walked away unscathed. He didn't even need that lousy job. Everybody had a good laugh. If anything, it made his reputation in the whole of Little Italy. Tony went on to bigger and better things. Look at how far he had come since then. Till now. Now, he had a lot to lose. Now it was no longer child's play. Now these were grown men, grown *business*men. Fear was their business and protection was their racket. This was serious and you had to consider the consequences.

He called up Harry Spritzka in New York. "Harry, I need a raise in pay."

"What for? I ain't payin' you enough? You're making fifty dollars a week!"

"Things are going good, right, Harry?"

"Yeah, there's a war on, you got a tiger by the tail, up there in Boston, Tony, but don't forget, I gotta make my profits; as long as you remember that, you got a job. How's the family, by the way?"

"Don't try and change the subject, Harry. The family's growing. Gigi's pregnant again."

"Oh, so that's it."

"Sure. Sure."

There was a pause on the line, as if Harry were thinking that he didn't know what "Sure, sure," meant, exactly, but he was figuring it out. "How much do you need?"

"Twenty dollars a week."

"You're out of your mind! I'll give you fifteen."

"Okay."

"Shit. I shoulda said thirteen."

"When are we gonna have a meet again?" Tony was thinking, *the less said at this point, the better.*

"Soon. Soon. I don't know, but, soon."

However, the New Year, 1917, had other plans. January seemed to pass without further incident. Caruso was coming to the city, to play Symphony Hall, with none other than Toscanini conducting, and Tony took Gigi for what turned out to be an unprecedented gala evening.

Tony LaStoria would remember this evening out for the rest of his life. His adoring wife clung to him, her head on his shoulder, readying herself to weep at the terrible sadness of the clown, smiling on the outside, crying on the inside; while the great man sang on the stage.

The opera that evening was Leoncavallo's *Pagliacci,* one of Caruso's triumphs. They sat back into their seats as Toscanini conducted them to the interior of that terrible story of the jealous clown who was the husband of a faithless wife. And when he came to the crucial aria, *Vesti La Giubba (Dress in the Motley)* at the close of the first act, the great tenor Caruso, in his role of Canio, dressed as a jester in a conical hat, with wildly gesticulating moustaches curled with wax, was preparing, on the outside, to play his role as Pagliaccio, the clown, in a play-within-the-play; *w*hile Gigi and all the audience, who knew the opera by heart, realized that, in truth, he is a jealous husband, with vengeance biting his soul like a tapeworm, as he prepares to use the play-within-the-play to catch out the lover with whom his wife, Nedda, is betraying him; at this climactic moment, when Caruso the tenor soared for the first time to the heights of the aria, bending into "*Ridi, Pagliaccio,*" "Laugh, Pagliaccio," his voice so expressing the perverse self-mockery of the moment, Gigi dug her head into Tony's shoulder, almost in terror at the pain of the clown's sorrow; and then, when Caruso returned again, to soar with ever more power and drama, for the second time in the aria, on the words, *"Ridi, Pagliaccio,"* this time conveying unmistakably with the blast-furnace force of his chest-bursting vocal the anguish of his jealous anger, Gigi dug her claws into her husband's arm, being soaked in every cell of her being with the tragedy of the clown, so that she went limp, as if slain by the music.

And yet, though the audience in their hundreds cringed and wept, Tony and Gigi felt it was to them alone, and to them only, that Caruso was singing.

That was the great man's magic. Chandeliers had no glow beside him. Because of that voice, you knew your own wife, like the wife in the story, was perfectly capable of falling in love with another man. And that this man that she would fall in love with would be none other than Caruso himself.

And you walked out of Symphony Hall afterwards to stagger head-down to the nearest trolley stop, knowing that all men, all women, be they husbands and wives, or saints in a cloister, were playing out their lives on the stage of the one great human tragedy, the common theater of our existence, here in snowy Boston, just as much as in faroff Berlin.

Chapter 8

The Invisible Enemy

Because of this performance, when they went to see the great Caruso, Tony bought a phonograph for their house, together with some cylinders of Caruso singing. Everything in the world, especially everything Italian, was on sale in the North End. The opera had restored Tony's spirit, renewed his faith. He felt magnanimous again. He felt expansive. He felt he had passed the crisis of La Camora, and that he had things under control again.

Then the Salutation Street police station was bombed, on a Sunday morning, the 17th of January, 1917.

It was only around the corner from North Square. The explosion was unexpected and deafening. The LaStorias were at Sunday mass at Sacred Heart when it went off. The parishioners poured into the street. The smell of black powder was in the air. Rubble and glass covered the pavements. It was the anarchists. A reprisal, for the arrests and imprisonments during the riots in North Square.

Nobody needed a newspaper report to reveal the facts. It was on everyone's lips instantly. Women were crossing themselves, thanking God that everyone had been in church. *It was in their neighborhood they set off a bomb like that.* What if they had been walking by at that very instant, on their way home from Sunday Mass, with the children by the hand?

It unnerved Tony all over again. What was happening to his world? The papers he read avidly every day for reports of distant explosions on the fields of France now informed him that twenty sticks of dynamite had been used in this blast, two streets away.

Every pane of glass from Commercial Street to Hanover Street was smashed.

Within a two-block radius of the station-house, debris covered every sidewalk.

Tony was living with a pregnant wife and two babies, across the street from the house inhabited, once, long ago, by Paul Revere himself, and he could only think that the times that try men's souls had returned, with a vengeance.

Thank God no one had been killed. The papers said the bomb had been placed in a jail cell, in the basement, directly below a room where three cops lay sleeping.

Only because the blast had blown outward, toward the station's lower wall, and not upward toward the ceiling, were the officers in the sleeping area above not killed instantly. But what next?

Those bastards, the Germans, answered that. They announced publicly, on the last day of January, that, as of midnight, on February the 1st, they were going to institute unrestricted submarine warfare against American shipping in the Atlantic. Ships flying the Stars and Stripes were to be sunk on sight.

Tony LaStoria felt the ground tremble underneath him. It was not that he was afraid. It was that he had no control over the turn of events. War fever spread through the North

End faster than the smoke from the anarchist bombing of the Salutation Street Station. People who had no official status on American soil, thousands of them, were turned into rabid patriots overnight. They were outraged. They took it as a personal affront.

The days of 1914 and 1915, when volunteers by the hundreds rushed out of the North End to take ship in Boston Harbor for the Old Country, to enlist in the Italian Army, were already ancient history. But who could have foreseen that not only would the boys never return, but that *three years later*, those not already dead and planted beneath the dirt of Europe would still be risking their lives in the trenches of the frozen Austrian frontier, washing their dirty feet in the ice-cold waters of the Po? *Would this awful slaughter never end?* And now, those bastards, the Kaiser, and the Emperor, were going to drag the USA into it! They had to be stopped!

Tony rushed to City Hall to sign up for his naturalization. If it actually came to war, here, (which God forbid) he himself, Tony LaStoria, might be subject to being taken from his wife and babies.

Of this he could not be certain, but on the other hand, there were no guarantees that it could *not* happen. As things now stood, he might be affected, while, as a non-citizen, he would have no say in anything. It was not just that he could not vote in an election: it was that Tony himself felt that, although he had gained status in the community, and was an important enough man in the North End, his lack of citizenship deprived him of the ability to speak out, somehow. This was deeply personal to Tony. Not that he was denied his rights. *But almost as if he denied himself his rights.*

But if he were naturalized, if he, like his own son, were an American, well, then, no one could deny him his rights.

Tony knew that it was a two-step process to apply for naturalization, that you had to go to the city hall, to the Office of Immigration and declare your intent, in writing, and then wait for a probationary period of at least a year, to attend your exam and receive your papers. There was no time to lose. *Why hadn't he done it long before this?* He had never felt any need to join any armed forces of Italy, but if he were called to the American Army, he would not refuse. He would not enlist, perhaps, as he could not bear to leave Gigi and the kids, but if he were called, he would then have no choice, and he felt that he would be proud to wear that uniform. *But he should then be a citizen, should he not?*

He was almost thirty years old, a man without a country, in a world at war with itself.

Then came the Zimmerman telegram.

It was March the 1ˢᵗ, 1917; the headlines in the papers that morning blared the existence of a communique, from the German foreign minister, to the German ambassador in Mexico, intercepted by British Intelligence. The message detailed a plan for the German Empire to enter into an alliance with Mexico if the United States entered the European war. In the event of German victory, Mexico was to receive her "lost" territories of New Mexico, Texas and Arizona.

The roof blew off the North End, as well as the rest of Boston, and the rest of the country. The neutrality tightrope shivering under President Wilson's tiptoeing feet snapped.

In his inaugural address, four days later, Wilson, having been re-elected in November of 1916 *on the promise to keep American boys out of the war,* was forced to tell the people there was now no turning back. "Our own fortunes as a nation are involved whether we would have it so or not."

That meant Tony LaStoria's fortunes as well. Whether or not he would have it so.

Two days later the Congress in Washington voted overwhelmingly to declare war on Germany.

Tony was now ready for anything, he knew not what.

But the next thing that happened was a phone call from New York City. He boarded the train the next morning at South Station and arrived in time for a meeting at the mansion on 91st Street, which had now grown to three stories.

Harry Spritzka told Tony that *he, Harry,* was enlisting! In the United States Army!

Tony was shocked. "What about Mimi?"

"She'll be all right."

"But, Harry, surely you don't have to go. Why don't you just spend a little capital—."

"You can't buy your way out of this one, Tony."

"How do you know?"

"Tony, I want to go."

"Me, too. But I got two little kids at home, and another on the way."

"Tony, I don't blame you."

"I'll go if they call me."

"Well, I'm not waiting. I'm enlisting. Tony—remember the old gang? My friends, down on Hester Street? Division Street? That we grew up with? We're all gonna join together."

"You're actually gonna do this."

"Nothing to it. I'll kill a few of those potato-mashers for ya, Tony."

Tony believed it. He remembered only too well the Harry he had known, the Harry Spritzka who wanted to kill—Tony felt that.

Whatever it was in Harry, Tony did not have it in him. But Harry did.

"What about Mimi? What does she say?"

"What do you think? She's got nothing to say about it. It's my decision. Nobody's askin' her!"

That was Harry, all over. Here they were standing in this magnificent mausoleum of a mansion having a meeting to discuss making more money to build the tomb taller, with the tomb-owner putting the meeting aside to throw a party to celebrate becoming a potential corpse so that he could make a widow out of the lady of the tomb and leave her to enjoy an even bigger mausoleum by herself.

Tony loved money as much as any man, but he didn't miss New York. Not now that he was here on 91st Street again. This was a place where he could never live again, a life he could never rejoin. He could be a nostalgic New Yorker every day, while he was in Boston, but he did not miss New York itself, the real New York. He missed Gigi and the kids.

The Selective Service Act was passed on May the 17th, and Tony registered for the draft. Registrations were held in local polling places. He had to go to a fire station on Fleet Street in the North End. They were told to keep that card on their person at all times. It was the first time Tony had been in a place where people cast votes in elections. He left with the card in his wallet, feeling enhanced somehow, ennobled in a way. Someday he would come back here, to vote.

In the end, he was never drafted. He did not know why, but he could think of a couple of reasons. The draft law had been written to register men from the age of 21 to 30. Tony was close to the age limit. And he had two children at home. Also, they had been told that if they were drafted, as aliens from Italy, they would be given the choice at that time of joining either Army. Tony had specified that he wanted to serve in the American forces, if called. Maybe that had something to do, somehow, with why he never was. *How would he ever know?*

Whether he was called into the Army or not, the war gave Tony LaStoria plenty to do. He, and everyone else, as far as he could see, like it or not, was drafted into what people began to call the War Effort.

At Tony's New York meeting at the mansion, Harry Spritzka forecast government contracts; and said he was going to make every payoff necessary to make sure they got their share. He told Tony to spare no effort to hire and train as many stitchers, for as many shifts, as necessary to get these contracts completed on time, or better, ahead of schedule.

But on top of that, he wanted expansion of their peace-time lines and civilian production as well. He was making Tony a General Manager. Tony was already a general manager, hiring factory managers in several towns and cities in three states, delegating further hiring to his hand-picked managers to staff the factories with stitchers and cutters and pressers, buying properties for the company for *Richard Paul* Stores, staffing them; but he hadn't bothered with the title, that's all. Now he was finding out that Harry intended to get his money's worth out of that pay raise of fifteen bucks.

Harry wanted new factory operations, coupled with new retail outlets, in cheap mill space in Hartford, Connecticut, Nashua, N.H., and Marlborough, Mass., as well. How was Tony to do that?

That was Tony's lookout. Harry would be elsewhere, starting with Camp Mills, in Mineola. But Harry predicted that people were going to have money in their pockets from this war, and he was right, as he usually was. And Harry Spritzka wanted his fair share of that pile.

President Wilson chimed in with his own mandates from Washington. He gave a speech stating that he expected that people like farmers, miners, lumbermen, nurses, teamsters, steelworkers and housewives were to go about their usual daily activities as if the outcome of the war depended on them.

Posters began to appear everywhere; the latest slogan was "Give till it hurts." Men in uniform were now collecting in the bars and restaurants, and special collections for "Our Boys" were being taken up at Sunday Mass.

The declaration of war on the Central Powers by the United States Congress was taken up as an excuse to start weekend parties in every big and small town and city. Half-trained units from Camp Devens were sent into Boston to mount parades, drums rolling and flags flying. People turned out to join the celebrations, lining the sidewalks. Everybody was waving the flag, even if it was only made out of paper. Smiles everywhere, happy faces all around. War fever was the epidemic of the day. At the Faneuil Hall Marketplace, an enthusiastic rally was held with speechifying by none other than Mayor Curley himself, who came down from City Hall to address mostly Italian fruit vendors, pushcart operators, and meat packers.

And then the worst thing that could possibly have happened came true. The Italian War Mission was invited to Boston by His Honor, the Mayor.

Pasquale Fabrizio was overcome with joy. Representatives of the King of Italy himself, Victor Emmanuel III, were coming to Boston!

Tony was dismayed. Now the old man expected Tony, as his well-to-do son-in-law, to troop down to the Copley Plaza Hotel by his side, for an early-morning Reception.

Tony was aghast. The Mayor had scheduled the War Mission, composed of Deputies from the Chamber in Rome, in addition to personal representatives from the King's palace staff, to arrive in Boston on a Monday, June 25th. He wrote to Tony's friend, DiBenedetto, that he expected the Boston greeting committee, including, of course, Italian citizens and Italian-Americans alike, from the North End, to appear at the Copley Plaza at 7.30 am, sharp, in "frock coat, silk hat, grey tie, grey gloves, and grey trousers," where an automobile convoy provided by the Mayor's organization would take them to South Station to greet the train full of Italian dignitaries when it pulled in from New York.

From there, they would spend the day on a whirlwind tour of the city, including a meeting with the Governor, Sam McCall. Who was indisposed that day. Leaving a man who had little else to do but to greet the Italian delegation: Lt Governor Calvin Coolidge.

Thereafter, Curley and the Italians moved on briskly to the Charlestown Navy Yard, for an inspection of United States naval strength, the Italians being the Americans' new allies; and also, the Fore River Shipyard, in Quincy, winding up at art exhibits at the home of Isabella Stewart Gardner, a visit to the world-renowned Boston Public Library, a series of speeches in the twilight on the Boston Common, followed by dinner and addresses, a concert, and dancing, back at the Copley Plaza.

It was an exhausting day. Tony would rather have been in Marlborough teaching farmer's daughters to run sewing machines, or in Providence, trying to hire competent cloth-cutters, or anywhere. Instead, the butcher, Fabrizio, expected Tony, the master-tailor, his son-in-law, to outfit him with all the necessary finery, none of which he had hanging in his closet. And thereafter, as a sign of respect, to accompany the head of the family (who, after all, was a Haymarket merchant) on the day's festivities. And of course to smile, and scrape, and bow, and shake hands, and make small talk.

What the world was coming to Tony did not know. But of one thing he was sure; or was it doubtful? Could it be that the old man, Gigi's father, had been right all along, in his glorification of that distant Piedmontese dynasty, the House of Savoy? Tony read the newspapers, in his office, religiously, at home, too, every day, even when he was on the road; he was well-informed, he thought, he was diligent, he kept up. How could he have been so wrong? It caused Tony agonies of self-recrimination to think his father-in-law could have had it right, the old moustache, the *via vecchia*, and he, Tony, the new generation, the new world, wrong!

It was the war, Tony decided. The war was confusing everything. From one minute to the next, you never knew where you stood, everything was changing so fast. One's mind, one's thinking, could not keep up with the speed of developments.

Unarmed American merchant ships were being sunk in the Atlantic by German submarines. A few years before such a thing would have been a fantasy concocted by Jules Verne or Edgar Allan Poe.

Aeroplanes were now not merely flying, (and, in defiance of all human logic, and previous history, staying up there!) now they were plunging to earth in flames, having fought desperate battles in the skies over Europe, shot down by other aeroplanes!

An invention by an Italian, someone called Marconi, a thing called a radio, was now being used at sea to save lives of endangered American sailors by other American sailors.

Automobiles were no longer the pleasure-craft of the ultra-rich; they were the engines of war, and had transmogrified into horrifying, terrifyingly-ugly tanks, bristling with armor-plate and cannons and machine guns, for blasting people's arms and legs to bits.

The whole world was going mad.

Hysteria swept Boston when German submarines were sighted lying in wait outside the harbor of New York City.

Again, in New York, no sooner had the US entered the hostilities, than Emma Goldman and Alexander Berkman, said to be leading foreign anarchists, were arrested. And in Boston, Luigi Galleani, named by the Justice Department in Washington as the foremost anarchist in the country, was arrested on the same day, June 15th, 1917.

Then the anarchists struck back. In Pittsburgh, an arson fire destroyed the Aetna Chemical Works, one of the largest munitions manufacturers in the country.

Most tragic of all, 116 girls, most of them teenagers, lost their lives in a massive explosion at the Eddystone Ammunition Corporation in Chester, Pennsylvania.

They died because they worked in the pellet room of the shrapnel building; and officials claimed that the anarchists who planted the bomb blew themselves up in the process.

Tony LaStoria made the sign-of-the-cross when he read this account in the newspaper.

He was sitting in his office in South Boston, in a factory he managed, where they did war-work.

He was reading an account where the factory manager in Pennsylvania was lamenting the fact that you could hardly employ five thousand workers in a munitions plant without employing foreigners.

Tony LaStoria could only thank God that he was not the manager of that factory.

And when he lowered the newspaper into his lap, it was only to reflect on another occasion he recalled only too well, which he would indeed never be able to eradicate from the print-shop of his soul; when young girls had their bodies burned, their dreams destroyed, their very lives lost because they had been sent to work on the ninth floor of a garment factory to help out their families at home.

For a long time, he sat there thinking of Laura.

All the doors were locked, and they couldn't get out.

Was this war any different than that?

The whole world was locked in with the rising flames and couldn't get out.

Toward the end of 1917, stretched to the limits travelling by train to outposts north and south of Boston, or driving the Buick himself on inadequate roads winding through every hill and vale and every town, city and village, spending days away from the family, sometimes more than a week at a time, trying to manage everything, Tony was left with Gigi approaching the birth of her third child, and her time was coming on.

Patsy and Maria were now 3 years old and one-and-a-half, more or less, and here was a third baby coming, in winter, at Christmas, in wartime.

Thank God for Anna-Lisa Fabrizio, their grandmother, and the midwives of the old neighborhood, over on Prince

Street. Without them, Tony and Gigi would have been hard up against it.

As much as Tony could easily have done without his father-in-law, he revered Anna-Lisa, his mother-in-law. That woman, she was a candidate for sainthood, in his estimation. How had he ever deserved a mother-in-law like that? He only knew that next to Gigi, he loved that woman more than anyone he had ever known, except Harry's Bubelah? Yes, that was it! Anna-Lisa Fabrizio, she was the second coming of his beloved Bubelah!

La Bambina Margherita, La Princessa, came into the world on the day after Christmas, 1917.

Little did Tony know, at the time, that she would become the family "anarchist," in her own special manner, the one who would attack and tear down everything, without having any idea what to replace it with.

And the irony was that Tony's nemesis, his father-in-law, was insisting that this latest addition to *his* family be named Margherita after the Queen Mother of Italy, Queen Margherita (who also had a pizza named after her!). The anarchist Queen of the corner restaurant! Many times in the faroff future would Tony have cause to recite this niggling thought to himself, in all its dripping ridiculousness. In the meantime, Tony, who insisted on speaking English to the kids whenever he was at home, because their mother always used Italian, quickly dubbed Margherita "little baby *Peggy.*" And Peggy she became, the rest of her life long.

The end of 1917 did not see the end of the war. It plowed into its fourth desperate year on rails of steel, powered by Big Bertha.

By now, Harry Spritzka had long since killed his first enemy. Tony received no letters, but he was in touch with Mimi, in New York, by phone, and she did. Of course, neither of them knew this at the time. It was not something Harry would write home about. But Tony could tell from the tone of concern and worry in Mimi's voice that there was more on her mind than she wanted to talk about.

How had Harry Spritzka ever deserved a wife who loved him like that?

Life was certainly a strange affair.

Sometimes Tony thought it was beyond him, a complete mystery, past anyone's human comprehension. That all you could do was wonder.

And then in the fall of 1918, with news of American military successes turning the tide in Europe, on the heels of a sudden euphoria that it might end, that they might actually emerge victorious, that this would after all turn out to be what Wilson said it was, the war to end all wars, due to American military might, to American sacrifice, to America saving the world: disaster struck Boston.

The enemy did not enter the city on foot, in German-made boots. It did not steal into the harbor in underwater craft. It may have come on shipboard, that's true—but it was an enemy that could not be seen.

Because it was the size of microbes.

The first sign was in August, late August, when sailors aboard a training vessel at Commonwealth Pier, on the edge of the North End, came down with the flu.

Nobody even knew about this, at the time. It was not reported because it was not regarded as significant.

It was not news until people began dying.

Then Boston knew that the specter of the Spanish influenza, which heretofore, had been confined to the European theater of operations, which they heard as distant thunder, in items tucked into the inside pages, or in letters home from the doughboys, had insinuated itself into their very midst.

And they were so very vulnerable.

None more so than a young family like the LaStorias.

By early September, thousands of soldiers at Camp Devens had contracted the disease. Overworked and undernourished, lying wounded on hospital cots, they were dying like flies.

Over-crowding, and close-quarters, were blamed for the defenselessness of the poor victims, who had already given so much, and now, died, not from the leaden bullet, but from the invisible bullet.

No place in Boston was as overcrowded, condensed, and jammed in as the North End. The Army camp, in distant Ayer, Mass., became the anteroom of hell, the North End, hell itself.

By October the influenza epidemic was rampaging throughout Boston. City officials had closed down theaters, clubs, and restaurants. Every venue where people gathered together. People were desperate to avoid contact. Tony LaStoria at first stopped riding in his car or venturing on the subway. Then he stopped going to work at all. Then he stopped going out. He spoke to everyone he had to speak to in his Division of shops and stores on the phone, which now never stopped ringing in the house. He stayed home, to help Gigi, who was frantic.

Gigi, whom he loved, who loved her children more than herself, who lived for them.

Tony was desperate. He could not let her lose them. He did not care if Government contract deadlines were not met. This was an emergency. Unprecedented. And no one knew what in the hell to do. Least of all him.

Although he had never been a church-goer, as such, when he did attend mass, if he went at all, he did so with his mind elsewhere. Back in New York, when he was younger, only to look at the girls (how many were his sins! of commission, of omission, of mere thought, which, venial or mortal, counted as much as any act). *Was this God's retribution?*

Now he paced back and forth with Peggy, the newborn, in his arms; not even a year old, the most vulnerable one; looking down at her for any sign of a sniffle or runny nose or fever. Gigi looked after the other two, but she would not even let her mother come over to help, for fear of contagion. She sent Tony out only to go to *Fillipo's Farmacia,* the only drugstore in the North End; but he came back empty-handed.

"There's no medicine," he said.

They both knew that the deaths in Boston now amounted to 100 people a day.

"Gigi, I'm praying. You pray, too. It's all we can do."

Gigi resolved to forget all about her fantasies of other realms, other gods. She found her rosary beads and tried to make it up to the Holy Mother, reciting endless Hail Mary's, as she walked back and forth, carrying Patsy, who was getting too big for this, exchanging him for Maria. They were both pacing. Tony was trying to talk to God Himself. Trying to reason with Him. To strike a bargain. God, why would *You* want to do this to *us?* What pleasure would it give You, to see us suffer this way? *It would be the end of us! Spare us! Spare us, and I will never forget You for it! I will uphold Your faith. I will go to confession. I will receive. I will be there for You, every Sunday, every day! Only spare us!*

November came, in the cruelest autumn of their lives, and they were saved.

They all got sick in the end, but none of them died.

Across the world, the numbers of dead were astounding. The papers, when Tony started reading them again, said 20 million to 100 million had died. You could not believe these figures. It was said that in the United States, half a million dead! In the greatest country in the world, with the best doctors!

You could not believe these figures. In the armed forces of the United States, 18,000 dead! Young, fit, healthy men, not just sick or wounded, legless or armless: young, fit, healthy men; who were conquering the world from their trenches; and who were cut down in the open, in their prime, by a hidden enemy!

Was it God's revenge on a human race gone mad? Did He heap slaughter on those who heedlessly, in violation of his every commandment, slaughtered one another?

Did He send an army they could not combat? An army they could not defeat? An invisible army, to obtain His revenge upon those who had scorned Him and turned their gaze away, to their own pleasures, to their own gratifications? To their own lust for death, glory, gold and blood?

These were the thoughts of a dreadful autumn that crowded out all reason from the mind of Tony LaStoria and every other parishioner who crowded the first Sunday masses when the churches re-opened, when the authorities in the city allowed that the epidemic was over, when the subways were suddenly mobbed again.

And as they huddled in church, (in astounding numbers, for the North End, which was the home of skepticism, of superstition, of backwardness, of alienation from Mother Church) they crowded, on their knees, to listen to Father Alissi, the pastor of Sacred Heart, tell them, as he celebrated a High Mass of thanksgiving, that perhaps now their lukewarm faith would be rekindled to a bright blaze. But, said the priest, "At such a cost! Of the lives of the dearly-departed among us!"

And the wailing of the women in that church that day was fierce, as fierce as the fire and brimstone of battlefields an ocean away.

Then the war ended.

As simple as that.

It was over, in early November, at the 11th hour of the 11th day.

As quickly as the War, *La Grande Guerra,* had come, in 1914, to a Boston looking elsewhere, in 1918, at the onslaught of the Spanish flu, it left again, on the eleventh hour of the eleventh day of the eleventh month, in a Boston looking elsewhere, licking its wounds.

Chapter 9

Nineteen Nineteen

In January of 1919, the 15th of the month dawned quiet and clear.

The awful autumn was behind them. Even the fireworks and parading surrounding the end of the war in November, which had temporarily lifted the spirits of the battered North End, were over now.

Without warning, on this uneventful day, the 15th of January, the molasses tank down on the waterfront collapsed, sending 2.3 million gallons of the sticky syrup flooding in all directions.

People were drowned in a black tidal-wave. Twenty-one died that day in the North End of Boston. The anarchists were immediately blamed for blowing up the tank, for causing death and destruction, and a massive mess.

Tony LaStoria was never so grateful in his life that his wife Gigi habitually stayed home all day with the children, and never ventured out unless it be truly necessary, or unless she were going to "visit America" with her husband. After escaping the Spanish influenza by some miracle, how would it have felt to lose a member of the family to a river of molasses, as some unfortunate people did?

Tony decided then and there that he was through with the North End.

"We cannot stay here, Gigi. It's too crowded, too dangerous. We have three children now. Where are we gonna find a backyard for them to play in? In this redbrick graveyard? If I have to live in my car, so be it! I will have to drive myself to work every day. But we have to get out of this town. We are leaving Boston, and that's that. There are other places to live, you'll see. We'll find someplace nice, and you can have a flower garden, I promise, instead of your window-boxes. It's not like you'll never see your mother again!"

Tony stopped himself when he said this. He had to sit down. It hit him like a thunderclap. *How had those words, those very words, those very particular words, escaped his lips?* who was always on his guard, never to allow himself to think such thoughts, never mind speak them aloud. He felt that he had brought his own mother straight into the room with them, and he was instantaneously haunted, assailed by the thought that he had callously abandoned his own mother, and that somewhere down the road, the road of life, the road which fate ruled, vindictively, in the name of revenge, he would have to pay.

Or else, why did she never write to him? why, in all these years? never so much as a letter? *In spite of all that Italy, and America, had been through, together, never so much as a letter.* Was it her revenge? Or did she simply stand on her pride and insist on him writing to her first? Or was it something else? Had she forgotten him? Did he, after all, cease to exist—in the eyes of his own mother?

Tony's friend DiBenedetto was not so sure about the molasses tank affair as the other editors in the city. Republican that he was, he was still even more Italian, by nature, and although he wanted to hold the city administration, that Curley gang of Democrats, responsible, in print, in his weekly, for their lack of oversight, he also wanted to find a reason why the anarchists were, after all, not involved in this.

DiBenedetto told Tony, "If I find out it was shoddy construction, or poor maintenance by United States Alcohol, or failure to conduct testing, or any such malfeasance there will be hell to pay! I will worry them like a dog on a bone! I will never cease! It's all too easy, Tony, for them to lay it at the door of the anarchists. And guess who gets tarred all over again with that brush? We do! Everybody in this town whose last name ends in a vowel!"

Nevertheless, the authorities had their excuse to go after the anarchists with renewed vigor.

They first banned the Mayday 1919 celebrations and marches which the anarchists and the Wobblies and the other left-wingers like the Debs Socialists held every year.

No one in Boston had forgotten that, back in '17, the so-called revolutionaries in Russia had succeeded in overthrowing the Czarist regime, which had lasted a thousand years, it seemed. If such a permanent state of affairs, virtually eternal, could be overthrown in a trice, only to be replaced by God knows what kind of Bolshevist reign of terror, why could it not as easily happen here? There were plenty who fervently wished it, living in their very midst! They had to be stopped. They had to be stamped out, no matter the cost.

Tony LaStoria's biggest problem was the clean-up. He struggled with might and main to eradicate every smudge and stain of molasses from his front steps, from the sidewalk, but it was an unequal fight. The stuff was tenacious. And he did not own the building.

That was another corncob stuck in his ear. Once they got out of here, never again was he going to be a renter. Why make someone else rich? Virtually overnight, Tony discovered he had a hunger for property. A man like himself, with his station in life, so hard-won, so all-devouring: he should have not only his own automobile, he should have his own land, house and home! Or why was he working so hard? To bring up his children in this stinking town, which he did not even like, but only tolerated?

And things were getting daily worse. In spite of victory, which was gained at the cost of the flower of its youth, the country had become bogged down in controversy over the Peace Conference at Versailles and President Wilson's League of Nations. The Italians of the North End were incensed at Wilson over the issue of Fiume, in the old country. The Italian government had been promised it would acquire this Adriatic city as part of its reward of expanded territories, as a member of the victorious Triple Alliance. But Wilson, under the aegis of his theories, peace without victory, the rights of small nations, and so forth, threw his weight against the Italians acquiring Fiume. And the residents of the North End did not like that one bit. Nor did the editor, DiBenedetto, who found in it another feather to add to his Republican war-bonnet.

In the aftermath of the war, the returning veterans who flooded into Boston were expecting to face renewed prospects, not unemployment, closed doors, and rejection. The same was happening all up and down the East Coast, and in the Midwestern cities as well. That was not what the returning vets of Boston had fought for. On top of a flood of molasses, there was a flood of rising prices hitting the city at the same time that government contracts were being cancelled. Then there were the Negroes from the South (Tony preferred to use this word because whenever he heard someone use the word "nigga," in that Boston accent of theirs, he felt that *dago, guinea* and *wop* were not far behind.) In the war years of '17 and '18, Negroes from the south, for the first time, had begun resettling in the South End and Roxbury, in search of jobs to fill during the wartime labor shortages. Now the returning veterans were dismayed that they had to compete for fewer jobs with more "niggas." You could join the Army and dig a ditch, all right, but you couldn't find anybody back home in Boston to pay you starvation wages to dig that ditch.

Then Wilson came out with a statement. He maintained to a reporter that, "if the Italians were going to claim every place where there was a large Italian population, we would have to cede New York to them, because there are more Italians in New York than any Italian city!"

Besides the arrogance, superiority, and superciliousness of that statement, it was ignorant, on the grounds that it was factually erroneous. Which was pointed out, with glee, in two languages, by the Republican, DiBenedetto, in the pages of *La Gazzetta*.

Then the anarchists responded, yet again, to attacks on them and everything else going on, with still more violence.

Their leader, Galleani, released from jail in Boston, had moved out of town, to Wrentham, southwest of the city, with his wife and kids (as Tony himself dreamed of doing.) At one point he turned up in Taunton, south of Brockton, partway to Providence and the Cape, to give an incendiary speech.

The very next night, in the nearby town of Franklin, four anarchists, all with Italian surnames, all thought to be Galleani's ardent supporters, blew themselves up. The papers quoted the police and the district attorney as believing the four men died in a botched attempt to destroy the mill of the American Woolen Company in Franklin, where there was a strike in progress. This was the very same company, the biggest in Milltown, which had led the mill-owners' opposition to the Bread and Roses Strike in that city, north of Boston, dating all the way back to 1912. The anarchists were everywhere, the papers maintained, South Shore, North Shore, Boston, Merrimack Valley, everywhere, and they had long memories, and they were out for revenge on what they called "the war-mongering capitalists."

Federal authorities now entered Massachusetts, and arrested three other men, charging them with conspiracy in the Franklin bombing. J. Edgar Hoover was the newly-appointed head of the General Intelligence Division of the new Federal Bureau of Investigation, at that time, so new that the initials F.B.I. were as yet unfamiliar to most people.

Hoover and newly-made Wilson appointee, A. Mitchell Palmer, who was now Attorney General of the United States, targeted Massachusetts as the leading den of iniquity, the hotbed of impending mayhem, promising to the press a "nationwide crackdown" on aliens, Bolshevists, radicals and anarchists, who were "roaming the countryside" disturbing the peace and terrorizing the citizenry.

The battle lines were drawn. The summer of 1919 was hot and steamy in Boston, not only weather-wise, but with demonstrations and counter-terror. Returning war veterans, ex-soldiers and sailors, alongside police themselves, and everyday citizens, chased parading radicals in Roxbury, including Italian followers of Galleani. Galleani himself was known to be under threat of actual deportation back to Italy, imminently.

The summer began with mail-bombs. One was sent to the home of Georgia's former Senator, Thomas Hardwick, co-sponsor of a 1918 deportation bill. It exploded and blew off both hands of the maid who opened it. More mail-bombs were found by the postal authorities before they could be delivered. They were addressed to Attorney-General Palmer, Postmaster-General Burleson, Chief-Justice of the Supreme Court, Oliver Wendell Holmes, a native son of Massachusetts; even John D. Rockefeller and J.P. Morgan. The newspapers clamored for action: they said the public was outraged. In Boston, fourteen demonstrators were found guilty of disturbing the peace by Judge Hayden in Roxbury District Court. The judge made statements to reporters, blasting "the foreigners who think they can get away with their doctrines in this country!"

A month later, the judge's home in Roxbury was virtually destroyed by a bomb placed against a main support column. The judge's son narrowly escaped being run down by the bombers fleeing in their getaway car.

Next day, Attorney General Palmer told the nation the Roxbury bombing was part of an organized conspiracy, hatched in Boston, and unleashed not only there, but in six other Eastern cities, including Washington, DC, with bombs planted, and timed all to go off simultaneously, within an hour of midnight. Palmer's own home, in the fashionable north-west sector of Washington, was bombed while he and his wife were asleep upstairs. They escaped serious injury, but they were showered with glass. The dead bomber was found under the steps of Palmer's house. An intact Italian-English dictionary was found nearby. It was believed the bomb had gone off prematurely, blowing up the bomber. He was tentatively identified as Carlo Valdinocci—a dedicated *Galleanista*.

In August, Galleani himself was deported.

The Justice Department maintained that a wave of fear and anger was sweeping the country in response to an organized, nationwide conspiracy to overthrow the American government. Wiseacres said the fear and anger were in response to the passage of the Prohibition amendment, back in January. The only reprieve the people of Boston had gotten to the unrelieved stress of 1919 was a grace period of a year before the police would begin to actually enforce the ban on drinking alcoholic beverages.

In September, the Boston Police Force, in the midst of all the uproar, had their own response: nearly 1400 Boston police officers went on strike after the 5.45 pm roll-call, angry that their wage increase demands had been denied.

That night, riots broke out across the city, mobs smashed windows, looting more than fifty stores, including the latest newly-opened *Richard Paul Discount Clothing* Store, 10,000 square feet of men's, women's and children's reduced-price clothing racks, sandwiched between R.H. Stearns and Gilchrist's, downtown on Washington Street, opposite Filene's and Jordan Marsh: owned by Harry Spritzka and operated by retail managers and staff under General Manager Tony

LaStoria. The rioters threw rocks, bottles, bricks and paving stones at picketing police officers, who lifted not a finger to protect the stores on Washington Street from the looters breaking their plate-glass windows to steal merchandise.

The unprecedented strike of public safety officers shocked the nation, and new Massachusetts Governor, Calvin Coolidge, elected in his own right just the year before, in 1918, just before the war ended in November, now entered the lists with the statement that "No man has a right to place his own ease or convenience or the opportunity of making money above his duty to the state." Governor Coolidge immediately sent in several thousand members of the Massachusetts State Guard to restore order on the streets of Boston.

But the police strike inspired more strikes across the nation, acting as a kind of catalyst. On September 20th, 300,000 workers went out on strike against Carnegie Steel, Bethlehem, and US Steel, in Pittsburgh, Chicago, Cleveland, and Youngstown, Ohio, demanding higher wages and better working conditions. All these strikes were as illegal as the Boston Police strike had been, and as police and state militias responded, violence and rioting broke out in several places.

In Massachusetts, under cover of night, and the general turmoil, local anarchists, still being sought by Federal agents, went on the run. Among those who departed for Mexico were two named Nicola Sacco and Bartolomeo Vanzetti.

The summer was over, but the year was not.

November of 1919 saw the second anniversary of the Bolshevist uprising in the former capital of the Czar's empire, in faraway St Petersburg, but this time, it was the Federal government in Washington, D.C. that issued forth with a pre-emptive stroke. On November 7, the precise day of the anniversary, deliberately, at 9 pm at night, agents of the Federal Bureau of Investigation, together with local police, executed a series of well-drilled raids, in 12 cities. They were under orders from Attorney General Palmer himself. It was his show. There was an election coming up in just about a year's time, and Palmer considered himself a candidate for President. He was prepared to round up members of the organization called the Russian Workers, but he was not prepared for every outcome that eventually came about. The papers next day were already calling these operations the "Palmer Raids." The attorney general had faced congressional committees questioning him in October, about the failures of his investigations into the wave of anarchist bombings. This was his reply to those who cast doubt on him.

But the other side did not cooperate: they did not go quietly to their prison cells or deportation docks. They and their friends protested that some were badly beaten during the raids; and more claimed they were beaten and threatened during questioning. The government agents had cast their nets too wide. They had brought in American citizens, they had arrested passers-by, they had taken some who admitted to being Russian, but who were not members of the Russian Workers. Some were teachers conducting night-school classes in space shared with the targeted radicals. The number of arrested far exceeded the number of warrants for arrest the agents had.

None of this was overlooked by their opponents, or the newspaper-selling press in general. The government had created a tinderbox. Of 650 people arrested in New York City, they managed to get the courts to deport only 43.

In all this time, Tony had not neglected to cultivate his connection with Harry Spritzka. Tony was responsible for a growing family now, he was its sole support, and he had ambitions to improve the lot of his wife and kids in the face of months of unrelenting turmoil in the city of Boston, and all over, coast to coast, so there was little incentive for him to forget who buttered his bread. If necessary, he would go to New York. These were difficult days in 1919, and the downturn in the economy, the masses of unemployed veterans returning from war-torn Europe, the migrations of Negroes from the South that were now re-drawing the lines of Northern cities, revealed the hollowness of the wartime prosperity.

Yet Tony's consuming reason for the railroad journey to New York to see his friend Harry, his old friend Harry, the lost companion of his youth, Harry, at that particular time, notwithstanding all these other reasons, legitimate and otherwise, was that Tony just had to know how Harry had done it, and why? How had Harry fared as an enlisted man, running off to join the American Expeditionary Force? And why?

If Tony were a betting man, which he was, he would have bet the house that his friend Spritzka was the last man on earth to run off and enlist. Tony certainly could not picture the whole affair as an instance of purely runaway American patriotism. There had to be something else. And because of Gigi and the kids and his burgeoning responsibilities, Tony had to know. God forbid that it might be vital to ensuring his future, and theirs, who depended so much on one Harry Spritzka. Even if he was no longer close to Harry—as how could he be? (each of them in his own way had turned his back on the other.) Still, Tony had to strive somehow to figure the man out.

Why had Harry never ceased tugging on the strings of his puppet, Tony? At one time, in both their lives, they lived under one roof. Now, with such distance between them, the strings were still there. Surely, it could not be from affection, from attachment to a lost boyhood pal. If Tony knew his man at all, Harry must have some plan in mind, some scheme. This was what Tony had to know.

When he went to visit New York in '19, Tony studiously avoided the old neighborhoods of Little Italy and Hester Street, or anything associated with his old haunts of East 72nd Street, and Uncle Eugenio's; and especially of anything to do with Washington Square, the Triangle Factory, the Asch Building, *Laura.* He stuck to the vicinity of Harry's mansion-building on East 91st, currently holding steady at three stories tall.

"It's that banker across the street—he built too high when he moved in," Harry told Tony. "He's shutting out my sunlight—and my view—I had no choice."

"Business must be good."

"You're nuts. It couldn't be worse. The war has ruined the garment industry. While Wilson got himself all excited over the war to end all wars—the whole economy went to pot—you think he cares? Hell, no. Can't wipe his own arse anymore."

Then Harry said, "Now don't give me them puppy-dog eyes. Your job ain't in any danger. I ain't throwin' in the towel. I need you up there on the job, for when we start expanding again. And that's what we're gonna do, Tony. Expand or die.

Soon as the country gets going again. That's the only way to make a nickel in this line of work, expansion. You're not gonna let me down, are you, Tony?"

"Of course not, Harry."

"Ah—I knew you wouldn't." But Harry's eyes turned aside. His mind was momentarily elsewhere. They were sitting in his home, his "pile," as he called it, but Mimi was not there, sitting with them; and Harry was avoiding eye contact.

"Harry, why don't you tell me about the Expeditionary Force? I mean, don't take this the wrong way, but before you left, you were braggin' to me about how you were gonna shoot a couple of potato-mashers for me. And now, it's like, you don't wanna talk about it."

"You wouldn't understand." Now Harry did look at Tony. "Nobody would understand who wasn't there."

"Are you all right, Harry?"

"Of course I am. Couldn't be better."

"Then what is it?"

"What do you mean?"

"Well—I never understood—why you felt you had to go."

Harry looked long at Tony. As if wondering, or debating, if he should say or not. Finally, he gave up, sighing deeply, and he said, "Because I'm a Jew."

That answer left Tony completely at a loss, as well as shocked into silence.

It must have shown on his face, because Harry said, not without kindness, "Look, Tony—that's another thing you wouldn't understand. Nobody would who doesn't have to live under the burden. Don't you realize that after all this, even after our service in this war, and I certainly wasn't the only Jew over there in Pershing's little gang—that we are not accepted in this country? And that we never will be? And Tony, it's that much worse over there!"

The look on Tony, of blank incomprehension, stopped Harry right there. "And if you must know—I did it for Mimi."

Tony was more mystified than ever.

"She needed a little break from me, Tony."

Tony felt suddenly very contrite, very humbled to realize that he may have misjudged Harry. That Harry might want Tony's friendship back, that he might tell Tony things he would tell no one else.

"Tony—how many kids you got now?"

"Three, Harry."

"Three. Goddam it, Tony. When you left New York, you were the last guy I would have picked to ever get married! Much less have three kids!"

"And you were the last guy I ever would have thought would have volunteered to get himself killed."

"Well, at least I got to take a few pot-shots at our enemies. And believe me, Tony, they are legion. And it ain't just here, or in the hallowed halls of the United States Army. It's that much worse in France, and worse yet in Germany. But, then, it's in England, as well. Another ally! Tony, it's everywhere. I honestly don't know what the future holds, but I know one thing. For us, for the Jews, we need a place of our own. Our own national homeland in Palestine, where we come from, Tony. That's why I gotta make millions! Without millions, how are we Jews safe? It's not just for myself. That's why you gotta help me, Tony."

This conversation Tony remembered distinctly, on the day when Chief of Police Puffy O'Brian was going on about the Elders of Zion, many years later, in the police station in Stoughton.

But at the time, in 1919, sitting in Harry Spritzka's mansion-on-the-make, the discussion continued, diverted into

Harry's specific ideas, which he needed to have Tony carry out, when Harry was ready to begin expanding factory floors, factory-outlets, and the *Richard Paul* chain of retail stores again.

And the day ended only when Harry rose to shake Tony's hand, reluctantly, as he seemed, at the end, to have something else he wanted to say.

"Three kids, huh, Tony? Look at this place. This magnificent pile. Tony, Mimi and I have no children. How am I ever gonna carry on the race if I have no children?—huh?"

"Harry, don't you love Mimi?"

"As much as I can ever love anyone, I suppose."

"I think you love her as much as I love my Gigi."

"We're a fine pair, we are, Mimi and me. A matched set of cuff-links."

"Harry—do you remember why I had to leave New York?"

"Sure. That girl."

"Well, you know what I mean, then. You know what I'm trying to say."

"What? What are you trying to say, Tony? Tell me something. You love Gigi as much as you loved that girl, what's her name? I don't even know if I ever knew her name."

"Laura," said Tony.

"Laura," said Harry.

"Harry, how am I supposed to answer that?"

"Life goes on, my friend, huh? We start all over again? Get the fuck outta here, you asshole. I'll call you in Boston."

Chapter 10

The Heart Goes Home to the Harbor

Through his friends, through DiBenedetto, but also through the Sons of Italy organization in the North End, and with the help of Father Alissi at *Sacred Heart,* Tony LaStoria was able to qualify for a mortgage.

They had been so happy, on the beach in Nantasket, on their one-day escape to the seashore, after Patsy's birth. Nantasket was located in the town of Hull. Tony wanted so much for Gigi to be happy again like that. So he pointed his house-hunting in the direction of the South Shore. The closer to Nantasket, the better, he thought. He wanted Gigi also to have her flower-garden as well as her children. To have a back porch, a front porch; not to be cramped into dark quarters without windows in the North End. He convinced her (so he thought) never realizing that it was she who had made up her own mind and was prodding him. Gigi had a way of twisting him around her finger without his being the least aware of it.

The family went house-hunting together, weekends, with the kids, in Tony's commodious 1914 Buick. Starting in Nantasket and working their way through the town of Hull, they came to Hingham. Tony remembered Hingham fondly from the days when he and the matchmaker, Brooklyn, used to go there to spend a Saturday afternoon visiting the thoroughbred horses in paddocks on the horse-farms that dotted the town. He and Gigi came across a beautiful place in Hingham, a two-family, on a shady street, Foster Street, right next door to Hull, on the seashore. Hingham in those days was a quiet, unobtrusive old-fashioned country town, south of Boston, not too far out, about 11 miles from the city line, but with land, land enough for flower gardens, and growing grapes, and planting tomatoes; the new house had an income coming in from the second floor. Borrowing two hundred from his father-in-law, Tony paid $400 down and took a mortgage for the other $2600 with the *Banca Italiana* in the North End.

By this time, Gigi placed all her faith in her husband. She who had always been the darling of her own Papa, Pasquale, now had forsaken him for the Papa of her *bambini*, Tony. In the crisis of the Spanish flu, the year before, it had not escaped her how much Tony loved his children, how attached and possessive of them he was. No matter how attuned to her parents she was, to her former life, she was now a mother herself, three times over, and she had to be certain of exactly who she depended on. Events frightened her. The thought of what she would do without Tony now terrified her. The North End was full of widows who had to wallow in poverty and misery trying to look after large broods of children—without a man—a man who now lay dead and buried, over in Italy, somewhere in France, under a flood of molasses, or in a collapsed drainage ditch in Boston, which only a moment before, he had been digging himself, by hand, by the sweat of his brow.

Life was too precious, and at the same time too precarious. Gigi had made her bed, and now she must lie in it. For good or ill she cast her lot with her husband.

Later on, years later, it seemed to them, in their memory, which Gigi and Tony shared mutually like a family photo album, it seemed to them that in 1919, when the family was still *più o meno* just starting out, both of them felt truly inspired, truly inspired when they discovered Hingham.

Hingham gave them a new life they had never imagined. Hingham rescued them from the perils and the ills of the City of Boston, its floods and epidemics, its over-jammed Italianized enclave of the North End.

Hingham back then was a coastal town, home to fishermen, with the prettiest little town harbor that you could find in that part of the world.

For Gigi, that memorable day on the beach at Nantasket, with infant Patsy nursing at his mother's breast, remained her touchstone. That was the day which lived in her heart, the day her husband had confessed the love for her that was hiding in his heart.

Nor would Tony ever be able to forget that walk into the ocean-water, from which he returned, as if re-baptized into life, by a saintly Laura; released, by Laura's vision, far away in the sky, in her angelic, heavenly form, from every vow; released, to return to his wife and child, to vow his new love, to his new son, and the woman who had given that son life, whose power and glory gave even to Tony himself a new life.

In Boston, the North End had been closed in, confined; they were on the edge of the sea, but could easily be unaware of it: Boston Harbor was hidden behind buildings, silenced by motorized traffic; the waterfront, too, was cluttered and obstructed, dingy and industrial, commercial with wharves and tugboats.

Hingham, with its quiet, shady streets, and its 19th-century, horse-drawn feel, was open to the sky, the sea; you could smell its salty fragrance. There were sailboats and fishing boats in the harbor, not barges. The town was prosperous in an old-fashioned way and dominated by old-line Yankee families. The people in the town who worked for a living were not laboring ditch-diggers, or stitchers who kept their heads down all day in a room with only window-light and incandescent bulbs. The working class of Hingham were farmers and fishermen who lived and worked in the open air and could look up and see the sky.

Here in Hingham Tony was quickly introduced to two new practices he had never before had the opportunity, or incentive, to pursue—clamming, and bird-hunting.

Being a boy from the mountains, originally, Tony had never lived on the seashore, till now. The few Italians who lived in Hingham, however, all made it a point to get to know one another, especially the new arrivals, and among them was a fellow called Pietro Dario, whom the locals called Pete the

Lobsterman. It was Dario who came to the house and introduced himself, and admired Tony's English, and took Tony by
the hand to show him the nice beach down on Summer Street,
where he and Gigi could take the kids bathing in nice weather,
and other places, like Steamboat Wharf and the Hingham
Yacht Club.

Dario was no Avellinese, like them. He came from a place
called Cesenatico, a sea-faring village on the backside of Italy,
along the coast of the Adriatic; Cesenatico was the home of
fishermen who painted an eye on the prow of the boat. Dario
did not share the same dialect as Gigi practiced at home, so
he had to try to get along in his halting English with Tony,
who helped him out. But Dario showed he was a generous
friend when he took Tony down to the ocean at World's End
to show him the place to dig clams undisturbed, with a screen
of woods behind you coming down to the water's edge, and
little competition. You could happily spend an entire Saturday
with the whole family there, digging. The kids thought it was
the best game they had ever played. And, then, how delicious,
the same evening, long-neck clams, stewed, breaded, fried, on
the supper table, fresh—and free, too. Tony thought he had
discovered a picnic paradise where you watched the sun go
down over the vast lands to the west while you and the wife
and kids pulled blankets around your shoulders and warmed
yourselves by the fire-pit dug in the sand.

Then there was Linden Ponds. A couple of miles inland in
Hingham was a low-lying marsh, dotted with a string of
small ponds. The biggest was called Linden Pond, the others
too small to have names. It was here that the local kids went

ice-skating in the winter; the rest of the year it was home to migratory birds; you could shoot duck, pheasant and quail there. Another of the local Italians, a fellow named Alliberto, showed Tony this place, and introduced him to a whole new way of life.

Tony had never forgotten the one picture of his father which he held in his mind still, after all these years, with a sepia-toned regret; and that was the picture of his father in Alta Villa, walking away from the house with a shotgun on his shoulder, heading for the outskirts to shoot rabbits for dinner. Tony retained for the rest of his days an image of his father's sturdy, mountaineer's gait, walking uphill, keeping his head up, surveying the spiky horizons, rolling along. The childish thought had then, in that long-ago moment, crossed Tony's mind: *will I ever be the equal of that man?* Now he had his chance, at last. With Alliberto's help, he soon equipped himself with the necessary—a 12-gauge shotgun for rabbits and pheasants, and an 8-shot 20-gauge which Tony called his quail-gun. And a kennel of bird-dogs.

Such a picture of himself, as a country squire, with a comfortable living from his important job in the big city, was something that had never entered Tony's mind for the least instant, in all the years he had spent in America as a city-dweller. But once he began, he could not stop. To have a house of his own with a spacious back-lot, which signified plenty of room—why, a man could spread out, a man could expand his family to include his best friend, the dog. No longer was Tony LaStoria defined by one angled side of a city square. In Boston you would not want to keep a dog chained up in the house. But here in Hingham, they could live together, in a pack, in a kennel, with their friends and family, and roam free through the woods and the marshes, chasing birds, and come home in the evening with their master, to be fed and cared for by the hand of man.

Another feature of the town of Hingham was its horsemen and horsewomen, its stables, its horse-farms, its thoroughbreds, too. It was fantastic to Tony to think that just a couple of years before, locked away in the North End, he had been deprived of the proximity of thoroughbreds. That was something he had put away, on the shelf, a part of his life that belonged to New York. Massachusetts was much more strait-laced and hidebound than the skyscraper city. It lacked the free-wheeling, breeziness of New York. Instead, it was dour and puritanical, and in place of saloons with dancing girls you had Sunday Blue Laws and looking down the nose on the very idea of pari-mutuel gambling on the ponies. So there was no such thing hereabouts as Belmont Park or Aqueduct Racetrack or Saratoga.

How incredible was it then to discover that there was in the town a family who came from Mayflower stock called the Radleys, whose head, Barrett Radley, the State Senator from Hingham, was a horse-breeder who raised thoroughbreds on a huge farm located on the question-mark peninsula tagged onto the tail of World's End like an afterthought: a fabulous place to raise and train horses, with stables and white fences open to the sky and the sea-air.

Tony went out there, just to look around, and breathe in the smell of horse manure again. He encountered another local Italian named Brigidi who was a groom, and who showed him around, pointing out the loveliness of the three picturesque dots in Hingham harbor, Button Island, Ragged Island and Bumpkin Island, which you could see clearly from the stables.

And Tony loved to think how, there, these pedigreed horses, the nobility of the species, could run free in the open air, and not exist as slaves lashed forever to an ice-wagon.

How enchanting it was that in this harborside town of old New England there existed a man such as Barrett Radley who, in spite of every obstacle thrown up by obstinate joy-killing Yankee inhibitions, which one would think were his particular heritage, was free-thinking enough to breed horseflesh to race, not in Massachusetts, but at Saratoga, Belmont, Aqueduct— even as far off as Kentucky.

Barrett Radley was not the only notable individual in this notable town. One did not have to look further than the town square, where there stood a statue of Abraham Lincoln.

When Tony asked why he was informed by Alliberto that, in fact, this was the town where the original American ancestor of Honest Abe came from, one Samuel Lincoln, an apprentice weaver. And there were other Lincolns in the town history, including the Revolutionary War General who had accepted Cornwallis' sword of surrender at Yorktown.

From the square in Boston where Paul Revere himself once dwelt, Tony had now come to the ancestral home of the country's best-loved President. And whose ancestor had been a member of the cloth trade. For someone like Tony, who loved America with the forever-fresh fervor of a *straniero*; who wanted more than anything, at this time, just after the Armistice, just at the beginning of the wild times of the Twenties, to belong; now he had found the place, in Hingham, the town where he could make all that dream come true.

And it seemed that Hingham was happy to collude in the conspiracy.

In the days of Tony and Gigi, the golf-pro at the Hingham Country Club was none other than Francis Ouimet, who had stunned the world back in 1913, when he defeated the invincible British champion, Harry Vardon, at the Country Club in Brookline, in the tournament that put the United States Open on the map of the country's mind. Another resident of Hingham, at the time Tony and Gigi moved there, in 1919, was Babe Ruth himself.

At that time, he was not yet the Bambino he became. He was a highly-regarded young pitcher, and slugger, on the World Champion Boston Red Sox, but they, in their wisdom, had only just discovered his batting prowess. In 1919, he broke the record for the league, with 29 home runs; although the year before, in 1918, when the team won the World Series, they had given him only 75 at-bats, and yet he hit eleven homers. In the '18 World Series, instead, they used him as a pitcher, and he won both games he pitched. But now that he had broken the home-run record, in '19 they sold him to the New York Yankees.

However, even Babe Ruth came in second in the race to win the passion and ardor of the local Italians. Man-o'-War, the thoroughbred, became famous in 1919 as the winner of his first six races straight, all in New York, where he was bred and raised by none other than August Belmont, Jr, himself, son of the founder of Belmont Park. It was Belmont Jr.'s wife who had given this noble thoroughbred his sturdy and inspiring name, in tribute to her husband's patriotic service when he went off, at age 65, to serve with Pershing in France during the Great War.

Like the other Italians around him, Tony LaStoria was not a particular fan of baseball as he had not really played it himself as a child. Like them, Tony was far more intrigued with horses, dogs, even birds. As he grew more and more into his newly adopted life as a country squire, he began to acquire pictures to hang on the walls of his new home. They might have been only inexpensive prints, but they were prints of pointers, retrievers, and racehorses. Highly-trained, and trainable, intelligent animals, as Tony would have it. Tony was no art-collector, but neither would he have a mere ballplayer hanging on his wall.

Still, Tony had seen Ruth play at Fenway Park when the editor diBenedetto took him there. So he went a couple of times, on a weekday afternoon, with Ferragamo, the cloth-cutter from the factory, treating his valued employee to a day at the park: it never hurt to find some way to let them know you appreciated what they did. In this way, Tony had seen Ruth play, but without really thinking about him, or even the game itself, which he did not truly understand.

Then Tony met Babe Ruth, in Ruth's own home, in Hingham.

It happened, that as long as Tony was beginning so many new ventures, from raising and training dogs and growing his own tomatoes; to making wine in the cellar from his own grapes, grown by him, on his own property (in all these things he was imitating the other local Italians, who showed him the example, and, of course, encouraged him to copy them); as long as Tony was branching out, he might as well dust off his old mandolin. The fact was, his new life made him happy. More than that, as he did not think, every day, or very often, in such terms, it made him satisfied with himself. Satisfied that he was becoming something. More of what he wanted to be. Approaching what he could be.

And so he could no longer ignore his music, which after all, had been a part of his youth in New York, but which, like so many other things, he had put aside, for reasons only too well-known to himself, but which he did not care to dwell on.

In any case, he hadn't picked it up for years. But now, in his new community, there was a demand, from the local Italians, for music, because in Hingham, they were not as close-to-hand to opportunities to hear Caruso or Toscanini that one had up in Boston. All the more reason to make your own music at home.

Just as they gathered together at one another's homes with their broods of children for endless large-scale heavily-attended summertime backyard picnics; just as they were devoted to the concept that they had to look out for one another, as no one else cared about them; so they had to sing and play the old tunes they hadn't heard since God knows when; songs which you certainly would not hear on the new-fangled radio, as yet in its crystal-set infancy. If they themselves did not keep these things alive and pass them on to the younger generation, who would? The music would die. Their way of life, their culture, would die. Yes, you could get recordings of Caruso, singing the same tunes, if you could afford the phonograph, but it was not the same. Not the same as pulling out the violin at the backyard picnic table.

So his friends encouraged Tony to play again, once they saw the mandolin in the house. And the next thing you knew, they had their own backyard orchestra, with guitars and fiddles. Then one day, a local Italian, driving by, heard them playing, stopped, and offered cash to them to play at the niece's birthday party. Soon, Tony and his little band was being hired out also by the local Yankee aristocrats who were having debutante balls and political campaign parties at the big houses overlooking the water in Hingham. The repertoire was the same as Tony used to play with Signore Siragusa's Sunday afternoon concert band in Mulberry Park, back in New York. Once you learn those tunes you never forget them.

However, things were changing, and the band changed with them.

At first, you didn't notice. After all, they had to get over the Great War first, and that was not easy, as 1919, in spite of Babe Ruth, was a down year for everyone, what with the veterans landing home with no jobs available to them, an economy in flux, anarchist bombings, a collapse on Wall Street, controversy over Wilson and the League of Nations, the Versailles Conference, and the Fiume affair, which outraged the Italians; the Palmer raids, the Boston Police Strike, which Governor Coolidge, that Vermont Yankee, ruthlessly put down; any and all manner of upsets.

They had just survived the greatest conflict the world had ever seen, as Tony, the newly-minted, homemade historian duly noted at the picnic table, and now they were emerging, like a caterpillar from a cocoon, as something they had never been: a United States on a world stage, an arbiter of the Peace of Versailles, looked on by the whole world, and themselves, differently, all because of the War. With expectations none of them could quite grasp, or foresee, or predict. And due to his own perspicacity, one Tony LaStoria was now a naturalized citizen of the United States of America.

One night a call on the phone came in from Babe Ruth's house. Somebody in his entourage at the big house he had out on Linden Pond. It was the dead of winter, but everyone knew the Big Guy liked a party—in fact, they had heard that it never stopped out there. So Tony and the Roma Jazz Band packed up their cases, jumped in the Buick, and headed out.

Tony did not go looking for an autograph. The Bambino was no Man o' War. They set up in the living room, and they were playing good that night. The liquor was flowing and the women were good-looking, dancing. Tony had a couple of drinks and got a big smile on his face. He saw Ruth out in the kitchen at one point, holding sway over an audience.

The band played on. They were hot—on the money.

The party was in full sway when Ruth came in and decided—what the hell did they need a piano for, when they had the band there? So he began to push his piano out the door. Everyone was roaring drunk. Despite his enormous strength, Ruth couldn't get the grand piano through the front door—the shape was all-wrong. Finally, in their delusional state, they figured out how to turn it on its side and with four or five helping, walk it through. They had it outside and were pushing it down to Linden Pond on its rollers when Ruth called to Tony and the band to come on along and play the accompaniment. Fortified with drink, Tony and the guys didn't even bother to pull on their overcoats.

When the piano had been pushed out onto the short rowboat pier in the pond, the boards and timbers had to withstand forty or fifty revelers, and the band, too, in addition to the grand piano, which now went splash! into the water—right through the planks of the pier.

They all ended up in the drink.

Tony finally turned up at home the next morning, still drunk, bundled up in his overcoat, passed out in the bottom of a wheelbarrow that his drunken friends pulled out of the garage so they wouldn't have to carry him up the slippery driveway.

Gigi just laughed. She thought she had never seen anything so funny in her entire life. Another legend added to the family album.

Chapter 11

The Trial of the Century

It was 1920 now, and the economy was recovering, women had the vote, even Tony LaStoria voted in his first Presidential election. A new decade was beginning and a new mood was seizing the country by the throat, a kind of hysterical reaction to the onset of Prohibition. The reality of it, replacing the future prospect of it, was starting to sink in. In 1919, even though the law had been passed and ratified, in Washington they knew that the country was not yet ready for it. But when it came, in 1920, when it was no longer a law postponed to next year, everyone soon found out that the whole country was willing to go crazy rather than not have a drink.

By the time the new Harding administration replaced the moribund Wilson, everyone knew that here was a President who certainly was not going to deny himself a little nip. *So, what the hell!*

By this time, little Patsy LaStoria was just beginning the first grade, at the age of six years, in the Hingham public schools. Maria and two-year-old Margherita were still at home with Gigi. Tony was commuting daily in his Buick to the warehouse district of the Fort Point channel in Boston to run Harry Spritzka's garment business at No. 10 Melcher Street, as well as all the other points of the compass he had to travel to from there. Gigi was about to have her fourth child. A boy, Eugenio, was born in late 1920, named after his father's not quite beloved but now grudgingly respected Uncle Eugenio. In 1922 came another girl, Gerardina, then a boy, Agostino, in '25, named after Gigi's favorite brother, and in 1927, Anna, the youngest, her grandmother Fabrizio's namesake. Tony and Gigi then had four girls and three boys. Gigi returned to the North End each time to give birth, each time staying a little longer to recuperate. She refused to give birth without her mother and the midwives of Prince Street.

In 1920, Tony was elected leader of the backyard band in Hingham, by acclamation. Again, it was his fluent English that made him the popular choice. And now they added trumpet, trombone and clarinet, and they were playing Paul Whiteman and Bix Beiderdecke. It was the new age, and Tony was styling their little band as the Roma Jazz Band, a snazzy combo of the old and the new. And a name he knew would look promising on a printed card.

Why not? Who would ever have thought that you would have a car in the driveway and a brand-new porcelain-white washing machine in the back hall, so the wife wouldn't have to scrape her knuckles anymore scrubbing sheets and tablecloths by hand on a washboard in a big basin? There was even a wring-er-contraption on top, where she could wring it all out before she had to hang it up to dry. *Whatever would they think of next?*

Tony and Gigi did not forbid themselves any of the new 'necessities': they could live without luxuries, they were not ostentatious, they were mostly homebodies, with a life centered around family. But who in this day and age of electricity was going to go against common-sense when it came to labor-saving devices? And so, if only out of pride, if nothing else, as befit his station in life, Tony was not going to deny his wife anything the insurance man or the Fuller brush salesman or the encyclopedia peddler wanted her to buy.

Thus the young and growing family of Tony and Gigi LaStoria were happily living in Hingham, on the South Shore, when Attorney General A. Mitchell Palmer in Washington launched new raids as soon as the New Year opened, on the 2nd of January of 1920. The raids of November 1919 were replicated, but this time there were 3,000 arrested. Those detained were held for various periods of time, but many had been taken, and had property seized, without search warrants, and their detention was spent in overcrowded and unsanitary conditions. The raids had covered more than 30 cities in 23 states. Again, targeting entire organizations, police and federal agents arrested everyone they found in meeting halls, including American citizens not eligible for deportation. Yet such was the wave of fear inspired by anarchist bombings, by the specter of the Bolshevik revolution in Russia, by the wave of labor strikes across the entire United States, from the coal fields of Western Pennsylvania to the apple orchards of Washington State, that most of the nation turned a blind eye. And to most of the nation, too, anarchists were indistinguishable from the tide of immigrant Italians.

The anarchists were now out for blood. On April 15, 1920, they struck on the South Shore, or so the police and newspapers later claimed. On that fateful day two unknown armed men held up the payroll office of the Slater and Morrill Shoe Company in South Braintree, shooting dead, with hand-guns, two employees. They were picked up by a getaway car, and escaped with $15,000 of the company payroll.

Back in March of 1920, a *Galleanista* named Andrea Salsedo, a printer in Brooklyn, had been arrested for questioning in the bombing of Attorney General Palmer's home in Washington in June of 1919. Besides the dismembered bomber himself, Valdinocci, no one else had ever been arrested in that case, which Palmer maintained was part of a widespread conspiracy of the anarchists. Salsedo was scooped up because the authorities had finally traced a leaflet they found after the bombing to Salsedo's print shop in Brooklyn. They held him incommunicado for questioning on the 14th floor in Manhattan, at the FBI offices on Park Row. Then he jumped to his death.

But the anarchists said he was pushed, after he had been beaten severely, and tortured, to obtain information.

They based this on the fact that Palmer and Hoover were proclaiming publicly that Salsedo had made important disclosures concerning the bomb plotters. The anarchists protested that it had been beaten out of him, and that he was then murdered to cover it up.

Finally, on May 5th, 1920, two Italian immigrants, Nicola Sacco and Bartolomeo Vanzetti, known to police as anarchists who had returned from self-exile in Mexico, were arrested on the South Shore. Sacco was taken where he worked as an edge-trimmer, in a shoe-shop in Stoughton, a South Shore town, inland, small and obscure, several towns away from Hingham; and Vanzetti, who was a fish-peddler, in Plymouth, by the ocean.

When arrested, the two anarchist friends lied to the police about what they had been doing on the evening of April 15th, 1920, when the two employees of the shoe company in South Braintree were shot dead by whoever it was who was robbing the payroll office. When they were arrested they had pistols and ammunition on them. They may have been in the process of hiding bomb-making pamphlets or even disposing of dynamite. They knew that the police knew they were anarchists who had been in Mexico together, after fleeing the deportation roundups of the militant summer of 1919, and they knew of the fate of Salsedo under interrogation. So they lied, and gave contradictory answers. Their questioners took this as an obvious sign of guilty evasion: they afterwards claimed that the two men exhibited "consciousness of guilt." But they were being questioned about their political activities, *not* about a payroll robbery in South Braintree.

On September 11th, 1920, to their surprise and consternation, indictments were handed down against Sacco and Vanzetti charging them with the murder of the paymaster and the guard in the payroll robbery in Braintree. The two anarchists proclaimed their innocence, saying they had nothing to do with the crime they were being charged with.

Nine days later, on September 20th, at noontime, on Wall Street, in front of the Subtreasury Building and the United States Assay Office, directly across the street from the banking house of J.P. Morgan, a massive bomb blast went off. A moment later, scores of men, women and children were lying in the street, covered with debris from thousands of broken windows and the jagged edges of torn facades of adjacent buildings. Panic and confusion reigned. The noise of the explosion had been heard throughout lower Manhattan and across the river in Brooklyn. Thousands of office-workers fled from adjoining buildings, in terror, and scores were trampled in the panic. When it was all over, a massive manhunt ensued. The bomb had been placed in a horse-drawn wagon and left parked at the curb at lunch-hour, with a timing device; the horse and wagon were blown to bits, and 42 innocent people were killed, without warning. A leaflet found by a mailman in a letter-box a few blocks away had a message printed in red ink:

> *Remember. Free the political prisoners*
> *or it will be sure death*
> *for all of you*

The authorities and the press assumed that meant Sacco and Vanzetti. Nothing dissuaded them as the anarchist movement all over the country mobilized in support of the two wrongly-accused men. Thousands of protesters, radicals and socialists, too, were arrested all over the East Coast from Washington to Philly to New York and Boston. Detectives visited five thousand stables on the East Coast, attempting to trace the horse used in the Wall Street bombing, in vain. Police did find the maker of the horse-shoes, a blacksmith in Little Italy, in Manhattan. The blacksmith told them he recalled that the day before the explosion a Sicilian man had driven such a horse and wagon into his shop and had a new pair of shoes nailed onto the hooves. But the bomber himself was never found.

The case of the two imprisoned anarchists, Sacco and Vanzetti, now proceeded to trial, and a trial that became notorious as The Trial of the Century. The Commonwealth of Massachusetts brought their case beginning in the new year of 1921, but not until May 31st, by which time the two prisoners had been roundly convicted in the newspapers and the court of Main Street America's public opinion.

Their trial was brought before Judge Webster Thayer, an old-line Yankee, in the Massachusetts Superior Court at the Dedham Court House, south of Boston, and by July 14th, they were convicted by verdict of the jury, composed entirely of American-born citizens, none of whom were peers of the accused men. Nor had the prosecution in the case brought a single shred of evidence connecting Sacco and Vanzetti to the crime they were accused of. Instead, the Prosecutor, Frederick G Katzmann, District Attorney of Norfolk County, and a graduate of Boston Latin School, as well as Harvard University, was allowed by Judge Thayer to present reams of redundant evidence day after day of Sacco and Vanzetti's anarchist ideology, their immigrant background, and their refusal to register for the draft during the war, none of which either man denied. Although eyewitnesses were produced to testify that they had seen two men commit the robbery and murders and then escape in a car driven by accomplices, who were those men? Not Sacco and Vanzetti, said Defense Attorney Fred Moore, who drew on funds raised by the Sacco and Vanzetti Defense Committee, and attacked these as false identifications with a vigorous cross-examining. No other arrests had ever been made and none of the stolen money was ever linked to Sacco and Vanzetti, or even recovered, for that matter.

By the end of the Trial of the Century, it was obvious to those who had mounted mass protest meetings all over the nation, as well as demonstrations in Rome, Paris, London and Moscow, and many cities throughout the world, that the Commonwealth of Massachusetts had succeeded in proving only that Sacco and Vanzetti were who they said they were: two avowed radicals, convicted not for breaking any laws, but for being immigrants, anarchists, and Italians.

So the 1920s passed, and it was all a blur, all a party without end, at a blasting, fevered upbeat tempo; Tony was busier than ever with all his activities, from work to play, fulfilling contracts, buying new buildings, hiring new staffs, opening new stores, training his bird-dogs, tending his tomatoes, expanding his vocabulary, expanding his jazz repertoire; and Gigi, with all her pregnancies and deliveries, between soiled cloth diapers and daily dosings of cod liver oil, one and another child constantly nursing a cold, a cough, the measles, the chicken-pox, weaning one infant, toilet-training another toddler: both of them were working night and day, ceaselessly.

Like all of his Italian neighbors, Tony was growing purple grapes and making red wine, cultivating red strawberries and starchy potatoes, raising green corn in the backyard garden, and Gigi was canning and preserving in mason jars to store on the cellar shelving right alongside Tony's glass gallon jugs of fermenting grapes.

Since he had his boys, she would have to have her girls.

On nights when Tony was home late, which was often, with all his traveling, she would hold off supper and gather the girls around her for cleaning and cooking and washing and sorting; but she also entertained and educated them, in Italian always, and with the old-fashioned deck of Napoletane playing cards, with which they played scopa, and, of course, the Ouija board.

The boys, who only scoffed at them, and would have refused to join in anyway, if asked or commanded, the boys she left to their English and their rough-housing. There was always the back of Tony's hand she could employ, when he got home, of course; and it was all-too-often necessary.

Another cross to bear. It wasn't enough to give them life itself, then you had to raise them, and feed them, and corral them, and put up with them. But she would not have traded it for any other sort of life. She was a queen in her own house. She need never go out if she didn't want to. Gigi was not the one who had to get naturalized and become American. She had her husband for that. She did not need to deal with the outside world. Tony was there to protect her from all that.

Even as he had his escapes, into the newspapers and his music, his dogs, his band, his clamming expeditions; his bird-hunting, his grapes and his strawberry-patch (even his once-a-week Saturday side-trip to load-up at her father's butcher shop, which he loved to do, as it made him feel that he was feeding his family, personally); even as Tony cultivated that game he played with himself of expanding his vocabulary in English, so Gigi cultivated her flower garden. For her and the girls. But really, for herself alone.

She had a long flowerbed, the entire length of the house and the driveway, from back to front. Daisies, roses, sunflowers; carnations, lilacs, daffodils and tulips. A gorgeous array of sun-painted colors. Tony could do whatever he wanted with the house and the yard, as long as she had her flowers. Tony had made his own life out of the discovery of Hingham, and so had she. Just as he had never before dreamt of playing a Paul Whiteman tune, so, in the old days, in the North End, she had never taken any notice of flowerboxes in the windows, up and down Prince Street. Nowadays each of them expanded his or her own vocabulary in their own way.

Gigi now had discovered that she actually loved nothing better than setting a chair out in the middle of all her beautiful flowers and sunning herself right along with them on a velvety-hot summer's day. Life was good, and they were rich. It was not that they had the all the money in the world: they were rich in joy, they were rich in children, they were rich in food, and wine, and song; they had all of everything, the joy, along with the pain. The roses, together with the thorns.

Eventually everything happened in the 1920s. Eventually Babe Ruth hit 60 homers. Eventually silent Cal spoke. Eventually Lindbergh flew the Atlantic solo in the Spirit of St Louis. Eventually Dr Robert H Goddard, in Massachusetts, successfully launched the first liquid-fueled rocket, though nobody knew about it. And eventually Sacco and Vanzetti were to find out what justice meant when administered by the Commonwealth of Massachusetts, but only after spending seven years incarcerated in the Charlestown Jail while the world clamored for their release, their case became a *cause célèbre*, and Italians and Italian-Americans in Massachusetts and all over the country were by turns defiant, outraged, and despairing; while the rest of society, in the face of the agitation over the plight of the two condemned men, by backlash, employing a wide brush, condemned by consensus, not just Luigi Galleani, not just Andrea Salsedo, not just Valdinocci, not just Sacco and Vanzetti, and

Al Capone, too, but all Italians in general as anarchists, crooks, criminals, gangsters and murderers.

Eventually Tony and Gigi's growing family were outgrowing the house in Hingham, and Tony was forced to consider whether there was some alternative, though he and Gigi were both loathe to leave Hingham, where they had been so happy. It was just that they could see now that a two-family house did not provide for them the room they needed, especially with new infants arriving every two years.

Unfortunately, for the older children, who were in school in the town, Tony could not find something suitable in Hingham itself with a price he liked. As busy as he was with Harry Spritzka's far-flung businesses constantly keeping him on the road, he was hard-put to find the time; they had too many kids now to conduct a leisurely search with the entire family on board the Buick; finally he found something big enough, with enough of a parcel to accommodate his dogs, his garden and Gigi's flowers, and with a detached garage for his still-new 1925 Buick (and with a price he liked) in another town. In fact, it was a deal he could not refuse: sale of their two-family home in Hingham would allow him to get into a roomy single-family, practically free and clear: an old garrison, side-facing the road, built in the 19th century, or perhaps even the colonial times before that.

He was soon faced with a revolt on the part of Patsy, Maria and Peggy, who claimed they would rather die than leave their friends, but eventually he prevailed when he proposed to accept their offer to perish, thereby reducing his grocery bill, and making the new place even more affordable, as well as less crowded.

So, eventually, in time for the 1925 school year to begin, the LaStorias packed up bag and baggage, children and animals, and moved several towns inland, removed from their beloved seashore, to a place called Stoughton.

A place which just happened to be where Nicola Sacco was working in a shoe-shop at the time of his arrest, that long-ago day in 1920.

And in 1925, something else happened.

On November 18, just before Thanksgiving, the family's "American" holiday, a man named Celestino Madeiros, then under a death sentence himself for murder, confessed that, while he was a member of the Joe Morelli gang, from down Providence, Rhode Island way, he had participated in the robbery and killings which Sacco and Vanzetti, still languishing in the Charlestown Jail, were accused of, completely absolving the two prisoners of the crime. Yet the Commonwealth's Supreme Court refused to overturn the verdict because under the existing rules of jurisprudence in the Massachusetts court system, it was Judge Thayer, and only Judge Thayer, who had the final power to reopen a case based on the grounds of new evidence.

At the Thanksgiving dinner table that year, the children, taking the license of the holiday, were freely complaining about how much they hated their new schools, especially the old-maid Yankee schoolteachers they had in Stoughton, who seemed to think Italian children were all barefoot and unwashed and had garlic on their breath. Their Pa, Tony, told them to be quiet and be thankful for what they had, on this day of all days: "You kids don't know how lucky you are."

It was in that indelible year of 1927, when they had been held prisoner in the Charlestown Jail for seven long years, that Sacco and Vanzetti finally reached their day of sentencing. Judge Thayer, on April 9th, at the Dedham Court House, sentenced them both to die in the electric chair.

In his last statement before the court, Vanzetti rose, to stand up and utter these words:

> *This is what I say: I would not wish to a dog or to a snake, to the most low and unfortunate creature of the earth, I would not wish to any of them what I have had to suffer for things that I am not guilty of. But my conviction is that I am suffering for things that I am guilty of. I am suffering because I am a radical, and indeed I am a radical; I have suffered because I was an Italian, and indeed I am an Italian; I have suffered more for my family and for my beloved than for myself; but I am so convinced to be right that if you could execute me two times, and if I could be reborn two other times, I would live again to do what I have done already.*

Chapter 12

Madonna and Child

Later in life, when Gigi looked back over the long saga of the turbulent Twenties, and, as she told Tony, combed over these memories, dwelling lovingly on some, discarding others with horror, it was her habit, and fondness, to remember those old, early days of her marriage and family as falling into three phases, each with its own sweet roses and prickly thorns.

The first was North Square, and here she no longer recalled anything but thorns: the Spanish flu and the Molasses Flood; then came nothing but roses, and that was Hingham; but that was followed by the years in Stoughton, when the Roaring Twenties went roaring right through their old garrison, which presented a gable-end facing the long and lonely stretch of the Pine Street woods. In her memory, aided by the Third Eye, which Gigi believed was as clairvoyant about the past as it was the future, she saw screen doors broken by her growing, overactive children, constantly in and out with a crash of slamming doors; never-ending heaps of laundry drying on the line; and her flowerbed wilting in November, after another hot and humid summer August, the roses dying, but the thorns still sharp.

At the age of seven, then considering himself all grown up, little Patsy LaStoria declared, at story-time, "It's just a fairy tale!" But his mother forbid him to say so to the younger ones.

"You used to ask me for it before you would go to sleep!"

"I know—but it's stupid!"

"You are the stupid one! Didn't you ever hear that children are to be seen, and not heard!"

In truth, she and Tony had come to believe that little Patsy, how should you say, that the boy was a little dumb, not up to their standard, a disappointment. At first, when he was born, they both, especially Gigi, had been so proud of him, and of themselves. Gigi felt, absolutely, that the first-born turning out to be a son was a sign from heaven: their union was written in the stars. For Tony, in his unseeing male pride, it confirmed his manhood. A boy signified to the world his virility and potency.

But for Gigi, something changed, when, barely two years later, as soon as the infant Maria came along, (and Gigi, who, after all, was still a new mother who had never yet had more than one to deal with) and she couldn't get little Patsy to stop hanging onto her skirts and wanting to be carried everywhere. At the time, Gigi was dismayed with him, and could not believe what a jealous little thing he was.

For Tony, the boy's clumsiness and slow-witted responses were magnified into a final verdict when the child simply could not learn how to tie his shoes.

And then there was the matter of his behavior. There was a time when "No!" was the only word he seemed to have learned.

Thank God that finally passed. However, they were still left baffled as to why little Patsy seemed so slow to speak up; he was having obvious difficulties with both Italian, and English. It seemed to confuse the boy terribly between his father insisting on English, and his mother sputtering the other lingo every time she opened her mouth.

Tony told Gigi the boy had to have English, or, when it came time for going to school, the kid was a goner. The fact was that the grownup Tony, even after all these years, was still agitated over all the trouble with truant officers he'd had, and that awful, disgusting truant-school they made him go to, during his own childhood in New York. In some ways, Tony could never forget an injury, or an insult. Real or imagined, it mattered not, but the thought lingered, the feeling festered, the grievance gnawed at him, it never went away, his whole life long. It was a particular fishbone in his throat that it was the truant officer who had torn him away from his beloved wagon-horse Fiorello.

Tony still thought of that poor beast often, which would cause his whole spirit to go into a crouch, as he remembered, all of a sudden, vividly, slumping down in tears, that night in the dark stable next to his fallen horse's empty stall.

So Tony had no intention whatsoever of holding his own children out of school. His mind was made up. It was simply too much trouble. And the children would have to obey, whether they liked it or not. That was why he was so worried about Patsy.

"The kid is so stupid!" he said to Gigi.

She also was in dismay, because in her heart, she had to agree. But her own biggest problem with Patsy was getting him to mind.

"You have to do something with that boy!"

"What?" he said. "My hand is sore from swatting his little *culu*. To tell you the truth, I think it hurts me more than him!"

Tony, the boy's father, finally resigned himself to the fact that he was terribly disappointed in Patsy. Now that the boy had been in school for a year and they saw the report cards from his old spinster Yankee schoolteachers, who marked Patsy down, down, down on conduct, and inattention, Tony took it as a personal affront to have fathered such a stupid boy, who obviously was never going to measure up to what you had to do in this life. "Fend for yourself," said Tony. "Like I always did! Like I had to." Confronting poor, uncomprehending Patsy, Tony would work himself up into a lecture. "Fend for yourself, or else, where would I be today?"

There the matter came to a final conclusion, and Tony, for once and for all, washed his hands of the whole affair. "All I know is, spare the rod, and spoil the child." And Gigi certainly did not disagree.

Then again, Maria, their first-born daughter, was also a disappointment to them, for entirely different reasons.

When Maria was born, instantly, they took one look: and looked at one another.

Instead of a darling little baby girl, a beautiful *bambina*, which especially Gigi was longing for, the new infant came out entirely too dark.

Tony said, "She looks like a walnut!"

Gigi said, "I know. I couldn't think of what it was, how to express it, but that's exactly the word. A walnut. But how? How? There's nobody on my side of the family."

Tony made a face. "Don't look at me!"

And that settled that, forever, and even longer.

Although they had been married by this time for only a few years, they felt that they had been through so much together. It seemed to them that they thought with one mind, spoke with one voice (they finished each other's sentences). Each one completed the other one's life, each one was the missing half of the other. Indeed, they could no longer conceive that they had ever been *not* together.

Poor Maria. Her disposition and mood seemed to turn out as brown as her skin color. Even her hair was deep black and shiny. Where had she come from? She was a morose child, never smiled or seemed to perk up. You could tickle her, and she had no response, she simply gazed up at you in wonderment, as if she were looking past you.

And so they decided Maria was a dreamer, pure and simple. She had her own life going on inside her. As she grew, it seemed that she preferred to be by herself. She played by herself. She never wanted to join in the other children's games. They were too noisy and rambunctious.

Maria did not want to share her doll with her sisters: the same kind of corn-cob doll, or newspaper-stuffed ragamuffin Gigi had been given as a child, dressed up in scraps of cloth Tony had brought home from the factory floor, and which Gigi sewed, on the Singer Sewing Machine Tony had given her, to make little dresses. Maria wanted to keep her doll and all her dresses neat and orderly. She hated for anyone to disarrange her things.

Unlike Patsy, Maria turned out fluent in both languages, easily and rapidly. She had a taste for words. And even at three or four, she spoke like a grown-up. And interjected her judgmental declarations, unsolicited, into her parents' supper-table conversations.

Maria, too, had to be informed that children were to be seen and not heard. She paid no attention. In fact, as time went on, she became, even at an early age, the third parent in the house. Gigi would find Maria repeating the same rules and regulations to her younger brothers and sisters that she had issued to them herself.

But more than that, Maria took it upon herself to be her mother's helper, from cooking in the kitchen, to hanging out the wash. You did not have to tell her. She gave her own assignments to herself. It was strange to have such a sullen and morose and withdrawn child functioning as an adult would, with responsibility, taking things upon herself, asking, and expecting, no thanks from anybody.

Gigi became terribly sad for Maria, blaming herself. She knew somehow in her heart she had communicated to this child her own judgmental misgivings: how, she did not know. Perhaps it was that reaction she had the first time she looked upon Maria; maybe it was in the mother's milk; maybe it was through the Third Eye, but somehow. The child seemed to have *intuition.* Gigi finally realized that what really had happened was that a little old man had come to live with them, disguised as a four-year-old girl.

Margherita, the third one, their second daughter, was a different kettle of fish altogether. That one was a handful. From the very beginning. Her grandfather, Pasquale Fabrizio, who had named her after the queen of Italy, was delighted. *"Il sangue non mente,"* he said to his daughter, Gigi, "reminds me of you!"

Gigi told Tony, "Watch out for that one. She's going to be trouble, not for me, for you."

"What makes you say that?"

"Ha! You don't know the half of it. Just wait till she's old enough, you'll see!"

Delighted, almost in spite of herself, Gigi called this one "Rita," a special pet-name she kept a secret, sharing it only with the girl herself, out of the hearing of others.

And indeed, by the time she entered the first grade, this "Rita" was more trouble for the teachers and the school and even the town of Hingham than anyone had bargained for.

Some said she had just jumped off a pirate ship. You could easily believe it. She behaved not like the Queen of Italy, but like *the Queen of the Buccaneers*. There was no piece of furniture Margherita sat on. Furniture was for walking on. There was no tree she didn't climb. There was no fence she didn't push over. She was quick-witted and had the tongue of a scorpion; but she was also sly. She never missed you watching her every move (she relished in it) but before you knew what was happening, she was already three skips ahead of you on the hopscotch.

People quickly labeled her a tom-boy, but Margherita had no intention of acting like a lady. In the fourth grade she caused a riot over a girl's basketball game in the town hall. By this time, because her teachers inveterately Americanized her name to "Margaret," she was known to one and all as Peggy LaStoria: a nickname she had given herself, or so she always said, since she would not credit either her teachers or her father. She was just not the kind to wait for the world to define her. The problem was: you could not keep Peggy down. You could scold her and chastise her and lose your wits altogether trying to devise ways to control her, but she always came back at you, usually from behind, where you least expected it, and where you had no chance.

Somehow, both Tony and Gigi also took incalculable pride in this child, overweening conceit, actually, although they were loath to admit it.

To Peggy herself, and the other children, they always maintained an exterior of stern reproval, but secretly, both of them blessed *the gods that be* for having sent this one.

Especially for Tony, Peggy put the twinkle in his eye. In fact, he admired her fearlessness, and could not think that he himself, in spite of his own history, had ever been that bold, as a child. It was clear to Tony that here was one who would never give an inch. Whereas, he himself, with such a growing family, so many bills to pay, such responsibilities every day at work, had become like a shadow of himself, hemmed in on every side, compromised, forever conceding.

As the 1920s began and soon became 'Roaring,' according to those newspapers which Tony relentlessly consumed on a daily basis, as Tony entered his thirties, he had to acknowledge he had turned into something even his own father could never have been. Tony's father was a master tailor. Tony aspired to be the same, but he was not. Instead, he had become a new kind of man, a professional *middle manager*. Neither the owner nor the rank in file, he stood in the middle, between two worlds. He obeyed the former, was obligated to the former, but he gave to the latter, he catered to them. In either case, he performed as a professional, quite aware that he knew what he was doing, and trusted his convictions, his own intuitions and instincts, his methods.

At home, on the other hand, he was the father, that was the role he played; but, increasingly, with so many children coming so quickly, like the old woman in the shoe, he simply didn't know what to do.

After Margherita, came Eugenio, their second son. Ah. Now here was a boy. Quiet. Unassuming. But intelligent. Not in a bookish way, in an everyday, common-sense way. If Eugenio broke a stick, trying to dig out an anthill in the backyard, he did not cry over it or try to fix it, he simply lost interest and moved on to something else. If something was too high on a shelf for him to reach, he did not stand on a chair, as Peggy would have: he waited for a grown-up and asked that larger person to get it for him. Eugenio seemed always to believe that eventually the world would come around to his way of seeing things. Personally, he was taking his time; no need to rush things. All in good measure. Keep an even keel.

Tony said to himself—ah, finally, I have a son. *He's like me. Smart.*

Gigi saw young Genie, as his father liked to call him, slightly differently. She saw more of the *vecchio coder,* the old codger, in him than Tony did. In this, thought Gigi, Gene was like his sister, Maria, except that he was genial where she could be dour.

His mother noticed that Genie, as he grew, was modeling himself on his father. His father would come home and sit in the biggest most important comfortable and upholstered chair in the house and have everyone waiting on him. Genie then decided that he could sit there, too, and wait, and eventually his sister Maria, or Gerardina (not Peggy, she was impossible) would bring him whatever he wanted. Till then, he could do without. But just like his father, Genie, even at eight years old, quietly expected it. It was his due. It was his place in the home, his role in life. Meanwhile, he sat back, taking in everything, missing nothing, little Napoleon planning his campaign, his arms languidly placed on the commodious wings of the armchair. His father's armchair. Sometimes he would give a direction: fetch me this or that. "Gerry—get me a glass of water outta the kitchen sink." Gerry ran to do as he asked. No need to say, *please.* And then, of course, as soon as the old man walked in, he would give up the chair to him, which, after all, he had only been keeping warm for his Pa.

Of all the kids, however, Gerardina was the apple of her father's eye, to use the American expression. Or, as Gigi would have said, and did, *pupillo dei tuoi occhi.*

First of all, she was a girl. Tony had been waiting for a daughter to come along who loved him, *without being asked.*

Somehow, it rounded things out. Somehow, it was the ultimate fulfillment.

Your mother, she had to care about you. Even if she hated you, or loathed you, or despised you, for any of a number of right or wrong or crazy reasons (which could happen, as Gigi and Tony both knew only too well) she still had to take care of you, or else face the utter condemnation and renunciation of the whole world. There is no one the world rejects so much as the mother who will not be a mother to her own child.

So-o-o—can you really trust a mother's love?

Your wife, your sweetheart, your chosen beloved, she may love you, right down to the ground, but still, she was an independent person. (You never forgot that *she* had chosen *you*.) And in truth, *you* had to worship at *her* altar. For that was the nature of married love. A wife, *you did not make her.* But a daughter—*her, you made.* In your own image. And that was all you had to do. Just plant the seed. What more could you do? A daughter who truly loved you was like a wind in the forest. *The forest surrounds you but the wind brings you comfort.* As a father, Tony had found out that the wind will blow where it will. The trees will grow according to their own pattern and whim, branching out here, there and in every wayward direction. You cannot predict. You cannot control. Like the tomato plants in his garden in the backyard in Hingham, and then in Stoughton, all Tony could do was to provide a tomato-pole to lean against, a sturdy piece of wood to curl around. In the same way, you cannot predict a daughter's love. *There is no more profound love in the world than that, a daughter's love for her father.*

So Tony concluded, after he had received this immense, unexpected, unpurchased and undeserved gift, from someone who came up only as high as his knee. In fact, he had known it from the very first instant. It was in Gerardina's eye the very first time she turned her gaze from her mother, who was giving her nourishment from her own breast, to register that it was her father, standing there watching them. Her eyes were adoring. Adoring brown eyes. And her hair was blond.

It was a confirmation of something Tony had long suspected, no, knew, in his own heart, concerning his lineage, his secret nobility. Tony had always heard that somewhere deep in the past northern princes had invaded the South, even Sicily itself. Everyone from that part of the world, everyone who had a stake in the peninsula of the Italian boot, because of their origins, because of family, spoke of such things, and marveled at the blond hair that cropped up in the landscape, both North and South. And the more learned, or just curious, among them would reveal that there had been at one time long ago a period of Nordic invasions and Viking takeovers. Was that where this one came from? For indeed, she was the fairest of them all.

It was not simply her hair color alone—it was also her fairness of complexion. Gerardina was as far as you could get from the black, shiny hair and walnut-brown skin of her oldest sister, Maria. Even Peggy, whose hair was dark, and who was the most obviously attractive one of them all (you could tell she was going to grow up to be a stunner); standing next to fair-skinned Gerry, Peggy's complexion was positively olive.

So, this child remained a marvel, and an enigma. It was not only that she freely and plainly adored her father; from the beginning, she deserted her mother's side, to go to him. Unlike Patsy, for instance, who, when he was little, kept clinging, beyond endurance, to his mother.

It was also remarkable that Gerardina did not compete with the others. First of all, there were too many ahead of her: Patsy, Maria, Peggy and Genie. At the supper table, they were like the hunting dogs that Tony decided to keep in a kennel in the backyard, as soon as they were settled in Stoughton, his beagles and retrievers, fighting over scraps. Gerry, as she was soon called, especially by the older, American-born kids, did not fight. She just held out her plate and waited for someone to notice her. Often, it was one of the pack of dogs, Maria most often, until eventually Maria had become a second mother to Gerry. And the one Gerry preferred to her own.

By the time she had five children, Gigi was becoming truly overwhelmed with the immensity of the endless amount of work that needed to be done, and the daunting mound of responsibility a mother had to carry on her back: the house to keep clean, dishes and clothes to wash, ever bigger dinners to prepare, school for the kids, clothes to mend and make, and, and, *everything.*

Yet even after they had five children, Gigi still wanted more. To Gigi, motherhood was her destiny. It was what she was made for. What she was put on this earth to do. It was her *accomplishment.* She wanted it. She even desired it. More than a husband's love, more than his passionate embrace, she actually desired pregnancy. For to Gigi, destiny, fate, predestination, these were not fantastical fallacies, they were real things that dictated and directed and determined what a person did and what happened to someone. Fate could not be detoured, destiny could not be disregarded; they came from the place where stories came from; her destiny was *who she was.*

Naturally, when she was a girl, she had pictured everything differently. Then it was all foolishness. Wedding dresses and bride's bouquets and secret whisperings behind curtains, conspiracies and parties and silly madnesses. At least, they seemed silly now. But then, at that time, she had not known the joy that becoming a mother could bring to a being. How could she have? How do you picture ahead of time, or even explain to one who has never experienced it, the profound *satisfaction* that comes in giving birth.

You only know, at the beginning, that you have an urge. In every house on every street, there is a mother. It's all you know of life. As a girl, how can you believe that you will not become one of them? And so a kind of inchoate urge forms within you. You do not think about it, and it has no name. You only know that something is driving you. Straight into the arms of circumstances that will bring you to the point. It has to do with boys, of course, and feelings, of course, emotions, and God knows what, but there it is, an urge. Like an itch you must inevitably scratch.

But that's all you know. You cannot know when all the silliness is over and you are left with your own body, that you can grow within it *a whole new world.*

For that's what a baby was to Gigi. A whole new world, with ears and eyes and all its parts, growing within *her.* Quietly gestating, without any effort—discomfort, yes, pain, yes, sometimes fear, all the time, worry; but seemingly without you having to do anything: just be yourself. Just exist. Just be there. As natural as a flower blooming.

For this tremendous gift she was grateful to Tony. Without him, how would she have ever known? That miracles are an everyday occurrence. That they are *inside* you. That they grow and develop and are born—within *you.*

And so Gigi had to keep him on the job. Tony was so beset with so many difficulties: the factory, the workers, that nemesis of his, *that Jew,* Spritzka, whom he worked for, the news of the world, the war in Europe, and then *Sacco and Vanzetti,* his mandolin, the little backyard orchestra, his newspaper, his cigarettes, his automobile, *the Sons of Italy*—and then, of course, in bed, at night, they had to go over the whole day together, scrap by scrap. By the end of it all the poor man was exhausted.

But in the morning, he was himself again.

And thus Gigi managed to remain almost continuously pregnant for almost 14 years in a row.

When she began, Gigi was young, and some might say, full of vinegar. She herself, later, much later, would look back and think of how stupid and clever, and foolish and wicked, and good and fearless, absolutely fearless, she had been, at that age, all at the same time—afraid of nothing. In her mind, she was much more afraid for her daughters, when they would have to grow up to face pregnancy and child-bearing and all the vicissitudes and volubility of living life to the full than she had ever been for herself.

Still, fear crept into their lives, all of them, Gigi and her brood of children, late at night, when the house was dark, when everyone was supposed to be sleeping, and all you could hear as you tossed and turned was, the sighing wind, and creaking wood.

Or, especially on those awe-inspiring winter nights, in Hingham, or in Stoughton, when the northeast winds were howling, the snow was blowing, and the miracle of electricity suddenly expired, like a candle which the breath of the wind blew out; when Pa had not yet returned home, and you knew the roads were dangerous, unplowed, and that he was out there somewhere, in a wilderness of blowing snow, in a blizzard, trying to reach them; and the children were worried because, gathered around the hot stove in the kitchen, with the lights out, and no radio playing, under candlelight, and the eerie shadows it threw on their faces, they could hear the ticking of the clock, like the beating of their hearts, and Pa was late, late, much too late.

And then he would burst in through the back door (with the sound of the wind howling, they never heard the Buick driving up, which he had left out front anyway, because he couldn't get in the piled-up snowdrifts in the driveway without shoveling it first) (and he would always walk around the back, on foot, plowing through the snow with his knees, so as not to alarm them, making noise with the front door banging open) and by the time he burst into the kitchen, he was a snowman up to his thighs! and he wanted to tear off his clothes to get at his soaking wet socks. And the children jumped up and rushed him, to grab him around the legs, while Gigi, at the stove, was crossing herself, breathing relief, thanking Christ, the Virgin Mary, all the saints, and the gods and goddesses, marble or real (she had caught the contagion of fear from the kids) and they were all yelling, "Pa! Pa! You're home!"

But besides fear, which one could dismiss, curse, or fend off, with excuses, apologies and rationalizations, there was, for Gigi, in those momentous years of child-bearing, worry. Which was much more insidious, stubborn, ineradicable.

It grew on her gradually. Because, after the fourth or fifth pregnancy, she could not remember now, she had begun to feel differently, within her body, not like herself; within her body, where the stresses and strains of the day-to-day and month-to-month changes you undergo, which you feel everywhere, from top to toe, but which arrive on a system of signals, registering in your mind though you cannot name them: *yes, yes, I've felt that before, nevermind, it's the same old thing;* the signals began to change. She could no longer trust herself. She no longer knew what was happening. Only that she was no longer her old self.

She had begun giving birth in 1914, and now it was 1928.

She had spread out. She was not now in the shapely form she had been. Her girlish figure was a thing of the past. This she did not mourn, as she was surrounded by love, and she knew that this love did not depend on her looks. She was suitable for her age, and her station in life. She looked simply prosperous.

Her husband still took her out and showed her off to his friends in a devoted fashion. They went to the movies (she adored Valentino), they still went to the opera and the symphony. She still loved to dress up, and looked well, and her husband's trade and connections provided her with the latest in style. She looked well.

But she did not feel well. She felt fatigued. Enormous fatigue. And something else. In the middle, the midsection. Looser. Floating around. It was as if the sinews of her knee had snapped, and now she had to walk differently, that sort of feeling. She felt a noticeable heaviness, down there, and sometimes had trouble moving her bowels, which was very worrisome to Gigi, as she loved to eat, and with so many kids to feed, was constantly cooking: enormous meals of macaroni and chicken, pastavazoule and pork-bones, steak and French fries, and meatballs, all the time, pork-and-beef and egg-and-breadcrumb and fennel-seed meatballs (she was not a butcher's daughter for nothing!) tantalizing herself, driving herself mad with hunger and salacious nibbling.

The doctor said, "Prolapse. Of the uterus."

He looked at Tony like he was a criminal.

They both knew something had to change. But it was hard.

They had been happy, deliriously, hysterically happy, without knowing it.

Happiness was simply not something they pursued. They were, in fact, quite happy to be sad. Each of them had known, in their own way, profound sadness, but they did not pursue that, either. Happiness, sadness, each came into the life of everyone in their own good time. It was unavoidable. It was natural. One could not be always *allegro*—sometimes *andante* overcame you.

For Tony, it was . . . a distant memory, of New York, of Laura, even of the horse called Fiorello; memories which, like his own shadow, never left him.

For Gigi, it was something else. Actually, a combination of things. For Gigi, it was all about her boy, Agostino.

He fell sick when he was still an infant. Gigi was beside herself. The doctor said he had done everything he could, and that she should prepare herself.

Gigi refused to accept it. She would will him to live, all by herself, move mountains if she had to.

It was 1925. He was a big boy. Bigger than any of the others. How could he die?

She took him to her mother's, on Prince Street, in the North End of Boston. She put aside her husband and her other children and devoted herself exclusively to little Agostino. Her mother's was much closer to the Massachusetts General Hospital than they were where they lived in Hingham. Just in case. Of emergency. Of course, she took him there. Maybe they were better doctors, more educated, than the family doctor in Hingham, a venerable old country doctor who had so many to take care of in the town that perhaps he was inclined to resign himself; perhaps he was too old and had seen so much, this Dr Stewart; or maybe he was one of those old Yankees who just looked down on the immigrant. You could never discount that factor. Look at the way he gave that look to poor Tony, who had done nothing wrong.

But the doctors at the Mass General were of no use to Gigi, either. The problem was intestinal. The boy could keep nothing down. Her own breastmilk was making him sick. She was reduced to formulas they told her about, one after the other, and she was forced to feed him in the crook of her arm, like a baby bird. The robust, big boy was in danger of starving to death. She and Anna-Lisa were worried sick. She and her mother would walk over from the North End each day. They stood over him and watched, night and day. Gigi was forced to start praying with all her might. She turned to the Blessed Mother, on her knees, in the hospital's Catholic chapel, she went down on her knees and asked Her to intercede, she beat her breast with *mea culpas,* swearing to the Virgin that she would finally renounce, for good and all, those other, forbidden gods and goddesses who had populated her girlhood imagination. Nothing worked.

Gigi blamed herself, that she had caused all this with her lack of faith, her misdirected devotion. It was the Holy Mother's revenge on her, She who had loved her own son so dearly, and had to take him down dead from the cross with her own loving arms. Yes, only the Holy Mother could know this sorrow. But was she, like the older goddesses, capable of being envious of a mortal's happiness, and wish to destroy it?

Then one day at the hospital, Gigi was sitting there in the corridor outside baby Agostino's door, looking forlorn, holding him in her lap, and an old Italian nurse, from the old country, chanced to happen by, one who could speak to her. She told Gigi to try undiluted apple-cider vinegar. She said something about enzymes which this contained that other vinegars did not—maybe that was the whole problem. Maybe he kept throwing up everything because his system did not contain these enzymes, to break down the food in his stomach.

Gigi was used to dosing the kids everyday with cod liver oil. But this apple-cider vinegar she had never heard of. The nurse told her it was well-known by the old-time mothers back in the old country.

It worked. Agostino was saved.

Gigi went down on her knees and vowed to the Virgin never again to turn away from her and promised always to exalt and honor Her above all others. Of course, it was a miracle. How was it that none of these Harvard-educated doctors could figure it out? How was it that a nurse from the old mountain grotto ways, with a small red cross emblazoned on her white nurse's cap, with a white cape on her shoulders and a flowing long white robe down to her shoetops, which proved her to be a nun of one of the visiting orders, who just happened to be there in the hospital that day, who, when she saw Gigi with her head bent over her boy, stopped to speak to her, and crouched down on creaky old knees to give her words of comfort, with a dark-brown wooden crucifix of walnut hanging from her neck; how was it that this old woman simply chanced to run across Gigi, who, a moment before, had been inside the ward with her mother, holding her half-dead baby boy in her arms, walking him back and forth to soothe his fretful whimpering, and was now seated mournfully in the hallway? The woman even addressed her in dialect, without ever having met her before!

It was, it had to be, a miracle. It was Mother Mary who had sent her, in answer to Gigi's plea.

Chapter 13

Serafina in the Tower

She sometimes called them her *incanti*, her spells. But she preferred to call them her *affascinati,* her *fascinations.*

Gigi remembered them coming even as a little child. But at that time, she told no one. She was afraid to. She was sure she would be punished. She knew that often she would go into a room and forget why, or what she wanted there. But this was far different. At first, she became aware of the *incanti* only because her big brother, Agostino, was giving her a ride in her father's pushcart, for fun: and the next thing Gigi knew, she was on the ground, seated, and felt like she was waking up from a dream, and her brother asked her, *how could you fall like that? I told you to hold on!* Gigi did not remember falling; she only knew she didn't know how she had gotten on the ground.

And because Agostino, whom she loved and admired, scolded her, she thought she had done something wrong, and she felt guilty, without knowing what she had done that was wrong.

After that, she paid more attention. She discovered that her spells would come upon her unawares, in the middle of something else, and that when she returned she would be amazed that she couldn't remember a thing, except that she was in the middle of dressing her corn-cob doll, or feeding the parakeet in the cage, and then suddenly she was *not there.* Where she went, she never knew. Only that, upon returning, she could remember starting to fill the seed-tray attached to the cage, and nothing more: but the tray was not filled, the door of the cage was open, the bird was flying free, when Gigi awoke.

Her mother, Anna-Lisa, witnessed it for herself, or almost did, when she blamed Gigi for letting the bird out of the cage.

It was then that big brother Agostino, Gigi's defender, protested, "It's not her fault." And the episode of the pushcart came out.

After this, Anna-Lisa was worried. She fretted that she would miss it. She had to see it occur with her own eyes before she would believe it. Then it happened at the supper table. As soon as Anna-Lisa saw it once, it started to happen more frequently. Then, it seemed, constantly. She questioned Gigi. She interrogated her. But she could learn nothing that way. The mother in Anna-Lisa only succeeded in frightening herself half to death.

Gigi herself was no longer frightened, however. She was receiving so much attention that she actually relished her affliction. It made her important, but more crucially than that, it told her that she was, indeed, *different.*

Everyone, that is, the butcher Fabrizio, the girl's father, and his own parents, the grandparents, upstairs, were *sympatico*, but *flemmatico*, and with a shrug, told Anna-Lisa not to worry, the child would grow out of it. Evidently, her husband

Pasquale thought children, if left alone, were as healthy as pigs; and the grandparents on Anna-Lisa's side, also upstairs, were simply beyond bothering, as senility was beginning to return them to their own childhoods.

But in fact, as Gigi entered into her adolescent womanhood and had her first period, the spells did decrease in frequency. But by this time, Gigi had learned to manipulate them. She would embroider them with her own imagination. She found many tales could be spun out of the question, "But where did you go?" These tales tended to come from the books her brother brought her, which she avidly consumed—especially her favorite, which would always be Bazzaro's *Storia di un'anima,* replete with its fantastical tales of half-human creatures and alluring river naiads, wreathed in golden mists and transparent clouds.

In truth, Gigi never knew where she went. Only that it was somewhere else, not here. *A world that existed right beside us*: like a door you stepped through. She would stop, or pause, and a grey mist would seem to come over everything, and then it would darken, and envelop her, and turn to black. And then she would wake up, and be startled to find she had gone again, and she still did not know where, or for how long.

When she grew up, and had children of her own, she simply turned the tables on them. Now she was Anna-Lisa, and they were Gigi, and she still could use her *fascinations* to frighten them, and thus, to manipulate them, and even control them.

She and Tony, the father and the mother, stepped into their roles as parents as if they were stepping into their shoes. They seemed to know instinctively that the best way to control the behavior of so many unruly children was to scare the life out of them. Although they talked about everything else, endlessly, they never discussed child-rearing between themselves. But then, bringing up children was natural, you were born to it, it was in your blood, in your bones; you did what everyone else did, and whatever felt natural, and that way, you were always right. Whatever the other one said or did, in front of the children, was always fine with each of them. They backed each other up. That was something the two of them found easy. Since the first day they met they always agreed on everything (Gigi made sure of that.) And, of course, as everyone knew, children were always trying to divide one parent against the other, trying to get away with doing something wrong, which they knew to be wrong, little savages that they were; or perhaps did *not* know, *little savages that they were.* Gigi and Tony were not about to let them get away with it. It was a parent's job to civilize the inner *bestia* in them.

Gigi was his wife, but she was also Tony's friend. That was one thing that Tony absolutely adored about her. In fact, she was the one who came along and finally, finally, gave him someone to talk to. That was something he was sure he had never had before, in his whole entire life (forgetting altogether his best friend, Harry Spritzka, and Harry's Bubelah, too, not to mention Litvak, the tailor, Professore Siragusa, his music teacher, Miss Morgan, the school librarian, even Domenico, the Iceman, all of whom took an interest in Tony and talked to him).

When the LaStorias went to bed together at night, that's what they did, talk (in addition to making babies, of course). They would talk before and after making the babies, and all the rest of the time, too. As long as they were in the same room, they would talk. But especially in bed, to review the day. They would cover everything, endlessly, until they were yawning and exhausted and had to roll over and fall dead asleep. Tony would tell Gigi every little thing that went on at work all day, or in the business, who said what to whom, who was happy and unhappy, who had a death in the family, or was expecting, where he stayed overnight last week, where his next trip was headed to, *everything.* Though Gigi had never met Harry Spritzka, she knew everything about him, what she liked and didn't like, and she told Tony so. She also knew all about Harry's wife Mimi and the size of her engagement ring and how many children did they have now? And Gigi would tell Tony all about her day with their son, Patsy, and then, their son Patsy plus their daughter Maria, and then when Margherita came along, their son and the two girls, and so on, with a brother for Patsy, named Eugenio, and next a girl they called Gerardina, God knows why. Eugenio, that second son, was named after Tony's uncle, whom he had not seen now in how many years? Since Zi'Eugenio had moved the whole family down to Camden, and all Tony's cousins, too, that's how long ago (Camden, New Jersey, that is) how many years is that now? *Where do the years go?* Finally, a boy came along, Agostino, named after Gigi's favorite brother, and, last of all, the baby of the family, pretty little Anna arrived, over whom everyone cooed and bubbled, except for oldest brother Patsy, who was by this time, fourteen years later, much too grown-up for such nonsense.

Naturally, Gigi was curious to know all about that seemingly fabled cast of characters who populated Tony's life before the advent of Gigi herself. That was a must. Indeed, she envied him his travels. What must it have been like to have crossed the ocean, by yourself like that, just a ten-year-old boy? Though born in Italy, back in her parents' home town of Volturrara, Gigi had been too young when their family's crossing occurred to have any living memory of it. Now in her marriage she made it her avowed purpose to compel Tony to confess everything about himself, absolutely everything. And he did, except for some things that he kept strictly to himself: how a gambler and a gypsy tramp had stolen his passage money; how he had fled from the touch of a young courtesan in a Chinese house of assignation; how his friend Harry had once involved him in the strange episode of the Englishman in the hotel room; how he had fallen in love with a girl named Laura and then witnessed her horrible death without being able to do anything to save her.

After all, had it not been Gigi herself who proposed that they each had secrets and, even before their first kiss, that it was only right and proper and natural that each of them keep their own secrets and need not share them with the other? Even before that first kiss?

And so, what was Gigi's secret? That she was so desperate to keep hidden?

Tony found Gigi's *affascinati* frightening at first; and then, as time went on, disturbing.

If you were sitting at the table, eating supper, with Gigi and all the children, the first thing you knew was: her head would go back. She could be in the middle of a sentence, and she would stop, as if she had lost the train of her thought. She would pause with the spoon of soup halfway to her mouth, and her head would tilt back. The soup would dribble on the table-cloth or her bosom. Her gaze would freeze into fixation, and if you followed her line of sight, as her head tilted back, you would see she was staring at the corner of the ceiling, where three lines converged. Then at the last moment, her eyes would roll back in her head. The kids would scream and hide their faces and start exclaiming "Ma-a! Are you all right?" But Tony's hand would shoot out: "Don't touch her!" After what seemed like forever, but was only thirty seconds or less, once her hand with the soup spoon went lax on the table, or the spoon fell on the floor, she would start to come out of it, gradually, not all at once. The children would be watching, holding their breath, entranced. It never failed to unnerve them. Then Gigi would blink, once, twice; then she would look at the person nearest (little Anna) (no, she was still too young) perhaps Gerardina: and give that one a wordless, questioning look.

Gerardina would say, "You went away again, Mamma!"

Gigi would say, "Oh."

Patsy, the oldest, always full of mischief, would say, "Aw—she's fakin' it again!"

His father would shoot him a look. "You show some respect!" he would command, in English. At the table, Tony always spoke to the children in English, and they would use it also, especially when they didn't want their mother to know what they were saying.

"Aw, Pa, tell me you don't believe in that stuff anymore, that's just for the little kids!"

But Tony would not. He did believe. He would look gently at his wife, and ask, "Where did you go?"

He always wanted to know. *He hoped someday he would find out.*

But Gigi truly did not know. To satisfy everyone's curiosity (which they would die of, in the end, she was sure) and to pacify the little ones, who seemed as scared as chicks in the nest, over time, she developed a reply. "I went to the place where stories come from."

All would then cry, "Oh, tell us a story, Mamma!"

"Not now. Maybe later. If you're good. Now first you have to finish your supper. And I mean clean your plate. Use a piece of bread, like this. "

The place where stories come from. Tony knew that was not the real explanation. But he would explore it later, at bedtime. It was one of their favorite topics together, one they never tired of. Tony, too, believed in his heart her spells were one of the things that made Gigi unique, and precious to him.

He never forgot the first time he witnessed, intimately, her going away.

It happened that time when they wandered down to the dockside on the waterfront ringing the North End, before they were married, when they were looking to turn their backs on the city, hover over the railing, and kiss each other, avidly, sur-reptitiously, beyond the ken of a censorious world. And as they gazed on the quietly lapping water swirling around the ankles of the pylons of the pier, their heads together, leaning on one another's temple, Tony felt Gigi's head slide back on his shoulder, and when he looked, her eyes were blank, as if unseeing, though they were staring upwards, and faroff, as if entranced by a passing cloud, and he felt a rush of alarm, but before he could think of what to do except keep holding her up so that she wouldn't fall, fifteen or twenty seconds had already transpired, and Gigi came back—as if nothing had happened. Suddenly, she came back! and Tony, amazed, perplexed, said, "Where were you?" and Gigi patiently explained that it was nothing, she hadn't bothered to tell him before, because it was nothing; in the family, hers, they were all so used to it, by now. The subject had simply never come up between the two of them. He had a million questions, then, and a million more now.

That story, the story of that day on the waterfront, became a part of their personal album of family legends. The children were endlessly fascinated about their origins: where they were born, when, what was the weather that day, what time was it, was it day or night? Why were they all born in the house on Prince Street in the North End, instead of at home? They were just like their father, a million questions. And one of their best-loved stories was the one about that day on the beach, at Nantasket, the one which ended, "And that's when your father fell in love with me."

However, there was another, different story that Gigi herself liked better. Perhaps because it was not real. Perhaps because she made it up herself. Perhaps because she had been given it, as a gift, and it really did come from *the place where stories come from.*

And that story was the tale of *Serafina in the Tower.*

First she would ask the little ones, "What do you want tonight? *Reynard the Fox*—or *Gloriana the Goose?*"

They would always clamor for *Serafina*—and she would always give in—unless she was tired of it, three nights in a row.

Some of them would not go to sleep at all, without a story.

"Now, Serafina was a princess: a beautiful young girl, with long blond hair all the way down her back, almost as long as the train she wore, which was attached to the pinnacle of her cone-shaped hat, you know, like an ice-cream cone upside down on her head!" Gigi would sometimes say the first thing that came to her, but if she changed anything important, or worse, omitted it, they would correct her. "But Serafina was a lonely young princess. Very lonely. Because she had been shut up in a tower, and she did not know why. She had only one window to look out on the world. And only one visitor who came to see her every day, and that was Alanzo, the Woodsman."

"Now, Alanzo felt very sorry for her—because every day she had no water to drink, unless he brought her water himself, from the well by the river. He was the only one who cared about her. And so every day he would fill her bucket and she would draw it up to her window."

"Because her window was up high in the wall!" the children would cry.

"Yes. High in the wall. And so one day, as she was taking a sip from the ladle in the bucket, poor Alanzo confessed that he had fallen in love with her. And Serafina cried, 'But, Alanzo, it's impossible!' And he said, 'Not if you send me a kiss!' 'But I am up here, and you are down there!'"

"Send me a kiss in the bucket!" the children yelled.

"And so Serafina left a little water in the bottom of the bucket and placed the kiss on top and sent the bucket down on the rope. But halfway down it bumped into a stone in the wall, and tipped, and the kiss ran out with the water."

"And just then a pigeon landed on the windowsill," said Margherita.

But Gerardina insisted, "No, no—it was a sparrow—pigeons are so dirty!"

"Anyway," their mother said, "Serafina picked up the bird and gave him a peck on the beak, and then threw him up in the air—and he flew, but he flew the other way! And poor Alanzo could not catch the kiss!"

"Then what happened?"

"Allora, you know what happened! Serafina took a sudden notion that if she blew him a kiss, that, of course, Alanzo would be able then to catch it!"

Then Gigi demonstrated how to blow a kiss from the palm of your hand, and the children imitated her, and eagerly gave the story an ending, all piping up in unison, "And so they lived happily ever after!"

Chapter 14

The Ballad of Puffy O'Brian

The door of the Stoughton Police Department opened, and Tony LaStoria was nearly bowled over by a uniformed policeman rushing down the front steps.

It was a rude introduction to a task he had little heart for. Left standing there, with the knob of the open door thrust into his hand, he hesitated, and almost turned back. He wished it were he himself jumping into the waiting paddy wagon and driving off, instead of the cop. But he forced himself to go on.

It was 1927, and Sacco and Vanzetti were still in their jail cells, awaiting execution, while the world watched as if mesmerized.

Inside, he said, "I want to see Puffy O'Brian."

He did not remove his fedora, an omission that did not go unnoticed by the desk sergeant.

"That's Chief O'Brian to you, mister."

"Your man almost knocked me down coming in here," Tony complained as he took off his hat, to gesture with.

"What's your business with the Chief?"

"It's private."

"He's a busy man."

"Not too busy to see me."

"Take a seat—if you don't mind."

"That's all right, I'll wait."

Tony seated himself on the hard bench opposite as he thrust the hat back on his head. He was in no mood.

In many ways, leaving Hingham, and moving to nearby Stoughton, four years previously, had thrust him into the middle of the Sacco and Vanzetti controversy. He had been happy in Hingham, a seaside town where he could take the kids clamming at the beach on weekends; a town where life was good, and Tony was popular, and spoken of by the town's elite as a homemade Toscanini, leader of the little band of gypsies called The Roma Jazz Band.

Stoughton was inland, landlocked; and moreover, the town where Sacco himself had been holding down a job working in a shoe-shop at the time of his arrest; which caused the local police to develop some kind of grudge. The notoriety of the long-running feud between the Commonwealth of Massachusetts and the leftists and liberals of the world because of the Sacco and Vanzetti Case left the old guard in the town feeling that their hometown of Stoughton had been tainted. And many blamed the influx of so-called foreigners whose names ended in a vowel for ruining the town's reputation, not to mention its property values. And then Tony had gone and got himself elected the President of the Stoughton chapter of the Sons of Italy.

But at the time he made the move, his family was getting bigger. He needed more room, more land, too, to enlarge his vegetable garden. A deal came along, and he couldn't say no because he made money on selling the house in Hingham, money which he could then put into a bigger, better place in Stoughton. Or so he thought, at the time. Sometimes he wished he hadn't. He thought he was improving things for his family, even sacrificing his musical pastimes for them, not stepping into an unseen sinkhole in a thorny briar patch.

The sergeant took his time sticking his head in an open door behind the counter. "Chief—some guy to see you."

"What's he want?"

Tony could hear every word they said—deliberately, he could only assume.

The sergeant returned.

"What's this all about, the Chief wants to know."

"That's all right—I'll wait here. I got all day."

The sergeant said, "I hope you're not gonna be one of those trouble-makers."

"I'm a tax-paying citizen of this town."

"The Chief don't like trouble-makers."

"You just tell him I wanna see him."

Tony realized they were lowering their voices when he heard the sergeant, at the door again, say "Speaks good English, Puffy."

Then the sergeant returned to unlock a hook-and-eye and hold open a half-door for Tony to pass behind the desk.

"Chief says to go right in, 'cause he ain't got all day."

Fedora still stuck on his head, Tony LaStoria walked into the office of the Chief of Police of Stoughton, Massachusetts, and came face to face for the first time with Puffy O'Brian, a man who was the constant subject of conversation, discussion and anecdote all over town, from gas station to breakfast counter; a man who knew it, and a man who did not dislike the idea.

Chief O'Brian had been Chief of Police in Stoughton for about six years. Tony LaStoria knew of him but had never had any occasion until now to meet him, talk to him, get to know him, or have anything at all to do with him.

Tony was averse to getting involved, and avoided anything to do with government, bureaucrats, officials, anyone with a title. He wanted only to be left alone. He knew that the Chief was a political appointee, and owed his job to his connections. It was no secret. But, *mind your own business, and let the world go to hell in its own good time,* was Tony's policy. Thus, Tony would have been astounded to think that O'Brian knew all about *him.*

"You know, you people burn my ass," said the Chief. That's how Chief O'Brian introduced himself. Tony had a little speech all prepared, but he was jolted out of his fantasy. "You walk in here like you own the place and ya think you're gonna run my town. Well, you people got another thing comin.' Don't you realize I got a lotta things on my mind and enough problems of my own keepin' the peace around here without babysittin' a bunch o' muley-mouthed rantin' and ravin' complainin' *gesticulatin'* wops like you and your rag-tag ragamuffin no-good dirty grease-ball friends?"

"Nice to meet you, too," said Tony.

"Take off your hat when you're talkin' to me."

"I'll keep it on, thank you. I feel a wind blowin' in here."

"Well, sit down, then. You're aggravatin' me, standing there, like you're lookin' for a hand-out."

Puffy O'Brian, sitting down behind his desk, was already as tall as Tony was standing up, and his bulk, even seated as he was, approached that of a pair of beer-barrels, stacked one on top of the other. His temperamental outburst was turning his already florid face redder, with blooming puffed-out cheeks, which buried his eyes beneath bleached eyebrows and a furiously pink forehead. The Chief was as baby-faced as an overgrown eighth-grader, but his stiff blond bristling crew-cut was already dotted with a silver patina.

As he took his seat, Tony could not help himself. "I resent the tone you're taking."

"You can resent all you want, it's my office."

"I'm a taxpaying citizen of this town."

"So what? That gives you privileges?"

"I got as much right to be here as you do."

"Izzat so? Tell me something, boy, where were you born?"

"I'm an American citizen and I got the papers to prove it."

"But you weren't born here, were you?"

"What's that got to do with anything?"

"Oh, that's got a lot to do with everything, boy."

"I'm a grown man, I'll have you know."

"Is that what you think? Well, I'll have you know, I've had my eye on you."

"What's that supposed to mean?"

"Oh, I got my eye on you, all right."

"I'm a law-abiding citizen."

"Izzat so? Tell me something. What do you do with them grapes you got growin' over in your backyard over there on Pine Street? Every time I go by your house over there, I look in your yard, see 'em growin' all nice and plump and juicy, all tidy-like, with the little arbor you built for 'em. Watcha doing with them grapes in your cellar, boy?"

"Those grapes are for me and my family, and what I do with them is nobody's business. It's not against the law to grow grapes."

"And I suppose you're gonna maintain you ain't turnin' them grapes into wine in your cellar every winter, huh?"

"And what if I am? That's for me and my family."

"Yeah, for religious purposes, I heard that one, too."

"And so what if I offer a glass of wine to company when they come over?"

"You gotta a lotta company goin' in and outta that house, that I know."

"People come to see me. I try to help them. They elected me the President of the Sons of Italy."

"And I know why, too. *Cause you're the only one in the bunch can speak a word o' good ole American, that's why!*"

"Now I know why people in this town call you bigoted."

"If I had my way, I'd put the whole lotta yez on a raft and push it out to sea!"

"You think people don't know what goes on at the Hibernian Hall?"

"You ever hear of a little thing called Prohibition?"

"You gonna sit there, Mr O'Brian, and tell me you're not cooking up a batch of home-brew in your bathtub, in your own house, right now?"

"Are you gonna maintain that you're not a law-breaker?"

"What about you!" Tony was becoming incensed.

"What about it, mister? You gonna arrest me? No? I didn't think so! But I can throw you in the clink anytime I want. I gotta nice little cell with bars on it reserved just for you, Mr LaStoria, right here in my basement, with your name on it, Anthony LaStoria! Right here in the middle of town, in the basement of the Stoughton Police Department. And don't you ever forget it!"

"You are one goddam son-of-a bitch, O'Brian."

"You bet your ever-lovin' grease-ball guinea ass I am!"

Tony was beside himself, wriggling in his chair. "You know, I don't know what to say! I cannot believe this. Can this be happening in America? I don't think people really realize what a—a—I don't know what to call you. You're like a pig, rollin' around in your own dirt!"

"Aw, shut up."

"Not only are you a bigot, you are a prejudiced, ignorant out-and-out bastard, and don't think the citizens of this town don't know it!"

"Oh, relax. You people get my goat."

" 'You people.' 'You people!' It sounds like a dirty word in your mouth!"

"Would you just please quiet down and sit on your hands or something so's we can get down to business."

"What business? What the hell are you talkin' about now?"

"I'm talkin' about all those radical Reds and anti-American organizers and dago anarchists going in and outta your house all the time. Them Sacco and Vanzetti sympathizers! Them bomb-throwers!"

Tony felt like a cement block had just fallen on his head.

It was thunderously obvious, all of a sudden, that this man was exactly what the *paesani* had thought him to be all along—an obtuse and immovable and irretrievably blind hater, consumed with persecuting them because he despised them!

Tony took his time answering. If ever in his life he wanted to measure his words, it was now.

He took his hat off. He leaned forward in his chair and put his elbows on his knees as he twirled the brim of the fedora round and round in his fingers. Finally, he looked up.

"I'm very disappointed in you, Chief O'Brian."

"What? Are you presuming to sit in judgment on me!"

"It's just that I came here hoping—wishing—that somehow we could have a reasonable discussion between us of conditions."

"Conditions, huh?"

"But you have painted my people—."

"So now they're '*your people.*'"

"—with a broad brush."

"You're just a sympathizer, like all the rest."

"My people are honest, hard-working people."

"All you people are consumed with this Sacco and Vanzetti thing! Well, let me tell you, mister, we're gonna fry those two bastards!"

"I did not come here to debate with you the merits–.

"Those two assassins! Those two thugs!"

"Sacco and Vanzetti have nothing to do with the vast majority of my people."

"You gotta lotta sympathy for those two murdering gunmen. Lemme ask you this, Mister LaStoria. How much sympathy did those two have for Berardelli when he was begging for his life that day on Pearl Street in Braintree when they shot him through the heart, one of their own fellow Eye-talians!"

"You got the wrong men!"

"Is that so? What do you know about it?"

"Everybody knows it was the Morelli gang from Providence!"

"From Providence, huh? Why? What's the Morelli gang doin' this far north? You know somethin' I don't? Maybe it's a good thing you came in here today. Maybe I oughta be questioning you, Mister LaStoria. What's your pal Phil Buccola, up in the North End–."

"He's no pal of mine."

"I know of all your friends and associates up there."

"He's a dirty Siciliano!"

"I know all about you and DiBenedetto, for instance."

"You think all us Italians–."

"So now you're an Italian?"

"I'm no Siciliano, if that's what you mean. I'm Avellinese, and proud of it."

"Yeah, and your father-in-law, what's his name? The butcher? He's got a stall up there, he crosses Buccola's palm every week, he wants to stay in business with his little stall in Faneuil Hall, he's another Avellinese, ain't he?"

"You're like all the rest. You think everybody with a last name like mine is the Black Hand."

"Aintcha? Ain't you payin' a little collection money every week to the boys?"

"I don't need to. I'm just a small fry to them. They don't bother with me. You and your laws and your courts and your Uncle Sam has taken care of that with Prohibition. So, now, what do they need with pennies, when they're makin' millions!"

"And newspaper headlines, too. I wouldn't be surprised if Al Capone's more popular than Hoover."

"Why not? He's does more for the people."

"Oh, yeah, he's another Mussolini—made the trains run on time."

"All my people want is justice, a little simple justice!"

"Did you know that Sacco was working at 3-K Shoe, right here in Stoughton, on the 15th of April, 1920. And that on the 15th of April, he took the day off, and didn't show up at work?"

"Facts, facts, facts! You people make a lot outta facts! You just twist them around to suit yourselves!"

"I know that fact because my pal Mike Kelley was the one who was good enough to give your precious Sacco a job here in the first place, after he was booted out of every other shoe shop in Eastern Massachusetts for his subversive activities!"

"You got nothing on Sacco and Vanzetti but circumstantial evidence like that! And the whole world knows it! From Rome to Buenos Aires, they know it!"

"Come to think of it, where were you on the 15th of April, 1920, LaStoria?"

"Those two poor condemned men have maintained their innocence for six years in jail now! And God knows, they may die innocent!"

"I'm kinda glad you came in here today, LaStoria. I needed to ask you a few questions!"

"I came in here today not to defend Sacco and Vanzetti but to protest the harassment you are subjugating my people here in Stoughton to, every day of the week!"

"Harrassment!"

"You heard what I said! What do you call it when my people cannot gather on the streets of their own town more than two at a time without your five-man police force prodding them with sticks to move along!"

"You ain't seen harassment yet!"

"My own children cannot go to school in this town without being subjugated to looks they get up and down. Did you brush your teeth today? Let me see your shoes! Let me see your fingernails! Their own schoolteachers treat them like they're unwashed animals!"

In spite of himself, Puffy O'Brian had to laugh. "Them old-maid Yankees on the School Department? Ladies Auxiliary o' the Black 'n Tans, I call 'em!"

"Yankee old maids, and the Keystone Kops! That's what we get in this town for the taxes we pay!"

Puffy O'Brian, in spite of himself, had to chuckle at the Keystone Kops, while he was reaching into a desk drawer. He then pulled out not a gun, but a box of cigars. "You smoke?"

"What's it to you? That against the law, too?"

Tony's face was overheated, as he frowned with suspicion, and twirled the fedora in his hands in such *agidu* that he was in danger of tearing the brim off. He was also mad at himself for being so agitated that he used the word "subjugated" when he meant to say "subjected."

"Have one. Panatellas." Chief O'Brian held out the stiff box across the desk to Tony.

Tony could not figure out what O'Brian was up to. "What makes you think I smoke?"

"I can see the pack o' Chesterfields stickin' outta your shirt pocket."

Tony smiled, a little chagrined.

"You know what they call you people around town?"

"No," said Tony, as he selected a Panatella.

"The Whiteshirts!"

Tony had never heard that expression.

"You know why? Because it's only people that are *trying to belong* that wear a white shirt every day of the year."

O'Brian had come around the desk and was holding out a lit match to Tony. Tony puffed the cigar alight. O'Brian said, "Good, huh?"

"It's okay."

"See? I told you we could have a reasonable discussion."

O'Brian returned to his swivel-chair behind the desk and returned the cigar-box to the desk drawer. Then he leaned back on his tilting seat and placed his hands with intertwined fingers behind his head. He said, "Now let's go back to the beginning."

Tony puffed. "Well, the real reason I came here today—well, I didn't want to—but the members of the Sons of Italy, they pay their dues, they elected my their President. They came to my house, the whole bunch, and they begged me to intercede with you because they are finally fed up."

Tony puffed and O'Brian puffed, and O'Brian said, "Oh, go on, do."

"Well, it seems that this week one of Gerardi's sons, the oldest, he's about sixteen, maybe, he was stopped in his own front yard by the cops in the paddy wagon. They just happen to be driving by and they screech to a stop and two of them jump out and collar the kid, in his own front yard! And demand to know why he's acting suspiciously. Is he trying to rob the place? The kid wasn't doing nothing. And they march him up to his own front door! And his father, Gerardi, opens the door—and there's two cops, got his son by the arms, wanna know, is this really your kid?? Well, that was the last straw!"

"You can't blame them. They're only doin' their job, protecting the lives and property of the local citizens!"

"Come on, Chief! They knew who the kid was!"

"Well, okay, you gotta complain about something. It's your job to complain."

"Can't you call off your dogs? At least get them to ease up a little?"

"See, Mister LaStoria, you gotta realize I got a job to do, too."

"This whole situation in this town is all just about Sacco and Vanzetti."

"Okay, we'll get to that. But let's backtrack first. Start at the beginning. What did you do in the War, LaStoria?"

"What did *I* do? What did *you* do?"

"I was a gunnery sergeant in the Massachusetts 37th, that's what. I did my duty. Over in France, under General John J.

'Blackjack' Pershing. Now, how is it that you didn't serve? 'Cause I know you didn't. I know more about you than you think I do. It's my job to know. Were you one of them draft-dodgin' anarchists?"

"If you know anything about me, Mr O'Brian, as you claim, then you know I have always been nothing but a factory manager, ever since I came to Boston."

"That's right. You run a sweatshop. Up in Boston. And every day you drive back and forth up and down Rt 138 from Stoughton in that Buick of yours, back and forth from town. Every coupla years, a new Buick. And every night you come home to your wife and kids. But what I don't know is, where do you go in between? For instance, I know you come from New York. Now, who's that guy you work for, who owns that chain of outlets up and down the Connecticut shore and up to Providence and Boston?"

"Harry Spritzka. He's a respectable businessman, and well-known all over New York, and his wife is connected to the Lowenstein banking family."

"Spritzka. He's a Jew, huh?"

"What's wrong with that? He's a friend of mine. Everything I have in life, everything my kids have, I owe to Harry Spritzka. And if you had any respect, well, Harry Spritzka is a veteran of the Expeditionary Force, the same as you!"

"Yeah." O'Brian considered his cigar. "He's a Jew. They're all Jews. Him and his banking circle."

"Mr O'Brian, excuse me for saying so, but you are one pitiful excuse for a human being."

"Just because he's your friend, and, by the way, has lifted you up outta the gutter and put you on Easy Street, well, of course, you'll defend him. But did you know that your almighty friend Spritzka is a member of *The Elders of Zion?* Did you know that, Anthony, my friend?"

"No, *Puffy!*—I didn't know that!"

"I can call you Anthony, right? That is your name, Anthony, right?"

"My friends call me Tony."

"Well, we ain't friends, yet."

Tony was genuinely bewildered. He had never heard of *The Elders of Zion* in his life.

"I suppose you wanna pretend that you don't know anything about all the conspiracies that go on against the lawful authority in this country, a loyal citizen like you—a loyal *naturalized* citizen like you."

"I only know what I read in the newspapers."

"Right. Right. About Sacco and Vanzetti, and everything else."

Tony did not know if he was smoking O'Brian's cigar, or choking on it. But he was fascinated to find out where all this was going.

O'Brian supplied him with the next hint.

"See, Anthony, I'm a loyal guy. And I got my friends, too, that I'm loyal to. And my friends just happen to be in high places. Once in a while, they ask me to do them a favor. Look into a thing or two, for them. They're pretty busy, on their own level, and sometimes they need an ear to the ground, so to speak, way down on our little local level. So, see, Anthony, just like you defend your guy Spritzka, 'cause of all he's done for you, and all you owe to him, which you can never repay, as long as you live, that's how loyal I am to my friends in high places."

O'Brian now sat up again and leaned his elbows on his desk and bit the cigar as he looked down, hulking, at Tony.

"The real question is, Anthony, who are you loyal to? Is your loyalty really given to the United States, or not? So-o, I did my duty in the war. I fought for you, so you could enjoy the freedom that you have, and even your friend Spritzka did his duty. So, Anthony, how is it that you didn't?"

"That was years ago."

"Don't matter. If I ask you right now to reach into your pants pocket and fetch your wallet and show me your Selective Service card, you know I got the right."

"That was years ago. I don't carry that thing around with me anymore. There's no war on now. There hasn't been a draft since 1917. That was ten years ago."

"But if I tell you to go home right now and fetch it, that, and your naturalization papers, you know I got the right."

"You got a lotta rights. What about my rights? I'm just as much a citizen of this country as you are."

"No you ain't. You weren't born here."

"Makes no difference."

"The hell it don't. Not in my eyes, it don't. And that's what counts. And you better remember that, my friend, Anthony. Cause you're livin' in my town. And I run this town, not you."

Puffy O'Brian leaned back in his swivel-chair again and considered the man sitting in his office, smoking his cigar, one Anthony LaStoria, one of the *Whiteshirts* who had invaded his bailiwick with their street pageants of obscure saints no one had ever heard of and their backyard sing-alongs piled high on picnic tables with foreign foods with unpronounceable names and their endless whining about their rights and their ignorant kids flooding our schools driving up the tax rates and their secret language that they use anytime they're in earshot and don't want us to know what they're saying about us and their speakeasy gangs and their notorious criminals and their stubborn defiance and their code of respect and their wilful disobedience of any laws they didn't like, and Puffy O'Brian said to Tony LaStoria, "How in the hell did you and Spritzka ever get together, anyway, a guinea like you and a kike like him?"

"You know, you shouldn't talk like that. How do you like it when I call you names?"

"What—you mean like—harp and paddy and thick mick? Don't worry, LaStoria, I know *exactly* how you think."

Tony smirked. In spite of himself, he had to smile.

Puffy O'Brian said, "So, you see, Tony—you and me—we ain't that different after all. You just remember I know all about that unlicensed gun you got in your house.

"That's a hunting rifle."

"I know, I know. You go puttin' rabbits and pheasants and quail on the table to feed that rabble o' kids you got. You got a license for that gun?"

"I got a license to drive."

"That one you gotta have. What about that kennel o' dogs you got back there in your yard, barkin' up the neighborhood? You got a license for them?"

"You people got a license for everything!"

"So now it's–'you people'?'"

"It's just another scheme for extorting the blood money outta the little guy."

"And you maintain you're not a lawbreaker."

"People are just trying to get by and feed their family."

"Well, Anthony. There we are. Question is, how we gonna fix this thing?"

"Whaddya mean—*Puffy*—fix this thing?"

"Things can always be fixed, Anthony."

"Yeah, I know that. I'm not so dumb as I look. So, now, the fix is in?"

"Well, shall we say?" Puffy O'Brian stood up to his full double-barrel height and came leisurely around the desk. He grinned and offered his hand to shake, and Tony, for the life of him, could not figure why they should now shake hands, as if they had just concluded a peace treaty, and were going to pose for photographs for the papers, but the Chief, grabbing Tony's slack, half-hearted hand, and gripping it, pulled him up, to walk him to the door, and with carefree insouciance, he threw his arm round Tony's shoulder, to usher him out.

"See, Anthony, here in Stoughton, we got this little thing called the Christmas Fund, you know, toys for the little kids, the needy ones, at the givin'-est time o' year. And all ya gotta do is make a little contribution once a week. And maybe ask your friends to maybe do likewise. Influential guy like you's got a lotta friends in this town, right, Anthony?"

The Chief stood broadly in the stationhouse doorway waving goodbye as Tony shoved the fedora down on his head and looked back, with the panatella sticking out of his teeth.

"Hey, paisan! When you gonna have me over for a big plate o' the wife's macaroni?"

Chapter 15

The End of Anna-Vittoria

In the black of night, after midnight, at the very beginning of the day marked down on the calendar as the 23rd of August, 1927, Sacco and Vanzetti were executed at the Charlestown Jail, in Boston.

After being held imprisoned for seven years, they were sent to their death rapidly and efficiently. Sacco marched to the electric chair a few minutes after midnight, at 12.11, and was pronounced to be without any life remaining in his body at 12.19. At the last, he had shouted, "Farewell, Mother." Vanzetti was allowed no more time to live, entering the execution chamber at 12.20, declared dead at 12.26.

He had said, "I wish to forgive some people for what they are now doing to me."

Their wake and funeral was anything but simple and quick. It took two days for 10,000 mourners to view the bodies in open caskets at Langone's Funeral Home in the North End. Tony LaStoria was one of those who slowly filed past, with his father-in-law, Fabrizio, and his friend, the editor of *La Gazzetta,* DiBenedetto.

On Sunday, the 28th, the funeral procession, which was being filmed for the Hollywood newsreels, wound its way to Forest Hills Cemetery, miles away. The funeral took a route passing close to the State House, which was where the Boston Police blocked the way, and angry, shocked mourners started a street-fight with the enforcers of public order.

Tony LaStoria was back home in Stoughton by that time. He felt that he was watched. This had become a feeling that would not depart. Chief O'Brian would be fully cognizant of his present and recent whereabouts. But to Tony, it no longer mattered. Like the vast majority of the people who shared his roots, his identity, as it were, he mourned the deaths of the two men, as a pity, and a stain, and an outrage, but, like them, he was not about to uproot his life in any further senseless protest, nor would he commit any violence in response to their execution. Neither would he, as a President of the Sons of Italy, a representative of people of his origins, faith and brotherhood, fail to pay his respects, no matter how it looked, to no matter whom.

It was a personal and private thing to Tony.

He had not revisited such deeply felt, turbulent emotions stirred up by death's unjust intrusion upon life since the moment he came upon and recognized Laura Antonelli's shoes at the temporary morgue down by the East River in 1911. He knew, as did DiBenedetto, Fabrizio and all the others, that a few—a very few—would seek vengeance. Only a few days before the final executions, there had been a bombing at the Dedham home of one of the jurors in the case. On the very day of August 23rd, the American Embassy in Buenos Aires was bombed. Demonstrators clashed with police not only in Boston but in Geneva, London, Paris, Amsterdam, even Tokyo. Wildcat strikes closed factories in South America, and miners walked out in Colorado. Three were killed in protests in Germany, and in Johannesburg, South Africa, demonstrators burned an American flag outside the American Embassy. Even at the wake itself, in the North End, a wreath had been draped on the coffins with a ribbon proclaiming,

Aspettando l'ora della vendetta . . . "Awaiting the hour of vengeance . . . "

Tony did not disagree with that. With everyone else, he was stirred to his depths with that avowal, and wished it, fervently. He had found that he simply could not help feeling that way. But, in the end, it was not his business. He had his own life to carry on, his own family to look out for, he was, and would be, burdened with responsibilities, virtually without end, at home, at work; so many people who depended upon him . . .

And so Tony LaStoria had to let this, too, pass from him. And as it passed, so did his last hold on the optimism of his younger days, the outlook that took it for a fact that things were bound to get better, as long as, well, look around at this country, the greatest country on earth, as long as he worked hard, well . . .

Not any more.

Astounding events were happening that summer of 1927, of epic significance, with an impact stirring every single person

in the United States, thanks to the wire services making news-photos iconic everywhere, thanks to newsreels in the movie-houses, to radio, to this new, fast, up-to-the-minute world of modern communications. In May, Lucky Lindy and his astonishing feat of flight, solo, transatlantic, instilled in every son of the land, native-born or not, a fiber of pride, the image of a home-grown hero, personifying a Spirit of St Louis; all summer long, the record run of the Bambino, Babe Ruth, set-ting a new standard every day, every time at bat. All of it was shadowed by the oncoming cloud of Sacco and Vanzetti, a purple shroud.

For Tony LaStoria, an overpowering reality had set in. He no longer knew what to make of where he had been, or where he was going. History itself had taken a detour. He had be-come so enamored of drinking in all the events of the day, in all their glorious panorama, in the newspapers, down to the last dregs, in the days of the Great War. Well, back then, things were black-and-white. You knew where you stood. There was right and there was wrong. America was right, and righteous, and her path was clear, and you could back her to the hilt, and even take the step of becoming a legalized American, without hesitation, and feel proud.

In the *Boston Globe,* and indeed, the *New York Times,* both of which Tony still followed avidly, to keep informed, to edu-cate himself, the renowned historian, H.G. Wells, was quoted as saying that Sacco and Vanzetti was a case "by which the soul of people is tested and displayed." One phrase arrested Tony's mind, when Wells called America "the most powerful and civilized Union on earth . . ." That phrase rang hollow to Tony. The part about *most civilized*—it wasn't true. *Not any more.* And so Tony found that the sense of pride he used to take, in pulling himself up, from an outsider to a citizen, from an *alien* to a man who *belonged*, this pride had been eaten away by seven relentless years of doubt, foreboding and dismay. It died, finally, in the electric chair at the Charlestown Jail.

In spite of everything, or perhaps in contrast, Gigi's latest pregnancy came to fruition, as usual, at her mother's house on Prince Street in the North End, in May of 1927, when she delivered the most beautiful child of theirs that she and Tony had yet seen, an opinion they formed and shared and agreed upon as soon as they first set eyes on baby Anna. They smiled at one another with the thought in their minds that at last they were finally getting it right. This infant delighted them so that they felt uplifted by naming her for Gigi's mother, Anna-Lisa, and never mind that the fatuous Anna-Vittoria, Gigi's noisome sister, would claim a share of reflected glory in the baby's name: let her, this was no time to quibble, it was cause for celebration, and the tide of emotion that swept over them was one of elation and fulfillment of long-cherished hopes, dreams and beliefs about themselves and their children.

It was a consolation to the child's father, Tony LaStoria. How could one be discouraged by the big world when in the small universe of the family such beauty and grace could be born into existence?

But Gigi's mother, the midwives, and the doctor, whom they had called in, were all telling Gigi that she could not have more children; that she was killing herself. She gripped Tony's hand tightly when they talked about this, and he had tears in his eyes. "No, no, no—we must take care of you now," he said.

Gigi was devastated. This could not be. She was supposed to have nine children. It was written in the stars. She herself had prophesied it. It was carved in adamantine letters in the book of life. In spite of the surge of pride prompted by the arrival of this most beautiful infant, Gigi became depressed. Never before had she felt this low after childbirth. Always there had been more of her vigorous, strong, youthful life to look ahead to. Now she could not lift her spirits above the bottom edge of a green windowshade pulled down. "No, no, no—we must take care of you now," Tony kept repeating. They were not the kind of people to dream up varieties of *amore;* they only knew one way to make love. To them, love between a man and his wife had only one purpose: to make babies, for it was their children who bestowed upon Tony and Gigi immortality, their children who enabled them to live forever, beyond their own deaths. These inchoate feelings, these suspicions, bordering on superstitions, never entered conscious thought; nevertheless, they were there. They were the solid rock, the foundation of their belief in life itself. They knew nothing about anything someone might call birth control. Why would anyone want to do that? To make love *without love?*

It was sad, it was tragic, but what could they do? They only knew one way to prevent childbirth, and that was to abstain. Gigi was going to lose him. She knew it.

After all the main events of that fateful year of 1927 had come and gone, after the first transatlantic telephone call was made, from New York City to London, after the Great Mississippi Flood, the greatest natural disaster in America history, after Silent Cal spoke, to announce "I do not choose to run for President in 1928;" after the Columbia Broadcasting system opened its doors and went on the air with 47 radio stations;

after a horse named *Bostonian* won the Preakness Stakes; after the Holland Tunnel, the first link between New York City and New Jersey, was opened; after Henry Ford unveiled his first new model since 1908, the Model A; after the American Helen Moody Wills won Wimbledon; after Jerome Kern and Oscar Hammerstein opened the original Broadway musical, Edna Ferber's *Showboat*; after Lindbergh's flight, and after the Bambino hit his 60th homer, and after Gene Tunney stunned the world in September by defeating Jack Dempsey in the infamous "Long-Count" Heavyweight Championship Bout at Soldier Field in Chicago; and after the execution of Sacco and Vanzetti: Thanksgiving came, as it did every year.

In the LaStoria family, this was their one great "American" holiday of the year, when Gigi cooked and served nothing but American dishes, which she learned how to do from the Fanny Farmer Cookbook: there was, of course, a 22-lb turkey (a lot of people to feed), mashed potatoes, and yams; stuffing, made with Gigi's own special touch, in which she fried up a whole loaf of American bread, diced small, rolled it in a bowl with chopped onions, garlic and seasonings, and then soaked the entire lumpy ball in liberal doses of vinegar before stuffing it into the turkey; oh how delicious it came out! a separate platter of roast beef, for those who did not care for turkey; also, one of roasted, sliced mutton-leg; (a bake-dish of lasagna, of course, Gigi's one concession, for how could they eat a big holiday dinner without any traditional Italian dish at all!); green beans and corn from the can; but also roasted chestnuts, jarred red peppers in olive oil, a bottle of anisette, and of course, jellied cranberry sauce, grown right here on the South Shore; and a variety of Italian pastries and cookies from almond biscotti to pizelle to creamy canolli, straight from Romano's Italian Bakery in Stoughton Square.

Over the years the tradition in the family had formed that on Thanksgiving Day, the two sisters, Gigi and Anna-Vittoria, like the Indians in the old days of the Wampanoag tribe on the South Shore, would smoke the peace-pipe, and get together at Tony and Gigi's house, for the holiday, so that their children could get to know one another as first cousins.

For in truth. Anna-Vittoria, against all predictions, had not devolved into spinsterhood, but had found herself a man to marry and give her children of her own. Gigi was acidly sure that this occurred because Anna-Vittoria was jealous of her younger sister, the popular favorite of their Papa, herself, the magnificent, the one-and-only *Gigi*; but she had to bury her thoughts and be on her best behavior for the holiday, for the sake of the kids.

The trouble was that awful and abhorrent husband of hers, Ennio Abruzzo. This could have been predicted, that Anna-Vittoria would have to scrape the bottom of the barrel to find anyone loathsome enough to actually couple with her. Ennio Abruzzo was a *contadino* who came from the steep-shouldered neighborhood of Acerenza, an ancient town in ancient Basilicata, between the toe and the heel, a town perched 800 meters above sea level, whose only redeeming feature was a broken-down old 11th-century Romanesque cathedral of dull camel-colored stone; a town which even featured an Arab sector, God knows how or why, since the truth was buried in the graveyard of time; a town, in which, if you stood in the highest street and looked down, the beautiful azure Mediterranean was but a blue haze in the distance. Ennio Abruzzo was a peasant from the hills who worked here in America as a seasonal farmworker, which meant that from October until April, he didn't work at all, but lived at home on Prince Street with his wife, children and in-laws, Gigi's parents, Anna-Lisa and Pasquale, who felt sorry for their daughter Anna-Vittoria, who had a husband who couldn't support a family. It was possible that the cranberry sauce on Gigi and Tony's Thanksgiving Day table in Stoughton had come from cranberries picked by this Abruzzo himself!

Tony did not care for Ennio Abruzzo because the man did not even attempt to make polite conversation at the dinner table when invited for Thanksgiving. The dialect of Basilicata was indecipherable to Italians from elsewhere, and ugly to their ears. What was the man taking about when he rhapsodized to himself about the famous native dishes of his hometown, which he called *maccaroun a desch't* (handmade macaroni) and *z'zridd* (lentils and beans with pasta); when he bragged about the local wine, the ruby-red *Aglianico?* The always meticulously clean-shaven Tony did not like the way the man waxed the tips of his moustache, either.

But there were two adorable children, a boy and a girl, to think about, first cousins of his own children. These were Guy, the older, and his sister Lorraine. Why on earth the pretentious Anna-Vittoria had given French names to their children Tony could not fathom. But in all fairness, the children themselves were innocent in the sight of God, and they could not help that they could not choose their parents, could they?

After dinner, washing dishes, the two sisters were whispering, in dialect, out in the kitchen. "I'm not having any more children, that I can tell you," said Anna-Vittoria.

"Why, what's wrong with you?" said Gigi.

"Never you mind. I don't have to tell you everything, do I? Besides, there's nothing wrong with me. It's that man."

"He's your husband."

"And you're my sister. And both of you love me, don't you!"

It's impossible! thought Gigi.

Anna-Vittoria, determined to get in the last word, said, "And you better not have any more pregnancies, either, if you know what's good for you!"

A few weeks later, near Christmas, when the kids were all on school-vacation week coming up, on a Sunday night, the little family of Gigi's sister arrived again in Stoughton. Back at Thanksgiving, the children had cooked up a scheme together that they should be allowed to spend a week in the country playing with their first cousins, as a special treat for their good behavior all year long; a wish that, of course, their parents, on both sides, hurried to grant, for their own reasons: Anna-Vittoria and Ennio, to be rid of them, Tony and Gigi out of sympathy and a sense of obligation to poor Guy and Lorraine.

On this occasion, Ennio Abruzzo seemed to have his mind made up that he was going to drain that whole gallon of home-made wine Tony placed on the table between them, which he had neglected to do, or been prevented from, last time, on Thanksgiving Day.

The evening wore on with the young cousins happily chatting and socializing, till Tony got up and excused himself, to go to the window of the dining room and look out.

"Hmm," said Tony. "It's snowing."

When he returned to the table, he advised Ennio to maybe slow down on the *vino* as it was looking like the roads might get bad. (He didn't want to come right out and say, *Don't you think you should get going?*)

Chief of Police O'Brian sent an officer over to knock on the front door of the LaStorias' house late that evening, actually, after midnight.

Tony had fallen asleep in his big armchair. Everyone else had gone to bed, the children to stay up talking all night, Gigi because of the big evening meal she had cooked, and consumed. Somehow, she always over-ate in the presence of Anna-Vittoria, who made her nervous and guilty.

Now Tony sprung awake instantly, because nobody ever knocked on their front door this late at night . . .

He flung open the door, prepared to scold whoever it was bothering them, only to find a cop standing there, shivering, shoulders covered in snow.

"There's been an accident. The Chief thinks you should come and identify the bodies. Sorry. We couldn't get here earlier because we had a tough time with the wreck. And we didn't know for sure who they were."

The police had pulled the bodies of the married couple from the death-car. Wintertime. Ice, tire-marks on the snow, and a tree. On the long straight and narrow of Pine Street in Stoughton, there was one curve where the road bent. This was where it happened. The bodies were laid out on the snow under police tarps.

Tony was distraught. Gigi insisted it was not his fault. Tony said, of course, they would take in their little niece and nephew, who were now orphans.

Prohibition was still in force, but the police did not make an issue of or carry out any investigating into the source of the wine. They knew the victims were Italian, or Italian-American; drinking wine was synonymous with the way of life of these people, as was law-breaking. The police had other things to do besides worrying about how many Italians killed themselves drinking and driving. For instance, those two anarchist murderers, Sacco and Vanzetti. Convicted of the brutal murder of two shoe-shop employees in a payroll office, one of whom was a fellow Italian immigrant! That will tell you all you need to know! After seven long years, awaiting execution, the case of the two Italian anarchist murderers had become, somehow, the "Trial of the Century," and an international *Cause célèbre*. This was what made the police officers of Stoughton, Massachusetts, shake their heads in disgruntled wonder when they thought about Italians, if they thought about Italians at all: the condemned prisoners Sacco and Vanzetti, and all the trouble their case, their incarceration, the protests, the agitation, had caused, and were still causing, the police. So what if these scum, these wops kill themselves off in a car? So much the better. *You can count on these ignorant dagoes to reduce the surplus population of goddam foreigners for the rest of us, all by themselves!*

They were sitting up in bed, as usual. For the thousandth time, or it seemed, the millionth, Tony told her, "It wasn't your fault."

And Gigi said, bitterly, holding back sudden tears, "It was *all* my fault! If you only knew how many times I wished it!"

"Gigi—you can't make things happen by thinking them."

"You know as well as I do, Antonio, that if you so much as think a thing—you can't take it back!"

"So—be careful what you wish for!"

"*She* should have married you, I know that. And I stole you away from her!"

"I would have never married her, *may God forgive me for speaking ill of the dead.*"

"She'd be alive today!"

"Why do you think I was trying to get out that window?" The thought greatly amused Tony, he couldn't help himself.

"It was all my fault those poor kids turned into orphans," said Gigi, "without a mother and father."

"Gigi! *cara mia!* Don't make yourself sick over it! Next thing you know, you'll be throwing yourself into one of your fits!"

"Ah! Exactly! Do you know what this is? It's *The Curse of the Third Eye!*"

"Oh, *mamma-mia!* Gigi! Oh, my God! You can't believe that!"

"Do you know what she told me?"

"Who?"

"Anna-Vittoria, who do you think? She told me she wasn't going to have any more children with that man! She didn't know how right she was!"

And a new fountain of tears poured forth.

Gigi LaStoria did not think about international affairs. She did not think about the local police. About such things she was more or less unawares. With a heavy heart, she took in young Guy, and little Lorraine, her sister's children.

Though she had insisted to Tony that he was never, never to think that any of this was his fault, because of the wine, which he merely offered to a guest, because, *allora,* that's what you do, still, Gigi blamed herself. It was *she* who had hated her own sister. *She* who had stolen her only sister's bridegroom from her.

And so Gigi LaStoria could take no satisfaction from the idea that she had been right, right to trust her powers; that her premonition, her foretelling, her future-sight, had now come true. It was her spells, her *incanti* that told her there was another world, a hidden world, with its own laws, its own gods, that governed this one.

She now had *nine* children under her roof, just as she had foretold, going back all the way to that long-ago day when she and Tony, with their heads together, were watching the water of Boston Harbor from the railing on the waterfront in the North End.

It did not make her feel triumphant; it made her feel cursed; indeed, she felt she had fallen under some kind of evil; yes, that was it, it was the twisting of fate into a perversion: Gigi's only sister had died so that Gigi could have her nine children.

Chapter 16

Fear Itself

Well before the end of the decade, Tony LaStoria was no longer buoying himself up on the swell of the 'Twenties. The end of Sacco and Vanzetti seemed to have driven the final nail into his sense of disillusionment. And 1929 was looming: he would be turning forty years old. *The end of the line . . . all downhill from here . . . might as well be put out to pasture for all the good you'll be, everyone knows that . . .*

In this manner, when the Crash did come, Tony was not alert to the consequences.

He thought, *so what if they're jumping out of windows down on Wall Street. Nothing to do with me.* That was a side effect of the general desuetude his spirits had lapsed into. Tony no longer thought he was going to change the world. Although the local Italian community in Stoughton had rushed to put him in charge of the local chapter of the Sons of Italy, again, *because he had the English,* he no longer thought that would make any difference; anyway, not as long as Puffy O'Brian was Chief of Police.

So Tony fell back in his big armchair at home, which embraced him in the grip of complacency: why should he worry? He was making money. He had a position and it was a lifetime sinecure, since he owed it all to Harry Spritzka, whom he had cultivated for this very reason. To Harry, but also to his own perspicacity, he owed this comfortable existence of his: respected, head of his household, sole support of his big family, pillar of his community, able even to take in two orphans not his own, God help us.

And so the idea that anything at all could happen to shake the *foundations* of the new life, this new *way of life*, that Gigi and himself had forged, (or simply fallen into, by increments, step by step during the past ten years) was beyond conceiving.

Tony could no longer picture the time when he was dependent on streetcars and subways to get around. New York City life, the early days in Boston, were that far in the past of his consciousness. The care and feeding of his automobile not only took up his time, it erased from importance any time before it. The car in the driveway was so convenient, so useful, so *necessary,* that one did not notice it.

Gigi could no longer picture the time when she had dreams of one day having her own life, her own house and garden, most of all, children of her own. Now home and garden and offspring were the overwhelming *everywhere* of her life, constantly underfoot, constantly in need of attention, demanding from minute to minute, so that it seemed she had never known anything else but loading the washing machine, hanging out the clothes, washing the dishes, cleaning the house, making the beds, directing everyone every minute on what to do next, right now, this minute, from stirring the sauce to rubbing out the stains it made on the tablecloth.

But how all this had happened, they no longer knew. It came on them so gradually that nobody could retrace the steps, from one pregnancy to another, one child to the next, one crisis to another.

And yet, would they change anything? Of course not. They were so much better off than they had ever been before. Look at the house. Look at how many rooms. Look at the size of the yard, now that they were in Stoughton instead of Hingham. Room enough for flower garden, grape arbor, tomato plants, a two-car garage for the car (so that Tony was able to use one-half for storage), a kennel for the dogs, a separate quadrangle in back of the house with metal pipes planted in concrete feet, and clotheslines for hanging out the wash to dry. Look at the modern conveniences, from running water, hot and cold, in the kitchen sink (a thing nobody had when they were children), to the indoor bathrooms connected to town sewer lines (not just one bathroom, but two) to the clothes-washer with the crank-handle wringers, to the modern, spacious icebox, to the coal-fired furnace in the cellar, to the gas stove, white now, not black, (no more cast-iron) to the phonograph, to the radio (now not a crystal set, but a handsome piece of furniture for the parlor, in a modernistic cabinet with doors).

Tony was not one to forbid himself either the latest gadgets or symbols of progress and prosperity. Once there was a powerful radio station in Boston, WBZ, beginning in 1925, putting out a kind of programming that quickly became an overnight sensation, that is, the novelty of music *and* news and even *weather forecasts,* and then *the radio chat hour,* where you never knew what might come up; and then shows that entertained you, like The A&P Gypsies, with bandleader Harry Horlick, whose theme song was "Two Guitars," Tony had to have a good radio. He liked to mine this show for gypsy folk tunes he could use for his new backyard band, which continued the tradition he had started in Hingham, though here in Stoughton, there were no mansions along the shore or rich patrons to hire you out. And then in 1928 a new nightly show debuted, called *Amos'n'Andy*, which made you laugh at life. Now Tony found himself hurrying home whenever his work and traveling permitted so as not to miss *Amos'n'Andy*. Tony had to have a radio, a good one, from one of the new radio stores springing up in every town, and he had to make all the kids sit down and shut up and listen and learn something, from an aria by Caruso on *The Voice of Firestone* to a re-creation of Einstein's discoveries on *Great Moments in History*. It was like a matinee at the movies coming into your own parlor.

How could you compare all this to being boxed into a narrow monk's cell of a building on Prince Street, in the North End? Why would you ever want to go back to that? No. Better to enjoy life a little, while we can, than to dwell on the horrors of the past. *Thanks to God, and my own two hands, those days are gone forever.*

Or so Tony thought.

Ever since they had gotten past the flu epidemic of 1918, and the unemployment woes of 1919, in the business, in his role as General Manager of what was now styled the New England division of *Spritzka Manufacturing and Diversified Industries*, Tony had been riding a crest of expansion. He had no time left over to think or reflect, as his task passed from managing a single factory in Boston, with only one downtown Boston retail storefront, to overseeing plants, and stores, all over Eastern Massachusetts, Rhode Island, and the south coast of Connecticut, not to mention the far north of Manchester, Nashua and Portsmouth in New Hampshire.

For that was the plan Harry Spritzka had held in mind all the while, in his feverish, impatient, planning way, ever since he had sent Tony to Boston originally. Whatever Harry wanted, Tony performed. It was Tony who had to turn Harry's brainstorms into reality on the ground. Nor did Tony ever realize the full extent of Harry Spritzka's machinations, the territory he covered, the enterprises he had gotten into. He knew little or nothing, for instance, of the operation of Harry's clothing manufacture from New York southward into New Jersey and down to Philadelphia. Tony knew only his own territory, eastern Massachusetts, Rhode Island, Connecticut, southern New Hampshire. Nor did he know, or care to find out, more about Harry's further branching, into other fields: real estate, banking, automobile insurance, finance.

Of course he knew of Mimi's background coming from a prominent Jewish family of New York bankers, brother Robert's expanding real estate developer projects and holdings in Manhattan and throughout the city and out in Long Island. But such matters, and such people, were as foreign to Tony as Australian aborigines. He knew of them, but to penetrate their mysteries was another thing. Tony had enough on his hands with his own expanding family at home, now that he had nine mouths to feed. And his duties as a middle manager now overseeing a burgeoning fiefdom of factories and downtown stores in far-flung cities across three states, no, make that four, took him away from home, away from the wife, the kids, the dogs, the grape arbor, the strawberry patch, the *Amos'n'Andy Show,* on long automobile journeys late into the night, to Worcester, Lowell, Milltown, Brockton, Fall River, Haverhill, New Bedford, Providence, New London, Hartford, New Haven.

In each place, Harry had developed a model. He instructed Tony to find the cheapest possible manufacturing space in obsolete or hard-luck red-brick mill buildings, those leftovers of an earlier epoch of the 19th century, usually located on rivers, originally powered by waterpower, re-purposed, but rarely renovated or updated. "Cheap space," Harry called it. But that was not the main thing. Although Harry wanted factory-outlets located on the ground floor of each premises in each town, the real object was to operate a downtown retail location, attractive-looking, expensive-appearing, but with discount pricing, at a corner location, accessible to trolley lines or buses. This was mandatory. For in Harry's experience, everything taught him that it was no use producing clothing to sell to middlemen; you could never obtain justifiable margins unless you owned the retail markup yourself. Why cut someone else in on the deal? If you were going to go to all the trouble and expense, expense, mind you, of growing all this corn, you better own the vegetable stand yourself.

There was no handbook for doing what they were doing. Neither Harry nor Tony went to technical schools or seminars or university to learn how to do this. They were making it up as they went along. There was no school of business at Columbia or Cornell that gave them their ideas. They invented it. They had been doing so, together, since they were teenagers in New York City.

This was what Harry taught Tony, when they had a chance to meet in person, for a catch-up session, which they did, from time to time, on at least three separate occasions, in Harry's rising mansion, on East 91st in Manhattan, during the 'Twenties.

Harry was the theory guy, Tony was the practice guy. Tony was really only interested in doing the same thing over and over again. Much of his value to Harry lay in this predisposition of his. Neither one of them examined it microscopically, but it came naturally to Tony. It's precisely what a tailor did with the sewing in his lap: the same dexterous motions over and over again. Tony left all the designing to Harry's powerful imagination, which forever delighted in detouring into schemes and manipulations. Because clothing was sold mostly to women, as Harry figured (they were the ones who dressed the husband and kids) it had to be fashion-driven: and you better own your own designers. They didn't have to be from Paris (they were living, and operating a garment business, in the golden age of French fashion) you didn't have to employ Jean Patou or Coco Chanel; but you better have your own guys, or women, who could copy a trend, and knock-off a pattern.

For things were forever fast-changing in the 'Twenties. One day women wore corsets, the next they dressed like men. After 1925, everything was above the knee. You better have an adequate women's section in your downtown retail storefront-on-the-corner, or you wouldn't sell any children's or men's clothing. You better have some feather boas floating around, and some cloche hats hanging on the racks. This type of thing did not really interest Tony. Designers were a pain-in-the-ass. He didn't want them in his manufacturing buildings. But Harry was the marketing genius: he realized that you had to have your own brand of clothing, something just a little bit different, a little bit distinctive, something that said *Richard Paul Sportswear*, like the sign over the door: after 1925, everything had to be *sportswear*. What Harry was building was nothing less than a pyramid: the foundation was costs, spread out wide all over the place, held down to the barest minimum possible, and the height and magnificence of the pyramid all came from other people's money, pouring in to purchase the finished goods, until the man at the top, Harry Spritzka, could obtain a commanding view, essentially, for free.

"So I see you got another story built on this place now," said Tony.

"They're still building higher around me!"

They were sitting in their usual places in Harry's second floor livingroom on East 91st, overlooking the corner of Park Avenue, Harry with his back to the bay windows, as he had seen the view before, which disgusted him anyway. And this way, the window-light allowed him to study Tony, who sat facing him. They no longer went out to dinner together. These were business meetings. For Tony, it was just like driving to New Haven, only a little further; and he could take the train instead of having to drive. If Tony got into anything personal, like Harry's children, Harry's attention would wander: he would look out the window, which signaled to Tony: *back to business.*

Between 1920 and 1926, he and Mimi had been blessed with four children, the last two, twins.

It bothered Tony that Harry was much more interested in statistics of volume production, employee hirings, sales totals, than talking about his children. How a man could have four kids, and be indifferent to the fact; not brag, not even bring up their names? Tony had to ask himself. But, like everything with Harry, that was the way it was.

"Real estate, Tony. That's the thing. That's gonna be our salvation. Take my brother. Now there's a smart guy, that Robert. Even I could learn a thing or two from him. As long as we own the buildings on the corner, where our retail sales are paying the mortgage for us, then, if anything ever happens, we've saved our asses, because we own the building. So we don't rent those buildings. Always own. If we can't own it, we don't want it. Find another corner."

Why Harry bothered with these repeated lectures was beyond Tony—except that he had always known that Harry liked the sound of his own voice.

And one other thing: with him, it's never how much we're making, what a good year we had. It's always, look at what we're losing if we don't do this, if we don't do that! No matter how much Harry Spritzka made, he was always losing more!

In hindsight, though it raised objections from the kids, the move to Stoughton proved to be fortuitous for the family when the Crash came. Where would they have put nine kids in the house in Hingham?

And when the Crash did come, suddenly, without warning, Tony went from adding, expanding and hiring to subtracting, shrinking–and layoffs.

Tony kicked himself over all this. *I should have known better,* he thought. *I should have known it couldn't last.*

But hindsight is one hundred percent. In reality, just as prosperity had come upon them gradually, and in the end result, completely effaced what went before, so did the end of the decade.

It was not as if they knew immediately, in October, in November of 1929. Certainly, the news from Wall Street, the talk about a "crash" of the stock market, was alarming. But nobody, not even Harry, whose eye for a dollar was acute, thought it was the end of something, or the beginning of something else.

Harry said, "Don't worry, it's almost the end of the year. Things'll pick up again, you'll see. Next year's right around the corner."

Nobody ever plans for contraction. In this life we love to lead, we think only of going up, up, up. Nobody ever dreams of one day landing in the gutter. It's nobody's ambition. It's nobody's idea of how things will be when we finally grow up. We only know "better"—"new and improved"—"Buy now, pay later." *So how in the hell could anyone have been prepared?*

There were signs, but they weren't road-signs, they weren't as big as billboards. You'd have to interpret tea-leaves; you'd have to be a clairvoyant to know ahead of time.

So, to say they had no warning was not completely true. It would be more accurate to say that they just could not imagine how bad things could get. Because next year was always right around the corner. And things were bound to get better.

But they didn't. Next year—turned out to be worse than last year.

After two or three years of this kind of thing, people began to lose hope. It began to seem like everyone they knew, in the neighborhood, in the town, friends, neighbors, even family, was out of work. Nobody had any money. You couldn't buy anything, only try to hang on to what you had. Why didn't somebody do something about it?

Tony had always seen himself as a benefactor. He had survived, through persistence, through connections, and his luck, and arrived at a position in life where he had the ability to give someone a job, in other words, help them out. As long as they were willing to work, he was happy to help. After all, you had to know somebody. Isn't that how Tony himself got to where he was? because he knew somebody? A big somebody. An important somebody. A somebody with money. And that gave Tony power, and influence, to sway people, even control their lives, but, also, to provide for them. That was the way of the world. Everything depended on the guy at the top.

Tony's position was in the middle of the pyramid. But he still reflected the glory. Because he, too, had the power to bestow upon a person, man or woman, with a family to feed at home, a job. These were not hand-outs, not charity. You had to work for your living, but that meant you were allowed to take pride in yourself. That was a boon you could bestow on people. Tony gloried in that feeling, that he distributed these benefactions, because he had risen up through his own hard work, because he had been just smart enough to get himself over to this country, and from the streets, learn enough English. Everything came from that; *that was the key, come to think of it.* That was why people turned to him, and even elected him as the President of something, because he was able to give them a job.

Now he had to take away the job.

He felt like a crook. Like a criminal. As if he had personally hoodwinked them. There was nothing he could say. He couldn't look them in the eye. He hated it. He hated himself. But what could he do? He felt like he was throwing them out in the street. He had used them and now he was throwing them away. To push his Buick from town to town and repeatedly close down a storefront, or a manufacturing site, to scale back to skeleton staffs, to have to say to people, "We have no orders, we can't sell what's already on the racks, what're we gonna do? eat the stuff?" To say, "I'm sorry," over and over again, in Worcester, Lowell, Milltown, Brockton, Fall River, Haverhill, New Bedford, Providence, New London, Hartford, New Haven. To drive from place to place, in the night, in the dawn, in the late afternoon, with darkness descending, to stay in a cheap room over-night, in a boarding house above a corner grocery store in an out-of-the-way place like Marlborough, where everyone depended on the last remaining mill-building in the town that was operating, and to spend the following day, in that building, putting padlocks on all the doors . . .

When 1929 arrived, Tony was just turning forty years old.

His oldest boy, Patsy, was already 15 years old. He had six more besides him. Tony thought of them by their American names, Mary, Peggy, Genie, Gerry, Augie and Anna, the baby. Then there were Guy and Lorraine, the children of his poor dead sister-in-law Anna-Vittoria. Every time he thought about it, Tony cringed. Their mother and father died in that awful burning wreck of a car-crash, on a night so frozen with ice that the policemen who tried to rescue them couldn't get any water going to douse the flames. Tony hoped those two poor kids never learned the truth of how their parents died. *What an awful picture to plant in their minds.*

Come to think of it . . . isn't it just the same image that was planted in my mind when Laura Antonelli died, her tender breathing flesh burnt to crisp black curling edges like newspapers discarded in a rusted old oil drum, all those years ago? He squeezed his eyes shut tight. Christ!

He and Gigi, then, had nine kids in the house, with ages ranging from going on four years old to fifteen, all depending on Tony.

As if he were not discouraged enough already, all Tony had to do was to think of those two poor kids, and of how, when he was ten years old himself, his own uncle, Zi'Eugenio, instead of shutting the door in his face, had taken him in.

And what did Uncle Eugenio have then? Another mouth to feed—with what? It did not seem possible that they could ever return to the way they were living then—in three rooms on Mott Street, in 1900—fourteen people.

But now the country had conceded that it was in a depression, an unprecedented Depression, with a capital "D"—the like of which had never been seen before, in living memory. And everyone was frightened. Worried. Nervous. The only thing left to them was to try to hang on.

As the calendar turned to 1931 and 1932, discouragement turned to despair. No one believed any longer in next year. The President himself had stated that he did not believe it was the government's role to intervene. No one was listening anymore.

But Tony took it upon himself to be the one in his own house who would make them listen.

In his parlor, in Stoughton, he convened them all, to sit around the radio, in a semi-circle, on chairs, cushions, the sofa, cross-legged on the floor. All the kids, all nine of them, even Gigi, though she protested she would not understand a word (always her convenient excuse)—(she understood more than she wanted to let on.) This time Tony had to over-rule her other excuse, too—"I have work to do!"

"We all have work to do," said Tony. "That's why you're gonna sit down and listen, like all the rest. Genie—get a chair for your mother to sit on."

When Genie had done that, Tony cleared his throat, then stood up from his chair (the kids called it his throne—no one was allowed to sit there but him, though Genie never had paid any attention to that taboo.) "Any of you ever remember me making a speech, eh?" They all shook their heads. The younger ones sat cross-legged on the floor thinking they were in for it now, the older kids, especially Patsy and Peggy, wondered what he thought he was up to. "Well, times have changed. We're in a Depression now, and that means we got a lotta work to do. I gotta grow more food in the backyard than I did before, because now, I'm the President of the Sons of Italy in this town, and with so many members out of work, I gotta help out my friends and neighbors by putting whatever food on their tables I can. They would do the same for me if the position was reversed. Don't ever forget that. We can't wait for the government to help us. If we don't help one another, who will? God helps those who help themselves. Don't ever forget that, either. That's all."

Gigi had to stretch a dollar further than ever before, and she made it her personal mission that none of the children on their street would go hungry, even if she had to give them all soup made out of nothing but pork-bones and rice. And Gigi did not care who the kids were, Italian, Irish, Polish: they even had a few Indians from the Wampanoag tribe still living in Stoughton and Canton: her back door was open to them all.

As long as Tony and Gigi had something, they knew how to share it, and they were going to expect from their own children the same. So it was not at all difficult to recruit more and more kids all the time for the back-door soup-line. And Tony had recruited his own boys, Gene and Augie, and their cousin Guy, and taught them to learn their way around the shotgun and the hunting rifle and the bird-dogs, and sent them out to the woods and the marshes around Ponkapoag for quail and pheasant and rabbits and even, yes, squirrel. There was food in the woods, and it was free. You didn't have to pay for it; so nobody need go hungry, really; all they had to learn was how to fend for themselves.

Thank God they were not cooped up in the North End of Boston: those poor people, what can they do?

Just as Tony sent out the boys with the hunting rifle and shotgun, so Gigi sent out the girls, Mary, Peggy and Gerry, and cousin Lorraine—not Anna, she was still so little. Gigi sent the girls out into the woods to pick berries, so they would be gone for hours at a time, sometimes the whole day, and come home again, in the picking season, loaded down by the bushel-basket. You would see them coming three-abreast with two bushels held by the wire handles between them, loaded up with blueberries and blackberries, so that when winter came, there was something to spread on a slice of bread, as Gigi marshalled her girls into making preserves to put up in Mason jars in the cellar.

With all his far-flung buildings in cities all over reduced down to skeleton crews, for maintenance and keeping an eye on things till business should pick up again, Tony was more at home than he used to be. But that did not mean he could work any the less. Whereas, he used to think *maybe when I've turned forty, I can slow down a little. I oughta take it easy, I'll be getting old,* when he was actually well into his forties, that's when the country went completely flat, and instead of reducing, he had to redouble his efforts. In the end, he needed those bird-dogs more than he ever had. They were no longer a luxury, a country squire's pastime, they now had to be turned into working dogs, who helped to provide for the family. And so he had to keep the bird-dogs happy, well-fed and cared-for, and yapping around his heels.

Patsy, at 15, was well beyond the age where you were eligible for your work-permit, so he was sent out not to shoot rabbits but to find himself a job so that he could bring cash money into the house for his mother, to help out the family. So Patsy had to quit school, and he found a job waiting tables at *Mamma Leone's* Italian Restaurant in Stoughton Square, but one night he came home early and told them he'd quit because Mamma's husband wanted him to bus tables and take out the trash for the same money, and he said he wouldn't without a raise in pay. His father jumped up and said, "What are you, stupid?" And he cuffed Patsy with the heel of his hand on the side of his head, right on his ear, so that Patsy's hand flew up to massage out the sting while he staggered, more from surprise, than from the force, and yelled, "Pa!" in a whining voice. His father then pointed a finger at him. "You're not so big I can't take you over my knee, you just remember that." Tony LaStoria threw his newspaper down on his chair, and stalked out of the parlor in a fury.

In the kitchen, he stood there turning round and round, fuming. He had never lost his temper with the children in quite this way before, that he could remember. But he had to make an example out of Patsy, or the rest of them might get it into their heads to ignore him and go their own way. *Funny how you could command a troop of dogs and get them trained to do exactly what you wanted, but with people! it's a different story.*

His daughter Peggy then came out to the kitchen and made a point of crossing in front of him to run herself a glass of water in the sink. She turned with the glass in her hand and looked at him, then she drank it down in one long, satisfying gulp, smacking her lips and issuing forth with a loud burp, tom-boy that she was. She said to Tony, "You gonna make me quit school, too?"

"How old are you, Peggy?"

"I'll be fourteen this year."

"That's old enough for your work permit, right?"

"Yeah."

"So what do you think? Or is there something special about you, that you can't help out the family?"

"Well, maybe it won't be so bad. I'll have a little money of my own to buy a lipstick for myself."

Her father turned purple. "You just bring your pay envelope home and hand it over to your mother, and never mind about lipstick!"

Now it was 1933, and there was a new man in office. A lot of promises; was it all just campaign hooey? Well, one thing was for sure: no President of theirs had ever invited himself into their front room for his Inaugural Address before the Congress in Washington. So, Tony had the boys gather the wood, and they started a fire in the fireplace, in the parlor, on Pine Street, in Stoughton, and Tony got his herd of untrained kids to assemble themselves, and, this time, to pay attention. And the man came on the Zenith console set loud and clear to reassure them that things were indeed about to change, and that they had nothing to fear but "fear itself."

When President Roosevelt was finished, Tony said to them, "Well, you heard what the man had to say." And he did not ask his children for their opinions, or open anything to discussion, or encourage a debate, or anything of the kind. In Tony LaStoria's world, in his family, there was a dictatorship of one, and he was the one. What Tony LaStoria expected of them was that his children would do what they were told.

So he said, "Now, look, nobody in this house is going on relief. Just remember, as long as you can work, you'll never go hungry. You look around yourselves and take a look at Patsy here. Maybe he's not the sharpest stick in the woodpile, but he can work."

Patsy had gotten a job in a filling station pushing a screwdriver and an oil-rag. But when he had gotten laid off, because nobody was buying gas anymore, Tony had taken his boy to work with him every day, and used him for whatever he needed done, from sweeping floors to machine maintenance. And he made sure Patsy got paid, and he made sure Patsy gave it to his mother every week; who, of course, gave him back a little change for himself, so he wouldn't have to feel like he was penniless and had to go around pulling out his empty pockets.

Patsy's Pa concluded this speech by declaring, "You're all gonna work, and help out the family, if I got anything to say about it."

Nobody moved a muscle. The combination of the President and their father was too much for them. Except for Peggy—who was sticking her tongue out at Mary.

Their father said, "And that goes double for you two."

But he was looking at Peggy when he said it.

Chapter 17

A Tale of Two Weddings

The children of the LaStorias, as they grew, never thought of themselves as poor. The Depression was for other people. Those poor people way out west in the dustbowl. Those poor fathers and mothers who were out of work, in Hingham or Hartford or Houston, Texas; the ones who had to stand in breadlines, or by fate or luck or whatever chance or circumstance were forced to beg for a living, reduced to soup lines to feed their kids. The children of the LaStorias later would boast that they had never missed a meal in their lives.

As they grew, in their house on Pine Street in Stoughton, the children of the LaStoria family, each in their own way, like branches off a tree, sought the sky, individually, and carved a crooked path, often wayward, seldom straight; but their common ground was their mother. She was the soil of their nourishment. She was the element in which they sunk their roots, in order to grow.

There was no getting around Ma. Now Pa, he was out of the house everyday. Even when he was not out of town on his trips, he came home only when the workday was over.

It was Ma who ran the house, beginning at daybreak, getting them all off to school, shooing Tony out along with them. She was there when they walked home for lunch, she was there after school, to listen to their stories, to scold and nag them for their transgressions. There was no way to hide from Ma.

But as they grew, they also saw Gigi, in their midst, at their center, with an evolving skepticism, because their mother was hopelessly outmoded and old-world, and clung to her Italian ways with, it seemed to them, increasing suspicion.

Sometimes it was hard to tell how much she knew, or whether she was only pretending. When they had *Baby Snooks* on the radio, or the *Follies of the Air* show, and they were all laughing, they could see their mother watching them for her cue to laugh: so had she not really understood? But at other times, she understood only too well, when she found them whispering their secrets in English, and she caught them up in Italian.

But it was tiring for Gigi. Raising so many children was wearing on the spirit. The first one, even the first two, were like a voyage with Columbus, discovery over every horizon. But after that, even with the third and the fourth, not only did you know beforehand what to expect, it was already stale bread.

After a time, because her oldest girl, Maria, aped her every action, and modeled herself as a little helper, or actually, a second mother, Gigi would let skip half the little tasks she used to perform, such as buttoning up their shirts and blouses for them, or ironing their handkerchiefs. Maria had beaten her to it, it was done already. Not only was the child attentive and obedient at school, she was a horse for housework. The girl never stopped, morning, noon or night. Maria did not play with dolls, she had mending in her lap; she darned socks and patched knees and elbows. God knows why this daughter had taken it on herself, but Gigi suspected it was out of pity. Maria was such a sensitive child, she knew precisely when her mother was worn out of patience, or tired beyond reason. Somehow Gigi resented this: she did not want pity, she wanted worship, she wanted respect, she wanted love, love, love.

Which was increasingly hard to obtain as time wore on. Gigi no longer liked what she saw in the mirror. She had become a shapeless mound of woe. It was awful. She supposed it was due to so many pregnancies. She blamed it on her prolapsed uterus. Who knew what effects such a thing had? How could you feel the same? Perhaps it played with your mind—perhaps it poisoned your emotions. Nowadays she no longer thought of having Tony buy her a nice new dress to put on. She no longer believed he even wanted to look at her. She did not want to look at herself.

After she had saved her darling young Augie from the clutches of death, and then became pregnant with Anna, accidentally, as she thought, Gigi actually became quite desperately worried. She had been warned (and Tony, too, feared it) that they had violated medical advice. But when Anna was born in 1928, both of them realized that was the end.

And so what then would happen to their love?

Gigi no longer went out to the movies or the theater; they were so far out of town, and she did not drive; Tony was always gone on a trip. Even to go to the corner store, which, in Stoughton, was a mile away, near the Square, she sent the kids.

So, on an evening at home, with the dishes done, she would gather the girls with her around the dining-room table for cards or the Ouija board.

The boys, Patsy, Genie and Augie, and their cousin, Guy, disdained such girls' games, just as they looked down on housework as woman's work, though they never refused to do it, if they were told to. But the girls, Maria, Peggy and Gerry, joined in. Anna was not yet old enough, but of course, cousin Lorraine was always included. All the children were past the age now for bedtime stories so Gigi had to invent other ways to keep a hold on them.

But as they grew older, she felt them slipping away from her. It did not escape Gigi that the adoring phase of "Mamma" and "Papa," on their lips, had given way to an abbreviated "Ma" and "Pa."

One night, as they were going to bed, Gigi said to Tony, "You have to do something about that Margherita."

"What is it now?" he sighed. The boys were so much simpler.

"She's having boys come over to the house."

"What? When I'm not here!"

"They don't have to run after her. She chases them!"

In his own mind, Tony was not so concerned about Peggy, as he preferred to call her. He thought of her as one who had an instinct, when it came to the opposite sex, of how to enthrall them, while *veramente*, she disdained them. That one surrendered nothing. She made *them* suffer.

But it was the idea that this daughter, who had been nothing but trouble from the start, was now violating a code, as unwritten as it might be. *She knows better. That's not how I brought her up! She has no respect! And she's too old now to go switching her bottom!*

"Well, what are you going to do about it!" he demanded of Gigi.

"You're her father!"

"A lot of good that does me."

"You're the one who always encouraged her!"

"Me!"

"Yes, you! When she wanted to climb a tree? You stood there and applauded. When she wanted to play baseball with the boys, you said, why not! Let her burn off some of that energy!"

"It seemed like a good idea at the time!"

Tony was trying his best to see the humor in the situation, but Gigi was not laughing.

"And so now you have to put your foot down!"

He turned to her, amazed. "I have to put *my* foot down? What have I been doing all these years? Whenever I come home, and I find you reduced to tears, almost! it's always me, always *me*, you turn to, when you can't get them to mind you. Why must I be always the disciplinarian?"

"Because that's your job. You're the father!"

"Some father." Tony was verging on a bitter reflection. Fatherhood in this day and age had become something abhorrent in the eyes of the world, the changing world. And so he said to Gigi, with a rancor he could not keep out of his voice, "That's the job *you* always assigned me to!"

Gigi was hurt, terribly hurt, by that throwaway remark. She said, "And another thing!"

"Oh, go on! What else! Let's start a list!"

"What do you propose to do about Maria?"

Gigi crossed her arms on her chest; she was ready for this fight.

"Her, too! That girl's an angel. You don't know how lucky you are!"

"Do you remember what year your angel was born?"

"Yes, I do. 1916. It was the year before the war, the year I signed up to get my papers, two years after Patsy!"

"Then you realize she's turning 20 years old this year!"

"What about it?"

"She's not married, is she? What do you propose to do about that? Her father, you call yourself! You haven't lifted your little finger for the poor girl. You think she's getting any younger? And how many do you spy, with your all-seeing eyes, chasing after her? Do you want the poor thing to see all her sisters, right down to baby Anna, married! while she sits on the side of the altar, holding their trains for them, mending their gowns when they get a rip!"

"What are you trying to say, Gigi? That's my job, too? getting Maria married off?"

"Do you think that poor young lady, as saintly as she is, is going to attract any attention, from anyone! You've convinced her, all her life, she's too ugly to even look at!"

"Well, whose side of the family does she take after? Not mine!"

"And not mine! We never had walnuts growing on our tree!"

Tony could have sworn he'd been given a respite, as Gigi was grinning, in spite of herself. But when Gigi saw the twinkle gleaming in her husband's eye, she reset her crossed arms, erased her face, and redoubled her fury. "Antonio!—this is serious. It's not funny. What do you think your precious 'Peggy' is going to do? Sit on her hands and wait for her sister?"

"Eh, she takes after you!"

That ended the conversation. Tony had touched on a very sore subject. He should have known better than to remind Gigi of her victory over her dead rival, Anna-Vittoria. (It was Gigi's father, the boastful Pasquale Fabrizio, the butcher, Peggy's grandfather, who went around proclaiming that this Peggy took after her mother, Gigi, and not that shriveled-up prune

Anna-Vittoria, thanks be to God!) Gigi sat there next to him in bed staring at Tony. She was looking intently. Sitting up in bed with her arms crossed. He was sitting on the edge of the bed; actually, his back was turned to her, he was looking over his shoulder, after removing his shoes; he was down to his tee-shirt, with the straps over the shoulders. Gigi's face was going slowly ash-colored. Her features were settling into stone, gradually draining down into a mask, like the visage of Medusa. She was looking at him while uttering not a word and he had the sinking feeling come over him that a mood of baleful evil was creeping into the bedroom, that she was forming in her mind some vindictive curse to throw at him.

Tony turned away, and sat there, disconsolate, in his shirt and trousers, for a long time, his palms flat at his sides on the bed, and for a long time he could not escape the feeling, which came into his mind in the form of a sentence, unfinished: *in all these years, we have never once so much as disagreed . . .*

It seemed a very long time he was sitting there, when he felt her hand on his back, caressing.

He turned, expecting to find that he had been forgiven, but she only said, "Come to sleep, Antonio. I know you don't love me any more. Not like you used to. But at least you could take pity on me."

Within the year, Tony had found a husband for Maria.

Taking himself to be no good at things like this, he secretly visited his father-in-law, Fabrizio, the butcher, for advice, without telling anyone. He found him on his deathbed, in the same house on Prince Street, in the North End. The old man had lost his wife two years before this. *That woman was a saint.*

Anyone who put up with Pasquale Fabrizio like she did deserved to be canonized.

It was about this time that Tony, unbidden, had begun to honestly feel a deep, aching sorrow for Gigi. His poor wife had lost her beloved mother, Anna-Lisa; and now, Tony could see, it would not be long before she lost the father she doted upon as well.

Pasquale Fabrizio had no hope of hanging on long enough to see the first wedding of a grandchild. But as a last gesture, he welcomed the chance to do this much, a little something. He said to Tony, with a forlorn look, "But what's the matter, son? Why don't you just call up Brooklyn? She's the one who brought you to Gigi. Or have you forgotten?"

"Papa—I haven't seen her for years."

"She's gone back to her own family? in New York?"

"Must have. Times go by. You lose track."

"Lemme see what I can do."

Though he no longer was at the butcher-shop every day, Fabrizio put in a call to the people who had taken over, and he located a likely man, who used to be his own customer, a guy who never said much, but who had that lonely look about him of a bachelor, a permanent bachelor. Pasquale could tell: he was always shopping for one, only one. Besides, he liked the idea that this one was a quiet fellow. He was a Calabrian. A little off the beaten path. English not so good. Everybody called him 'Charlie,' but his name was Renato Laverna. He was maybe thirty years old already—a good eight or ten years older than poor Maria—but perhaps that was a reason why he would not pass up this chance. Evidently, no one else wanted him; he was not exactly a charmer of ladies. Pasquale and Tony both shrugged. The man had a good job, also permanent. He was a tailor at the alterations counter in Jordan Marsh. Tony had met him there once, and he knew that people laughed at him for his broken English—when Renato Laverna spoke of his well-known workplace, Jordan Marsh, it came out *"Giorgio Marscia."* But in the Depression, that was a good job for a man to hang on to. At least he would be able to support her. The fact that he was in the same trade as the family counted as a plus to Tony.

To everyone's surprise, Maria fell madly in love with him. For about six weeks, she retired to her bedroom, in order to write love poetry. Her brothers and sisters, her cousins, too, went about holding a finger to their lips, astounded. They could not believe the change that had come over their sister. She spent hours in the afternoon on the edge of her bed just looking out the window at the trees and flowers and once in a while writing a line or two in her notebook with a pencil. She no longer went around the house looking for tasks to do that no one else would ever think of, such as trimming the claws on the feet of her father's bird-dogs.

When it came closer to the wedding, they first had to attend a funeral, and at the wake they held in the narrow house on Prince Street, Maria was on her knees before her grandfather's open casket, weeping as she prayed, while Peggy kept a furiously stoic face on, Gerry looked pained, and they all, except for Peggy, crowded around their mother Gigi, who was destroyed with grief, and needed people to help her in and out of her seat.

Tony thought for certain this was going to spoil the wedding, which was scheduled for the same month, June of 1936.

At the wake, the boys breezily crossed themselves and went looking for drinks and shoving-matches in the other room with the uncles, Agostino and Aldo, whom they rarely saw anymore.

And then, at the wedding, Maria looked absolutely beatific in the white dress Gigi had sewn for her by hand. Tony was amazed. Never before had he walked a daughter down the aisle. She looked radiant on his arm. In spite of the cost of this extravagant wedding he was throwing for her, with all the family and guests, he was actually glad of every penny he had spent. No man could have ever deserved a daughter as saintly as this one. In every fiber of her being she lived up to the Holy Virgin she had been named for. In all his life, Tony had never thought he could be as proud as he was at this moment.

When guests at the wedding saw Gigi crying, they assumed they were the usual tears of the mother of the bride at a daughter's wedding. They could not know that Gigi had found her niece Lorraine inconsolable in the back of one of her Uncle Tony's rented limos, weeping, with her brother Guy's arms around her. Lorraine was refusing to come into the church. Her Aunt Gigi, with a bouquet in her hand, leaned in the window. The limo was parked outside St James' Catholic Church in North Stoughton, the wooden church which formerly was a stable. Lorraine simply told her aunt that she was sorry, but she had been overcome by the thought that, if she were ever married, her dead father, Ennio Abbruzzo, would not be there to give away the bride. So no one suspected when Gigi forlornly went inside for the ceremony that her tears were flowing not from joy but from grief and guilt.

Meanwhile, Tony, the father of the bride, was thinking that his daughter Maria looked absolutely beautiful. He was so happy for her. Everyone that day was saying they could not believe the change that had come over her. Where was the dour, round-shouldered drudge they thought they knew? A young woman of crushing innocence glowing with adoration had taken her place in the night!

Within a year, the newlyweds made Tony and Gigi grandparents—and Maria named her first child, a boy, Anthony, after her father, who felt honored, and at the same time, chagrined to know that he had never understood the depths of his daughter Maria's feelings.

And, Tony thought, she looked absolutely beautiful. He was so happy for her. Everyone that day was saying they could not believe the change that had come over her. Where was the dour, round-shouldered drudge they thought they knew? A young woman of crushing innocence glowing with adoration had taken her place in the night!

Within a year, Maria and Charlie made them grandparents—and Maria named her first child, a boy, Anthony, after her father, who felt honored, and at the same time, chagrined to know that he had never understood the depths of his daughter Maria's feelings.

But now Maria was gone. Just when Tony was beginning to appreciate what he had never realized he had (and Gigi, too) Maria was gone to live in Watertown, next door to Cambridge, across the Charles River from Boston, where Charlie Laverna had bought a two-family house on quiet, tree-shaded Dewey Street, just off Coolidge Square, where the landmark Bell Telephone building was, so it would be only a short walk to get to Mount Auburn Street where he could take the streetcar to work at '*Giorgio Marscia.*'

For Tony and Gigi, it left a hole in the house on Pine Street in Stoughton.

The squat, old-fashioned garrison, big as a barn, that stood sideways on the lot with the gable-end facing the long, loping two-lane country road that was Pine Street, where Tony had moved the family when they were all so much younger; where he had congratulated himself time and again on his own shrewdness in having purchased a 2-story home with bedrooms upstairs practically for cash without any bank mortgage, at a time when no one had foreseen the oncoming Depression: now, with one daughter gone, though the others all remained, that house of his felt so empty.

And that was true of the rest of them, too, even her mother: when Maria was gone, that was when they missed her.

Not to be outdone, Peggy found herself a husband within a year of Maria's wedding. *She found him at the racetrack.*

It happened this way: back in 1935, something occurred in Massachusetts that Tony, in his wildest imaginings, had never thought possible. Pari-mutuel betting was legalized in the Commonwealth, by an act of the legislature.

Over time a verdict on Massachusetts had settled into Tony's mind. He had come to see it as a hidebound backwater where Sunday blue laws and long Puritan noses turned the pleasures of everyday life into a mess of foul porridge to be stuffed down people's throats. Nothing new and progressive ever came out of Massachusetts, where the governor was an Irish crook and the Senator a Saltonstall. *Sacco and Vanzetti*—there's your proof right there. A place where somebody like Fiorello LaGuardia could be elected mayor of a great American city—*that was New York.*

But now right here in Massachusetts the Depression had forced their hand. They were so desperate for revenues from anywhere, by any ways and means, that they had to stifle their fire-and-brimstone souls. And out of those same souls, which were like snakes in a snake-pit shedding their skins, crept their foul and devious Yankee greed, to win the day. Finally they had to admit to themselves, with scalding chagrin, that people like Tony LaStoria were sending their betting dollars out-of-state, via the bookie parlor and Bell Telephone, to Belmont, Aqueduct, Saratoga, and now, worse yet, to Lincoln Downs in Rhode Island, or Rockingham, in Salem, New Hampshire—both of them right across the state line!—and carloads of loot were now escaping there daily, by state-approved roads.

So much for revolutionary slogans about taxation without representation upon which this Commonwealth was founded. It was a brand-new day for Massachusetts. First the income tax—and now, pari-mutuel betting. Cotton Mather was writhing in his grave.

And for Tony LaStoria, at long last he had something to look forward to: a day at the races.

Suffolk Downs, in East Boston, opened on April 15th, 1935, an easy drive under the harbor, in the brand-new Sumner Tunnel. No more long grey days spent sitting in offices in more-or-less shut-down factory buildings wondering when you could hire again or, worse, when you might even get some goddam orders come in.

Now the focus of the day, a desultory walk to a lonely local diner for an endless lunch-hour with a lousy white-bread sandwich, was replaced with, overnight, Post-time! the Daily Double! at Suffolk Downs.

Not since the days of the Harlem River Speedway, a long, long time ago, had Tony been able to stroll about the paddock just to gaze at those beautiful animals, the thoroughbreds. Now, instead of exporting racehorses out-of-state to Kentucky from the horse-farm of a wealthy Mayflower descendant in Hingham, they were importing the best horseflesh in the country, to race right here in Boston, and the biggest names among the riders, too. For Tony, it made him realize that something had been missing, in his life, some attraction, some stimulus, some fun, for once.

And so, in the name of spreading the joy, he drafted his son, Patsy, into the position of constant companion, at the racetrack, every day.

That was a place where there were a lot of strangers, and some characters you really didn't want to know, and you had to have someone to talk to, that was half the enjoyment. At the track, you were best to stick to your own, or at least, people you already knew.

Patsy was actually somewhat thrilled his father had finally found a use for him. Finally he could receive the pleasures of the old man's benediction, and a place in his father's life which he had always coveted and yet been denied because he was thought too stupid. Well, he was not too stupid to press pants. For some time now he had been pushing a broom, going for coffee, and pressing pants for his father in the shop at Number 10, in the South End. Tony had devised a job for his oldest son by taking in pressing from the overflow from cleaners downtown, down on Washington Street.

So now, every day, they traveled to work in town together from Stoughton. In luxury. Tony had bought a brand-new, used '32 Buick sedan, back in November of '34, when FDR, who was by now a local household-god around their way, was riding high on the scale of saviors-of-the-downtrodden. The new car was to celebrate the Depression ending by Christmas;

which never happened. But in the meantime, Tony was tired of scrimping to get by and he was going to ride in style till happy days were here again.

And now, his son Patsy discovered an incentive to improve his reading, which, in school, he had never liked, as a subject, and had always done poorly in. Now, every day in the car, while Tony did the driving, he had to go over the green sheet with him, so they could make their picks for the Daily Double. His father had Patsy read out loud the handicappers' reports on the horses and jockeys, and then, *Voila!* Patsy found he *liked* to read: in fact, he didn't mind it at all!

When Peggy LaStoria caught wind of what was going on, due to Patsy's big mouth, she was not about to be left out of the party. Just as she was bound to get herself let into all the boys' games when she was nine years old, now, she wasn't going to be left out when she was eighteen. So, one day, she just showed up at the track, with some young fella on her arm.

Which was fine with Patsy, as he usually had a current love interest following him around, who just happened to run across him at the track (Patsy figuring his father would never notice).

In spite of what his father thought about him, Patsy had always been popular with the girls. It started back in the fourth grade, when he used to invite himself into the jump-rope line at recess. In the 6th grade, his last at school, when the girls were just figuring out that boys might like them as much as they liked boys, he was surrounded by girls, before school, after classes, on the fire escape, in the hallways; to the chagrin of the other boys, who could not figure out how he did it. When he worked at the gas station in Stoughton, there were always a couple of them hanging around; his girlfriend of the moment, and a girlfriend of hers. And the following week, it would be a new girlfriend. Patsy was very fair and democratic about it: he gave all of them a chance. They liked him because he made them laugh. He was a tease. When the girls started wearing bras, something new in the thirties, he offered to take their measurements. They were thrilled-to-giggles, though they pretended to be shocked. Patsy always made sure he had one of Pa's tailor's tape-measures in his pocket. He would loop it around them and pinch it together behind their backs, and they would stick their chests out. He better give them a good reading, too. From there, with their arms raised high, it was easy to shoot them a tickle in the ribs, and then run like hell, with a girl falling over in hysterical laughter, trailing. Patsy would tell them outrageous stories, usually beginning, "I had a dream about you last night. I was kneeling in front of you. It was our wedding day, and I was slowly, slowly, ever so slowly, pushing the garter up your leg. Your left leg. Like this: higher, and higher, and——." or "I had a dream about you last night. We were sitting up in bed together, reading French diaries, naughty French diaries, very naughty." "Oh, Patsy, you know you can't read French!" "I don't have to. I was reading your mind, and you were translating. Why, Janey, I'm shocked!"

This particular day at the track, Peggy showed up and just slipped herself into a seat beside them in the grandstand, with her boy-for-the-day seated alongside her.

Her father leaned over and said, "You know—ladies are not seen here without an escort."

"Why do you think I brought Scooter here with me?"

"Scooter?"

"Well, I wasn't gonna ask *you* for a lift!"

Tony was thinking no good could ever come out of a young man they called Scooter.

"He's got a car!" She had caught her father leaning past her to give the boy the up-and-down. "A nice one, too. Don't worry. You ain't gonna scare him away. I got him trained. Told him all about you."

The next time she showed up with an altogether different boy.

"You're gonna get a reputation," her father said.

"I hope so," she said.

The next time her father said, "What happened to the last one?"

She said, "I ditched him. Couldn't cut the mustard. I let 'em know, from the start, I'm a very expensive date. If they can't come up with the scratch, they can't come up with the catch."

In the end Tony became hopelessly resigned. To his son's surprise, one day he consulted Patsy about it, when they were in the Buick together.

"What do you know about your sister?"

"Pa! She's a nice girl! Take it from me. I know! She's my sister! She's your daughter!"

"She's a disgrace, that's what she is!"

"She doesn't mean any harm. She can't help it! Look at her! In those suits she gets those guys to buy for her! Va-va-va-voom!"

"They buy suits for her?"

"And flowers! And wine!"

"She's eighteen years old!"

"Don't worry! She'll be married soon, and she'll be offa your hands. You know—she's got the itch. She'll be somebody else's problem. And I do mean problem!"

His father stopped watching where he was driving, to give Patsy a long, insinuating look.

"You and her! Birds of a feather. Both of youz got the same itch. How many times have I told you, when a young lady walks by—you gotta ogle her? For Chrissakes—you look like you're gonna break your neck, sometimes! Don't you know how self-conscious that makes the poor girl feel?"

"Pa—they like it!"

"And then, the whistle! Whaddya think this is?—*the Old Howard?*"

But Patsy was right. Peggy was soon married. Because she fell in love. Of all things. At the racetrack.

His name was Henry Fabiano.

She spotted him one day standing at the rail for the seventh race. He was standing straight with his back turned to her, both hands placed on the rail; not hunched over, like most of the men, or with a rolled-up newspaper or scratch sheet in hand. He was looking into the far distance all the way down the track to the sixteenth pole, stretching his neck, rather like an eagle, or a hawk, searching for prey: or so the thought came into Peggy's mind. He had his profile turned to her. He wore a fedora. And he had on horn-rimmed glasses. She had never seen him before, but she wanted to know who he was.

It was easy for Peggy to meet a guy at the track. They were usually pre-occupied gamblers, but they would talk to you. When they got around to noticing, they paid attention to her. Patsy and her father, especially him, would get tired of sitting by the time the seventh race came around, and towards the end of the afternoon, they would drift, like a lot of other people, from their seats, down to the rail.

The finish line was where it got exciting. Bodies pressed together—everyone trying to catch the exact moment—winner by a nose, lost by a neck.

Peggy ditched her date-for-the-day ("Wait for me here!") the next time she saw the man with the glasses at the rail, when the seventh race came. She managed to squeeze herself in, several bodies up the rail from him, where she could watch him, face-on, as he watched the end of the race. He was impervious: lips pressed together; not jumping and shouting and gesticulating as the other men were: he was observing. What was he doing there? She was consumed with curiosity. She noticed he had a moustache, a pencil-thin upper-lip affair, that made him look like Gable, but the horn-rimmed glasses gave him an intellectual air. She was intrigued.

She got herself prised-in next to him before the next race. The rail was still crowded. He didn't know she was there. He had some kind of abstracted air about him.

Peggy said, "So, who do you like in the eighth?"

"Huh?" He looked down at her—and quickly away.

"The eighth race. Who do you like? Got a tip for me? I'm flat, and I could use a winner."

"Oh, I don't gamble."

He said this without bothering to look at her.

She was intrigued now even further. If he didn't play the ponies: "So, what the hell are you doing *here?*"

"Oh—I'm a sportswriter."

He still did not deign to converse with her.

"Boston Post? Globe? The Daily Record?"

"Oh, no, no, no." Now she had his attention. "Nothing like that. Suburban paper. You've probably never heard of it."

So he was modest, too. She liked that. Most of the guys who tried to impress her were blowhards.

She said, "I never met a sportswriter before."

"Really."

It was clear to Peggy that with that one word he had dismissed her from his mind. And that bothered her.

She said, "Why don't you and me go over to the clubhouse—and I'll buy you a drink—I wanna talk to you. I wanna find out all about you."

No young, pretty woman had ever said such a thing to Henry Fabiano, certainly not at the racetrack, or anywhere else. So he went with Peggy LaStoria to the clubhouse. And they were married three weeks later, in Wilmington, at the Town Hall, in the town where Henry lived, where he had grown up, north of Boston, and where he was the owner of *The Wilmington Gazette,* a townie's newspaper, a weekly: owner, editor, news reporter, typesetter, delivery-driver, paper-boy, sweeper-upper, and–sports columnist.

When Peggy brought Henry to the house on Pine Street in Stoughton to present him to the family as her husband, a week or so after the wedding, her sister Gerry, now fifteen, was dumbfounded; little Anna, nine years old, was delighted, but disappointed that she had missed out on being flower-girl; Maria, who everyone had now decided to call Mary, was away at her own home in Watertown, which was why they had all changed her name: she was no longer the Maria they had grown up with. Gigi, who loved a love-story, and could say to Peggy, remember when you used to ask me for *Serafina in the Tower,* or you wouldn't go to sleep at night?—Gigi was ready to embrace Henry Fabiano as a new star in her firmament, as well as a new son in the family. The boys, Patsy, Genie, Guy and Augie, especially 12-year-old Augie, were suitably impressed with Henry's blue-serge suit and his shy way of being his own intelligent self without trying to show he was smarter than they were. Augie was absolutely thrilled to meet a sportswriter.

And Tony, father of the bride, met up with her in the kitchen, where he had gone to hide after spending a suitably polite length of time in the parlor affecting to chat, in monoyllables, with his new son-in-law. Peggy chased him out there.

"What's the matter, Pa, you don't like him?"

"I like him—I like him—I'm happy for the both of you."

"But—."

Her hands were on her hips.

"But—." Tony shrugged. "What do you want me to say? Don't make me say something I don't wanna say."

"You're disappointed."

"I'm disappointed."

"In me."

"Disappointed. That's one way of putting it."

"Hey—at least I saved you all that money you woulda had to spend on the big church wedding."

"Please—don't insult me."

Peggy dissolved into tears and fled the room.

Tony looked down at the half-empty wineglass, standing on the counter, the stem pinched between his thumb and first two fingers, as if to tell him he wanted a cigarette—.

He looked around for the crumpled pack of Chesterfields.

He hung his head and muttered, "Ah—the bride is crying."

Chapter 18

Father Coughlin Speaks

As far as Tony LaStoria was concerned, that was the breaking point. He no longer knew anything. Not the struggles of the past. Not the querulous present. Not the meaning of his own life. Was this what it all had come to? But most of all, he no longer knew where they were all going; nor would he strive and struggle any longer to peer into mysteries of the future. For what if you really could see there? What if you really knew?—what was to come? The truth was that Tony did know, or suspect, what was to come, and it was never far from his mind, or anyone else's.

You could not live through the 'Thirties without hearing rumbles of distant earthquakes. It was as if you were living with an underground radio of constant static pocked with messages struggling to get through, all of them troubling, forcing you to want to push them away. You were just counting your blessings that you had come through the Great War, the flu epidemic, ridiculous disasters such as the molasses flood, which mocked humanity, even the sudden disappearance of prosperity, now a distant memory, replaced with *what? The Depression?* It was too much to hope for, that there would be a return of optimism. But to live from day to day, hand to mouth, with this sense of calamity coming over the horizon—of its *inevitability*–.

On top of that a source of friction had invaded their home itself—a loudmouth foghorn of demagoguery. It was none other than Chief O'Brian, who had now departed the police force, and turned up as a physical education instructor at Stoughton High School.

Ever since Tony had confronted him face to face on that fateful day at the police headquarters, O'Brian had invited himself to Sunday dinners, on Thursday evenings. Why not? Everyone else in Stoughton was welcome at Ma LaStoria's back door! Puffy O'Brian expected, however, to be wined and dined like a foreign potentate. He was there to experience the lavish delights of that good old south-of-Italy home cooking: he complained vocally that all he ever got at home was *boiled patatas.*

And Puffy O'Brian, from the onset, made a point of being continually complimentary to Gigi, who pretended to not understand a word. The Chief enlisted the children to translate for him, and communicated the rest with the cartoonish faces he made, smacking his chops, rubbing his ample abdomen. Gigi in return cordially detested him to his face, while behind his back complaining to Tony, who protested that it was none of his idea, but what could he do? "I don't invite him. He invites himself. What do you want from me? He's a guest!"

Puffy O'Brian had noted the new second-hand Buick in the driveway, and the up-to-date Zenith console in the parlor, and he was there to celebrate the end of Prohibition with a glass of Tony's wine, re-filled from the gallon jug from the cellar. O'Brian was not shy about holding his glass out. And he was also there to keep collecting for the Christmas fund, which turned into a year-round project; it was always something: cleats for the football team, bats and gloves, catchers' masks, a poor Irish family, down on their luck, that Puffy knew of, the Stoughton Square soup-kitchen—the list lengthened month by month.

"Maybe it's better this way," Tony said to Gigi.

"He's a *scroccone*," said Gigi.

"I know, I know," said Tony, "but the kids like him. They think he's funny."

"He's funny, all right. He's a *sanguisuga!*"

"Eh. He's a bigshot in the high school now. Maybe it will do the kids some good." Tony knew an argument he wasn't going to win when he saw it. So, he decided to play the superstitious card. "Besides," he told Gigi, "he knows people. Big people, important people." He made his eyes big and with two fingers tight together pulled them across his puckered lips. *"Ma silencio—segreto!"* And he thrust his chin out at his wife.

After satisfying his baser needs at the dining table, Puffy O'Brian would adjourn himself to the parlor, and kindly invite Tony along. They would sit there in their respective armchairs, two patriarchs of the desert nomads, and expansively puff on after-dinner cigars. Eyeing the radio, and, being so concerned for the welfare of the eternal souls of the LaStorias, Puffy would gently suggest that it was time for the Father Coughlin hour. While the good priest informed them of the worldwide conspiracy of the Jews, Puffy would elaborate with nods and pointed cigar to make sure that the message sunk in: we are all Catholics in this together, with a world of kikes and darkies against us. O'Brian would never fail to remind the assembled audience of LaStorias of the origins of Coughlin's radio ministry. "It was the Klu Klux Klan, burned a cross on the lawn of his parish church in Michigan. That was back in '26." Puffy would then nod, knowingly.

Boston's own Cardinal O'Connell was still, in the 'Thirties, industrious in his indignation about the local immigrant population from Southern Europe—by which he meant *the Wops*. It particularly stuck in the Cardinal's craw that in these hard times, the Protestants were sending their missionaries into the North End to proselytize the wayward. And horror of horrors, amongst the Italians there were only too many open ears. It was up to him, Cardinal O'Connell, and the local parishes, and all good Catholics (by which he meant the Irish) to go on the offensive.

This was a mission that Puffy O'Brian took seriously. He was there to make sure the LaStoria children were attending Sunday school at St Brigid's, where the Irish nuns could get hold of them. Poor little Anna came home one Sunday crying, asking, do they really burn you in hell? In everlasting fires of damnation? Gigi had to try to convince the poor girl that there was a heaven, too. The Irish sisters of the Order of the Holy Union kept at them with hell and sin, and commandments and catechism, terrifying the Italian first-graders with tales of the black stain on their souls: *Original Sin.*

The children of the LaStorias were already beset with the troublesome issue of nationality. In school, you had to know who was a Kraut, who was a Polack, who was a Canuck, and so on. And the kids were continually asking their parents—how can you tell one from another?

Gigi was wont to say, "You see that big, fat puffed-out face on O'Brian, all blotchy and red-nosed?—that's the *Irlandesi* for you!" But recalling Tony's admonitions on this subject, she would retract herself and lecture the kids on how to treat company when they came to your house; while at the same time looking over her shoulder for the devil.

Originally, Father Coughlin had gained an enormous following, numbered in the millions, all around the country, because he had promoted a populist platform of his own, calling for monetary reforms, the nationalization of the railroads, and protection of the rights of organized labor. His radio hour was not picked up by CBS for national broadcast until 1929, but then he began his attacks on the socialists and communists, while managing to blame the capitalists for making these godless alternatives attractive to the American people, in their sufferings.

When Roosevelt ran in '32, Coughlin coined the catchphrase "Roosevelt or Ruin!" on his radio show. Already a star, a featured guest of the Congressional Committee to Investigate Communist Activities, Coughlin managed to boost his popularity astronomically by thundering out on his program, after the first hundred days of the New Deal, "GOD is directing President Roosevelt!"

However, by 1936, his tune had changed.

It was undeniable that the developments in Europe were taken by Americans as not only a specter to dread but also a phenomenon to applaud. Mussolini had made the trains run on time. Hitler was rebuilding a moribund Germany (although that was troubling to many who recalled the Hun and his atrocities in the Great War).

Father Coughlin drifted to the right with the rest of them. He also was a factor encouraging the drift. His show had become so influential that now the Roosevelt administration, and even the Council of Catholic Bishops, wanted him cancelled. His radio rants had begun to attack Roosevelt, Capitalists, and Jewish conspirators.

This note caused a shiver down Tony LaStoria's spine. Every time Coughlin said "Jews" on the radio, it reminded Tony that O'Brian had seemed to know all about his association with Harry Spritzka: from *before* the first moment Tony stepped into his police station.

What were his sources? Where did someone like Puffy O'Brian, in a little-noted place like Stoughton, Massachusetts, get his information, about goings-on in New York City? About something as foreign, alien and supposedly secret as *The Elders of Zion?* Only Tony himself knew the depths of outrage that he felt in his own soul at the time they slaughtered those two poor *paesani,* Sacco and Vanzettti. But what if people like O'Connell, Coughlin, worse, O'Brian, could peer into his soul, could read his mind? What if he gave himself away? What if he said something, inadvertently, or out of carelessness, or forgetfulness? Better to keep his thoughts to himself. Or better yet, agree with everything Puffy O'Brian said. In any case, if he needed to scare Gigi into behaving herself with Puffy, it might be well to recall that he could bring up *The Elders of Zion* at the right time, if need be. What Tony LaStoria did know was that there was *good reason* to be fearful. Hitler was threatening to annex Austria. France and Britain were making their belligerent noises; or providing Der Fuhrer with their permission: hard to tell which, from one day to the next. The waters were treacherous. Voices were shouting on all sides, and you could trust none of them. They all contradicted each other, and themselves, including Father Coughlin, who was famous, or infamous, for just that, constantly reversing course. And every country, every politician, every man was divided against himself. This was 1937, and who knew if they would all be at war again by 1938? And what would happen then, to Tony's three sons? It mortified Tony to think that, in the Great War, he had not been called upon to serve, even though it may have been through no fault of his own. It left him open to the very accusation Puffy O'Brian made to him that day in his Police Chief's office: *what did you do in the war, Anthony?* Yet his sons would have no such exemption: they were Americans, and God forbid there was a war. To go back to the beginning: *had he done the right thing coming to America in the first place?*

About his daughters, he didn't worry. They were spared, as long as they lived in this country. Thank God they weren't growing up in the old country. Look what happened over there the last time. No woman was safe. Tony realized with considerable chagrin that this fortuitous circumstance of their birthplace was nothing they would ever thank him for: not his daughters, excepting Gerry, who loved him. In any case, because of Peggy, he had written off even Gigi, he knew, to his sorrow. He had to admit that he had failed all his life to understand women, and that he expected he never would. He was so much more comfortable around men. Even Puffy O'Brian was more congenial company than the females in his own family these days. But his sons, they were precious to Tony.

Oh, how could you go through life half-right and always wrong? With every decision you ever took coming back to haunt you?

Of course, Tony did not depend solely on O'Brian in the parlor, or Coughlin on the radio, as he tried to navigate his way. He would have been remiss by his own lights not to consult with Harry Spritzka.

But that troubled him, too, these days. Of course, it was impossible to go back to their old times together. Tony knew that and he knew that Harry knew. Each of them would have thought it silly. They had become, after all, grown men, with families and, yes, responsibilities, which they were accustomed to, as befit them in the station of life each had attained.

But also, from what Tony knew, and had learned during The 'Thirties, by Harry's own admission, Harry, his wealthy benefactor, fit the profile outlined by O'Brian and Coughlin *only too well.*

Not that Tony was anxious to see Harry, or spend time with him. First of all, a trip to New York was not the same anymore. It was almost onerous to walk the streets there and to have to see the Big Apple crestfallen by the Depression to the point of selling wizened little rotten apples on the corner. And how could you not say that sitting in Harry Spritzka's mansion, his rising mansion (which now had reached four stories) was not a rebuke in itself? Tony would be sitting there drinking the man's liquor and thinking, *how is it that one man can luxuriate like this when so many are dressed in the rags of want and care? Talk about biting the hand that feeds you.* Whatever he thought, whatever he did, Tony, in his own eyes, was virtually criminalized by his dependence on Harry. Why was he, of all people, so fortunate as to enjoy every privilege, when others were suffering, simply because he knew Harry. And yet, and yet, it would be the height of foolhardiness to throw away his advantage. If he did that, how then would he ever meet his own responsibilities to the seven children he had brought into this compromised world, not to mention Anna-Vittoria's boy and girl?

Moreover, Tony did not want Harry looking too closely at his own activities, especially, after 1935, when he spent almost every afternoon when he was in Boston at, not the office, but the track. His position had become reduced to something like that of the caretaker of an ancient nobleman's neglected country place. He roamed empty halls and clipped hedges with a pair of shears. That was why he spent his days at the track. From sheer boredom. From the emptiness of his unproductive routine.

And yet, Harry Spritzka remained loyal to him, Tony LaStoria.

Never once had the man ever dropped to Tony so much as a hint of a layoff, either to his face, or on the telephone, where it was harder to fool people because your tone, your voice, betrayed you. Instead, Harry talked always of the flow of orders: when the orders returned and they were back in business, they better be ready.

Meanwhile, how had *Harry* managed, in the world-wide Depression, Tony wanted to know.

Being the friends they still were, it gave Harry the chance to boast, for once, of *his* perspicacity.

"Real estate, Tony. My brother was right, the whole time. I just didn't want to see it. Stubborn, I guess. I wanted to do everything my own way—I'd show him!–I had to fool myself into thinking I knew it all. Well, I don't. And another thing. Stay away from the stock market. Bonds and securities and municipal bonds and the government, Tony, ain't never gonna go outta business. And then, there's my wife's family. The banking Lowensteins. They steered me right. When banks go down and the tellers are jumpin' outta windows, it's because they took bad advice. Somebody sold 'em a bill o' goods. When the Crash happened, when all the banks were going down, me and Robert and Mimi were buying! Ten cents on the dollar. Buying and holding. Waiting for the golf club to swing back the other way. And I do mean club. In more ways than one. For what is a man without his friends?"

Here Tony received the well-known significant look, and the wink was not necessary. Tony understood.

The rest of Harry's talk, during the three or four sit-downs they had in the Thirties, was about all the menace of Europe.

Here, Tony paid close attention because, in his eyes, Harry was a veteran, who had seen first-hand the *Ancien Regime* drown itself in an orgy of blood-letting, and therefore knew whereof he spoke.

"I'm worried, Tony. Frankly. Our people are in a weak position. You know that Einstein has come here? He's at Princeton. And Freud is now in Britain. So, we don't lack information. We know what is going on. We just don't know how far Hitler will go, in the end. Or whether anyone amongst the Great Powers will have the spine to stop him. Or worse, will bother their heads to stop him. Which is problematic for the Jews, because it makes you stop and think. The truth is, we can only depend on ourselves. That's why it's more important than ever that we get the Balfour Declaration realized, not in theory, but in actual reality, on the ground: the Jewish homeland, in Palestine."

There it was—*the international conspiracy. The Elders of Zion. Plain as the nose on your face.*

On the train-ride home, Tony could think only of the doom of the next generation.

And when he looked at his son, Augie, this gangly colt, twelve-years-old, who took after his sister Peggy, with his passion for games and teams, he felt apprehensive.

Chapter 19

The Indian in the Woods

From the very beginning, Augie had responded to Tony with ears as alert as one of his father's bird-dogs, with an avid desire to please in his brown eyes, and with virtually a wagging tail.

As a toddler, he followed his father everywhere, from kitchen to parlor to garden to garage, clambering onto the seat of the automobile. The boy had an insatiable curiosity. He had to know every minute what his father was up to. "Pa—where ya goin'? Can I come?" Tony hated to tell the boy no, he could not, because he could see all his hopes collapse in his eyes, and he would turn, and trudge off, whereas he had, a moment ago, trotted up. Tony would have to enlist his other son, Genie, to take the kid for a walk or to play with him. Patsy was too old and disdained his two younger brothers; he arrogated to himself the privileges of the oldest. Genie and Augie were close enough in age to be buddies; and Genie was always the kind to take his little brother under his wing.

Tony LaStoria took the pride of a mother lion in these two boys. As disappointed as he had been in his first-born, Patsy, his affection for the two who succeeded was overweening. He who had never had a brother of his own, growing up; whose only comparison, as an only child, separated from his parents, had been his cousins Enrico and Luigi, so much younger; or more, the street companions of his boyhood in New York, the likes of Knickers, Long-Johns, Il Gatto. Of course, he could not leave out of mind his brotherhood with Harry Spritzka, for he knew, it must be said, they were in fact, for a long time, brothers under one roof, if not by blood. Yet even Harry Spritzka's place in his life could not excite in Tony the penetrating bond he now, too late for his own childhood, formed with these two sons; the brotherhood that got under his skin, the connection that only males of the family can feel for one another. Truly it was said, as his father-in-law Pasquale Fabrizio once had it, *il sangue non mente.*

Of all his children, Tony thought of young Eugene as the one who resembled himself the most. He was the one who studied his father and modeled himself on Tony. When he was still quite young, Genie said to his father, "Teach me how to sew, and how to run the machine. No, I don't want to be a tailor: I'm going to be the boss, like you." Genie's mind was made up. He was going to be a boss, because his father, in his eyes, was the big boss of everybody, and Genie wanted to be just like him.

Augie was a horse of a different color. Nobody knew where that kid came from, not Tony, not Gigi, not his sisters, though all of them, across the board, stood up to take note, dazzled by him.

From the start, he grew straight up, as spare as a birch, as lean as an arrow in flight. And yet as he grew he turned out to be, like the knots in an oak tree, impenetrably strong. Where other people had flab, fat, and soft tissue, under the upper arm, in back of the thigh, this kid grew hardened muscle, without trying. His body was as obdurate as a rock, as smooth as a stone from a river.

Tony observed, with considerable secret satisfaction, with wondering awe, that somehow, in some mysterious way, the mountains of Alta Villa, the rock upon which that ancient town, built originally in the darkness of lost times as a defensive redoubt, a refuge from foreign invaders, from Greeks, from Saracens, from Spaniards, from roving troops of *banditti*, from Norsemen, from, no doubt, the Romans themselves: somehow the bastion-rock of the high mountain places of his own origins had been translated into flesh and blood and emerged generations later in this boy.

Thank goodness his mother, Gigi, had saved him from perishing as a helpless infant.

The boy soon showed his independence. He had inexhaustible reserves of energy and had to run, run, run all day to tire himself out. There was no challenge he could pass up; climbing a tree, clambering the old-time stonewalls of the neighborhood that were leftover from colonial times, crossing a brook on stepping stones without getting his feet wet, scaling the most formidable cliffs or rock-walls he could find; one day, Genie had to climb up on the roof of the garage to get Augie down; Augie, who refused to come down; Augie, who challenged him to come up; and don't you know, poor Genie fell off and broke his arm.

When Augie heard him cry out in pain, then he jumped down, to help his brother, in one leap. No hesitation. His brother was hurt.

Genie had tears in his eyes at the sudden sharp pain. Still, he never forgot the form and grace and fluidity with which Augie had leapt off the roof, one arm high in the air trailing his body, for balance, his feet pointed toward earth and poised for the collision, his knees bending as he landed, to take the shock—he was like a big cat—but with the flair and litheness of a toreador or fencing-master. Genie yelled at him, "If only you had done that when I told you to! I wouldn't've got hurt!"

It all came naturally to Augie. He never thought about it. If anything, it was too easy. He could not understand why anyone could not do it, if he could. He never could understand why the boys at school made such a big thing out of him, always wanting him on their side, telling him he had to be captain of this and leader of that. He didn't want anyone making him into anything. He just did things for the sheer sake of doing them.

When his father, Tony, was at his wit's end what to do the boy, he suggested to Augie that he chop wood for the fireplace; there was a whole stack at the side of the garage; why didn't he try that? Augie was only 8 or 9 years old, but his father gave him the little hatchet and showed him how split the short pieces that were fat enough. "Just be careful and remember, Augie, you can slice your leg off the same as splitting wood."

He should have never started the boy on that. Soon he was going out to the woods that surrounded every house in town in those days, when they were closer to the 18th or 19th century than they liked to think in Stoughton, and out in the woods, Augie was chopping down whole trees and dragging them back to the yard through the trail that led out the back. Nobody could say the kid wasn't a worker. To him it was just exercise. Then of course, there were the ball-games the kid loved. Anything you could play with a ball was certain to attract his attention.

His sister Peggy was the one who introduced him to basketball, and got her brother Patsy to get off his lazy duff for once, and hang a bushel-basket on the apple tree in the back-yard for Augie to practice on.

Peggy told him that when he got to the fourth grade, they'd let him try out for the school team, and bragged to Augie that back in her day, back in Hingham, she had been the ace of the girls' team, that time when she got in all that trouble for fighting on court in front of the whole town?

Augie complained that the basket was too low on the apple tree and the crooked branches gave him no room, so he re-hung the basket on a straighter maple at the edge of the woods at the far back of their yard—after he ripped off the lower branches with his bare hands. Of course, you had to have a backboard, too, which he chopped and hammered and nailed up himself.

Those woods were an attraction for Augie. Patsy might like to jump rope with girls, and Genie might like to curl up with a book in a chair on the piazza or the back porch (they told him he was going to ruin his eyes reading) but for Augie, it was the woods. For one thing, his father was always disappearing into them with his dogs. Augie wanted to grow up as fast as he could so that he could go with them, to find out everything they were doing, and then, do it himself.

Augie was only four years old when the 'Thirties began, but he still wanted to go along. Not being able to, because he was still too little, only made him want to know, all the more, and grow, all the more, so that he could find out what was in there. His father told him he was going with his bird-dogs to Ponkapoag to shoot pheasant. And sure enough, he would come home with 2 or 3 birds for the table, whether pheasant or quail. Ma and the girls would pluck them and roast them, and were they ever delicious! Pa told Augie there were also deer and wild turkey buzzards in those woods. Pa said that he didn't shoot deer because it was too much trouble to skin them and gut them for the table, *and you didn't shoot what you weren't going to eat.*

There were plenty of other ways to get meat for the table, and venison, besides, was not to everyone's taste. If you were starving, that would be one thing, but they certainly were not starving, and Tony still shopped at the meat counters in town at Fanueil Hall, where his father-in-law used to cut meat, and, family provider that he was, brought loads back every Saturday to Stoughton in the big trunk of the Buick. Tony himself enjoyed foraging at the open-air markets of the city as much as he enjoyed hunting in the woods around Stoughton. In both cases, he was providing for his family. But he promised to teach Augie all about how to handle the shotgun and the rifle as soon as he was old enough, and he did. Genie wanted to be like his father because he was a boss of buildings and people, but Augie wanted to be like him because he was a hunter.

Tony himself wondered where he got his own liking for it from. All he could think of was the memory of one day seeing his father going off down the street in Alta Villa, in the early, early morning, with the dewy mist still steaming from the ground, with the shotgun under his arm, and turning off the road into the first open field. His father had brought home rabbits for the dinner table. So, in spite of himself, and his long-standing grudge, he must take after his father, after all. *And what does that tell you about life, eh? That in the end, after all, you turn into your own father?* Tony shuddered. *What a grisly fate!*

Tony told this story about his father to young Augie, adding that there were rabbits in these woods, too, just like back in Alta Villa. Thus Augie got the idea that he came from a long line of hunters and ought to, by rights, follow in their footsteps.

And then, there was the lure of Ponkapoag, which from his earliest times, had become, for Augie, a mythical place.

One day, when he was still only twelve years old, Augie marched off with his father's 12-gauge shotgun, carrying the gun the way his father taught him to carry it (muzzle-down, stock under his right armpit, right hand holding the forestock so that the barrel was pointing away and he didn't accidentally shoot himself in the foot or point the rifle at anyone who could get hurt) heading through the woods for Ponkapoag, which was only about four miles away.

If the woods had had neighborhoods, or better, townlands, Ponkapoag would have been a townland of its own. It was an expansive stretch of low-lying marshlands surrounding on all sides a body of water called Ponkapoag Pond. Like everything around the South Shore towns of Eastern Massachusetts, the unsettled areas retained their old-time Indian names from the days of the first white settlers from England; so Ponkapoag, which everyone pronounced, "Punk-a-pog," was a place of its own in the woods, amorphous as it may be, but certainly not mythical, as everyone in Stoughton and Canton knew what it was and where it was, even if, vaguely, they couldn't trace its boundaries for you.

Augie cut through the woods at the back of their house on Pine Street and came out to where York Street snaked around and started heading north towards the Canton line. Ponkapoag straddled the two towns. From York Street, Augie hooked up with Indian Lane: he was familiar with the shortest ways of getting there. He came out to the pond about where the Appalachian Club was situated. From there he picked up the

Ponkapoag Trail, which was just a path through the trees, and followed along till he found a likely tree overlooking a spot of water where he thought he had seen deer before, coming down to drink. He was going to taste what venison tasted like if he had to shoot it, skin it, and cook it himself, out there, in the woods.

And there he was leaning against his tree making himself one with the tree-trunk and making himself unseen by any deer, with his rifle stock at his feet and his fingers curling around the barrel as he watched, ready to lift the gun into firing position, as quietly as possible, his mind alert, but pushing away other thoughts that were extraneous and, from time to time, intruding: when he became aware of a feeling that he was being watched.

Augie turned his head and there was a man there, with a rifle, watching him.

He was leaning up against a tree, being unobtrusive, just like Augie.

The man approached. *There goes my deer,* Augie thought. Then he thought, *well, I'm not doing anything wrong.* And then, *I'm in trouble.*

But the man was friendly enough. He smiled at Augie, and said, "Hi, young fella."

"Hi."

"What's a young fella like you doin' out here all by himself on a nice day like this?"

"Hunting deer."

"Oh. I see. Well—you won't catch any deer that way."

"Why not?"

"Because you don't know what you're doin.'"

"Yes I do."

"No, you don't. Listen. You want to learn how to hunt deer? Well, you just come back with me to the clubhouse and I'll show you everything you got to know."

As they began to walk together, the man asked the boy what his name was.

"Augie," was all the boy would say—he felt for sure he was in trouble now.

"Well, Augie, nice to meet you. My name is Tobias Haskins."

Mr Haskins explained that he worked at the Appalachian Club, and that he was the general all-around man for the club and the grounds and the pond, and that this was not deer season, that was just two weeks long at the end of December, and do you have a license? No, well, you have to have that, and you're allowed only two antlered deer per season per hunter, and anyway, don't you know, you never, ever go deer-hunting alone—how old are you anyway, Augie?

"Twelve."

"That's a good age for learning something, Augie. First of all—what are you gonna do if a deer runs at you? They're bigger than you are. And a lot stronger. Do you know how strong a deer is? You'd be one dead twelve-year-old—if you didn't know enough to run away, or dodge 'em. Secondly, how's a boy your age gonna dress a deer outdoors in the woods all by himself—supposing you did get one?"

"What does that mean—dress a deer?"

"Well, that means how you prepare the deer for eating."

"Oh, my father taught me that—you don't kill an animal unless you're gonna eat it."

Mr Haskins stopped and looked at Augie. "I don't know if you know exactly what I meant. Has your father taught you how to dress a deer?"

"Uh, no—whatever dressing a deer means–he thinks they're too much trouble."

"Hmm. Well—I see I got a big job on my hands here."

"Can I tell you something?"

"Sure. What?"

"You look just like my Pa."

"I do? Why? Your father an Indian?"

"No. He's Italian!"

"Oh—that explains it."

"I don't think it's your face or your eyes or anything. I think it must be your nose—you have just exactly the same nose as him. Are you really an Indian? With a name like Haskins?"

"Why, what's wrong with that? It's a good name. You think I should be called Chief Bear Ass, or something like that?" Haskins chuckled when he realized that joke only worked in writing.

Augie thought he was laughing because he meant the other thing, so he laughed, too, out of politeness.

"Well," said Haskins, "—now you know my name—you still haven't told me—who *is* your father?"

"Tony LaStoria. From Stoughton. Or originally—well—"

"Oh, yes, I do know him. He's up here all the time, with his dogs and his shotgun."

"So you know him. He never told me about you!"

"Well, next time I see him—."

"Don't you dare tell him about me! He'll kill me!"

"So—he doesn't know you came up here by yourself today? Hmm. I didn't think so. He doesn't strike me as the kind."

"He never told me he knew an honest-to-God Indian!"

"Well, he probably doesn't really know that part."

"Wait'll I tell him!"

By the time they reached the Appalachian Club, Augie had learned a great deal that he had never even thought to ask—that you needed to have a mentor demonstrate for you how to dress a deer, that you couldn't learn something like that out of a book, so, naturally, you had to have someone show you, on the spot, which meant you had to have killed a deer, which was another reason why you never hunted deer alone, especially for the first kill, and that, in olden times, all the young Indian boys were taught all about these matters by their fathers and older brothers, and that yes, they hunted with bows and arrows, but then the English came, and of course, they had guns, so the Indians had to have them, too, and that, these days, there weren't that many of them left, but that Tobias Haskins lived in Mashpee, down on the Cape, where there was a whole tribe of his people, the Wampanoags, although his little group was called the Pocassets, they were still Wampanoags, and the rest of them were out on the islands, Nantucket, and Martha's Vineyard, which Tobias Haskins called Aquinnah, which Augie took to be one of those Indian names, like Nantucket, or Cohasset, Ponkapoag, too, for that matter, and that the Wampanoags still held a pow-wow of their tribe, once a year, in the summer, in Mashpee, on the Cape, where they had re-started the annual pow-wow way back in 1924, that was even before Augie was born! and that, yes, Haskins was a real Indian name, you see, there was so much inter-marriage going on, if you know what that means, back a hundred years ago, and anyway, who did you think was here before any of the Europeans came, young fella?

Augie raced home that day and thought his feet had hardly touched the ground, he covered the four miles he had to go so rapidly, thinking all the time, seeing himself as a young Indian boy who had just been initiated into a real hunters' clan, and he couldn't wait to tell Pa all about it—.

But he stopped himself. *Better not. Maybe I should just keep this all to myself.*

So that Christmas of 1937, there was Augie, with his first kill, deer season having opened on the 15th of December, on the back steps at Pine Street, giving away venison steaks to all the neighbor-kids, and nobody knew how he had done it. And he wasn't telling. All he would say was, "It's for me to know, and for you to find out!"

And so venison steaks were added to the local legend of Augie LaStoria, alongside the tale of the longest home-run ever hit out of the Stoughton High ballfield, and the 99-yard punt return that won the 1940 Thanksgiving Day football game for Stoughton versus arch-rival Canton, when Augie was just a freshman.

Chapter 20

The Rules of the Game

It was Coach Puffy O'Brian who recruited Tony LaStoria's kid, Augie, to the high school teams in all three sports.

At one point in his illustrious career as Police Chief in Stoughton, the town fathers, that is, the three-man Board of Selectmen, composed of the oldest Yankee stock the town had to offer, old white-haired Jeremiah Thompson, alongside geriatric specimen John Ellsworth Higgins, and the slightly less-petrified Amory Sedgwick, came to a momentous decision, for the good of all, and the general betterment. Now these leaders of tradition and defenders of the status quo tended to lump in the Irish Catholics in the town right alongside the Italian Catholics, so they had no compunctions about firing Puffy. However, in their wisdom, they ruminated and concluded it might be best not to piss off, or, ahem, alienate, the other five Irishmen on the police force; therefore, they "promoted" Puffy to the position of School Department Physical Education Director and, crown on his head, High School Football, Basketball, and Baseball Coach.

It was Puffy O'Brian who gave the Stoughton High teams the nickname *The Black Knights,* after the Cadets of West Point. It was Puffy O'Brian, and certainly not Tony LaStoria, the boy's own Pa, who went out in the driveway to throw the ball around with the kid. Augie had first met Coach O'Brian in the kitchen, and the dining-room, of his own house, while he was still Chief of Police; but in the heedless way of a growing boy, he had forgotten all about that. To Augie, the man was simply "Coach," and counted along with Tobias Haskins as a mentor, a word Augie had learned from Mr Haskins. All this was unbeknownst to Tony, the boy's father. Where Tony LaStoria grew up, on the Lower East Side of New York City, his own "mentors" were someone like Professore Siragusa, or maybe Litvak, the tailor. (Like apple, like tree, Tony, too, had been expanding his vocabulary in English since the day he first met Miss Morgan in the school library of PS 150.) But for Tony, this whole business of team sports was just something outside his own experience of life. It was like expecting his son Augie to love playing the mandolin.

The most legendary exploit of Augie LaStoria's youthful passion for sports occurred one day at the basketball cage at the Y in Stoughton, where the high school team was practicing for a game that Friday night versus Randolph. It was a Tuesday, and Coach wasn't there yet, and Augie, who as a freshman, was already six-foot-two, was standing at the foul line, bouncing the basketball, and gazing absently at the metal hoop attached to the square wooden backboard.

The practice of jumping the ball after every basket had been eliminated back in '37 by a rules change, so the game of 1940 was much faster and more exciting than ever before. Augie was hogging the ball. His teammates crowded around. "What?" they were saying.

"Shut up!" he said. "I'm thinking."

"Thinking what?"

"I wonder."

"What! What!"

"I wonder—if I could just stand under the basket—and jump high enough to just—drop the ball in?"

"Can't be done."

"Impossible."

"Whaddya mean, impossible?" Augie protested. "Some guys playin' this game are a lot taller than I am. For cryin' out loud, it musta been tried somewhere, sometime, by someone. You just ain't heard about it, that's all."

"You gonna try it, Augie?"

He said, "Remember when we used to hafta jump ball all the time? You ever see me lose one?"

"Nope."

"That's right. And you know why? 'Cause I can *jump*."

Augie tried it, and it worked. Just the way he thought. It was a little difficult—but if he coaxed the ball just up on the edge of the rim gently, and pushed with one finger, right at the apex of his jump, by timing it just right, the ball would roll in, or fall in.

"Wow! Did youz guys see that! Do you know what this means? I wouldn't even have to shoot the ball! I could just drop it in! Come on. Let's see how it would really work, say, if we're in a game, like, you know, fast, everybody running. Let's run a play or something. Or, whaddya say we try it out on a lay-up drill, see how that would work?"

Augie was excited and he got Jimmy Robillard to feed him the ball six or seven times. And the more he did it, the more he got his timing down, and the distance, and the jump, and everything! And he was running around feeling ten feet tall.

"Lemme tell ya, boys, *this* is fun!"

"Yeah, but you're not gonna use that in a real game!" It was Coach O'Brian, who had just walked in, and the other players were yelling, "Coach! Coach! Augie just invented a brand-new move! Ya gotta see this, Coach! He calls it his drop-shot!"

"Yeah, yeah, yeah. I seen it already—twice. All right, now, huddle up, all o' yez." They circled around him, including Augie, who was flushed and happy, and breathing hard. "Now look, Ace." Puffy O'Brian was proud of his star *atha-lete*, whom he had personally discovered, as he let everyone in town know, but he liked to pull the strings himself. "It's just a trick shot, that's all, Augie. Why ya always gotta be showin' off?—huh? Everybody already knows you're better than anyone else! Now, you can't do that in a regular league game, and that's that. Whaddya wanna *embarrass* the other side?"

That's the way it went around Stoughton. Everybody knew Puffy O'Brian and Puffy knew everybody, and what Puffy said, that's what went, that was the law.

It was a lot easier to swallow when he was just the Coach at the High School than when he was on the Force, but the kids all respected him. After all, he'd been in the war; and so, he coulda told them a thing or two. And the way things were going, over there in Europe, maybe they oughta listen, too.

It turned out in the end that Puffy O'Brian was a good influence on Augie LaStoria: probably because he almost got Augie killed.

It was the '41 Thanksgiving Day game against the Stoughton Black Knights' traditional rival, the Canton

Warriors, and the other side won the coin toss. Augie said to himself, before the kick-off, *I'm gonna get that ball-carrier. He better not catch it, or he's gonna be sorry.*

So Augie ran downfield under the ball and the poor kid was catching it. Augie had him set up in his sights like the kid was the ninepin and Augie was the bowling ball. All of a sudden, out of nowhere, somebody Augie never saw, not even out of the corner of his eye, wallops him, right in the kisser, while he's charging full-speed, focused only on the man with the ball. An uppercut sends Augie ass-over-tea-kettle and all he could remember was a vague sense of a looming shadow about three times as big as he was standing over him, and the next thing he knew—the ballcarrier fumbled, it gets kicked around, and Stoughton recovers, all the way down to the five-yard-line, and the boys all are yelling, "Line-up! Line-up! We're going in!" Augie's the single-wing tailback, and he lines up all right, but he doesn't remember being in the huddle, and while he's thinking about that, the center snaps the ball right back to him, and Augie fumbles it right back to Canton. All his Stoughton teammates crowd around, peer into his face, and there's blood running out of his leather helmet, all down Augie's face; so they push him away, and start yelling, "Get over to the sidelines!"

And Augie stumbles over, but Coach O'Brian sees him coming and starts screaming, "Whaddya doin! Get back in the game!" and almost swallows his cigar.

And Augie doesn't know where he is, but he starts trotting back to the huddle on wobble-legs, and his side starts yelling "We got the ball again! Get in there!" and Augie dutifully totters towards the goal-line with the ball in his hand on the old Princeton off-tackle dive-play that their playbook calls the tackle-offset, and Augie drops the ball, and costs them another touchdown (the second one) and all the guys are yelling,

"Coach! Coach! He's hurt! Get him outta here! Get 'im outta the game! He's killin' us!"

So Puffy O'Brian lifts up the leather helmet sagging over Augie's brow and sees a mass of blood, and he says, "Ah—go sit down!"

And he spends the rest of the game marching up and down the sideline swearing a blue streak at Augie, telling him to just walk it off. "Okay, now get ready, you're going back in, where's your helmet, come on, just shake it off, what happened, ya got your clock cleaned, huh?"

And at halftime he was steaming, yelling at the whole team in the locker room, "I'd love to get youz turtlenecks in boot camp, in the army, how do youz pansies think you're gonna survive that, if ya can't beat Canton on Turkey Day— when they're handin' ya the game!—huh? Canya tell me that! Yez wouldn't survive the first five minutes! Yez'd be shittin' yer pants getting off the bus!"

And Augie, when he was sitting on the bench, and he was finally getting the feeling his head was clearing, at last, and he had, at length, a cogent thought, it crossed his mind to say to himself, *Well, bub, let that be a lesson to ya. No matter how big you think you are, there's somebody out there bigger than you are.*

And Augie remembered that, later, when some people were shooting live rounds at him, and he was the deer and they were the hunters.

Chapter 21

Black Sheep, Lost Lamb

All their lives growing up, the LaStoria kids had always heard that they were lucky they lived in New England because they were so far north that hurricanes never reached them. They pitied the poor people down south. On the September day that "The Hurricane of '38" hit Boston, it was completely unforeseen.

What happened to the LaStorias was that two sisters, Peggy and Gerry, that very afternoon when the Hurricane hit, were splitting a box of popcorn at the show in Porter Square in Cambridge.

After Mary's marriage to Charlie Laverna, Gerry had slipped into the role of family caretaker once occupied by her big sister; she was trying her best to help out her mother with little Anna around the house, and her father, too. Tony had been chastened by his recent contretemps (another vocabulary addition) with both Mary and Peggy, each in its different way; and nowadays he was finding something he needed in Gerry, a daughter who had genuine affection for him; *perhaps the one who really cared about him?* might have been his thought. This time he was trying to be sure not to overlook a four-leaf clover, the way he had with his firstborn daughter Maria.

As for Peggy, though he would never admit it, a queasy feeling of revulsion lingered on from his wedding confrontation with her. As her Papa, he hovered between *black sheep* and *lost lamb.* How do you reject your own flesh and blood? How do you cast them out, how do you ex-communicate them? *Can you divorce your own daughter?* Tony LaStoria needed to feel that he was not that callous. Yet he rejected Peggy, he disowned her, he wouldn't be satisfied with himself if he didn't. *She had no respect.* He needed a daughter such as Gerry (who idealized him, he knew, but still) *look at the alternative. Look at Peggy.*

Because Peggy had hit on the Daily Double at the track, earlier in the week, two days before the Hurricane that nobody knew was coming, she wanted to spend some money on something new to wear at that darling little Scottish shop, in Porter Square, that carried plaids and woolen things. And because Porter Square was easy to reach by bus from Wilmington, where she was, at this point, living with her husband, Henry Fabiano, in *his* hometown, she called up her sister Gerry, long distance, at the house on Pine Street in Stoughton. Though her older sister Mary was actually closer by, in Watertown, right next door to Cambridge, she was no fun at all, and would only be censorious with her. Peggy knew that Mary more or less shared Tony's judgmental view of Peggy and her marriage to Henry Fabiano. After all, Mary had been perfectly fine with having her Papa find a husband for her. Peggy's wild behavior and complete rejection of propriety and traditional ways, not to mention their mother Gigi's feelings, called into question Mary's own choices, and made her look stodgy, and Mary didn't like that. Peggy's other sister Gerry, on the other hand, was still young and impressionable, and more importantly, still liked Peggy. Gerry was not, at the moment, on the outs with Peggy, nor Peggy with her, as she was with most of them.

So, could Gerry meet up with her? Because, you know, "it's no fun going shopping alone." And they could go see a picture, because "you know, I hate to go to the show by myself." And another thing, "that picture I wanna see, *Condemned Women,* is showing at the *Rialto.* That's another reason to be in Porter Square tomorrow. Listen, Gerry, it's bound to be shocking. It's got Anne Shirley in it, and that dreamboat, Louis Hayward, plays the love interest, who turns out to be the prison doctor! So, whaddya say, Gerry, you gonna skip work tomorrow, or what?"

Gerry, like the others, had left school when she was 14, in the 7th grade, when Pa told her that she had to leave school to help out. She had gone to work at the Tyer Rubber Company in Stoughton, where she started chumming around with a new best friend, a Polish girl named Hildie Razilko. She and Peggy were on the phone, long distance, from Wilmington to Stoughton (Peggy's shopping trips were always planned ahead of time, like Pershing's invasion of Mexico). Gerry loved Peggy, who was now 20 years old, 4 years older than she was; a grown-up woman, and married, to boot, whereas Gerry was still a kid, by comparison, in her own eyes, just turned 16, and so Gerry said, "Listen, I don't know, Peggy, you better hang up, isn't this costing you a bundle?"

"But you know I hate—."

"I know, I know, but I don't wanna get in trouble."

Gerry's girlfriend, Hildie, whose family also lived on Pine Street, further down, towards the corner of York Street, happened to be hanging on every word, on the other side of the telephone, and she whispered, "I'll cover for ya. I'll tell 'em you're sick." Gerry frequently had Hildie over for supper. Basically, they were together day and night, and Hildie was dying to find out all about the shocking movie, *Condemned Women,* even if she couldn't see it herself, because she knew Gerry would tell her all about it the following day at work. Gerry knew Hildie wanted to see it, too, just by her expression when she overheard the movie's title, and the teasing note of naughtiness in Peggy's voice. So Gerry said, "Can I bring Hildie?"

"No, I don't like that girl," said Peggy, on the phone, and then she thought, *oh, no, what if she's right there?* So she hastily added, "Besides, I can't spring for three, whaddya think I am, a bank?"

"That's not very nice, Peggy," said Gerry, defending her downcast friend.

"Well, I'm not very nice, am I? Just ask Pa. Come on, Gerry. Don't let me down, now, I'm counting on you! Besides, my treat!"

"Oh!—." Hildie was waving furiously at Gerry, and mouthing the words, *it's okay, it's okay, you'll tell me all about it the next day!* So Gerry, into the phone, said to Peggy, "All right, all right, stop twisting my arm," adding, "I don't know where you get the money to just spend like that!"

"Where do you think? From my husband. Or else, what' he good for?"

The two sisters made arrangements to meet in Porter Square, getting off the buses, at which trolley-stop, what time, and so on, and then Peggy proclaimed, "Good-bye!"

"Good-bye!" answered Gerry, and she hung up. "Oh, Hildie, I'm so sorry."

"Nah, nah, nah, who cares? If that's the way she feels about it, who needs her? Just tell me all about it, the next day, at work. I gotta say, though, that sister of yours, she's a scootch!"

The next day neither Peggy nor Gerry, in the morning, had any idea of any such a thing as a hurricane coming. There were no forecasts of anything. Pa LaStoria drove up to Boston for work, just as usual, in his Buick that morning, with Patsy. Nobody had any forewarning, really; and certainly no warning of a hurricane; nor would they have known one had they seen one. The last one that had reached as far north as New England had occurred in 1893, and none of them had ever even heard of that. To them, hurricanes were something you heard about hitting Florida, or Louisiana, places like that, at worst, Cape Hatteras, in other words, *down south.*

So that morning, Gerry met Hildie on her front doorstep, after her father left, and as far as her mother knew, she and Hildie were going off to work together, as usual, at the Tyer Rubber Company.

Whereas actually Gerry caught the trolley in Stoughton Square and wound her way by streetcar, with transfers, up through the Blue Hills Reservation, through Milton to Mattapan, up into downtown Boston, changing at South Station for the subway over to Harvard Square in Cambridge. It was a long, but pleasant, ride, because she was accompanied by a good book, *Anthony Adverse,* which she had been dying to read ever since the movie version, with Fredric March and Olivia deHavilland, which Gerry had seen, at the *Central,* in Stoughton Square, came out in '36.

Though in so many other respects, they were opposites, personality-wise, like her big sister Peggy, Gerry was a fanatical follower of the Hollywood movies. You always read the book first, if you could, or often, the movie made you want to read the book. In this case, Gerry got a blue-bound hardcover copy of *Anthony Adverse,* well-worn, with little threads hanging from the spine, from the Stoughton Library. It was so much longer than the movie. In fact, the movie barely told half the story; so Gerry was glad she had seen the Hollywood version first. Growing up in the 'Thirties, it was hard to be immune to the allure of the silver screen, when all around you, there was so much hardship: it was cheap, it was there, it was everywhere; for an afternoon you could let go of all your troubles, and slip into that darkened cave with the ghostly bluish beam of light, and be taken away.

Anthony Adverse, being a terribly long novel, was the perfect thing to take along on her endless streetcar journey; and it was so fascinating, and compulsive, that Gerry did not actually notice that it took any time at all before she was seated in a diner in Porter Square for a late breakfast with Peggy.

After which it was shopping for stockings, skirts, capes and blouses, and hand-bags to match, at The Tartan Shop, then lunch, of course, and it was already one o'clock in the afternoon before they were seated for their show to start. Peggy paid for everything they bought, even the things Gerry picked out that she liked, even the lunch, and the tickets for the show.

Gerry was thinking *big sister's certainly generous with throwing around Henry Fabiano's money!*

The one thing about the movies with Peggy that Gerry could count on was the running commentary of nudges and elbows. Peggy just could not shut up and let you watch. And of course, it was now late September of '38, and Peggy had already been a married woman for a whole year, and so they had a lot to catch up on.

"That man," said Peggy, referring to Henry, while digging into popcorn and gazing at Louis Hayward on-screen, "I swear, it ain't blood running in his veins, it's printers' ink."

"Peggy!"

"Well, he's at it morning, noon and night, and its seven days a year, I mean a week—oh, didja see that? That's him, Louis Hayward, I'd like to hitch a ride with him."

Gerry giggled, thinking of the famous scene with Claudette Colbert thumbing a ride by hiking her skirts up. A voice behind them tried to shush them. Peggy swerved her head and shot looks like darts. "Ah—blow it up your fanny!" After that, they were not bothered.

Gerry said, "Sheesh—where'd you learn your manners?"

"At the track," said Peggy, as she reached for popcorn. "Same place that paid for your breakfast. And lunch."

"Okay, okay. I get it. But where do you get the money for the track?"

"Same place that paid for your breakfast. And lunch." Peggy sighed. "Well, anyways, little sister—it's got so bad, I hate to let him touch me."

"Peggy!—you've only been married less than a year!"

"I just hate to get all smudged up, is all."

"At this rate, how're you ever gonna last a lifetime?"

"Ever hear of the divorce courts, kid?"

"Peggy! You're as bad as the girls in the picture!"

"I make him wash his hands with that tar soap before I let him touch me."

"I don't believe a word I'm hearing."

"So—you don't want me to let you in on a little secret, then."

"Peggy, no!"

"Ah, but, yes! At least I think so. I been feeling funny lately. Well, worst comes to worst, at least we'll get another shopping trip out of it. But, you know, Gerry, I'm gonna hate getting big. What if I lose my figure and I can't get it back?"

The only warning they had of what was to come was when they felt the building shake, or thought they did; but it must have been their imaginations. Then when the double-feature let out, around four o'clock, and they descended from their balcony seats down to the lobby, they could not believe what they saw through the rattling glass panes of the doors. The few trees along that stretch of Massachusetts Avenue were lying flat on their sides—and all the telephone poles. It seemed as dark out there as ten o'clock at night. The wind sounded like a streetcar going down the Harvard Square tunnel: deafening.

"What's going on?" Peggy demanded of the girl behind the candy counter, who was shivering as she clutched a thin sweater around her elbows.

"I don't know, but it doesn't look good to me."

"Well, hell—how're we supposed to get a streetcar home?"

A voice said, "There won't be any streetcars running in this, honey."

The patrons of the show were gathering to huddle together inside the rattling glass doors, which were rippling like wax paper, when somebody else said, "I don't think it's such a good idea to all stand here in front of all this glass."

Another voice agreed, "Yep—they could blow any second."

"God—never saw such a wind! Look at it! Rain going sideways!"

"We better all get back inside."

And so the two sisters joined the rest, and later, the line to the office, of people trying to make phone calls to home.

But the phones evidently weren't working anyway, all the lines must be down, what was the use? They were socked in for the whole night, it was looking like, and nothing on hand to even eat but licorice sticks, and who knew what they would find in the morning, or if they would ever get out of there. And to think you had to use the rest rooms in this place, not just for a piddle, but to wash your face and comb your hair, oh, it was just too much!

They had no idea of what had hit them, of what was going on outside, in the rest of Cambridge, or in Boston. So how could they have pictured the bridges down, the roads flooded out, the boats pushed into house-fronts, sitting there in the dark: the real dark, after they, too, lost electricity.

Peggy put her feet up, and then down, and then up again, and Gerry was just plain miserable, thinking of all the trouble she was going to be in when her father found out where she had spent the night.

They were as much prisoners as the "Condemned Women" of Hollywood. Only for them, it was no fantasy, but the real thing.

And neither one of them ever stopped to think for one second that Tony LaStoria and Patsy LaStoria and Henry Fabiano were all, at that moment, out in automobiles, trying to get through blocked roads in a devastated night, worried to death over a wife, over a daughter, over two sisters, and the problems of how to get through to them, or whether they would find them safe when they did.

At least their Pa, Tony, had found out where they were from Hildie Razilko. Lucky for him he was in his office in South

Boston and by some miracle, the phone lines to Stoughton lasted long enough for him to call through to Gigi, at home, to let the family know that he and Patsy were fine and planned on staying put for the night; at which point he incidentally found out that no one had heard from Peggy and Gerry, stranded, in the storm, they supposed, in Porter Square, Cambridge. Which Gigi only knew about from Hildie. Hildie had gotten scared for her best girlfriend Gerry, out in this, this *hurricane,* and phoned the LaStorias' house, and got Anna on the phone to explain to her mother; even though she felt like a rat, who was going to get Gerry in trouble with her Ma and Pa.

Having been indoors all day in the stout seven-story redbrick mill-building at No.10 Melcher Street, the kind of building not even the worst hurricane anyone had ever seen could blow away, Tony LaStoria took his son Patsy along with him, to buttress him in the Buick, to give him another pair of eyes, and make a search party of it, as he thought it best to get out there in the storm in case his children needed him: his nemesis, Peggy, and his darling, Gerry. How could he and Patsy just sit there safe and sound when they, silly females that they were, might be in peril?

Henry Fabiano, home alone in Wilmington, worried sick about his lost wife, who had not thought to let him know where she was going for the day; whom he found missing when he got home from his office at the *Wilmington News;* his lost wife, whom he cared for, in his desperately-dedicated, near-sighted fashion, the only way he knew how to be, about anything (his work, his home, his hometown, his weekly newspaper, sports, the news, his life, his wife): where was she? Where *could* she be? his lost wife, who had not called him all day, who might be anywhere, in this awful storm, who perhaps had been unable to call him, who might at this very moment need him, need his help.

Desperate, thinking the worst, Henry Fabiano dashed out in the windy downpour to the neighbor's house across the wide lawn, soaked and slushy. Young Franny, Peggy's girlfriend next door, said Peggy had said she'd be back long before Henry ever left the office, not to worry, you know him, married to the job. Well, didn't she say where she was going? No, she just said she'd be back by five. At this point, Franny was frantic about her own newlywed husband, who hadn't got home yet. Henry Fabiano promised her that as soon as he found Peggy he would then set out to locate Franny's husband, but, look, he'll be home any second now, you'll see.

Starting from Wilmington in his second-hand 1932 Model-A Ford, driving, peering through the inundated windshield, at downed power-lines, uprooted trees, and overturned buses, having no idea where to begin, Henry Fabiano was out there *alone,* with all the phone lines down. And Henry thought *if I know her, I better try Suffolk Downs.*

Chapter 22

Bulletin

To Tony LaStoria the idea of war, the reality, seemed inconceivable. His newspaper habit had never for a day flagged since the last war in Europe, through floods, epidemics, strikes, the upbeat 'Twenties, the Sacco and Vanzetti saga, or the downbeat of the Depression. Tony kept informed. It was 1940 and the war in Europe was far down the road to catastrophe, the Germans just waiting for Christmas for the collapse of the woebegone Russians. England, all assumed, was next on Hitler's timetable. As for China, that was a distant newsreel, so far away, it wasn't real.

Yet it was so hard to get your bearings, to make up your mind what to think. They were feeling beneficial side effects from the conflagrations in Europe and the Orient. The epic doldrums of the 'Thirties were fading. The predicted upswing in orders, *predicted by Harry Spritzka,* had materialized: they were here, it was happening. Tony's New England division of Harry's business network was now a foundational bulwark of what Harry and his brother Robert had newly dubbed The Manna Group, a conglomerate of manufacturing and industrial service companies, real estate trusts, banks, and automobile insurance agencies, owned and operated by an umbrella entity called Spritzka Brothers.

It seemed the countryside over that everybody had a job again. What previously had been shrinking was now expanding. Thanks to Roosevelt and Lend-Lease and the British, who were desperate to get their hands on everything America was willing to sell to them, everybody had money in their pockets. The war was not real. *This* was real. The war was a Saturday serial they put on at the show before the Double Feature.

In the house on Pine Street in Stoughton, the table was set for Gigi LaStoria's Sunday dinner at two in the afternoon, everyone knew, so they timed their arrivals. Augie, who was 16 now, was still living at home, although it seemed he was never there, except, naturally, for Sunday dinner. Anna, the baby of the family, their special pet, was 14. Gene was twenty-one, old enough to have a nice steady girl, an attractive young Greek girl called Celia Constantinos; but Patsy was already 27, and had married a girl named Mary Carlotti, who came from Somerville, where the young couple were living with her family.

This Mary, another Mary in the family, besides their own Mary in Watertown, was pregnant with Patsy's first, and, although she was feeling so uncomfortable in her seventh month, Patsy had hauled her all the way down to Stoughton on the streetcar lines. After all, it was Sunday dinner. What better time to show off?

Gerry was 19, unattached, and seemingly, in no rush. She had her hands full, between her girlfriend Hildie, her job at Tyer Rubber, which was now running three shifts, six days a week, and her housekeeping chores, inherited from the role first carved out in the family by her big sister, Mary.

Gerry was, day to day, more worried, troubled and bothered with her mother. Gigi seemed lackluster and careworn compared to her old self. Gerry's mother had grown so overweight she could no longer pull up her own stockings. She needed Gerry's assistance in the mornings to get going. It was like pushing a formless pillow into shape. But she was still the one who wielded the rolling pin, and she had Gerry up at six in the morning on a Sunday to help with rolling out the dough and cutting the macaroni.

Gerry would have loved to lie in bed, where she was re-reading *Gone with the Wind,* for the third time, and was in the middle of *The Grapes of Wrath,* again. She could never read just one book at a time. Her sister Mary was home in Watertown with her husband and two children, that Sunday, as usual. That husband of hers, the Calabrian, Laverna, was not the most sociable. It seemed to Gerry she hardly ever saw Mary anymore. She wouldn't know her nephew and niece, Mary's kids, they'd be grown so big, if she ever did see them again: Little Tony, now 4 years old, named after their Pa, Big Tony, and baby Gerry, age 2, her own namesake. Gerry thought she ought to go up there to Dewey Street and pay her namesake a visit, but when did she have a minute to herself? When and if she did have such a minute, either her girlfriend Hildie or her sister Peggy were pulling her away to see some latest Hollywood extravaganza at the show: *Meet Me in St Louis,* which Gerry had now seen at least four times, although, for Judy Garland, she would gladly go seven more. Seven was her record, and that was *The Wizard of Oz,* in, oh my God, *Technicolor.*

The following summer, it was a rainy Sunday in August about a quarter of two when Peggy walked in the back door on Pine Street in Stoughton.

Patsy said, "Look what the cat dragged in!"

Peggy said to him, "Hiya, Fatso!"

"Hey, only Pa gets to call me that."

"Married life suits you, I see." Peggy pulled out a chair and deposited her overladen handbag on the table. Which raised her father's disgusted look. Which Peggy did not fail to notice.

Her brother Gene was there at Gigi's big dining room table with Celia, now his newlywed wife, since their June wedding. So were Augie, now 17, and Anna, still the tender age of 14, and also, seated next to them, Gerry's girlfriend, Hildie Rizilko, whom Gerry frequently invited over for Sunday dinner. Gene dutifully tried staying out of the Peggy wars, so he asked what he thought was an innocuous question, just to make small talk: "Where's Henry, parking the car?"—referring to her husband, Fabiano, the editor.

Peggy ignored him and leaned over to Patsy's wife Mary, who was looking miserable at the thought of food. "So, kid—you're expecting. I know how you feel." Then she turned to Gene. "What did you say, brother of mine?"

Gene sank in his seat. "Nevermind."

"Well, for your information, I left him cutting his toenails."

"Peggy!" Gerry was setting out the plates and dishes.

Her father turned to Peggy and said, "When you gonna learn to behave yourself? Can't you see we got company?"

"Pa!" said Peggy. "I didn't know you were talking to me. No more silent treatment then?"

Her Pa rolled his eyes, and clicked his tongue–tch!-leaving unspoken the thought, *I shoulda known better and kept my trap shut.*

Peggy looked at Gene, and said, "No, seriously—I left him."

Gene was puzzled. "So, how did you get out here to Stoughton—on foot?"

"He dropped me off in his car, dumb-bell, just now."

They all looked at one another, uncertainly. Did she mean what they thought she meant?

"Well," said Peggy, seeing their unanimous bafflement, "just because we're getting divorced don't mean we ain't talking to one another, unlike some people." When all their faces began registering degrees of shock, Peggy added, petulantly, "What can I say? Married life didn't suit me."

"But what about your children?" Gigi, her mother, blurted out, in dialect.

"They're with him. They'll be all right. They'll be fine." Peggy and Henry had their first, Henry, Jr, back in '39, and their second, Ronnie a year later. Peggy was in a hurry to get pregnancy out of the way. Her one concession to motherhood was that she didn't want Henry to be alone in the world, without a brother or sister, the way her father Tony had been: *and look how that turned out.*

Her father put down the Sunday *Post,* in which the front page carried a report on the Libyan front, where the Italians of Mussolini's Army were being bulldozed by the British, and said to Peggy, in the voice he used to signify excommunication, "There's no divorce in this family."

"Why, Pa, didn't you hear? Lincoln freed the slaves. Maybe one of these days, he'll get around to the women, huh?"

Gigi's pride and joy was the oversized dining-room table with the scrolled and carved lion's-paw legs and the removable leaf in the middle. This was the table where she stood supervising Gerry setting out each course, on Sundays, and holidays, until everyone begged her, Ma, sit down, eat, you're always the last to sit down. The dinner, lentil soup first, then followed by her big steaming yellow bowl of macaroni, spaghetti and ravioli, with meatballs and sausage, then the main course, which today was a roast leg of lamb, with potatoes and onions garnishing, and finally, to help with the digestion, *insalata.*

At these big family Sunday dinners, Gigi would sit down when she was ready to call it a day and start to relax, her family gathered, the dinner lasting all afternoon, and she was just going to sit down at last, when she detected the word "divorce," a word she certainly did know, and which bothered her; not because she condemned the idea, piously, or because any Pope, bishop or parish priest forbade it, but because it meant that one of her children was in trouble, and what could you do about it? *Prepare to shed tears? Push more food onto their plate?* Gerry was about to start dispensing the soup when her Pa, Tony, stood up and walked out, taking his newspaper into the parlor with him. A gesture whose pointed meaning was not lost on any of them.

Gigi spoke Italian to her daughter Peggy, thinking that this way, at least Gene's poor bride, Celia, the Greek girl, who was so nice, wouldn't have to hear, and told Peggy, "See what you did now?" nodding at Peggy's father, whose abrupt departure had sent her a message. "Oh, you can never leave well enough alone."

However, Peggy knew her mother was not really mad at her. Gigi was simply not able to take the side of anyone other than her own child. Peggy knew also, somehow, that Gigi was secretly admiring of this daughter's boldness, her spirit: after all, thinking of herself and Peggy as two sisters, two of a kind, Gigi thought: *il sangue non mente.* Long ago, between Gigi and Peggy, their compact had formed around the idea that both had to put up with *him,* this Tony: one because she was married to him, the other because she didn't quite know if she hated her own Pa or not.

Gerry tiptoed into the parlor, wiping her hands on her apron. "Pa—you want me to bring you something in here?"

Her father looked up at her from his paper with eyes as big and brown as one of the bird-dogs in his kennel. The thought of this daughter, who, as he conceived it, honestly loved him, not out of duty, but out of some kind of affection, some empathy or sympathy; this daughter, who was so genuinely and ingenuously *simpatico* (in contrast to that other thing, Peggy); to think of his daughter, Gerry, in this complex of conflict and emotion sometimes brought home to him the tenderness of love when it is tinged with pain. "All right, Gerry. Just bring me a plate, I'll put it in my lap. And the mopina, the big one. I'm bound to spill all over myself." He looked down forlornly at his usual white shirt. "And put on the radio for me." She now set about to do his bidding, and he added, with a resigned, self-pitying note of complaint, which only Gerry's ministrations could have brought out of him, "I don't want to have to listen to her in there."

He watched her go, saddened even further at the mixture of such feelings combined of pity and awe as this good daughter roused in him, which resided, in turmoil, right alongside a consciousness of his own ridiculousness; and, he reflected, only too bitterly, that he himself had aided and abetted that other one in reducing him to this. *Could I at least have avoided stepping in the pile of* cucca *right in front of me?*

He put his newspaper down. He had lost his appetite. He was sitting there, dinner in his lap, paper put aside, and he was picturing his daughter Peggy, thinking of her as if she were one of his dogs, a bitch, and one who had bit the hand that fed her.

A few months later, just after Thanksgiving, on an early December Sunday, when winter still seemed like it might not set in this year after all, Tony LaStoria was sitting in the same chair in the same parlor after the usual big Sunday dinner, sitting by himself, dozing, waking fretfully, with the newspaper fallen in his lap, the noise of his family, still gathered around the table, murmuring out from the dining room, including the annoying stridency of his daughter Peggy who, since her separation from Henry Fabiano and her children, had installed herself back home while she was "between jobs," in her own description; when, on the radio, the voice of Charles Daly from New York seemed to interrupt another program with a one-line bulletin.

"The Japanese have attacked Pearl Harbor by air, President Roosevelt has just announced."

Tony did not stop what he was doing, thinking, feeling, until the radio seemed to suddenly fall silent for the longest time. Which never happened. Dead air. That caught his attention. Then he asked himself—*did I hear what I thought I heard?*

He had been sipping his usual after-dinner cup of coffee, which he always took to cap off the *vino* he had taken with dinner. Now he put down the spoon in his right hand, on the saucer with the coffee, on his little side-table. He dispensed with the newspaper still lying in his lap, folding it up neatly on the floor next to him, and he stared at the Zenith console radio, across the parlor by the end-table next to the sofa.

The regular announcer's voice came on, introducing the usual 2.30 broadcast of CBS' *The World Today,* from New York.

Ever since the war had started Tony had been gathering and collecting diligently every drop and morsel of news and information he could, and the radio was a strong runner-up to the newspaper in his pursuit of the sources that kept him updated; and, also, this show gave him a way to allow himself to feel somehow his old connection to New York, which was, and always would be, his city.

That connection, that old, worn-out loyalty, these days was not to be disregarded. It was where Tony LaStoria had begun, with America. His roots, his sense of identity. It had been such a facet of his dream, so many years ago; once, it had meant the world to him, New York. For love of that city he had given up even his native land of Italy. And now was not a time, in the passing scene, with everything menacing that was going on in the world, to bury your head in the sand. Tony and all the other regular members of the Sons of Italy in Stoughton were furious at President Roosevelt. He had been demoted from the pedestal of sainthood he held during the Depression, in their minds, because of his insulting comments back in May of 1940, when Mussolini had taken Italy into the war on the side of his ally, Hitler, and the Axis Powers.

Roosevelt had been scheduled that very day of Mussolini's announcement to give the commencement speech at the University of Virginia in Charlottesville, because his own son was graduating from law school there. And that was the occasion when he uttered the infamous quote, "On this tenth day of June, 1940, the hand that held the dagger has struck it into the back of its neighbor."

Overnight, it was all anyone could talk about. The print trade quickly dubbed it "the stab-in-the-back" speech; bad as it was, that managed to make it even worse.

In Stoughton, the bitter after-taste of the Sacco and Vanzetti affair was close at hand, always ever-present, because Sacco had lived in the town and worked at a shoe-shop in Stoughton. The locals would not let go of it. The whole town was divided, for and against, over that case. Even now, so many years later, when the townspeople had wilted in the Depression, only to emerge onto hopeful days, trumpeted by war-clouds on the horizon, they would not let you forget: *Sacco and Vanzetti.*

So sensitive was their assessment of how they were perceived in the town that the local Italians were electric and vocal in their resentment over the President's "stab-in-the-back" thrust.

They considered themselves betrayed. And by whom? None other than their savior, Roosevelt, whom they had anointed as the democratic prince who delivered them from the Depression. It was Roosevelt himself who now had turned into their Judas.

They, the Italians, were the ones who, in fact, had been "stabbed in the back."

Though the President had never actually uttered those four words in his speech, everyone swore he that he had. And who could ever forgive the image of the "dagger?" Even Tony LaStoria himself had to admit that his boyhood friend, Harry Spritzka, on the day of their very first meeting, so many long years ago, had admonished him, before they began that fateful fistfight—*no knives!*

This was the worse calumny of all, to revive, at such a time, the age-old spectre of the Americans' unshakeable superstition that every wop carried a knife in his pocket and was ready to slit your throat, for car-fare.

And as if to confirm his unwavering duplicity, the President then proceeded to try to woo the Italians back into the fold when Columbus Day came around in 1940. The November elections were then at stake: *and now, Roosevelt needed your vote!*

The Italians all over Boston and Eastern Massachusetts trooped to the polls to reverse their previously unyielding faith in their savior by voting overwhelmingly for Wendell Wilkie.

Tony LaStoria, as the long-time President of the local Sons of Italy, nowadays had a double duty to keep himself informed and up-to-date. After all, what was he to say to all the worried Italian parents in town, or up in Boston, where he had his General Manager's office? The ones who were so worried that their beloved sons, who meant more than the world to them, would be dragged into a horrific foreign war that was none of nobody's business, certainly not theirs!

Then there was the fine line you had to dance because you knew that in their hearts of hearts, your people were also secretly proud of Mussolini, and of what he had done for the homeland, and Italy's stature in the eyes of the world. How many times had you heard the phrase repeated, 'He made the trains run on time!' At least there was one place in this world where Italians could hold their heads high! And so, they were actually rooting for the home team, as it were! *What a rabbit stew! How do you advise them?* How do you help them fend off their worst nightmares and simultaneously not feed and inflame their absurd visions of glory? *What about this ridiculous devotion to the revival of the Roman Empire! Because that's exactly what it was, ridiculous!* What a time to be caught in! You better not have your pants down this time.

This new war, this horrible, shameful, obsessed ritual of re-opened wounds, of bloodletting and slaughter, was not like the first time. It was no longer the other fellow who had to be dragged off to save the world for democracy. *This time, they were coming for you, for your sons, for your flesh and blood!*

And so it was that Tony had restructured his Sunday dinner around the 2.30 broadcast time of *The World Today* on CBS. His practice now was to finish his second course at the table, in time to join the show in the parlor, and only come back after the half-hour program was over to resume the meat course.

But on this Sunday, of all Sundays, Peggy had upset his regimented routine.

And so he was not paying attention when the first announcement abruptly ended.

Until the silence.

Now, he put everything down, crossed the room, and turned up the volume, then resumed his seat, sitting forward, his elbows on his knees, on edge, listening.

Charles Daly in New York was introduced by the announcer at the resumption of the beginning of *The World Today.*

It was the regular introduction; same as every week; sounded normal: Tony was listening to every word. The announcer concluded, "Go ahead, New York."

Daly then began by repeating the same line, "The Japanese have attacked Pearl Harbor by air, President Roosevelt has just announced." But he added, this time, "Pearl Harbor, Hawaii," and also continued with a second sentence, "The attack also was made on all military and naval activities on the principle island of Oahu."

Daly had mispronounced the name of the island, but it did not register with listeners, who were saying to themselves, *where?* He then interrupted himself to announce that they were going to a report by Albert Warner, in Washington itself.

Tony yelled out, "Patsy! Genie! Come here!"

It was something in their Pa's voice that made the three sons of Tony LaStoria set aside knife and fork and rush in with cloth napkins still tucked in their necks. They thought they were going to find the front room on fire. The women all followed, after catching the chairs the boys were tipping over. The patriarch pointed to the radio. "Listen!" Patsy listened, then yelled

"Turn it up!" Augie went quickly to kneel by the end-table and adjust the knob. And the voice from Washington continued, "The President's brief statement was read to reporters by Steve Early, the White House Press Secretary. A Japanese attack on Pearl Harbor naturally would mean war. Naturally, the President would ask Congress for a declaration of war. There is no doubt that such a declaration would be granted."

Everyone crowding into the parlor now erupted. "I don't believe it!" "Those sons-a-bitches!" "This is it!" "We're in it now!" "Those little bastards!—how could they!" Celia slid in behind Gene and snuck her head through his arm. She was crying already as he put his arm around her. Tony yelled out, "Shut up!—everybody!" Patsy was red in the face. He was expecting opposition and he was not in any mood for it. "Pa—we gotta go! We're enlisting!" His father said, "Shut up and listen, will ya!" Patsy turned to his brothers. "Gene, you with me in this? Augie—you're not old enough!" Tony said to his son, "Patsy!—you don't know what you're talking about! You're not going anywhere!"

The voice of Warner from Washington droned on. "The two Japanese, Namura and Kurusu, are at the State Department in a meeting with Secretary Hull. Hostilities seem to be opening over the entire South Pacific. Regardless of what the diplomats are saying, Japan has now cast the die. Yesterday, Japanese troops were steaming for Thailand. It was based . . ."

No one was listening any longer. The whole house was in an uproar. Everyone talked at once. Gigi had finally made her way over and was trying to stretch her neck to see above all the others jammed in the wide arch to the parlor. She knew it was terrible, and she was trying to locate Tony's face to gauge how bad it was, the news. Then Tony was yelling in English to her, "It's all right! It's all right! Come in! Come in!" He was waving his hand for her to enter. Bodies parted to let her through. Tony grabbed her hand and pulled her over to sit in his own seat. He turned to Patsy, furious. "You—*stubido!* You wanna break your mother's heart? Now—settle down, all of you— let's at least try to listen and find out what the hell is going on!"

Patsy stood up to his father. "Pa! we know. We *know.* Today, yesterday, tomorrow, what does it matter? The pot's boilin' over, it's been on the simmer for awhile. It was gonna happen in the end no matter what. Now it has. And somebody's gonna hafta teach those little yellow dogs a lesson. And it looks like it's gonna have to be us!"

Augie yelled at Patsy, "I'm going with you guys! You can't keep me out!"

Gerry locked her arms around Augie, her little brother, her favorite. "No, no, Augie, you stay here with us!" She knew in her heart she had already lost Patsy and Genie.

Gene looked down into the eyes of his sweetheart, Celia, and said, softly, "Merry Christmas, baby, huh? Some present the bastards are giving us."

The other women in the room, Gerry, young Anna, Patsy's wife Mary, were now seeking one another out, locking arms in a three-way embrace, to support one another so that they could stand up in the riptide of emotions coursing through them.

Peggy stopped them all in their tracks with her comment. "Jesus Christ—I wish I could go!"

Absurdly, they all laughed, except her father. He said, "Patsy! Go get my gun outta the closet! Give it to Peggy! Let her go! Hirohito won't stand a chance!"

While the rest of the room erupted, Tony LaStoria turned to his wife, and for the first time in years, he knelt down before Gigi, and clasped her in a big embrace, as tight as he could. He buried his head on her shoulder, to try to stop up the tears he felt surging up. Then he pulled back, and held her face in his hands. She was openly weeping. She looked at him as if she had just found him again, after having not seen him for years. She looked at him as if her three sons were not standing there at all, in the same room with her, but had already been taken away and lost to her, and were dead and buried in their graves. Gigi looked at Tony and asked, "È vero?"

"Si, caramia—mi cara, cara amore. È vero."

Chapter 23

Sons of Italy

Soon after that Sunday, too soon, right after Christmas, it seemed, or perhaps at the beginning of January, 1942, something happened that gave a shock to all the LaStorias, and to Tony a grievance, a scab to pick over, that ever after never quite seemed to quit itching. It was none other than Puffy O'Brian himself who came to the house, on another Sunday, with a job of bearing bad news to carry out.

Over the years, the Coach and erstwhile Police Chief had been a visitor for Sunday dinner before. But more often, he'd been there mid-week; he loved *pastavazoule,* especially when Gigi put in the pork rinds and preceded it with a bowl of *minastra.*

This was a different occasion, and at the dinner table Puffy was plainly not his usual, affable, beer-swilling self. He seemed rather nervous and said little and avoided looking at the family. Finally, Tony pulled him aside into the parlor, by the elbow, and said, "What is wrong with you today? You jumpy or something?"

Puffy said, "First, Tony, I don't like to do this. You gotta believe me."

"Do what, Puffy?"

"The only reason I agreed was to try and make it easier on you and the family. They thought that because you and me were friends, and I'm always over your house, and coachin' Augie, and all—."

"Puffy, you're drivin' me crazy."

"I'm gonna tell you. But first, you gotta forgive me."

"Forgive you for what?" Tony stopped himself. "I forgive you."

"You swear?"

"I swear. Come on! Out with it!"

"Well, Gigi's gotta come down to the station tomorrow morning and register as an enemy alien."

Tony bent forward slightly, threw his arms out a little, frowned, and said, "All right." He was stunned and the words escaped his lips before he knew what he was saying.

They resumed their places at the table. Puffy kept his head down. Tony looked at his dinner but he was abstracted, at a loss to know his own thoughts, his own feelings, as the sense of a deep, and profound, vindictive anger crept over him.

At the station the next morning, it became clear to him that some things were, after all, unforgivable.

Gigi emerged from behind the closed door of the back room in the stationhouse and her face was a mask of tears. She approached Tony looking down at both hands while she kept rubbing her fingertips against her thumbs. She looked up into Tony's eyes, and said, in Italian, "I'm such a big danger to them, they had to fingerprint me."

When the police brought the finished ID card, with her photo pasted into the corner, to her back door, she saved the picture-card all day, waiting for Tony to come home from work.

When they went to bed that night, she thrust it at him, saying, "Look!—how they made me look!—like Al Capone or something."

By this time, they had two sons enlisted in the United States Army. That made no difference. Gigi had never felt so humiliated in all her life. Tony was aggrieved all the way down to his soul. The pendulum had swung. And when it swung back, this time it took their last son.

It was April of 1942, long past deer season, when Augie went to see his friend Tobias Haskins at the clubhouse at Ponkapoag. Colonel Doolittle's raid on Tokyo was the big story in the news that day. Augie said to his mentor, "Mr Haskins, I just gotta join up—before it's too late! The war's gonna be over before I get a chance!"

"I hope so," said Haskins.

"You know—I never asked you this before—but—were you ever in the Army?"

With all his heart, Augie wanted it to be true. So many times, in his boyish imagination, since he had first met the Indian, he had replayed over and over Haskins performing all the heroic deeds he'd seen Gary Cooper perform as *Sergeant York* in the Ardennes Forest. Only Haskins was half-naked, with a tomahawk in his hand, and wearing a Mohawk haircut and war-paint.

"I did serve one time. It was back in '16. General Pershing and me took a little look-see kind of a ride down south of the border."

For a moment, Haskins let his guard down, and Augie perceived the twinkle of satisfaction in the smile that creased his countenance. Augie thought, *he must be remembering.*

But then Tobias Haskins recollected that this was serious business they were discussing and reverted to his usual impassive blankness. Augie summoned up his best impression of being over-awed. "I'll bet you guys showed that old Pancho Villa." Augie was hoping to hear all the details. He wanted to know everything. This was his chance to talk to someone who'd been there. "How come you never told me about it, Mr Haskins?"

"Nothin' much to tell, Augie. All I remember is lotsa sand, and flies. Flies all over the place. Flies everywhere."

Augie waited, while trying manfully not to appear as over-eager as a puppy, but it became clear that the mask had come down over the older man again. He had to respect that. Still, he knew a veteran. That was something he didn't know the day before. (He was completely forgetting about Coach O'Brian, in his rush of enthusiasm.) Despite himself, Augie's youthful exuberance filled in the pause. "Well—I need your advice, sir, because, you know, I gotta enlist."

"How old are you, son?"

"Old enough."

"Exactly how old is that?"

"Well, I just turned seventeen. But I can't wait, Tobias! Seventeen—that's a whole year gone—wasted—I could be all done boot camp and training and all, and be in action by that time!"

"Well, son, just remember, over there, it's deer season all year round, and the deer are shootin' back at you."

"But, Tobias—you did it."

"Yes, I did. But I was 25 back then, Augie, a grown man, and I knew what I was getting' into."

"You don't think I do?"

"Well, I think you're gonna get your eyes opened, that's what I think. And right now, that's just what you need."

"So, why did you do it?"

"Augie, I needed the job. Plain and simple. To tell you the truth, I wasn't amounting to anything, back then, and probably, well, if it wasn't for Jim Thorpe, and all the publicity he got in those days, well, put it this way: for a while there, Indians were respectable."

Augie looked at his friend with a frown. "Mr Haskins— you've done all right for yourself."

"Yes, I have. And if it wasn't for bein' a veteran, who knows if I would ever have gotten this nice cushy position I got here with the Appalachian Club."

Haskins put his arm around Augie's shoulder and started to walk with him. The last thing he wanted to do was discourage the boy. He had acquired a genuine liking for him. But it was his obligation to set the record straight, as far as distinguishing fantasy from reality. "Augie, my friend, I'm glad all that was 25 years ago. I'm glad I'm too old now for this go-around, because this one's gonna be bad. We're gonna lose a lotta people in this one."

They walked in silence for a while, and Haskins became lost in deep concentration. He said to himself, *in old times, in the tribe, we would have raised up a young man to be a warrior, with everybody behind him, step by step, until he was ready, because we put him through all the tests, and made him prove himself. Nowadays, they just push 'em out there to face the cannons.*

Augie went to see the Army recruiter in his office at the Post Office in Stoughton, and the recruiter asked him the same thing as Haskins—*how old are you?*

Augie was ready. "I'm seventeen, sir."

"Well, you still need parental permission then."

"That won't be a problem, sir."

"Well, here's the form. And look—you don't call me sir—I'm not an officer. Might as well get used to it. But there's something else I wanna know, and I ask this of every recruit. Why are you choosing Army? And I need a real answer. We don't want rejects from the Marines."

"I wouldn't go for the Marines, sir."

"Why not?"

"I don't wanna be just a grunt." This time Augie remembered to not add, 'sir.' "I wanna learn something. I have thought it over and I like the range of training in different things the Army offers. I been thinking, Signal Corps. I like technical stuff, you know, modern, the latest. I've read all the brochures, and, well, it's the best Army in the world. And I wanna be with the best."

Augie thought that was quite a speech, and also, that he better quit while he was ahead. He never mentioned the real reason he was thinking: *Sergeant York was Army.*

As he was leaving, the recruiting sergeant said to him, "You're big for your age."

And so Augie knew that he was in. The Army was sending him its first message from the Signal Corps.

Still, Augie was quite willing to go strictly by the book, and so he was careful to get one of his football squad teammates to forge his mother's signature on the permission paper.

His actual mother was completely dismayed. She did not understand how Augie could have done this to her. Her last boy! The one she herself had saved, as an infant, that day in the corridor at the Mass General. They had already robbed her of all her dignity and self-respect, and now they wanted her baby, too! Never mind that he was six-foot-two, he was still her *bambino!* But him, he, himself, he *wanted* to leave her. He was excited! She hated to say anything that would hurt his feelings, but she wanted to say to him, *what did I ever do to you to deserve this!*

At South Station, they all gathered to see him off. Gigi had been through this scene already twice before with Patsy and Genie. Each time she had dissolved in tears and needed to be held up. This time, the whole family was there, even Peggy (of course, at the last possible minute). Augie was their darling. Only Anna was younger than he was. His three older sisters had made him their pet the entire time he was growing up, only to tower over them. And then, when they had to look up at him, they saw Adonis, played by Tyrone Power. Not Errol Flynn. Not Gable. Tyrone Power. How could anyone *not* fall in love with him? He could slay a girl with one look. And the thing was, he paid no attention whatsoever to them! Compared to his own brother, Patsy, this one was an altar-boy! The only constellations in his sky were the DiMaggio brothers and the 1940 Boston College Sugar Bowl squad led by Chuckin' Charley O'Rourke, the greatest quarterback who ever lived, according to Augie. Mary didn't count, as she was so isolated with her own household over there in Watertown, Anna was too young, but Peggy and Gerry were thick as thieves, and they both said to one another, they were scared to death in case some girl did get a-hold of him! He'd be putty in her hands!

At the last moment, his father took him aside.

"I hope you know what you're doing," Tony said.

"Don't worry, Pa. I know how to take care of myself."

"I'm not worried about you. I'm worried about your mother."

"Pa, you take care of her, will ya? She knows how I feel."

"How does she know? Have you told her?"

"Pa!"

"If you don't write to her, every single day, I'll come down there, personally, myself, and know the reason why."

"I will, Pa, I will."

"You better. Just remember, the Army is full of heroes. They don't need you to show 'em how. Do what you're told, keep your nose clean, but don't volunteer for nothin' and nobody."

"All right, Pa, all right." Augie wanted desperately to get away onto that train.

Tony LaStoria looked up at his son, and the last thing he said was, "You're too big a target, you know that?"

"Pa, will ya stop worryin'! I gotta go now. The train is leaving."

And then he was gone.

Sadly, the LaStoria family turned to go. The emptiness they felt was as large as the cavernous vault of South Station. Everything that could have been said had been said. They had no more words left for one another.

That day was only the beginning of Tony LaStoria's worries. Or near the beginning. His worrying was already well underway. Perhaps it began that Sunday in the parlor—December 7th, on the radio. The moment he put aside his newspaper, he felt it begin. *What are we gonna do now? As if we haven't been through enough—now they gotta throw this at us?*

And so in the aftermath of Augie's departure, after he had put his last son on the train to God knows where or what, it was time at last to make occasion for something which had been bothering him, ever since that decisive Sunday.

At the Sons of Italy Hall in Stoughton (built by the members themselves, a wood-framed white-clapboard building which could easily have been a Lions or a Kiwanis or even a Boy Scouts, because it fit into its surroundings almost like a, God forbid, Unitarian Church) all of Tony's concern about fitting the Sons of Italy into the war-effort, in the face of the government clampdown on enemy aliens, had to be addressed, as Tony felt, by the members.

And so, as President, he reluctantly climbed on the stage and stood above them, assembled in the same folding chairs they put out for their banquets and dance recitals, and the distaste he felt for this self-imposed task was coming back on him in his mouth.

"Now, look," he began, "we're all in this together. I have something to talk about with you and so I asked you to come tonight for this meeting because it's very important that we take care of this now. We should have before now. I have a proposal to make. I think we should pass two resolutions tonight, and give publicity to both through the local paper, because, as you know, and I don't need to tell you, the townspeople of our town are looking at us, and we need to make a statement—a definite statement—that they can't misinterpret or misunderstand or twist. So, number one, first resolution—we hereby conduct all our meetings in the English language only—and we gotta make this public."

A member began to protest in Italian, and Tony cut him off—in English.

"Bacigalupo—you ain't liked anything we did in the last 7 years, so we don't need to hear from you, we know what you think."

Tony turned to the rest of the 25 or 30 present, all men, and said, "Now I want a show of hands—a unanimous show of hands."

Bacigalupo muttered, "Who does he think he is—Mussolini?"

Tony said, "When we publish this item in the papers, it's gotta say, 'A *unanimous* vote was taken' passing the resolution—get it?"

When all raised their hands except one, Tony lost his temper. "Baci—you get your hand up there! I don't want you going around town telling everybody, 'you know, I wasn't for it—it wasn't really unanimous, like it says in the paper!'"

Tony waited till Bacigalupo sheepishly recognized that everyone was looking at him, and he was alone, and finally, reluctantly, he raised his hand.

"Second resolution," said Tony, "and this one we gotta act on. On Sunday, right after 11 o'clock mass, in the parking lot in front of this building—and the reporters will be notified to be here with cameras—we're gonna burn the Italian flag."

There was a rumbling of discomfort and seat-shifting at this startling proposition.

Tony said, "Anybody here not a loyal American? Tell me now. I wanna know. And another thing: the rest of the town wants to know. There's a war on, and we gotta live here in this town. Or, you do, for the duration. Myself, I got three sons in the armed forces of the United States, so you know where I stand. But the rest of this town's gotta know just exactly where we all stand, in an unmistakable way. And this is it. Now anybody wanna stand up and say they're against the rest of the country? I know, I know. I feel the same way as the rest of you about everything. They came and made *my wife* register as an enemy. We're all in the same boat. But if they can do that, how do we know if tomorrow, they're not gonna come and take our homes and tell us we have to go away and live behind barbed wire surrounded by armed guards somewhere in a camp outdoors in tents or barracks like they're doing to the Japs out west right now! If you're German, or Jap, or Italian, in this country right now, you're not safe! And I might as well tell you right now that I can't stay in Stoughton. I got government contracts coming outta my ears up in Boston, and they're rationing gas. I can't afford not to be at the shop on time every morning. We're running three shifts, and we're making uni's for the troops! So, for God's sakes, if this is the last thing I ever do for you—let me do this for you!"

And so, on Sunday, the press came, not just from Stoughton, but from Brockton and Boston, as well, and took their photographs, and the burning of the Italian flag by a Sons of Italy organization in Stoughton was widely publicized as something of a sensation, and afterwards, copied by other posts in other surrounding towns, as far away as Worcester and Providence.

Soon, not too long afterwards, the LaStorias were living on the bottom floor of a two-family on Kimball Road in Watertown, around the corner from their daughter Mary and her family on Dewey Street.

It was a short walk to the end of the street in Coolidge Square where Tony could catch a streetcar into Harvard Square, jump on the subway and proceed from there to South Station, where it was another short walk to work, across the Summer Street bridge on the Fort Point Channel to the shop at No. 10 Melcher.

There had been no time to sell the house on Pine Street in Stoughton. They had to leave that in the hands of an agent. For the first time since North Square, 24 years before, they were renters, while Tony looked for something to buy.

The worry on Gigi's mind was, how would the boys find them when they came home for Christmas? That was her hope, her wish, that they'd be home for Christmas, so everybody told her, and she fervently believed it. So she made sure Gerry wrote each of them letters with their new address and telephone number, every day for three or four days in a row; and after that, every week, at least once. Gerry humored her because she was worried about her mother.

Gigi seemed not herself these days. Her boys were gone and her life was over. She missed her flowers. She had an incurable loneliness for the house on Pine Street where they always had a houseful and there was a constant hub-bub of coming and going. Now she had to be cooped up in somebody else's flat in a town where no one knew her and she had to sit in the window and look out not on her beloved sunflowers but on strangers' faces going up and down. She missed her mother and her father, long dead now; but what about the living? They were gone, too. She looked forlornly at Gerry, who was always there, there for her: who else? But Gigi could take no consolation in her daughter, and even Tony, when he was in the house, seemed to have withdrawn into a corner, and was always preoccupied.

Their youth was gone. Spent, like last week's grocery-money. They were old people. The world had forgotten them. With so much dire suffering in the world falling down on the heads of innocent millions, why should anybody care about them? And then, there was the constant dread of the mail, and the telephone. What if the next letter, the next ring of the phone, brought the message so many had to hear? Gigi could not bear the thought. What a horrible time in the history of the world to be old. She had dreams: *they were handing her a telegram. She could not read it. It was in English.*

But Gerry was worried about her father, too. There was only one topic nowadays safe to raise with him: the horses. Gerry loved him so much that she felt very desolate that he could no longer enjoy his day at the races surrounded by his three sons. Although she had been there herself, to Suffolk Downs, only once or twice, in their company, she had seen with her own eyes her father come to life as he shared with them his love of horseflesh, his enthusiasm for the race, his interest in following all the statistics and records enshrined in the green sheet. When the results were flashed on the infield tote-board, it was as if Tony's own eyes lit up. The animation that overtook her father, how they argued among themselves, and worked themselves up to a fever-pitch, back and forth right up to the very last second when they had to make up their minds once and for all which pony to place their two bucks on! For Gerry, it was a window into a man's life. It was how they felt, how they thought, how they acted, amongst themselves, men among men, *when they forgot you were there!* No wonder her sister Peggy could never bear to be left out. And now all that was taken from him. There was no son with whom to share the daily double, the Masscap at Suffolk Downs, the big match race, Seabiscuit versus War Admiral.

How her father had loved that horse, Seabiscuit. And therefore, Gerry did, too, even though she was at the track in person only rarely, now that Patsy, Gene and even Augie were gone. But Gerry was at home on Kimball Road. She would get a call just before noontime from Pa, from his office, to go down to the Boylston Spa and see Tomaselli the bookie, to get in Tony's wagers at Saratoga, Hialeah, even Santa Monica, whichever was in season. And when the meet was on at Suffolk Downs, they got the local radio broadcast of the seventh race at home every afternoon, with Babe Rubinstein calling the featured race of the day; and Gerry was always there to pencil in the results on Pa's notepad by the phone.

Because of the way things had worked out, Gerry was not in the frame of mind to be overly critical of the choices her sister Peggy seemed to have made. Her husband, Henry Fabiano, was long gone; he enlisted at the earliest opportunity, in the Marines, no less, and as far as anyone knew, he was somewhere in the South Pacific. Not that he ever wrote to his wife, Peggy—or, ex-wife Peggy. That was something even Gerry was still not sure of, what exactly had happened there. It was now late 1942, and Gerry was 20 years old, yet all she knew was that her 24-year-old sister Peggy conducted herself as if she were a single woman on the loose in a big city, a major American port, during wartime, and serving as the personal hostess, appointed by herself, for the entire complement of young guys in the service who had liberty, shore leave or a weekend pass, on any particular night.

After all, they were young, and this was the time of their lives. Nobody was gonna give them a second chance. All they had to do if they didn't believe it was to look at their mother and father, Tony and Gigi, to see that *youth didn't last.* And these were days when there was some kind of strange alchemy in the air. They were building boats faster than they could count them down at the Quincy Shipyard; the Charlestown Navy yard was full of sailors working on ships in drydock. They were no longer stranded in the outskirts in a place like Stoughton, where nothing ever happened. Downtown Boston was hopping, it was *The Hub!* There was Army and Navy and Marines all over town. Peggy didn't need a job; she didn't have time to work; there were only too many young fellas willing to spend their service pay on her, to buy her dinner and drinks, things to wear, perfume, jewelry. And Gerry enlisted her services, too, as an escort for her father, on a Saturday afternoon when they could cajole him out of his foxhole full of newspapers to go out to the track in East Boston. Their father no longer looked askance at Peggy's antics. He had seen for himself that she knew her way around not just the track, but the men who spent their lives there. Wherever Peggy was, that was where the party was. She knew how to entertain them, keep them amused, keep them interested, and yes, fascinated—but yet, at arm's length. Peggy had a little black book of phone numbers that was as thick as a rug. She had a pocketbook full of change for cabfare. If you didn't do things her way, you didn't spend five minutes in her company. She always had a steady guy she would play for a month or two, before replacing him, and inveterately, she made sure he knew that he had plenty of competition. She played one off the other. She would hang on the steady's arm, her driver for the day, her escort, and flirt with the other guys, right in front of him. Peggy knew what was what. She knew how to say, *Hiya, how ya doin'?*—and also, *Get lost, brother.* Her father wondered: *you could almost believe she grew up on the streets, not in a home with a family at all. She's a goddam gypsy!*

In the meantime, Gerry was at home with their mother every day as she sat in the window gazing out on the flowers that were not there. She was there every evening to make sure Pa had a hot supper as soon as he got home after another long day of overtime.

When their father needed help at the shop, he gave orders to his daughter Mary to get back to work. Pa needed good stitchers, and they were hard to find. With his overload of war-time government contracts, he needed someone he could trust to do exactly what she was told exactly when she was told to do it. When they moved into Kimball Road in Watertown, they were back in touch with Mary, who was no longer separated from the family, miles away in Stoughton, with no car with which to get out there.

Mary's husband, Charlie Laverna, was still working his day-job at *Giorgio Marscia*, altering gentlemen's cuffs and sleeves and pant-legs. The Calabrian had no ambition to ever be or do anything else, unless it was to tend his tomatoes out back of the house on Dewey Street. Unlike Mary's brothers, he was not running off to enlist; he was happy to wait to be drafted, if they ever got around to him. Mary was not sure he had even registered—but as he was the father of their two children, she was not about to make any issue out of that. She needed him for the money he brought into the house.

But, still, Mary was disappointed in married life; and re-membering how he had always slighted her in his own mind, her father, Tony, made up his mind to rescue her from her doldrums, by getting her out of the house and back into the work-force, so she could have pocket-change of her own, and not have to go begging her husband. Which caused a big fury on the part of the Calabrian, as he was adamant that no wife of his should be out of the house. She should be home, where she belonged. Mary told him to shut his mouth because her father needed her. Soon enough, she was promoted into a position as a floor-lady at No. 10 by her Pa, and that was a little more money in Mary's pocket.

Thus it happened that on top of caring for her rapidly aging, woe-begotten mother, Gigi, Gerry was the daughter who got appointed by the rest of them to be the family house-mother, and had Mary's two kids, little Tony, now 6, and attending the Coolidge School, one block away, in first grade, and little Gerry, still only 4 years old, over on Kimball Road each day to look out for them, to wash, and clean and clothe and feed them, while their mother was at work at No. 10. All this was carefully stage-managed by Pa in order to get the whole resources of the family involved in war-work with maximum efficiency. That was his whole reason for leaving Stoughton to move to Watertown, to be close to Mary and close to in-town.

The bottle-cap that fell in the soup was, of course, daughter Peggy. That one was of no use whatsoever to her Pa. In fact, everyone agreed, without ever saying so, that flame and gasoline should be always kept well asunder as far as those two were concerned.

But in fact, it was another task heaped on Gerry, the good-girl. For Peggy had indeed not sent off her husband Henry to the South Pacific without obtaining from him at least a couple of keepsakes. Which came in the form of her two sons, Henry and Ronnie.

Henry, born in '39, named after his father, and Ronnie, named after Ronald Colman, from the movie *Lost Horizons*, born a year later, were in need of a mother's care morning, noon and night, which to Peggy was an afterthought. She was far too busy in her exciting new life to be bothered with the boys, and she knew she could count on her little sister Gerry to mother them for her. So Peggy simply left them at the house on Kimball Road in Watertown. After all, there was no room for them in her tiny beachfront flat on Revere Beach Boulevard, out on the far end of the beach, towards Point o' Pines.

And since everybody in the family thought Peggy should get a job and quit freeloading all the time, she needed to be near her source of income, in the bars along the beach, where she waited on tables and bar-tended for the loose change, tips, and boyfriends it brought in.

Now, Peggy reasoned, little sister Gerry was as yet unmarried, and besides, she had baby sister Anna there with her every day to lend a hand after school, plus, Gigi, their mother, and the children's grandmother. Anna, now 16, was in her junior year at Watertown High, so who better to help Gerry and Gigi care for her Henry and Ronnie in addition to Mary's Tony and Gerry. *So-it all worked out—didn't it?*

Pa LaStoria was not worried about Gerry. She was a brick. She was, in his eyes, the strongest of them all. It was sad what had happened to Mary, in her marriage with the Calabrian. Pa could see that Mary, his neglected one, was happier out of the house on a daily basis, six days a week. Peggy was completely beyond anyone's control, even his; maybe even her own. He could not worry about her. Long ago, he had written her off, and they both knew it, and had signed their truce on that basis. The only alternative had been open warfare. And that, Tony LaStoria concluded, was not an option. It was wartime, and everybody had to make sacrifices.

Trouble was, his wife, Gigi, poor thing, was not up to the task any longer. Even Tony, though he didn't care to look too closely, could see that.

Each night, when they stopped off the trolley at the corner of Mount Auburn and Arlington Street, getting home to Watertown late, as usual, from working overtime again, Tony and his daughter Mary, would walk home together, first the one block to Kimball Road. Mary would then pick up Tony and Gerry and walk them another block over to Dewey Street to her own house, where they lived on the second floor so as to pick up a little more from the tenants by renting out the first floor (the Calabrian knew how to count his pennies).

Each night, when they stepped off the trolley, it was as if, another day done, Tony, weary, had come to the end of nothing. No longer did he have Patsy sitting next to him in the Buick to drive to work up in Boston through the Blue Hills. No longer did he have Gene at his side daily to be his second-in-charge at the shop at No. 10. Augie owed his mother a letter, which hadn't come yet. Mary was wrapped up in her own thoughts, going home with two kids by the hand to a house that felt like an argument. The only one left that Tony could depend on was Gerry; who seemed to know what to do on her own without having to be told; *who seemed to think just like he did.*

Chapter 24

Tony and Harry

Government inspectors were crawling all over the shop at No. 10. They were making rain-gear for the Army, winter-overcoats, and fatigues. Everything had to come up to spec. Ever since the upswing in war-work, Harry Spritzka had rediscovered the New England branch of his far-flung enterprises. Now Harry had resumed crawling up Tony's back by telephone. Not that he ever came to Boston, or had ever seen the buildings Tony had picked out for him to buy in so many places dotted all over the map of three states, no, four. More than ever, Tony could tell from his tone, his telephone-manner, it was all just numbers to Harry, and every one of those numbers had a dollar sign in front of it. For years, during the Depression, the phone connection between them had fallen dormant. When there were no orders, no contracts, there was no Harry. Now, he was on the line in advance of every contract, with all the facts and figures and deadlines worked out ahead of time.

It was all mysterious to Tony. If he knew Harry, the man must have suffered prodigiously during the downtimes over the money he was losing. Harry had always bled more for a nickel lost than he bloomed for five thousand gained.

But Tony LaStoria neither knew his old friend Harry Spritzka nor did he understand him. For one thing, Harry was not the same young wild-eyed entrepreneur he'd been in his teens. Service in the first war had changed him. Nearly losing and then saving his marriage to Mimi Lowenstein had changed him. Having four children had changed him. His brother Robert had saved him from his own tendencies, but Harry himself was responsible for having the newfound sense to listen. Robert found little brother Harry eventually to be a worthy partner and they went into business together, founding the Manna Group. This was finance, wealth creation, and strategic business-formulation that was simply beyond Tony LaStoria's ken.

The two brothers brought their real estate and garment manufacturing and sales enterprises together to form the Spritzka Organization under the umbrella of the Manna Group but they did not stop there. They diversified. Robert specialized, especially during the Depression, in buying failing businesses and turning them around. Everything from ball-bearings to bicycles. He focused on the acquisition of the vertical chain of supply in a field of manufacture: for instance, with bicycles, he wanted to own the tire-makers and the bicycle-chain-makers and the people who made the spokes and the fenders. (Tony would have been astonished to find out that the Tyer Rubber Company in Stoughton was a wholly-owned subsidiary of a holding company that was owned by the Manna Group, in other words, by Harry and his brother Robert; Harry, of course, had never thought he needed to mention that to Tony.) Robert's strategy was to buy everything he needed to make an article from himself, run everything at a loss, and take the tax benefits. Along the way, he taught Harry how to take his skills in making clothing and apply them to making pancake mix and perambulators.

By the end of the thirties, the Manna Group had survived the Depression quite handsomely. The Group owned the Superior Bank of Chicago and a chain of hotels called the Empire Regency, built in cities everywhere from Denver to Detroit, Kansas City to Cincinnati, in each town, across the street from the main train station. Robert owned 31 per cent of all the five-story apartment blocks in New Orleans and Harry owned two-thirds of all the hog-processing plants in Arkansas. The brothers brought their sons (who were now, during the war, of an age to be in the service, like Tony's sons) into their business, holding places for them while they served in the officer corps of three branches after their graduation from Harvard, Princeton, Cornell and Yale. There was Robert, Jr in the Marines, serving at the Pentagon, and Louis, in the Army overseas in England as liaison to General Harold Nicholson's war-planning staff. Harry's twins, James, who was called Jay, and Jerome, were in the Navy, serving on board submarines (Jay) and aboard jeep carriers, or baby flattops, in the Atlantic (Jerome). Harry's two daughters, Nancy and Jean, were students, Nancy at Vassar, and Jean at Smith.

The Harry Spritzka Tony once knew, who manufactured clothing, had moved on, and now manufactured money.

Although he protested that he had no time, that it was impossible, that he couldn't get away, even for a minute, Tony, in spite of himself, welcomed the call that finally came when Harry directed him to get his ass down to New York for a meeting, face to face.

On the train, Tony had plenty of time to think about it, and everything else, as well. Looking out the window on the same flat scenes he had dismissed as depressing so many years before, when he first came up to Boston, he realized at length what was bothering him so much. It was his sons. Not Gigi, not Mary, Gerry, or Anna, who were safe at home, whom he saw every day; not Peggy, with whom he had mostly cut ties altogether; the women in his circle were safe enough, cosseted in a familiar routine. They were not subjected to the perils of war-torn Europe, of ravaged Italy herself. But could he say the same about his three sons?

No. There, everything had worked out to the exact opposite.

Would it have been any different for Patsy, Gene and Augie, back in Italy, had their father, hypothetically, never come to the United States? Of course not. It would have been worse. This, his faculty of reason told Tony, was true. But reason only went so far.

There was something else that was beyond the mind of man to comprehend. And that was: how it could be that a man was condemned to raise three sons he loved better than his own life, only to be called upon to sacrifice them: to heap their bodies on top of a raging funeral pyre and watch them burn? This was more than any God, so-called, should ask of any man.

And this was what Tony LaStoria was travelling to New York City, to a mansion that now stood at seven stories, to talk about with Harry Spritzka.

For who else was there with whom he could talk about it? Who else but someone he had known all his life who was now, as a father of sons in the service, in the same precise predicament. As always, Harry's life was running on parallel rails with his own.

And who had Tony known longer than Harry Spritzka? Who knew Tony when he was a child? Who shared life with him on the streets of New York? Not his wife. Nor his sons or his daughters. There was only one person in the world who knew anything about where Tony LaStoria really came from.

It was now early September of 1943. It was 32 years since Tony had walked away from his life in New York City and left Harry Spritzka sitting there in his office in the garment district on West 37th. Tony's sons, Patsy and Augie, were somewhere in England, while Genie, after having survived North Africa, was now, for all anyone knew, in Sicily with General Patton.

"How can there be a God, Harry?"

They were seated in their usual places, a glass of wine in the hand of each. They had finished hashing out every last detail of every last contract. Now they were left with each other, face to face *as it was in the beginning, as it was now, and always would be.*

"See, that's where you and I differ, Tony. This war we got here is right up my Jehovah's alley. Because my Jehovah is a god of his Chosen People. He's not a sacrificial lamb, hanging on a cross, ready-made for the slaughter. And my Jehovah's gonna lead his people to a Promised Land. Not in the hereafter, Tony. Literally. In the here and now."

"This—is what you believe, Harry?"

"I don't believe it, Tony. I know it."

"You look around at the suffering going on in the world right now, and this is what you see?"

"Tony, I got sons in the service at the moment, just like you do. They hadda go through Princeton and Harvard first, but now at least they're officers."

"Aren't you worried half to death about them, Harry?"

"They're in no danger, believe me. Not where they are. They're in somebody's staff-officers' billet in the rear. They're not in the front lines like I was in the first war. But, Tony—look—I got back in one piece. So will your sons."

"I wish I could believe it so easily. I get worried. Sometimes I get an awful feeling."

Harry shrugged. "You're their father. You're gonna get these feelings. You feel responsible. Somehow, it's all your fault: you shoulda done something different. Tony, there's nothing, nothing we coulda done any different than what we did. Just pray they don't come back crippled or maimed or something like that."

"Harry, don't even make a joke."

"Tony, there's worse things than death. Worse things than death."

"How can there be anything worse than what they're doing over there to your people. Harry, you must know. Up in Boston they had it in the papers that they were rounding up Jews and—."

"I know, I know. Everybody knows it, except the American government, and Winston Churchill."

"They had it, Harry, on page 12 of *The Globe*, on the inside where nobody's gonna see it. And the figure I saw there, that they gave, 700,000 dead—Harry, how is that possible?"

"It's possible. It's possible."

"Aren't you worried about Mimi's people back there?"

"Oh, no, no. We got them all out years ago. No, her people are bankers, after all. They had resources. After all, we've known that this was coming for years—didn't you?"

"Who could've imagined?"

"But it was Hitler's stated policy. He told the world, in advance, what he was gonna do. You just didn't want to hear it.

That's why it's so important for us to get the Jewish homeland out of all this. Because if we didn't know before, we know now: nobody's gonna take care of us but ourselves, and our lord God Jehovah Himself, and the righteousness of His mighty staff."

"How Mussolini could have ever put poor Italy into bed with that Hitler."

"But that's why we're having a war against the man. There's no other way to stop him. If you really understand, Tony, politics, history, people—as they really are—you realize it had to come to this."

"I just don't understand it."

"Well, Tony, at least we know one thing. Hitler can't win this war. You wanna know why? I'm gonna tell you why. Hitler can never win this war for one simple reason, because he's got the Jews against him."

It was small consolation to Tony, Harry's certitude. Like with everything else, Harry's mind was made up. You couldn't penetrate that thick forehead with a dozen howitzers. Tony, as he rode back to Boston, alone, on the train, crawling up the coastline of Connecticut in the low-lying twilight, dozing with his temple leaning on the cold glass of the train-window, sometimes opening his eyes, to see—nothing—nothing he hadn't seen before. The same dreariness, the same emptiness it was thirty, thirty-five years before . . . *who's counting?* Frequently nodding off, only to startle himself awake, with the jolt of the train bumping along the *da-da-da, da-da-da,* lulled to sleep again by the cradling sway of the coach side to side, rocking, gently rocking, *rock-a-bye baby on the treetops, why haven't we heard from Gene? Augie's a good boy . . . writes every day . . .*

almost . . . can't tell us where he is, but . . . why haven't we heard from Gene? It's been three months. Patsy, I know, got himself a cushy job directing traffic in the MPs . . . how that guy does it I'll never know . . . and I used to think he was so stupid. But Genie? Where is he? This very minute. Is he all right? For all we know, he could be lying somewhere bleeding his life out this very minute . . . last we heard, North

Africa . . . Sicily . . . Genie . . . where are you?

Chapter 25

Return to Alta Villa

Sgt. Gene LaStoria saw Italy for the first time veiled in a dress of translucent fog, and she appeared to him as a fabled shore. His ancestral homeland had always been, to him, imagined, never known. Born of Italian parents, but born and raised in Massachusetts, he was an American soldier who spoke fluent Italian, mainly because his mother spoke no English. His father came from Alta Villa Irpina, a small town, high up in the mountains, near Avellino; which meant that, at the moment, as he peeked over the top-rail of an LST, seeking just a glimpse of that imagined land, at this moment, his father's hometown, hidden up there in the distant looming wall of mountains, was only about fifty miles away.

The fog did not last. Like a curtain suddenly moth-eaten, it was perforated with artillery explosions, blossoming smoke-bubbles, cloud-puffs without thunder, unheard beyond the roar of landing-craft motors and churning ocean (but promising to be audible soon enough). These formed a tilting horizon rocking violently with every buffeting wave as their vessel rode up and down.

It was 0830 on the first day of the Allied invasion of mainland Italy, Sept 9th, 1943, *Operation Avalanche.* Four waves of infantry in LCIs which had gone in before their craft, starting at 0330, had by now secured the beach.

The day before, on the 8th, the men of the invading US Fifth Army had been told that Italy had surrendered.

Mussolini had been deposed back in July, arrested by the secret police of King Victor Emmanuel III, and imprisoned in barracks. But now, on the 8th of September, his replacement, Marshall Badoglio, head of the Italian Army, appointed Prime Minister by the King at the time Il Duce was deposed, issued his own Proclamation, which declared an Armistice to be in effect between the Italian armed forces and the Allies.

Italy was out of the war.

Partly for this reason, the Americans landing on the beaches in the Gulf of Salerno were expecting little or no resistance.

And also, in the back of their minds, having been through this before, this limbo of waiting to land, riding in a seesawing LST, where it was hard to see over the top at what the hell was out there, as they prayed, or scribbled their last letters home, to hand to the coxswain, to hold for the regimental chaplain (just in case), they were hoping for, they were *expecting,* the same greeting they had received that day back in July, in their invasion of Sicily: an unopposed landing.

Sgt. Gene LaStoria, of Stoughton, Massachusetts, tossing in his LST toward the beach at Paestum, south of Salerno, was not writing any letters home. This was his third landing, after North Africa and Sicily. What would he say to them? I'm OK, how are you? Next line: *War isn't something you want to write home about like you're on vacation.*

With the 36th Division on the right flank, southwards of the widening mouth of the River *Sele,* and the 45th Division on the near bank, stretching north toward Salerno, guarding the right flank of the British Tenth Corps, to their left, Sgt. LaStoria had fondly hoped this would be a repeat, not only of Sicily, but the even easier landing at Algiers, in French North Africa, now almost a whole year behind him.

Before the landings, in spite of the overwhelming armada of heavily-gunned Allied warships, both British and American, out in the Gulf of Salerno, which some thought numbered as many as 450 vessels, and included two British battleships, plus an American heavy cruiser, the *USS Savannah,* not to mention four British aircraft carriers, there was no naval, or for that matter, aerial bombardment of the landing beaches, to soften them up.

Somebody up at the very top, one of those genius generals of theirs, for all they knew, Mark Clark himself, had decided that a pre-landing bombardment would have eliminated the element of surprise.

Any one of 90,000 troops, sailing for three days in land-ing-craft from embarkation points in Bizerte, Oran and Mes-sina, could have told him, surprise was lost on the day before, September 8th, when a high-level German bomber took a lei-surely camera-flight over the whole fleet.

Nevertheless, the general belief among the soldiers of the line was that this was considered a routine landing by the muckety-mucks. Why do we bother to have an intelligence arm? The first thing you learn in this war is—*you only know what you can see in front of you.*

It was a little strange then, as the very first waves were approaching, to hear a loudspeaker on the beach announcing, in English, *"Come on in and give up. We have you covered."*

Still, when they hit the beach, nobody in sight.

They did not know that the commander of the 14th Panzer Korps, with three divisions of armor and infantry, including a paratroop division, had placed his forces lying in wait for them 3 miles inland, ready to counter-attack, under orders from his boss, General Von Vieterling, who also had the LXXVI Panzer Korps, with three more divisions of tanks and grenadiers, to the north, looking down on them from the vantage of the flanking hilltops, 450 feet high, that ran right down to the water's edge, pincers enclasping the city of Salerno.

Sgt. Gene LaStoria, of Stoughton, Massachusetts, riding in his LST toward the beach at Paestum, south of Salerno, as a non-com member of Lt. Waco's platoon, and manning, with three other men, a self-propelled 37mm cannon, could be sure of only what was directly in front of him: the back of a helmet.

So, what was he going to write home? Pa, I'm alright. Ma, I'm scared. He supposed they knew that. *And I'm pissed off.*

That was also true. And felt better.

When they hit the sand, they sank in four inches.

They looked back at the huge double-doors of the LST swung wide-open. Vehicles were already rolling down the ramp, starting up, and motoring out of the way over a steel carpet of wire mesh which Army engineers had rolled out for them to form a beach-roadway, so that they could get their heavy vehicles, tanks, armored-cars, self-propelled guns, and jeeps, over the sand and up to the paved shore road.

Paestum, it was plain to see, was a resort town, having been famous for its sandy beaches since Roman times.

Right in the middle of their sector, on the flat marshy land that started right behind the shore road, was the ruin of a Doric temple, complete with classical fluted columns, still standing.

Sgt LaStoria could see that it was as ancient as other places he'd seen in North Africa and Sicily, but he would have needed a Baedeker in his hand to tell him it had been placed there in the 6th century BC by Greeks, and had later served the Romans as a Temple of Neptune, god of the sea.

Now, at this moment, before the august remnant of ancient civilization, all up and down this same shoreline, as far as the eye could see, was the most modernized, mechanized army ever created, pouring out of row upon staggered row of LSTs, with gaping mouths vomiting motorized vehicles onto the sand.

After landing, Sgt. LaStoria and his crew, with the rest of Lt. Waco's platoon, assembled in a long single-file strung out along the beach road, which, like beach roads all over the world, followed the shoreline, as close to the water as it could, as it needed solidity underfoot to stay in place, a commodity the men of the Fifth Army were to find in short supply, thrown, as they were, into a fluid situation.

The job of Sgt LaStoria's crew was to function as mobile anti-tank support to regimental infantry, and their platoon of four half-tracks under Lt Waco was attached to an infantry battalion, and assigned to the 141st Regimental Combat Team, or RCT, and the first orders they were given instructed them to seek out and establish a defensive camouflage position, inland.

They could not stay where they were, lined up, bunched like that, as they were extremely vulnerable to both German artillery and Luftwaffe attack from the air. They had to vamoose out of there fast, and find some place inland, and there, await reinforcements, orders and support.

Sgt LaStoria's original unit had been decimated in the Kasserine Pass fiasco in Tunisia. At the time, the sergeant was in hospital in the rear with dysentery. He missed seeing any action in that brutal defeat, and thus, thereafter, he had been transferred, as a replacement, to the 36th Infantry Division, a Texas outfit. In Sicily, they had more or less a Sunday stroll under General Patton, all the way up the road to Palermo. Now he assumed, like everyone else, that today would be the same, *but you never knew.*

It was only by chance that Sgt LaStoria's vehicle was the first to turn off the beach road and set out across what appeared to be a marshy, low-lying field towards an unmarked road leading *where?* they could not tell: everything before them was too flat, and no buildings could be seen.

He happened to be in the lead, and the other three half-tracks of their platoon fell in behind him as battalion infantry advanced across the marsh towards the distant road.

Back on the beach, they had seen dead bodies, under olive-green tarps, already lined up to be taken away. They had crossed the sand where, two feet past the high-water mark, they had seen craters, small ovals, scooped out, where somebody had stepped on a mine. Injured. Legs or feet blown off. Killed. They didn't know. But they knew enough not to ask themselves.

Stretcher-bearers had taken away the wounded from that field of fire so that the engineers could clear it, and then the Army engineers with their mine-detectors had also been by to clear the mine-fields, by the time Sgt. LaStoria's platoon were deposited on the beach by their LST.

But now they were going down this unoccupied road, when up ahead, over a distant rise, came a German Panzer IV tank. And behind it, in single file, were four others.

When Sgt. LaStoria saw them, he saw a gun-flash from the lead tank. He heard machine-gun clatter. A tower of water and marsh-grass sprayed over their vehicle, soaking him. When he was able to lift his head, he realized what a narrow fix they were in. He fired his 37 mm gun. He yelled at his loaders to feed him. He fired again and got a lucky shot that shattered the tread of the lead tank, which was just turning off the road as its turret swiveled to hold aim directly on his forehead. If his shot had hit where he aimed it, it would have bounced off the Panzer IV's armor-plate. The tank jarred abruptly as it halted, stuck fast, giving Sgt LaStoria only an instant to think before he'd be fired upon again. After disabling the lead tank, his only hope, he thought, was to keep up a rapid, steady return-fire, reloading and firing as fast as they could, while the other enemy tanks attempted to fan out from the road behind the first one, now stuck.

Sgt LaStoria expected at any moment to be blown to bits. His 37mm M3 gun, mounted on a lightly-armored half-track, was facing German Panzers re-fitted with long-armed 75mm guns that could defeat any Soviet tank made, not to mention American M4 Shermans.

Already, in seconds, this was worse than anything he had seen or contended with in North Africa or Sicily. If this was his baptism, he was Christianized instantly.

Just then, the British battleships offshore, and the American cruiser, opened up and were thundering shells over their heads at coordinates being called in by the infantry spotters. High overhead Spitfires, Seafires and Lightnings were suddenly battling Messerschmitts in the air. You could even see Vesuvius glowing in the distance. Instead of being outnumbered and overwhelmed, the Krauts seemed to be counter-attacking in force. Sgt LaStoria and his crew had stumbled, or blundered, straight into it.

Sgt LaStoria screamed at the driver below him to back it up, quick, and the driver did, till they were back over a little hump in the road, behind them, which they had just, a moment before, crossed over.

Their vehicle was a halftrack. It had a long-nosed cab on the front end, basically a General Motors ¾-ton 4X4 truck cab, with a miniature bull-dozer scoop attached to the front bumper, like a plow, but it had tank-treads in the back, under a flat-bed built up with so-called armor-plated sides, an enclosure which housed their gun. It was called the M2 halftrack. Sgt. LaStoria had to stand up back there and fire the gun. He had two privates in his crew who were his loaders, and the corporal was the driver. His only hope, he thought, was to back up and hide himself behind the hump in the road, so that most of their vehicle became shielded, buried behind the hill, from the line of sight of the enemy. Going by the book, he took up this position, in defilade, to protect his outmanned half-track and his crew, while keeping their gun still able to fire over the top of the crest in the road. In the fix they were in right now, he would have to fire through open sights.

They were in a fight. And it was the first time, for the 36th Division.

Sgt. LaStoria found out quickly why this Division had been labelled as untested. They were a pack of fool tobacco-chewing

Johnny-Rebs, drawlers and hillbillies, the whole pack of them, yelling, not singing, *The Eyes of Texas Are Upon You*, as if they thought that was how you won the war.

Sgt. LaStoria's mouth was dry and he felt like he could have swallowed the ocean if only he could get a drink.

Pfc. Johnny Granger and Pfc. Billy Stanton, two real Texans, were his loaders, and Cpl. Steve Doaks was the driver. He himself was standing on the platform of his rotating 360-degree exposed turret, so-called, and his loaders were feeding four-round clips into the 37mm M3 gun manually.

Sgt. LaStoria was sweating. The morning haze had burned off and it was now sweltering on top of everything else. *Exposed is what you call it, all right,* he was thinking. He was not trying to destroy anything, only discourage them, and somehow hold them off.

In theory, they had been told, their M3 37mm gun could fire 120 rounds per minute. They were finding out fast that they could only wish this were true.

And the three of them in the back, as well as the driver in the cab, were literally sitting on top of all the high-explosive ammo which they needed to fire back to try to save themselves.

Behind them and around them their other three half-tracks and the infantry spread out and took what cover they could and they slugged it out toe to toe with the enemy at a range of three hundred yards, with machine-gun and carbine fire coming from both sides rattling your rib cage, shattering your hearing.

They stood there almost an hour with their platoon, stranded, feeling like they were firing a toy pop-gun at a concrete bomb-shelter. If it hadn't have been for the long-range guns of the fleet, which were pock-pocking the enemy front with balloons of bursting big eight-inch shells, if it hadn't have been for the three hundred yards, who knows if they would have made it.

Finally, anti-tank guns from the 45th Division, who were lost, because their LST had somehow drifted off course and come in to land in the wrong place, south of the *Sele*, soldiers who were only looking for their friends, found instead Sgt. LaStoria and Lt. Waco, and decided, as long as they were here, to come to the rescue of the eyes of Texas.

They claimed that the white smoke-screen the Navy had laid out after dawn, which had been intended to help hide the landing craft from German artillery and air, had instead blinded or confused the helmsman on their LST.

So, this is sunny Italy, Sgt. LaStoria said to himself.

They had been in a fight for their lives, and survived. For one morning. And they could be expected to have more of the same. But now it was afternoon, and it was blazing hot.

Instead, there was a lull. But that ended about three pm, when three Stuka dive-bombers came screaming out of the sun down onto the beach.

The platoon was now parked in the shade, keeping the peace, trying to cool off, and the terrific explosions they heard were a mile away, behind them, on the beach.

Nevertheless, the sound of those Stukas was enough to make a sane man lose his reason. Thereafter, at intervals, the dive-bombers returned.

But the platoon was in dry-dock, in a defensive mode, and in no mood to go seeking out the enemy on their own without orders. Which in any case would most likely have been the wrong thing to do, and gotten them in trouble with the really smart tacticians and strategists who were running this show. So they were content to sit and wait it out, while they enjoyed the cacophony of jarring sounds which meant that other sectors were taking their turn getting baptized.

It appeared to the untrained eye that their invasion had stalled. That was the Army for you. *Hurry up and wait.* However, that first night, they were treated to a real fireworks display.

Dogfights broke out over their heads. They could lie there under the black-out star-canopy and watch red and white tracers whizzing through the black canvas of the sky. Out in the bay, the Germans had sent over high-level bombers, taking advantage of the darkness, which took away the air-cover for the armada of the Allies sitting in the water. The long-range fighter planes of the Fifth Army had to take off from fields in Sicily, too far away. Taranto, in the boot-heel of Italy, had a perfectly adequate airfield much closer, but the British Eighth Army had only just landed there this morning, simultaneous with *Operation Avalanche* hitting the beaches south of Salerno. The British had not yet secured the airfield which was their objective. Now the whole sky lit up as broad as daylight as, at first, by ones and twos, flares, ghostly red and fading to grey and white, sped into the sky, leaving snail-trails behind, only to quiver, quail and die, by the dozens; and yet it built up rapidly into such a barrage that a gauzy veil of light pulled across the heavens. While below in the orchestra pit, the guttural opera of exploding bombs thrown down by high-level Junkers 88s and Dornier 217s achieved the furious splendor of Wagnerian thunder.

Captain Strickland came into their bivouac and told them he was recommending them for a unit citation for their action on the road and read out to them his official dispatch. "Lieutenant Waco and his men, having only one 75-mm self-propelled mount available for his platoon, engaged thirteen Mark IV special German tanks—."

That's an outright falsehood, Gene LaStoria thought. *There were only five I saw. What kind of an outfit is this?*

"–they destroyed three tanks and materially assisted in the destruction of two others—."

More lies. And they were Panzers, not Mark IVs . . .

"—subjected to near cannon and machine-gun fire," the Captain continued, "they displayed conspicuous and extreme bravery under fire."

Gene LaStoria did not feel very brave. He felt lucky to be alive, and scared to death. He vividly wished never to go head-first into such a withering trap again. But he no longer had any illusions of avoiding it either.

He said to himself, *you're dead already. Might as well face it. Just look around you— this is the landscape of oblivion.*

He had joined the Artillery, he thought. A nice, safe distance from the vicinity of enemy infantry shooting at him. Maybe hanging around some nice airfield somewhere on a perimeter defense and whiling away the time patching up torn trousers-legs with a needle and thread, for the guys. Like back home in boot-camp. *No such luck.*

The battle went on for three days and nights. First they advanced, then they withdrew. The Germans then advanced, and next, pulled back again. The firing flared up around the ruined temple and then it shifted to the tobacco factory. The two armies traded that little parcel back and forth, as it was a focal point, several stout buildings arranged in a circle, very thick walls, much like a medieval fortress.

The Germans wanted it to set up as an artillery post to shell the beach. They would attack in force each night, and the Americans, each night, would withdraw, not caring to take the casualties it would cost to hold onto it. Then the Germans would set up and pepper the beach for awhile.

When daylight returned, first thing, the Allied bombers would start dropping 500 lb bombs on the big, circular target of the tobacco factory, and the Germans would have to get out to save their guns.

While the two sides jabbed at one another, the build-up on the invasion beach went on.

The US Fifth Army was bringing ashore everything it had, undeterred, trying to beef up. The chiefs of this tribe, the ones who wore the war-bonnets, had 90,000 personnel already on land, but they wanted 160,000, as fast as they could. At the same time Von Vieterling and his Panzers were bringing in reinforcements, getting ready for who knew what. Allied air reconnaissance thought they might be trying to go on the offensive soon.

By now Sgt. LaStoria and his crew were rapidly becoming inured. The scream of the dive bombers still shivered your spine, but you had learned how to tell, from the sound, how close or far they must be. You could tell the direction and general vicinity of the German artillery shells by the hoarse whistling sound they made flying overhead. You no longer cringed or covered your head at every sound. The German 6-inch mortar-shells were the worst. The Cement-Heads lobbed them in a high arc in the air, and they came straight down, with a kind of a sad sigh, like a bored child, weary of play.

By now you knew exactly when you had to dive under the truck-wheels. Necessity is a stern, but quick, teacher.

Maybe one of these days, one of these sunning-themselves higher-ups would figure out that the key to this whole thing is firepower: who can out-gun the other guy. *That's the only thing that'll make you keep your head down.*

On the third night, Gene went along with some other guys to visit the Chaplain, Father DeSimone, in the chaplain's tent, to congratulate him, because the story had gone the rounds that the padre, who insisted that he could go anywhere the boys could, because he was under the protection of "Somebody high up," had been forced to swim a river the night before to save himself from the Germans.

While the chaplain was laughing and re-living the tale and his audience was back-slapping him, asking for blessings, as the man of God had proven to the unbelievers that he was indeed *connected,* the priest noticed Gene wasn't smiling, and took him aside to ask him if there was anything he could do. Gene told the chaplain, "I'm too old for this war, Father."

"Why, how old are you, Gene?"

"Well—I been here three days, and I feel like I've aged forty years. So, that would make me 63. See what I mean, Father? Too old for this war."

Then a corporal they didn't know came in to say he was looking for Sgt. LaStoria. It was now September 12th.

The corporal drove him in a jeep to an abandoned building still standing down on the waterfront in the town of Paestum itself, a building Mussolini had built at one time to distribute food to the poor.

And there Gene LaStoria found himself in an office with two other GIs named Pullino and Langelli, called to attention in front of an American Army major named Conroy; a Captain from the Italian Army, dressed in their splendiferous uniform; and a British officer named Langhorne, who had a Scottish accent.

The Scotchman was British Navy, and Gene wondered what the hell could be up.

The three GIs were instructed to speak only Italian, and answer the Italian *Capitano's* questions about their families, their backgrounds, where they were from, and so forth, whether they had grown up speaking Italian at home in the house with their families, and so on, questions about their parents, especially, and where they were from, their original home towns in Italy, and so on.

When they were finished with the questioning, the Captain stuck his finger in Pullino's chest, and said "Napolitano," and then poked Gene LaStoria, and said, "Avellinese."

Langelli was dismissed from the room when the Scotchman queried the Italian and the Capitano said, "No. *Siciliano.* No fucking good."

The British Navy guy, Langhorne, then congratulated Pullino and LaStoria, who looked at one another, "for *volunteering* for this absolutely essential mission behind Ger-r-r-man lines."

They were told only that they were to be assigned as artillery and air spotters up in the mountains. And that everything they heard from now on had to be held in strictest confidence and absolute secrecy, for reasons of military security.

Then the two American GIs were separated.

Aware that his father came, originally, from Alta Villa Irpina, a town outside the city of Avellino, Gene LaStoria had even imagined that, as long as he was going to Italy, maybe if he got leave sometime, he might venture over there to see what it was like; he would have loved to have a little time to poke around; imagine their faces back home when he told them he'd made it to the old hometown!

But recently he had forgotten all about such pipe dreams, because the actual reality on the ground had turned out to be so vicious and intense.

And he had had no idea that Avellino itself had been occupied by the Germans, since the 22nd of August.

But these days, everything was so confused. In your foxhole, you didn't know what to think when you saw, not just British and Canadian officers observing the front, but Italian Army units going by in trucks, in full-battle dress; Greek Army, French paratroopers, even American engineering battalions composed entirely of Negroes, staffed by white officers; and even representatives of King Peter of Yugoslavia!—and what else—but Japanese infantry! *And they were Americans!*

So, Gene LaStoria had to admit to himself, why should he be surprised to be pulled out of his unit, hand-picked, just because of his fluent Italian, and the local accent he had consumed, imitated and adopted, without even knowing it, from his mother?

Things stranger than that, which nobody in a million years would believe, were now accepted daily occurrences all around you, in this crazy war.

By now, he expected nothing out of Italy but heat, sand, flies and mosquitoes. The dream, of a quaint, picturesque "Old Country," was gone.

But nothing could have prepared him for this.

It was explained to him that where he was going, mechanized units could not go.

Then Sgt. LaStoria was told to take a nap and he was fortunate he was so dog-tired that he fell asleep, because he was awakened after four hours, and then given only one day, crammed with 24 hours, in which to be trained on radio operation, Morse code and airborne bomb-spotting.

He was trained on a US Army standard-issue SCR-300 tactical field radio. "So simple a child could operate it."

He was given requisition-form-sized sheets made out of silk, on which were printed three columns of 4-letter codes, with which to communicate bombing coordinates for aircraft, or else parachute coordinates for supplies by air-drop.

He was given his own three-letter code-name for radio transmission—DOM.

Twenty-four hours turned into eighteen and then exhaustion and nerves set in and he was allowed to sleep again.

In the pre-dawn hours of September the 14th he was awakened and hot black coffee was poured into him and for the first time he was given the outline of the mission.

He was to be in the vicinity of Avellino no later than three days from now, the 17th, when American paratroopers were to be dropped, in a midnight operation.

And in the meantime, before that happened, he was to locate a group of Italian partisans in a mountain hideout among a set of caves somewhere above and beyond a terraced hillside of olive groves outside Ospedaletto d'Alpinolo, approximately 4 miles due northwest of Avellino.

That was the purpose of his radio.

Once he had located this partisan outfit, he was to act as their liaison with Allied command and help them to carry out their assignments in support of Allied operations by calling in parachute drops of arms and ammunition.

Avellino was about 20 miles due north of Salerno, he was told, and it was garrisoned by infantry and motorized units of the brand-new German Tenth Army, who were said to be looting the place, as they had Salerno.

Meanwhile British bomber forces from no less than 5 British Navy aircraft carriers belonging to something called Force V, out in the Gulf of Salerno, with A-10s and Bostons, and the Americans, with B-24s, B-25s and B-26s, from landing strips in Sicily, were bombing the living Christ out of Avellino, where the Germans had conveniently congregated for them.

The Germans kept pouring in, however, because they were trying to re-group, being chased northward from Brindisi, Taranto and Potenza by the British and Canadian Eighth Army.

Intelligence thought their aim was to man and fortify prepared defensive positions north of Caserta along a line they had dubbed the Winter Line, in order to mount a winter defensive campaign intended keep the Allies from ever reaching Rome.

The whole purpose of the Salerno landings had been to send the US Fifth Army island-hopping around the German flank to try to get in behind them and cut off all their forces in the southern toe and heel of the Italian peninsula. For reasons known only to some inscrutable god of war, or, perhaps, the British Eighth Army's General Bernard Law Montgomery, 1st Viscount of Alamein, this didn't work, and now the Germans were furious at everybody, and fighting rear-guard and holding actions in order to fall back. They were especially incensed at the Italians, who, by surrendering, had turn-coated on them, and they were taking it out on the civilians of the towns and cities, in reprisal for their betrayal by the remnants of Mussolini's armed forces, who were now fighting *for the Allies* and *against them,* under direction of Marshall Badoglio.

And even more, the Germans were infuriated and incensed by the actions and operations of the local Partisans, functioning behind the shield and cover of their own mountain valleys and peaks, in hideouts and cave-networks, beyond the reach of regular troops. The Partisans knew those hills better than any of the other combatants.

Sgt. LaStoria was to establish contact with his targeted guerilla-group, in order to coordinate their activities, and get them to aid, abet and assist the American paratrooper operations, once the Yanks, as the British Navy guy called them, had made their midnight landing, scheduled for the 17th.

Three days from now.

In between Salerno and Avellino, twenty miles distant, civilian refugees from the bombing, looting, and fighting, were flooding the roads everywhere. They were fleeing the destruction of Salerno, to hide, on farms in the countryside owned by relatives or friends, fleeing while they were the targets of German wrath, and Allied bombardiers, both.

Nobody knew where to go or what to do, except that they knew it wasn't safe for men of any age, mothers with children, kids or the old folks, to try to stay in Salerno, where different parts of town, or separate neighborhoods, changed hands, between the Americans, British and Germans, four times in four days.

The refugees were trying to avoid the highways, which the Germans were strafing. They crossed farm fields and followed creeks, brooks and riverbanks, streaming northward, trying to reach safety in the mountains, which were precipitous, rugged and high, only a few miles inland.

Sgt. LaStoria was told he would be given a wife with a child, and a donkey with baskets, and to blend in with the refugees trudging and climbing from stone to rock.

Her name, he was told, was Amata Toscana, but he didn't want to talk to her.

He had only three days to cover the fifty miles from Paestum to Avellino and find people he didn't know, while at the same time, he did not know, exactly, where they were.

As far as Gene LaStoria was concerned, she was only there to provide a cover story for him, just in case.

This whole thing was crazy.

He had to pass as a local if they encountered any Germans. For which reason he intended to avoid them at all costs.

Meanwhile, all he had for his own protection was an automatic pistol, to be secreted in his civilian clothing, and to carry out his mission, a radio set hidden in a basket on the donkey.

"Excuse me, sir," said Sgt LaStoria, at the end of this pre-dawn briefing, when it was still only 5 am on the 14th of September.

Gene LaStoria was being handed a pile of civilian clothing and being asked to change quickly, by a British naval officer, because the woman was waiting outside with the donkey.

Gene was still in his own uniform and he was looking at Major Conroy, of the US Army, who had been in the room the entire time, but said nothing.

He didn't expect to make it through this. So he had nothing to lose.

"Excuse me, sir," he said, addressing Major Conroy. "I can't do this."

The British officer looked at him. "Mutiny is not an option here, laddie."

Major Conroy folded his arms and regarded Sgt LaStoria. He said, calmly, "Are you trying to refuse the mission, Sergeant?"

The British officer looked at Conroy and said, "This man was r-r-ecommended to us, Major."

Gene LaStoria exploded. "By who!"

The Major didn't bat an eye. He said to the Sergeant, "By Capt. Strickland, your C.O."

"Son-of-a-bitch!" said Gene.

"Well, he did want to cite you for your performance on the opening day of *Avalanche,*" said the Major.

"I know that, sir, but this is different. I was just reacting then. I did what anyone would do in the same fix. Nothing special. I'm no hero. But, sir, this is a suicide mission. You're asking me to take off the uniform–."

"What about the paratroopers who have to drop in those mountains at night, Sergeant? That's not a suicide mission? Do you know what happens to your radio when we drop it from an airplane? How would you like to be the one responsible for them being out of radio contact while they're up there in the mountains, beyond the reach of any help?"

"But, sir—you're not asking them to take off their uniforms!"

"That's why you've been carefully chosen, Sergeant. Because you can pass for a local. They can't."

Sgt. LaStoria looked back and forth between the two of them. "You two guys are sending Pullino on this same mission, ain'tcha? You're betting on at least one of us getting through! Ain't that right?"

"We can't divulge any information to you on the other man's mission," said the Major.

Gene noticed that the British guy was staying out of this little discussion, letting the American handle the American. Whereas before, he had done all the talking, all the instructing, all the planning.

Gene said, "Major, sir—ya gotta excuse me—if I don't speak up for myself now, I'll never get the chance."

"I understand," said the Major. "But we don't have all day."

"But, sir—it can't work this way! Do you two guys really want me to get that radio up there, or not? Because you gotta give me *transport* if you want it there by the night of the 17th!"

"Out o' the question," said Lt Langhorne, abruptly.

Gene knew immediately that this was the naval officer's little cooked-up disaster, and that his chance, his only chance, was to get the Major converted. So he said, to both of them, "Do you guys even know how far it is from Paestum to Avellino? It ain't no twenty miles! Ya gotta at least get me to Salerno. Give me a head start! Give me a chance, gentlemen!"

The British Lieutenant looked at the American Major to save him. "You're the Intelligence man, Major. What do ye say? I'm just Naval Party 874."

Major Conroy sighed heavily once, looking down over his folded arms. But he came up in his fighting stance.

"Just what exactly do you propose, Sergeant?"

"Sir, respectfully—ya gotta give me a jeep or something if you expect me to make it!"

"Och–ye want to ride in style, do ye?" The Lieutenant.

"Out of the question." The Major.

"Well—at least a motorcycle, or something."

"A bye-cycle!" The Lieutenant's face lit up.

The Major's eyes narrowed in thought as he appeared to consider this.

Gene said, "Do we have a map here?"

"Aye–military maps," said the Royal Navy man.

"An ordinary road map, I mean."

The Major said, "I believe I do have something in the room here—pre-war—Berlitz." He went to open a desk drawer.

Gene said to the British Lieutenant, "What's Naval Party 874?"

"Combined Operations Communications Unit, attached to higher echelon headquarters," Langhorne replied.

"Oh, I see," said Gene, realizing the guy expected him to be suitably impressed. "That accounts for the radio stuff."

"That's Top Secret, by the way. Ye can never tell yer mother."

Major Conroy was unfolding the map from the booklet, spreading it out on the conference table.

Gene pointed, "Okay. First get me to Salerno. That's a must. I can't go through the lines here in this area because it's fifty miles the long way around. But if I start from Salerno, I got a chance. Let's see—how far is this, marked here—let's see, from the scale—I'd say, 35, 40 kilometers—how far is that in miles?"

The Major pointed out that the book said it was only 38 minutes, by auto, Salerno to Avellino.

"Shit. Wish I could use a motorcycle. But, maybe a bicycle is better. Less noisy— attract a lot less attention. You got some saddle-bags, Major?" Gene glanced at the Lieutenant. "I guess you're right. The bike is the way to go. How heavy is that radio, anyway?"

"Och, 'tis a feather, fifteen pounds," said the Naval man. "The answer to yer other question, well, I'm not verrah good at kilometers, actually, but I would say it's, mebbe, twenty-three and a half miles."

"Okay. So the bike is the way to go. If I have to, I can hide it easy. Cover it up with leaves. If I have to, I can ditch it, easy. Hard to ditch a woman and a donkey. I can throw the bike down and make myself disappear."

Major Conroy was leaning over the table with his hands planted and so was Sgt. LaStoria. Their heads were together, over the map. "Well, Sergeant—can you make it?"

"In three days, sir? I can make it. My father walked all the way from Avellino to Naples, once, on foot. 'Course, he was only ten years old. And he didn't hafta carry no radio. And he hitched rides, too, on farmers' wagons, goin' his way. That was in 1899, sir. But he told me all about it. Jesus—wish he could see me now. Wonder what he'd say if he knew I was about to drop in on his native town as an American tourist, all expenses paid by the government?"

"He'd say, good luck, son," said the Major. "Yeah. *Buona fortuna.*"

The three men were all smiling now, each one remembering his own father.

Gene said, "Now, what about getting me to Salerno, sir? Didn't I see a whole bunch of jeeps and motorcycles parked outside here when I pulled in?"

"Might be something we can use there."

"And, Major, I swear, sir, if you get me killed on this mission, I'm coming back and haunt you, every night, for the rest of your days."

Standing in between Sgt. Gene LaStoria, in Salerno, and Avellino, his destination, was the LXXVI Panzer Corps, three divisions, one of them the Herman Goering Panzer Division.

If Salerno were counted as sea level, Avellino was a full 2000 feet above it. That was the kind of precipitous climb he faced on his bike.

This wall of mountains had been an obstacle to the Greeks, the Romans, the Vikings, the Saracens, the Spanish and the French, in times past, and it was an obstacle to the British, Americans and Germans now.

The British Eighth Army, under their General Montgomery, had landed 300 miles to the south of Salerno, at Reggio Calabria, on the toe of the boot, all the way back on September 3rd.

But on the day Gene LaStoria landed on the sandy beach at Paestum with the Texas 36th Division, Sept 9th, Montgomery called a two-day halt in his advance, due to the difficulty of the terrain.

And the Germans withdrawing northward before him were then suddenly available to be called in by their commander, General Von Vietinghoff, to reinforce his six divisions facing the US Fifth Army, which was now over-extended on the beaches, and for three to six miles inland, along a 35-mile front, from Paestum to Salerno.

Therefore, the Germans were able to counter-attack in force.

Gene LaStoria was not aware of all this intelligence on Sept 14th, at 5 am, when he threw their little party into an unscheduled re-planning, but he was hurriedly briefed by Major Conroy on the highlights as they all went outside, and he and the British Navy man climbed into an American jeep, to be piloted by Lt. Langhorne.

That's how Sgt. LaStoria found out about the Hermann Goering Panzer Division. He was getting ready to set out on what he was certain was a suicide mission.

All he really knew was that his ears and eyes told him that for two days now the other side had been attacking furiously, and might very well be about to throw his side back into the sea.

Lt. Langhorne steered the jeep onto Highway 18 north and headed for Salerno while it was still dark. The Germans were again bombing the Tyrrhenian Sea from on high, but in the person of Langhorne, the British Navy was having a breezy old time of it in their bouncing jeep.

As dawn crept up on them over the mountain ranges on their right, to blossom fully at about 0630 hours, they were zig-zagging. Every crossroads they came to, they were re-directed by MPs.

They were told first they couldn't go *there* because Jerries held an area, and then told they couldn't go *here* because the Krauts were dug in over *there;* everything seemed to be a mass of confusion.

At one point they found themselves in an unoccupied orange grove, so they stopped for breakfast, and Gene LaStoria filled his peasant's pantaloni-pockets with walnuts and figs. How he was going to open the walnuts he didn't stop to think. Portable food was what he was after; he didn't count on living to see his next meal, but if he didn't, he didn't want to go out on an empty stomach, either.

Lt. Langhorne cheerfully explained that Naval Party 874 had a radio station set up inside Salerno, fully staffed and completely equipped, and so, that was where they were going. That was supposed to make everything all right.

They got there, but what should have taken, oh, 45, 50, 55 minutes, tops, on a beach day with traffic, took them four hours.

If they hadn't stopped to get advice on what was up ahead from a group of Italian women walking the side of the road while balancing on their heads with one hand bundles of household belongings wrapped in bedsheets, they never would have gotten there.

Even stranger was another gang they passed with the girls, old men and boys carrying bulging suitcases, while the bundles on top of their heads this time were all burlap sacks.

Where in the hell did they find those?

Finally, they were outside the station of Naval Party 874. Langhorne had been there before, while they were setting it up, and so he knew exactly where it was, in a 4-story square-shaped dirty white block-building on a corner beside high railroad embankments which carried a trestle and formed an overpass over a bend in the street at the city outskirts.

When they got there, a British platoon was trotting at double-quick time around the curve, heading for the underpass with rifles at the ready. And uniformed British swabbies in denim, with their sleeves rolled up, having received orders to evacuate, were piling out of the radio station block, filling American trucks in the lot behind it with everything from microphones to filing cabinets.

Sgt. LaStoria got his bicycle out of the back of the jeep and set off under the railroad bridge in a hurry, waving off Langhorne, and hoping to catch up to the bog-trotting British platoon, which he soon passed, pedaling as fast as he could.

All he could think of was to get out of here quick and get to somewhere where he could think.

There were trees and side-streets, one straight road through a suburb of nice homes, looming over which was Hill 419, the big mountain flanking the southern rim of the city all the way down to the sea, which the Major had told him to avoid: German mortars and artillery were dug in on the heights so that they could shell the harbor and anything that moved.

Gene stopped. He had to think, at all costs.

He thought at first he'd be much better off to wait till darkness to try to get around that Hill 419. But what if that cost him too much time? He would love to be invisible, covered by night, but what if he himself couldn't see out there in the dark?

He had three days to get there: rapidly becoming two and a half.

The parachute drop was for midnight of the 17th. That would give him extra time.

But, then again, this place Ospedelletto d'Alpinolo, was beyond Avellino, so he needed that extra time back. And Major Conroy had warned him strictly to avoid Avellino itself at all costs, as intelligence confirmed with aerial photos that it was full of German troops.

He decided that he just had to keep going in daylight, and hope to at least get out of Salerno's vicinity before nightfall on the first day.

He would need to sleep. And so he would have to hide, off the road. And so, he reasoned, he would have to sleep at night; when there would be no streetlights anyway, and black-out in any farmhouses or outbuildings: he just didn't know what to expect.

He had memorized that page in the Berlitz book that showed Highway 30 blending into Highway 88 and taking the happy motorist up the hills to Avellino. That's where he had to go, Highway 30: jump on that at the end of his current long stretch, and he would be on his way.

He just had to keep going while daylight lasted, probably till about 7.30 or 8 o'clock at night (out of uniform, he was back on civilian time) and meanwhile, keep his eyes peeled and fastened way ahead, on the lookout for anything bad, ready to ditch at a moment's notice.

If there were any people home in this suburb, they were in the cellars. They certainly weren't out on the road with him.

Or maybe they were smart enough to have evacuated already?

He could see perhaps half a mile ahead at the most because of the rises and dips in the road surface as he pedaled.

But he could use his ears.

The sound of the battle increasing and decreasing went on all afternoon. He could tell the Navy out in the bay was hitting the Germans hard. It was non-stop, the sound of the big guns. But the German 88s and 75s and tank-cannons and anti-tank-57s were also voluminous; it was clear from the battle-noise that the Germans were attacking.

Maybe that was good—for him.

Then he came to a flat space, just before the junction of Highway 30, which he was expecting to be up ahead shortly.

To his horror, he could tell the sound of the enemy artillery was coming out of a stand of woods, right there at the level road-junction.

Had to be. Where else would they be, with their mechanized blitzkrieg?

Shit. What to do?

Suddenly he realized there was the sound of his own guns out there, too, firing on the Germans.

It was just gut instinct, but his gut told him to go talk to the boys.

A picketer had him in his sights as he approached another grove of trees walking his bicycle. The soldier yelled, "Halt!"

Gene held his hands up high, and called out, "Hey, buddy! Let me come in. I'm a friend!"

"Keep your hands up—away from that bike!"

"Listen! My name is Sergeant LaStoria. Let me come in. I need help."

"Okay, buddy, I don't know who you are. But you come on ahead, slow—very slow. No false moves."

"Can I push the bike?"

"Leave the bike there and remember, I got a trigger-finger."

Sgt. LaStoria slowly walked in, no longer sure it had been the wisest move.

But his "buddy" let him walk ahead of him with a rifle at his back while they went to find the Lieutenant of the platoon; the Germans were firing on the platoon's position, while they fired back.

Sergeant LaStoria told the Lieutenant that he would like them to step up their coverage to rapid fire to make the Germans keep their heads down while he raced past them on his bike through the road junction where the Krauts were hiding in the stand of woods.

"You crazy? You expect me to believe this story about a mission? How do I know you're not running away—a deserter?"

"Okay. I'm a deserter. Shoot me."

"Ah. I don't feel like shooting you. You got dog-tags?"

"They made me take 'em off. Can I put my hands down?"

"Did you pat him down, jerk-off?"

"No, sir, I did not."

"Well, do it!"

"Sir—he has a weapon—it's GI issue. It was in the waistband behind his back."

"You shit-head, you coulda got me killed! Why do you have this weapon, mister, hidden that way?"

"I might need it to shoot myself when I get captured so the SS can't torture me and get all my secrets outta me."

"You're a wise-ass, aren't you?"

"I come all the way over here and ask you for help and you give me the business."

"Where you from?"

"Massachusetts."

"Somebody get that kid from New Bedford over here, what's-his-name."

After a little while, the kid from New Bedford came running up. After the Lieutenant gave him the picture, he said to Gene LaStoria, "Where'd you say you was from?"

"Stoughton, Mass."

"Oh. Okay. What kinda people live in New Bedford?"

"Portuguese, everybody knows that."

"That's right, Lieutenant. Okay. Uh. What road would you take to get to New Bedford from Stoughton?"

"138."

"That's correct again, sir. And he sounds like he's from home. Say pahk my cah."

"Pahk my cah."

"Say—wahm me up, baby!"

"Wahm me up, baby!"

"That's it, sir. He's legit."

The lieutenant said, "I don't know. Sounds crazy to me. Maybe it is everything you say, but–."

"It's a crazy war, sir."

"Say that again. Well, if you wanna take your life in your hands like that, I suppose it's the little we can do. Why did you say you got picked for this again, friend?"

"Because I speak good Italian. My mother never learned how to speak English—so we had to. My name is LaStoria."

"Say something."

"*Stai un stubido culu.*"

"What's that mean?"

"You're a stupid asshole."

The Lieutenant laughed. "Okay, jerk-off—go your way. We'll give it our best. What a crazy war. Give him his pistol back. But keep him covered till he's outta my sight."

Gene LaStoria went into his racer's crouch on his creaking old bicycle and sped through the intersection as fast as he could, once he thought he had timed the tennis-match of artillery firing back and forth to the peak of its volleying.

He was close enough to the kraut battery to see the muzzle-flashes and the smoke.

He made it through, and immediately came upon a long downhill, where he coasted and let his legs rest and threw his arms out in a big V-sign. He didn't care who saw him. He had made it, and he felt so much better.

After that, he knew that he would have to get through two little towns before branching off to the left onto Highway 88.

The first was Baronissi, and the second was called Mercato San Severino. All you had to do was read the road-signs.

Ah. Peacetime.

He figured that at this point he was already about four miles outside Salerno, and it gave him a tremendous boost because he was sure he had now cleared the German lines surrounding the city, and it ought to be clear sailing from here all the way up to Avellino.

Baronissi and Mercato San Severino were too small, and off-the-main-track, to billet the Krauts. Their numbers required cities like Salerno and Avellino. Of the two, Salerno was much the bigger and, as a sea-going port, more important. But Avellino was still, on its own, important enough to give its name to a *provincia,* and a surrounding population. That was how the Italian Capitano had identified Sgt. LaStoria for this mission, after all, as an *Avillenese.*

Now he checked his watch, and it was already 3 pm on the 14th, and so, he figured, that gave him only maybe four hours of daylight left, 4-1/2 if he was lucky. He started to use his watch to time his downhills. He could coast very quickly, 30, 40 seconds at the most, and part-way up the next hill, then he had to pump like mad; and finally, whipped, climb down and push it; till he could coast down, and rest his legs again, very briefly.

This was not going to change, he knew. The mountains that were really only hills of 450 feet in height, or so, down in Salerno, around sea level, were now already 800 feet high along both sides of the road; that is, to his east and west, as he was going north, and the sun was going down over the tree-tops on his left, so that the road was already covered in shadow, except for patches of sunlight where there were gaps in the surrounding forest.

This was the countryside, and it was rugged. Any farms were small, and mostly growing fruit such as apples, or olives, and the land had to be terraced to do it.

Over to the east, really tall mountains hovered, with jagged peaks and pinnacles, like icicles standing upside down. It was some kind of massif that he had noticed stood out in green on the Berlitz road-map.

Gene's father, Tony LaStoria, had once told him that when he was a kid growing up in these hills, there was an old Italian proverb everybody used to recite: *After we climb one mountain, another looms into view.*

Gene was finding out quickly just how easy it would have been, for anybody who wanted to, to lose himself in this part of the world, as long as you knew how to survive in the forest. To his west, where the sunlight was fading to blue rapidly over the tree-tops, there was another massif: according to Berlitz, as he recalled it, a round green shape, where his final destination of Ospedelletto d'Alpinolo was a dot, right on the edge of the round mass.

One other thing he had noticed, when he had looked at that Berlitz map, which he had mentioned also to Major Conroy and the Naval guy.

Very close to Ospedelletto d'Alpinolo, to the east of it on that map, lay Alta Villa Irpina, the hometown of his Pa. In his own mind, just in case he wanted to bail out on this mission, not saying that he ever would, but just supposing he would have to, or, for some reason, was forced to: then he wanted to keep Alta Villa Irpina in his sights: for some reason (and now was not the time he cared to analyze it) that was a comfort to know, for Sgt. Gene LaStoria.

And the other thing he had to remind himself about, now that he had already had the thought cross his mind *I might wanna ditch this whole mission and disappear in the woods* was *what the artillery lieutenant had said about "a deserter." For one, if I don't get that radio delivered, my handlers, the Major and the Scotchman, they'll know: they'll find out as soon as those paratroopers land. Which means, basically, I gotta watch out not just for the Germans, but for the Americans, too. Fucking Christ. I'm caught in a vise here. They're squeezin' me on both sides. This is a goddam suicide mission.*

But at the moment, he had no more time to think about it, because he was already approaching the hill-town of Baronissi, and it was only six o'clock!

He figured he was way ahead of schedule, because he thought he was already at least seven, maybe eight miles, beyond Salerno. And he only had 23-1/2 miles to go! (according to Langhorne, he kept telling himself).

He didn't want to allow himself to count the extra uphill miles it might take to get around Avellino and over to Ospedelletto d'Alpinolo, and maybe beyond, to find that partisan camp, wherever it might be. He did not want to daunt himself.

Thank God for that bicycle. Thank God he hadn't let himself get saddled with that donkey, and a wife named Amata!

How he relished the thought of telling his own wife, Celia, back home, how he had almost gotten married again in Italy! *By order of the US Army! What a hoot that would be!*

Looks like a nice, pleasant little town, Baronissi. Everybody staying indoors, what with a war on.

He was going down the main street when a local woman motioned to him from the doorway of her little row-house. He got off, and went over with his bike, and she invited him in with a pail of goat's-milk. He leaned his bicycle up against the wall.

She told him to bring it in if he wanted to find it again. The woman was tiny and old, and he wanted to hug her; boy did that milk taste good! Then he found out what she wanted. It was goat's-milk in exchange for the latest news. Clearly, he was not from Baronissi! She'd never seen *him* before. Therefore wherever he was from, whoever he was, he must have information from the outside world, and she was all excited to get the news. What was going on? Where was he going, with that *bicicletta,* where had he been that morning? In Salerno! *Santo Christo,* what's going on? It became obvious that she was all excited because the Americans were coming and the war would soon be over! Where were they? Tomorrow, they would be here, no?

He thought he might just spend the night here, get off to an early start, tomorrow. It was clear that she thought he was from somewhere nearby: *Alta Villa, did you say?*

He made some quick calculations, time-wise. He asked her how far to Mercato San Severino. She said 12 kilometers, and he had to figure that in his head. He did not want her going round later claiming to the other townspeople that an American had just passed through.

Then, in exchange for the goat's milk, out of his pocket, Gene pulled walnuts, to offer her a treat; the old lady's eyes got big, and out from a drawer came a nutcracker: *which solves that little problem,* thought Gene, and he was about to say something when he realized he better stifle himself quick because, *oh shit, I've forgotten the word for 'nutcracker.'*

In the early morning, Sgt. LaStoria figured maybe 4 am or so, when he could not sleep any longer, he lay there thinking, in the woman's house, *I was pretty stupid, after all.*

I forgot completely about that radio.

What if she noticed his bulging saddle-bag? He had gone out to use the outhouse in the back garden. Could she have looked? *dumb!—better not do this again.*

He began to worry so that it prevented him going back to sleep.

He was having second thoughts such as, *you know, asshole, you don't really know who's who, up in these hills. What if you're so trusting you don't realize you're talking to somebody who might make a phone call and, bam! that's it for you! They come and get ya! The war ain't over yet, ya dumb bastard! How do you know there ain't Fascisti still runnin' around up here, you gonna trust 'em all, because they're Italians? like you're strolling down Hanover Street or something, waving hello to all your aunts and uncles? What a dumb-ass you are!*

And so he got off to an early start on the second day of his journey, if for no other reason than to escape these morbid thoughts.

And as soon as he was outside again, moving again, he felt so much better.

And in the earliest light available, he started timing himself with his wristwatch again. The climb was getting harder. The hills going up were not as long, but they were steeper.

Going down was like, well, like pictures of the ski-jump he'd seen in the papers, or the newsreels, from the Olympics, you know? *Whoosh!*

And then, the deflation of the uphill. Having to climb off your bike and push your way uphill again: all the more conscious now of the 15 pounds of canvas-covered radio tubes in the saddlebag.

But that was all right, because he was 23 years old! Because of boot-camp, because of active-duty, he was in the best shape of his life. He was not really tired. He'd got a good rest in the old lady's place after all; he wasn't yet fatigued.

And it occurred to him—*he'd left the war behind!*

There was nothing and nobody but him on this road. He was the only fool out there! No cars, no trucks, no military traffic!

It was exhilarating. He realized that he was soaring. He was having an adventure. What he had pictured to be impossible, he was doing.

He wished his brother Augie could see him now. *He was an awful kid for Ponkapoag, practically lived in the woods. Wish he was here. He'd be a big help to me right now. He'd know exactly what to do. Wait'll I get home and tell him this one!*

He stopped to think: that he had gone from the trough of town at 4 am to the high-altitude giddiness of the forest of 8 am! He'd have to start working on maintaining his vigilance, and not get carried away with himself.

Only 12 kilometers to Mercato San Severino!

Then he lifted his head, coming over a hill-top, and there it was! already! He checked the time—10 am on the 15th! He was making it!

This place turned out to be half the size, if that, of Baronissi. Where the other had been a hill-town, this was a mountain-scaling fortress. At the very top of a big hill by the side of the road, off the road, so to speak, although you could see it from here, a mile off, with the ribbon of Highway 30, snaking up to the cliff-dwellers at the top. This little mountain reminded him of *The Pimple,* down on the beach, near Paestum, where the Krauts had dug in with their mortars and pill-boxes, a free-standing mound that rose out of the middle of nowhere.

From a distance, Mercato San Severino looked exactly like that!

When he got to the middle of it, he realized that he'd missed his turn-off, to Highway 88, back there somewhere. He could see that Highway 30 took a right-angle hook onto a due-west path in the middle of Mercato. He would have to ask those old guys, over there, playing cards at the table outside the trattoria. They told him he would find Highway 30 intersecting 88 outside the town. Just take the hook in the road. Where you from, anyway?

Alta Villa Irpina, said Gene.

Oh, yes, I know it, said one.

Never heard of it, said the other.

I've been in Silentina Irpina, said a third.

They started arguing about how to get from here to Volturrara Irpina, and Gene hopped on his bike, and left them there.

Once he found Highway 88, he realized he was more than halfway to Avellino. *This was too easy.* He knew he should be feeling alarmed, or on-guard, or something, but he was feeling too good to care. Something in this mountain air was puffing out his chest.

The old men had indeed warned him, back in Mercato, about all the Germans occupying Avellino.

If he expected to get home to Altavilla Irpina, watch out.

They gave him tips on how to get around the city, contradicting one another, starting another argument, but, what the hell else did they have to do?

Anyway, he wasn't going there, but to Ospedelletto d'Alpinolo.

He checked the time again, and suddenly it occurred to him, *oh, fuck, oh, shit, here I am with a nice American GI issue A-11 Military Spec wristwatch on my left wrist, made right back home in Waltham, Mass, checking the time!*

He stopped his bike, half-way up a steep hill, took off the watch and hurled it as far as he could into the woods.

The next day was the 16th, and he found himself looking down on Avellino through the trees.

He was absolutely bike-dragging tired. The last 8 miles or so, on Highway 88, he figured, since Mercato, all lonely mountain road winding around and up and down, had been some serious climbing.

Still, Avellino was in a valley. A high, mountain valley, true, but the hills and mountains around it nevertheless were higher still, and gave you a vantage point, from which to look down on the city.

He could see the troops, the trucks, the armored vehicles, slow dots, moving around. As long as he could see them and they couldn't see him, it was all right. He had absolutely no desire to be down there amongst that city. He would swing way around the place to the west, as the old men of Mercato had advised, and make his way up to Ospedelletto d'Alpinolo.

He was way ahead of schedule. A whole day. But he wasn't there yet, and he would have to cross a major road leading from Avellino down to Napoli, and Napoli, he knew, was still occupied by who knows how many Krauts, perhaps thousands. After all, it was a city of four million souls. What worried him was the traffic that he guessed must almost certainly be passing back and forth between Naples and Avellino on that linking highway he'd seen on the map.

He decided to ditch the bike. He'd carry the radio, on his back if he had to. He would go the rest of the way on foot. After all, it was only three or four miles outside Avellino, where he needed to get to.

If he ditched the bike, it would enable him to wait till nightfall to go on, and under cover of darkness, he could get across that highway.

Yup. That was the way to go.

Gene turned away with his bike, turning his back on the city below, just as his hearing detected faroff the faint grumble of aircraft which then began rapidly, steadily increasing: *our boys, on the way to hit Avellino.*

He lost the bicycle where he thought it could not be found, got as far away from it as he dared, and carried himself and his canvas bundle as deep into the woods, off the road, as he dared to go, while being able to find his way back.

He found a place to bed down under a mossy, fallen tree-trunk, covering himself and the SRC-300 in leaves, putting his pistol next to his cheek where he lay, a log under a log, and went to sleep for the rest of the afternoon.

The last thing he remembered thinking, before he fell asleep was *Pa came down this mountain, on this same road to Naples . . . 44 years ago . . . huh . . .*

When he walked into the camp of the Partisans, Sgt. Gene LaStoria had his hands raised high in the air, and told the sentry they had posted, *"Buon giorno. Sono un amico."*

They were in a forested mountain crest about three miles west of Ospedelletto d'Alpinolo, at a spot which was precisely located on the hem of a massif, which went straight up as soon as you passed through the camp.

That day, when he got there, the mid-morning of the 17th of September, 1943, everybody in that camp was anti-Fascist, and livid at the Germans in Avellino, and expecting the Americans any day now.

As Sgt. LaStoria walked into the camp, hands held high, the sentry with a rifle pointed at his back, armed men now came emerging from tents and lean-to's, a grim-looking set of partisans, with the determined, hungry look of mountaineers, of wiry long-distance hikers.

When he indicated to them to take down the back-pack from his shoulder, and they had unwrapped the SCR-300, the *American* radio, they gave him directions, gladly, to the hide-out of their chief, who was called *Il Giustizia*.

Having met their first American, these guerilla fighters were beside themselves with excitement, carried away with mixed and complicated feelings of relief, fury, joy, anger, revenge, feeling liberated of pent-up emotions of fear, hope and despair which had lasted years upon years, to this very moment.

Sgt. LaStoria hadn't mentioned his name then, as, in the excitement, it hadn't seemed to come up, nor had they asked, and he had avoided mentioning Alta Villa Irpina, as he was anxious to get to only one place, and didn't want complications, after all this, and what he'd had to go through to get here.

Gene LaStoria, too, was feeling a tremendous relief, as well as an immense emotion of triumph. He had reached his personal mountaintop. He had made it.

He was never going to forget this feeling, so help us, as long as he lived. He would have it always, to fall back on—this moment.

At this point all Sgt. LaStoria wanted to do was to get on with it and finish what he had come here to do. When he had entered the Partisan camp he had asked the sentry for the man in charge. Now it was that man, the first armed partisan he had encountered, who directed him.

When he got to the tiny level space before *Il Giustizia's* hide-out, with the sentry levelling his rifle behind his back, he still had his hands held up high.

Around them the mountain top fell away on all four sides.

It was heavily wooded, except for this tiny level space, tramped down by many feet till the grass was worn away to form a bald spot. From this camp, the Partisans could see anyone approaching from any direction, while they themselves were hidden behind a screen of trees that rendered them invisible.

Lining the level space was a semi-circle of holes in the rock, little caves, and makeshift huts and lean-to's, thrown up by the hand of man, who tried to tame nature and bend her like a mistress to his service, and out of these huts, hatless men in uniform came running, shouting, "It's a Yank!"

They were British airmen, four of them, with their ranks and insignia ripped off, POWs who had escaped from the Italian Army prison camp, in Barletta, on the Adriatic seacoast south of Foggia, all the way across the Appenines to the east.

They began excitedly asking Gene LaStoria if the British Army had yet reached Foggia, as they fully intended, they assured him, retracing their steps back the same way, fifty miles, as soon as the Allies captured the airfield at Foggia—and be flying again!

Two men approached wearing bandoliers.

Gene LaStoria expected this was the leader of the Partisans he had asked for—but which one? The first one, he addressed.

"*Buon giorno. Sono un soldato Americano. Ho venito come un amico and, uh, e ho porto un radio per su gruppo a usare.*"

Gene had taken his hands down and was holding one out to shake with the first partisan, when the other stepped in front, saying, "It's okay—we speak English here."

Gene replied, "But I need to practice my Italian."

The man said, "Why? You going to stay awhile?" Everyone laughed.

Gene said, "Well—if you let me."

The Partisan leader took Gene's hand, shook it, smiled and said, "Welcome."

Gene pumped his hand, and he was smiling vigorously as well. "Mi piacere. I mean— I'm happy to be here—believe you me!"

More Partisans were beginning to crowd around, pressing the British airmen milling on top of Gene and the group-leader, and hearts were swelling through this assemblage of men, smiling on a mountaintop, as they all felt a current of camaraderie run through them that was virtually tangible, right down to their fingertips.

Gene LaStoria spoke seriously to the group leader as they shook. "What is your name? Who am I speaking with?"

His second answered for him. "*Questo è Il Giustizia.*"

"Oh—Justice," said Gene. "That's a good name."

"Yes," said Il Giustizia. "It's a good code-name for me."

Gene tried to make a joke. "Better than *Il Duce,* eh?"

They all chuckled, and grimaced, out of politeness to the newcomer.

Il Giustizia said, "That name we don't talk about. That one, we spit on. We have just learned yesterday that he was rescued on the 12ᵗʰ by the Waffen-SS, in a raid by Skorzeny. Hitler sent them, personally. Mussolini is now free again."

"I didn't know," said Gene. "I'm sorry."

"Well—and why did they send you? And, from where? How did you find us? If you find us, others can. We must talk. Let's walk."

The British servicemen and the rest of the crowd now dispersed quite a bit in order to give the two of them a little privacy.

Gene told Il Giustizia, "I am from the US Fifth Army. I'm a sergeant. My regular unit operates a 37mm halftrack; anti-tank weapon, for infantry support. But I was kidnapped by Intelligence, American and British, to be sent here. Now the thing is that tonight at midnight, the 82ⁿᵈ Airborne will make a parachute drop in this area—top secret—and we need your help and support once our men are on the ground. That's why I was sent and why I have the radio, the SCR-300 your men are looking over back there, so that we can coordinate drops of supplies to our men and your *gruppo*."

"And you were choosed—why?" said Il Giustizia.

"Well," said Gene, "it so happens that I grew up in a home in Massachusetts where our mother only spoke Italian. So, we learned it as kids, and so—we've been speaking the local dialect you have here all our lives—and that's why I was selected by the Intelligence people—they were looking for somebody like me who could pass as a native, to get this radio up here. As you know, or maybe you don't know, these combat-radios are too fragile, and too important, too valuable, to be dropped by parachute. So, my mission was to get it here safely to you before the 82ⁿᵈ Airborne drops in on you tonight."

"I see," said Il Giustizia. "And you succeed. You are to be complimented."

"Well," said Gene, with a heavy sigh of relief, "I'm just glad I made it. I hate to think what our boys would do to call in bombing coordinates without a radio up here." Feeling expansive, feeling welcomed, by the reactions of these rugged mountain-men, and yes, congratulated, by their leader; feeling the seductions of the camaraderie this unusual manner of meeting these men generated, which would never have happened in peacetime; Gene LaStoria was suddenly over-washed with a sensation of belonging here, of having come home, of the serendipity of the situation, and so he volunteered a little something about himself. "You know, sir, it just so happens that my father comes from Alta Villa Irpina, and that's, what? Four or five miles from here?—ten kilometers? Yup. Forty-four years ago, to the day, who knows, my father ran away from home in Alta Villa, to go to New York, by himself when he was only ten years old."

Il Giustizia stopped him, with a hand on his arm, and said, with great curiosity, "And what is your name, my friend?"

"I'm Sergeant LaStoria—Eugene LaStoria—Eugenio. They call me Gene—back home." Gene's enthusiasm faltered, and his voice trailed off. The two Partisans were reacting to his name.

Il Giustizia had gone ashen grey. The face on his second was turned ghostly pale.

Gene said, "What's the matter?"

Il Giustizia said, gravely, "We are holding two men here. They are hill-town, how you say, mayor. The former mayor of Ospedelletto d'Alpinolo and the former mayor of Alta Villa Irpina—the Fascist mayor."

For some reason, Gene's heart fell. It was not anything he guessed. It was more the ghastly appearance of the two partisans.

Something was deadly wrong—and for the life of him, Gene could not figure out what it possibly could be—but he had an awful sense of foreboding come over him suddenly.

Then Il Giustizia clapped his hands together once and looked at his partner, practically with glee, as he did a little rocking dance, heel to toe.

"It's perfetto!" he said. "It's opera! It's classical drama! Puccini or Verdi would die for this plot twist! Bring them out!"

Two men with hands tied behind their backs were led out of a caged hut and placed before Sgt LaStoria.

Gene was still mystified but he did know that this was not good.

Both men were aged and stooped. They appeared to have shrunk from misuse or neglect.

They were meek, not defiant—resigned, it appeared.

Il Giustizia said, "This one is Bruno Merloni, formerly the fascist mayor of Ospedelletto d'Alpinolo. And this one—formerly the Fascist mayor of Alta Villa Irpina—is Enrico LaStoria."

Gene heard the name, pronounced as it was by Il Giustizia, with loathing, with vehement contempt, and he went to jelly all over.

In his worst nightmare he could not have imagined–this.

Finally, he managed to say something. "Why are their hands tied behind their backs?"

"They are scheduled for execution."

"Why?"

"Do you know what these two men have done!" thundered Il Giustizia. "Have you ever heard of *Il Confino?* This one—" he pointed to Merloni—"turned his entire native town over to the very profitable racket of housing the internal exiles sent to him by Mussolini! And this other one—LaStoria—denounced my brother Mario and caused him to be kicked to death by Fascist thugs with their shodded feet and boot-heels."

With all his might, with every ounce of his being, Gene LaStoria wished he had never been sent here, to stand here, on this mountaintop, to be here now, to hear this.

It was a singular shiver he felt. Like a shadow gliding right through your body. It was the raven's wing, *il fato.*

He said, to Il Giustizia, "By what authority do you do this?"

"By the authority of history!"

"You call this *'Justice'?*"

"Let me ask you something. You say you come from Massachusetts? Then, you tell me, what justice did Massachusetts give to Sacco and Vanzetti?"

Slowly, Il Giustizia circled the wooden figure of the American sergeant.

"You come here!" he shouted, "and you think we are ignorant! You think we know nothing! *nothing* of the world! I will tell you now that we know well the names of two martyrs of *your* 'justice,' by the name of Nicola Sacco and Bartolomeo Vanzetti! The question is, do *you* know them—do *you* remember them—for we have *never* forgotten!"

Gene LaStoria protested. "I was seven years old when that happened. Of course, I remember it. But I had nothing to do with it! Nor could I have done anything! I was a child! But I will tell you that my father—."

"Your father! Oh, yes, we remember him, too. He was the one who ran away. They've been talking about that for years in Alta Villa! And do you know why? Because, the superstitious say, *the boy must have to know something that we didn't!*"

"May I talk to the prisoner?"

"Talk away! It won't change anything! *Sentence has been passed!* But you talk here. Where we can see you! And by the way—did you come to our camp unarmed?—I don't think so—I don't think even the American Army is that stupid. Were you searched when you came into my camp?"

"No," said Sgt. LaStoria. He suddenly realized just how awfully impossible his position was.

But he felt he had to speak to the prisoner. If there was any chance—any chance at all that he was not really who Gene thought he was, *and was afraid he was*—he had to find out.

Sgt LaStoria said to Il Giustizia, "I have to tell you that I am armed with a sidearm which is in my waistband at the back. Now—I will turn my back to you both and also raise my hands in the air and I think you should have your partner here dis-arm me."

When that had been done, Gene LaStoria turned to face Il Giustizia once again. "Now I wish to say one thing to you before I talk with your prisoner. I came here to carry out a mission assigned to me by my superiors, and I have a duty to carry out that mission, and I believe that you do, also, Il Giustizia, *con respetto.* Other Americans are going to drop out of the sky onto your mountain, at night, tonight, at midnight, to aid in your cause, and they will need your help. Therefore, although you have my sidearm now, I will need it back. You and I have to cooperate, and to do that, Il Giustizia, we have to trust one another."

Il Giustizia said, "Listen to me, my friend. You say you have come to help us now. But I say to you—where were you in 1922? Where were you in '25—'26—in '38? At Munich, eh? If you people do what you are suppose to do, back then, maybe none of us would be standing here now! You could have saved the world!—from such misery! From such pain! And suffering, and death! Si, death! Instead, you save yourself!"

Gene LaStoria sighed heavily as he lowered his hands. "May I speak to the old man now?—your prisoner?"

"Speak away!"

Gene LaStoria turned to the old man with the white hair who was called by the same name as he was and led him by the elbow over to a rock, where he sat him down; and Gene stooped on his haunches before him, almost in supplication, as it were; and Gene asked the old man, in his best dialect, "Do you have any children?"

"No."

"You don't have a son named Antonio?"

"There was a boy by such a name, but he's no son of mine."

At that moment, Gene knew that this man was his grandfather.

He knew because he had always wondered why his father never spoke of his own father—the grandfather of his sons—the *nonno* of his daughters–who sat cross-legged before him now, for questioning. Why had his father never even mentioned his father's name, not even once? . . . *there were never any letters from the old country . . . nor did I ever hear of Pa ever writing a letter home, even to his mother . . . it was as if they had never existed, Pa's parents, as if Tony LaStoria had rolled down off this mountaintop like a rock, like a stone—not a child, from his mother's lap . . .*

Sgt Gene LaStoria could see now that they, father and son, *had disowned each other! Like father, like son . . . for—haven't I seen with my own eyes Pa disown his own daughter Peggy, the same way?*

"What happened to your wife?" Gene asked. Maybe he would find her, and perhaps the women in the family would turn out to be another story, perhaps turn out to be human, even.

But the old man with the snow-white hair pulled straight back from a widow's peak, hair exactly like his own father's, hair like combed silk, said to him, "*You*—can look for her in Rome. I haven't seen her since 1905. If I were you, I'd look in the cemetery."

So—she, also, had run away. The old man's wife. My grandmother I've never seen.

Gene said, "Did you do any of the things Il Giustizia said you did?"

"Of course we did. It was our duty!"

It was apparent on Gene's face that he did not want to hear this answer.

His grandfather then said, "If I were you, I'd watch out. Don't trust that man."

Gene was glad the old man still had sense enough to lower his voice.

"You don't know who he is. Justice! His name is Cosmo— Cosmo Perugini—his father was a pig-farmer! And do you know who the son is? He's *Partito Socialista di Unita Proletaria!*—he's a Communist! Why do you think we had to do what we had to do?"

Gene heard this and had to conclude that the situation he was in was completely hopeless. He said, "Is there anything I can do for you?"

"There is nothing you can do for me! My life is over. Go away! Why did you come? I only want to die."

"Don't say that–!"

"I will say it! We are all under sentence of death! You, too! Yes—even you."

Gene LaStoria turned his face away, raised himself up with his hands on his knees—like a catcher, in baseball, at the end of the ninth inning.

He went back to the man called *Il Giustizia*.

"I ask only one thing of you—and then I will take back my sidearm, if you please. Don't worry. I promise my solemn oath that I am intending only to do my duty here and carry out my mission, which is to help you. I ask one favor of you. Let the old man go. Not for the sake of justice. As a favor to me. As a gesture to a friend. To a comrade in arms."

"Why should I do that?"

"I don't know. Because I ask you to."

Il Giustizia took aside his second and they conferred some distance away.

Gene LaStoria could see his lips form the words, in Italian, the Americans will not *always* be here . . .

Gene LaStoria stood there. He was no longer a sergeant in the American Army. He was a grandson who had just met his grandfather for the first time. And wished with all his heart and soul that he had not. As brutal as it was, he could no longer hide the truth from himself. *His own grandfather was on the other side in this tortured and god-forsaken war.* And he, Gene LaStoria, was trying to save from execution—*one of the enemy.*

Il Giustizia returned.

"Okay. Isn't that what you Americans say? I will do this for you. For you. Only for you. Only for that reason. Against my better judgment. Against everything I have ever fought for. I don't want to do it, but I do it for you. I will also shake your hand. We are friends—we are comrades. We fight together— for the right. Give him back his *pistole*. To fight side by side, we must trust one another."

When the old man heard that he was to be released, he looked to the heavens and, raising his hands, he gave out a shriek, the howl of an animal in agony, the perverted grief-struck wail of a man forced to go on living when he had just spent his last mortal breath accepting death.

His grandson, if he lived for an hour, a day, a hundred days, a hundred years, his grandson, Gene LaStoria, as long as he lived, would never be able to forget that sound, nor would he want to remember the wretched wringing of that protest of the heart.

About the Author

Eugene Christy is a novelist, poet and musician currently enjoying retirement in his home in the Berkshires. His maternal grandparents Antonio Scioscia and Giuseppina Fabrizio came from Alta Villa Irpina, near Avellino, in the South of Italy. He has studied under Sean O'Faolain, James Dickey, and Larry McMurtry. Appearing as Gene Christy, he was previously known around the Berkshires as the singer-songwriter and accordian-player who led The Dossers, the Irish-themed pub-band trio featuring Bill Morrison and Rick Marquis. His current project, six years in the making, is called The Twentieth Century Quintet, five novels telling the saga of Antonio LaStoria and his descendants through three generations in America from 1899 to 1972, to be published by Adelaide Books, New York, in 2020 and 2021.